6/25/13
$14.99
B&T

9/13

With drawn

Praise for Mary Kay McComas's
What Happened to Hannah

"Hannah Benson is a memorable character of uncommon strength. From the unthinkable horror of the past to the glimmering possibility of love in the present, *What Happened to Hannah* is a stirring novel of family and redemption."

—Kristina Riggle

"Blending poignancy with humor, crafting characters as real and recognizable as your next-door neighbor, Mary Kay McComas weaves stories that brighten the heart."

—Nora Roberts

"I love Mary Kay McComas. Her books are honest and real, and transport you to a place that feels like home."

—Patricia Gaffney

"It is hard not to be moved by the tender love story that emerges from the depths of violence in this haunting and touching novel. You will never forget *What Happened to Hannah*."

—Jessica Anya Blau

"A touching tale of trauma, healing, and family. . . . McComas builds the relationship between Hannah and Anna deftly, showing how hard it can be for strangers who happen to be family to know each other."

—*Publishers Weekly*

"Mary Kay McComas has written a poignant tale of the prolonged effects of domestic abuse."

—*Daily News* (Iron Mountain, Michigan)

By Mary Kay McComas

What Happened to Hannah

something about sophie

MARY KAY McCOMAS

WILLIAM MORROW

An Imprint of HarperCollins*Publishers*

P.S.™ is a trademark of HarperCollins Publishers.

SOMETHING ABOUT SOPHIE. Copyright © 2013 by Mary Kay McComas. All rights reserved. Printed in the United States of America. No part of this book may be used or reproduced in any manner whatsoever without written permission except in the case of brief quotations embodied in critical articles and reviews. For information address HarperCollins Publishers, 10 East 53rd Street, New York, NY 10022.

HarperCollins books may be purchased for educational, business, or sales promotional use. For information please write: Special Markets Department, HarperCollins Publishers, 10 East 53rd Street, New York, NY 10022.

FIRST EDITION

Designed by Diahann Sturge

Library of Congress Cataloging-in-Publication Data has been applied for.

ISBN 978-0-06-208480-4

13 14 15 16 17   OV/RRD   10 9 8 7 6 5 4 3 2 1

For Doss, in our 35th year—I still love you more

Acknowledgments

I'D LIKE TO THANK MY AGENT, DENISE MARCIL, FOR ALWAYS BELIEVING in me. I believe there is a special place in writer heaven for an editor like Esi Sogah—for her editorial skills, but mostly for her true love of stories. And my pals—Nora Roberts, Pat Gaffney, Elaine Fox, Mary Blayney, and all the ab-fab ladies I know in Washington Romance Writers—well, it wouldn't be any fun at all without you.

something about sophie

Chapter One

"SHE'S COMING." ARTHUR'S COUGH WAS MOIST AND RASPY. HE winced with the pain it caused him. "Soon. She's coming."

His face was pale and withered. There was a tremor in his hands as he picked at the hospital linens; his eyes watered from both age and emotion, and his lips were chapped. He was, in a word, pitiful.

"Bad idea, my friend." His guest sat, sure and relaxed, reflecting on the man Arthur once was—tall, blond, golden; handsome and charming; a pillar of the community, loved by all who knew him. But not unlike the mighty and magnificent stone pillars of ancient Greece, time and life took its toll and toppled him, leaving this sad ruined visage of what had been. "You shouldn't have sent those letters. Nothing good will come of it."

"Still no remorse?" Three words, then he gasped to catch his breath.

"No. I can't be sorry for deciding to protect the lives of many by not speaking for one."

"Two."

"Fine. Two. We did what we could for them."

"Not enough." His thin, frail body hacked out another cough that racked him head to toe, leaving him exhausted. "Not enough to save our souls."

"Yours, you mean. Not enough to save *your* soul. Mine's not going anywhere for a while yet and neither are the people you'd be leaving me with to take all the blame—not fair, Arthur. We had a deal."

"Please."

"How about we both write long heartfelt letters to her? I'll leave them with my attorney to be delivered after my death. Both of them. How does that sound?"

"She's coming. Monday. She said. Tell her . . . then. Beg . . . forgiveness."

A large, resigned sigh came from his companion, who stood and walked to the far side of the bed, avoiding the green tubing delivering extra oxygen to Arthur via a nasal cannula and the IV fluids passing through a monitor into a port in his chest. A warm hand came to rest on the paper-thin and deeply bruised skin of his right arm.

"You know, Arthur, I like you. I always have. You're a good man. This business aside, we've worked well together over the years. We were a good team, don't you think? We had a lot in common—the same interests, the same goals. I thought we'd successfully managed to forget about what happened that night."

"No. I never forgot."

"Of course not."

"I still hear it. She screams. She cries. They laugh."

"I know. I know. What happened was horrifying and . . . vile, but getting involved would have destroyed us, our reputations, our families. Everyone we love would have suffered. We'd have lost everything."

His upper body vibrated through a nod. "She did . . . lose everything."

Another sad, fatalistic puff of breath. "Who knew when you announced you'd contracted the big 'C' you meant conscience?"

"Please."

"I know this is important to you, Arthur, but—"

"I left it," he interrupted on an exhalation. "For her."

"What? You left her what?"

"My life." His sad, tired eyes met his friend's. He rolled his head back and forth on the flat pillow behind his head. "Not enough."

"Here, let me help you." The pillow slipped from under Arthur's head and he watched as hands, slightly younger than his own but still strong with good health, plumped it with vigor. "Hospital pillows . . . cover a thin brick with a pillowcase and who'd know the difference, huh? Okay, let's see if this is more comfortable." A gentle hand supported his shoulders until he felt cool linen on the back of his neck. The movement triggered another coughing spasm that strained the veins and tendons in his neck, turned his face a queer shade of reddish purple.

"Good God, can't they give you something for that?"

"Makes me sleepy."

"At this point that might be a blessing."

Arthur barely shook his head. His voice was raw and weak. "Afraid to sleep."

"Wha— Oh. You're afraid you won't wake up?"

Instead of nodding, he simply lowered his eyelids to hide his misery and fear.

"Then I'll just assume that the next time we meet you'll thank me for this."

Arthur's stomach heaved in urgent awareness, his eyes bursting open in panic to glimpse a second pillow descending toward his face. He raised his arms to block it but he was too slow; grasped and clawed at it but he was too weak. He tried to shout out and coughed the remains of his breath away with no means of sucking in more—the prongs in his nose gouging and tangled. Great strength arrived from nowhere as his body's instinct to survive took over, twisting his body, thrashing his legs in a desperate attempt to break free. His muscles began to sting like fire, little popping noises exploded inside his head and soon all that was left was the muffled voice of a long-ago confidant.

"I'm sorry, Arthur. I really am. But you haven't given me any other choice. You know that. I have too much to lose. You understand, don't you? Nothing's changed for me. I can't let anyone destroy everything I've work for. Not her. Not even you, Arthur. Shhh. Don't worry. No one will know. I'll take care of the girl when she gets here. I'll keep the secret." The pressure on his upper body and face increased drastically. "Let it go, my friend. Just let go. . . ."

Chapter Two

SOPHIE SHEPARD HATED HOSPITALS. THE SMELLS, THE COLORS, THE chairs, the peculiar silence under the noise. The only things she disliked more were funeral homes.

And here she was, walking softly to keep her flip-flops from flapping on the too-shiny floors and echoing down the eerily empty off-white halls of yet another unfamiliar hospital in another unfamiliar town—searching for yet another mother.

She cringed. Okay, so that wasn't funny. She knew exactly who and where her mother was. What she wasn't sure about was why she'd let some stranger talk her into driving eight hours to discuss a birth mother she'd never been too interested in, in the first place.

Was her general lack of interest in this woman abnormal? She couldn't possibly be the only adopted person so happy and satisfied with the life she got that she thought of it as a gift from a woman who, for whatever reason, hadn't been able to raise her herself? Life was complicated. For everyone. She read once that there were people who studied such things and describe the human condition as a never-ending tragedy—because life was short and always ended in death. But frankly, whether her life was an accident, a burden, or part of another woman's tragic existence, she was glad to simply exist.

Very Pollyanna of her, she supposed, but she did agree that life was short and she worked hard at not complicating it with things she couldn't change.

"Hi. I'm looking for an Arthur Cubeck?" The helpful smile on the nurse's face drooped a bit and she pushed her chair away from the counter, glancing at the three other caretakers nearby, then swiveled to look over her shoulder uncertainly.

Sophie's gaze followed to a man in a white lab coat standing on the other side of the nurse's station. His attention gravitated in reluctant stages from the laptop in front of him, straight into her eyes; lingered a long second, and then he looked back to quickly save his data, close up the small computer, and head around the corner toward her.

She released her breath in a gust and frowned at the clammy print of her hand on the counter.

He was not a particularly handsome man. Tall, fit, trimmed dark hair, clean shaven—nose, mouth, arms, and legs. Truly ordinary. Until he came around the corner and bore holes through her with his eyes in a most extraordinary way. She couldn't even tell what color they were yet, only that they were the most intense she'd ever come in contact with. Direct, observant, something that was hard to put her finger on, and very appealing.

"It's Koo," he said without preamble. "Arthur Koo-beck."

"Oh." They were green. Plain old green eyes, same as hers, but bursting with fire and life. She split the air between them with her hand. "I'm Sophie Shepard."

"Drew McCarren." His hand was warm and strong and covered hers completely. Plus, it wasn't one of those light, limp-wristed encounters men tended to bestow on the weaker sex. His handshake was as bold and honest as his eyes. "You're not a relative of Arthur's."

"No." She laughed. "Otherwise I'd know how to pronounce his name, wouldn't I?"

His lips bowed and he gave a nod; humor registered in his features. She was—just briefly—dazzled.

"He wrote to me," she said abruptly. "A couple of times. He wanted to talk, to tell me something. He asked me to come. I wasn't going to." She heard herself gushing but couldn't stop— she was too busy quelling an urge to lay her soul out on the counter, exposed and vulnerable, for him to see. How weird was that? "I didn't know who he was, obviously, and I wasn't at all interested in what he wanted to talk about, so I wrote back and told him I couldn't make it." She faltered under his scrutiny and glanced down. He wasn't judging, merely listening; but knowing that *he knew* the man was elderly and ill, and she'd refused him, felt awkward. "When he wrote and told me he was sick and he needed to get something about me off his chest, well, he made it sound important, so as soon as school was out I decided to drive down."

"You're in school?"

"I teach. Kindergarten."

He gave a quick nod and took a quiet breath. "Well, Sophie Shepard, I'm sorry to say it but Arthur Cubeck passed away Saturday."

"Oh." Her disappointment was a surprise. But the tears that pressed and stung the backs of her eyes were a shock. She looked away, muttering, "I'm sorry."

After a moment, he asked, "Are you all right?"

She nodded, then shook her head. "I could have been here sooner. Friday, Thursday even, but I stopped over in Washington, D.C., to sightsee. I'm sorry I missed him."

She was sincerely sorry, and let down that he'd taken his story about her with him. So, she was human; she could admit it. The old man's desperation had stirred her curiosity; her curiosity had aroused vague emotions from her childhood. A childhood during which she had, from time to time, wondered why: *Why didn't she want me? Why'd she give me away?* A childhood, too, filled with the kind of love and happiness that can soothe and heal a wounded psyche until all that remained of the question was a faded blemish, like a tiny scar from chicken pox.

But still, she was human.

When the doctor simply stayed with her, saying nothing, she looked up. Kindness and empathy. That something in his eyes that was hard to put her finger on? It was understanding and compassion, and it was as deeply ingrained in the character of this man as his DNA.

"Are— Were you his doctor?" He confirmed it. "Would you know if he, Mr. Cubeck, happened to leave me a letter or a note maybe? You know, to ease his mind?"

He looked doubtful but glanced over his shoulder at the nurse, who'd been quietly keeping abreast of the conversation. She shrugged.

"We'll look into it. Will you be around awhile?"

"It's a long drive home. I thought I'd stay over tonight and head back in the morning. Will that be long enough?" she asked the nurse, assuming that *looking into it* would be more in her job description than his. "Or I could leave my address and you could mail anything that might show up?"

"Sure." He pulled two business cards from his shirt pocket, handing her one with the blank side up, then reached for the pen in his lab-coat pocket. "You can put your information on that card, and here's another to take. Call me in the morning, or if you have any other questions."

She nodded, finishing up her cell number, and swapped cards with him. "Thank you, Dr. McCarren."

"You're welcome, Sophie Shepard." He smiled, but it was more like a reassuring pat on the back. Huh. Not even a quick, short flirt. Bummer. He turned to the laptop he'd set on the counter and opened it up.

No longer in the warmth of his gaze, she felt an air-conditioned draft blow cold on her face from a vent in the ceiling. Even reason returned, when she started to walk away.

An attraction? To a doctor? Who, no doubt, spent most of his time in a *hospital*—more than four hundred miles from home! She glanced at his card: Internal Medicine. And directly under that: Hematology/Oncology. Great. She burped a single breathy laugh and thought about banging her head on a wall. A *cancer* doctor? Hers was the most remarkable talent for being attracted to impossible men.

"Ms. Shepard." She turned back to him—way too eager. "Do you have a place to stay yet?" She shook her head, swallowing, trying to dislodge her tongue from the roof of her mouth. "Halleron House is a nice B&B. Turn left out of the hospital lot. It's about seven blocks straight down Poplar, two blocks passed the church. Tell Jesse I sent you. I get compensated for everyone I send her."

"Thanks. I will."

Clearfield, Virginia, is one of those picturesque little towns that are featured on the lids of chocolate boxes and Christmas cards—not too unlike Marion, Ohio, where she was from; a tad smaller perhaps. Located in the western Piedmont area of the state, it was tucked away in the foothills of the Blue Ridge Mountains. The closest major point of interest was less than an hour northeast, the large college town of Charlottesville. The University of Virginia was founded by Thomas Jefferson;

but more importantly, it's the home of the Virginia Cavaliers—more fondly known as the Wahoos according to the boastful billboards down scenic U.S. 29 South. It also features a large renowned medical center and a law school ranked tenth in the nation according to her dad, who, twenty-five years earlier, graduated from UVA with a degree in psychology. He stayed on two more years to get another degree in sociology, to marry her mom, and to receive the best gift a daddy could ever dream of. Her. Sophia Amelia Shepard.

And *that* was her favorite bedtime story, even now.

Halleron House was exactly where the doctor said it would be—a large white Victorian house with a square turret and rose-colored trim. The flower beds, showing every sign of having a bumper crop this year, were tidy and neat; the grass in the yard meticulously manicured inside a black wrought-iron fence. Lacy green ferns hung from the eaves of the front porch—the two fan-backed wicker chairs and the swing with pretty rose cushions were painted white. It was chocolate-box-top perfect.

"Ms. Halleron?"

"Call me, Jesse. You must be Sophie Shepard." She was a tall, medium built, going-gray-haired lady with soft, welcoming pale blue eyes and a bright toothy grin. She wore jeans, a gray plaid oxford shirt—and looked as neat and well groomed as her house. "Drew McCarren called and told me a pretty little redhead might be coming. Come in. Come in."

The entry featured a freestanding staircase with white risers, wooden steps, and a balustrade with thick heavy newels; polished rosewood wainscoting ran down the hallways on either side. Draped in a slightly worn runner rug of ruby, navy, and beige, and set off by big hydrangea blooms in a vase on an ornate table nearby, Sophie felt as if she'd stepped back into the early nineteenth century.

"Welcome to Clearfield. Just set your bag down there. I'll give you the ten-cent tour before I take you up to your room. Where are you from?"

"Marion, Ohio."

"Well, that's a ways. I'm sorry you came all this way to meet Arthur and missed him—such a sweet man. Dining room. The kitchen is through that door or you can come straight back through this hall. His funeral is the day after tomorrow. Apparently, they have to wait for a couple cousins from Florida to get here and his son, Hollis, who was here last week for a few days but then missed Arthur's passing—he needs to make special arrangements with his work, I hear. He lives in Texas now with his family and owns several fast-food franchises." She frowned. "I can't recall which ones just now, but I guess he does fairly well with them. Arthur was always bragging about him. I call this the parlor." She waved a hand at a cozy room with a homey mix of traditional and antique furniture. "And my office is through there. Down this hall is a TV family room that you're welcome to use if you don't mind tripping over my son. His room is back there as well. There's a small library upstairs with a TV in it, too." She took a breath. "Drew mentioned that you're a schoolteacher?"

"Kindergarten." She wasn't sure what it was about the word exactly, but she found that simply identifying herself as a kindergarten teacher always seemed to automatically distinguish her as being a stalwart sort of person—patient, strong, steadfast, and brave. Chirpy, playful, and giggly, too, unfortunately—but then, she didn't believe any singular word was perfectly perfect, so to speak.

She rushed to pick up her suitcase before Jesse could. The woman's smile came easy and warm before she started up the stairs.

"That must be a satisfying job. All those eager young minds,

soaking everything up like sponges. That's quite a responsibility, being a young person's first experience with school."

"I love it. I learn a lot from them, too."

"I bet you do." She topped the stairs and turned back to
Sophie. "Did you know Arthur was a minister?" She shook
her head; her suitcase was too heavy to be conversing between
huffs and puffs. "Not my minister. He was a Unitarian. An
interesting religion, from what I've read about it. It's not a
very imaginative faith, but then you have many big think-
ers and writers who believe in it. Like Longfellow, Thoreau,
Whitman, if I'm remembering right. And Dickens, Louisa
May Alcott, Sylvia Plath . . . a tragic example, but you also
have Alexander Graham Bell and Charles Darwin, too, so
there must be something to it. And Arthur would have been a
shining example for any religion he chose. A wonderful man.
You could always count on him, for anything. Poor man—his
wife and teenage daughter were killed in a car accident years
ago. Hollis was ten or eleven and Julie was eight, I think. Arthur raised them all alone. Never remarried. He lost Julie a
few years back—more than any one man should have to toler-
ate, yet he was always the first to show up and *really* help in
times of trouble. He wasn't simply a lot of lip service, if you
know what I mean. You're my only guest at the moment, so
you can choose your room. One overlooks the front, the other
the back; otherwise they're much the same. Both have their
own bath."

Sophie peeked at each room—one yellow, one blue, both
large, lovely, and comfortable looking. "Front, please. I like
yellow."

"I do, too. It's cheery."

She stood smiling in the doorway as Sophie looked around.
She had a soft spot for chatty people who took over that first
gawky get-to-know-you dialogue, who take all the effort out

of meeting someone new and put you at ease. She also loved a good gossip, as long as they weren't discussing her.

"Jesse, your home is beautiful."

"Thank you," she said proudly. "It's a work in progress. I bought it fourteen years ago and I've been fixing this and that ever since."

A hesitation in her voice turned Sophie's attention to the odd stare and thoughtful frown on her face. "What is it?"

The woman shook off the stare but the frown remained. "The strangest thing: for a moment there, the way you tipped you head, I think . . . it . . . you reminded me of someone. I don't even know who, it just seemed familiar."

"One of those creepy déjà vu moments?"

"*Oui*. Aren't those weird?" They laughed. "And for the record, we have no ghosts here. You're safe as can be."

"Good to know."

"I'll leave you to settle in. There's coffee in the kitchen, or tea if you like. I'll be baking Drew's pie."

"Drew's pie?"

"That rascal. Every time he sends someone over here, he comes knocking at my back door for a piece of my cherry pie." She laughed and confided, "I mass produce them every two or three months. I give a couple to neighbors, but I freeze most of them for this very reason." She smiled. "Plus, I get to look forward to his visit. I used to babysit the McCarren kids for Elizabeth once in a while—he was always my favorite."

"He seems nice."

"He is . . . and more." She started to leave, then popped her head around the door. "Do you have allergies?"

"No."

"Shellfish?"

"Love 'em."

"Good." And she was gone.

* * *

Jesse made a delicious Crab Louie for their supper. Her son, Mike, didn't eat green food. Period. He was fifteen with dark shaggy hair and braces on the big grin he'd inherited from his mom, was thin and bony, and had the biggest feet Sophie had ever seen. He ate four cheeseburgers, ketchup and mustard only.

Between the meal and after dinner coffee and dessert, the doorbell rang and Jesse went to answer.

"Is it awful having strangers in your house all the time? Does it bother you?"

He scrunched his nose. "No. Not most of the time. I've gotten used to it, you know? And she likes it."

"It's only the two of you."

"Since I was one. He skipped—my dad?"

She nodded. "Sorry."

"Can't miss what you never had, right?" He didn't sound the least bit bitter. He was either an excellent actor or Jesse had done a good job of being both parents for him. "But Mom says he was tall, six-six maybe, so that's something."

Well, yes. It was, but what? she wondered, though she didn't have to ask.

"Basketball."

Apparently, she was beginning to look incredibly dense because he laughed and flipped his palms up—it was obvious. "I love basketball. I play all the time. I'm usually the combo guard, but if I get fast enough and tall enough, I want to play swingman. Like Kobe Bryant and LeBron James." He gaped at her. "How about Michael Jordan?"

"The shoe guy?"

Sophie held her giggle until the boy looked dangerously on the verge of convulsing—and then they both laughed. That's when Jesse returned, followed by a dark-suited gentleman with a horseshoe of silver hair around the base of his head and silver wire-framed glasses. His expression was formal but warm, guarded but still easy to read. He was excited to see her.

"Sophie, this is Graham Metzer."

"Hello." He nodded and smiled and she looked to Jesse for further instructions.

"He's Arthur Cubeck's lawyer and he'd like to have a word with you."

"Oh. Sure."

Clearly bursting with curiosity, Jesse took her coffee and her son—who grabbed two apples from the sideboard to hold him until dessert—and left the room.

"Mr. Metzer, would you like a cup of—"

"Ms. Shepard," he said, cutting Sophie off in his haste. "I couldn't believe my ears when young Dr. McCarren called to ask if Arthur had, by any chance, left a letter for you with me. This is good luck, indeed."

"Really? He left a letter?"

"No, I'm afraid not, but he did leave you something in his will."

"His will?"

"That's correct. And you being here saves us the time of having to notify you by mail, but, well, Dr. McCarren mentioned that you were planning to go home in the morning. Ohio, as I recall."

"That's right."

"I rushed over here to find out if you could possibly stay, until after Thursday morning, which is when the family would like the will to be read. It *is* unusual to have a formal reading of the will these days; this is a first for me. Generally, a copy of the will is simply given or sent to the deceased's personal representative and all beneficiaries named in the document; also to any known disinherited heirs who might contest the will, before we admit it into probate. But it was Arthur's, Mr. Cubeck's, request that the will be read aloud to a gathering of his entire family to avoid any misunderstandings." He hesitated. "This is also peculiar in as much as the will itself hasn't been altered in twenty-five years—reviewed and reaffirmed, from time to time, but not altered—and apparently the family is ignorant of its contents. Highly unusual. Particularly in these circumstances."

"What circumstances?"

"Arthur's age and the length of his illness. As a rule, the will and its contents are part of one's *getting their affairs in order* as one grows older or becomes infirmed, and the family has at least a vague awareness of its contents. I'm not accustomed to this sort of high drama."

"High drama?" She knew she was repeating him but none of it was making sense.

"Secretiveness," he said, like that one word ought to clear it all up. He hesitated before he asked, "So, will you come? Thursday. My office on Main Street. About ten A.M.?"

"I guess so, sure. But I don't understand. I'm not family. I don't even know the family—or even Mr. Cubeck, for that matter. I'd rather not intrude if I can avoid it." *Plus,* she wasn't too hot on the idea of having whatever information he had about her birth mother announced to a bunch of strangers.

"I understand." He shifted his weight uncomfortably and looked nervous. "Arthur didn't make your presence a requirement, and, unfortunately, I'm not at liberty to explain the conditions right now, but I can tell you that he left you . . . well, an extraordinary gift. For not being part of the family, that is."

"Like what?" He pressed his lips together and shook his head. "Oh, right." She sighed. "Well then, I guess I'll see you Thursday morning, Mr. Metzer."

"Thank you. I hope it's not too big an inconvenience for you."

She stood to walk him to the door as he didn't seem inclined to chat over coffee. "It's not inconvenient at all. I'm taking sort of an *aimless* vacation, I guess you could say. Especially now with Mr. Cubeck gone. So all I need to do is call my dad and let him know I'll be staying here longer than I thought, and check to see if Jesse will keep me a couple more days."

"You know I will," came her holler from the TV room down the hall. "You can stay as long as you want."

She grinned at Mr. Metzer, enjoying the idea that small towns in America were all alike: her backbone, her greatest asset, and her richest source of unswerving constancy—in so many ways. "Well, all right. I'll call my dad."

She let the man out, said good night, and was closing the door when she caught Jesse in her peripheral vision. "That was weird."

"Is everything okay?" It wasn't a casual question; she was genuinely concerned.

"Arthur Cubeck left me something—more than a letter—in his will. And I didn't know he existed six months ago."

"Oh. Wait a second." She dashed through the hall door to her office and returned a moment later with a refolded newspaper, open to the obituaries. "This might help. See? There's a nice picture of him. Taken a few years ago, but he hadn't changed much until the last year or so. Chemo, you know."

She did know. "Thanks, Jesse. He . . . He looks like a kind man." She squinted at the small picture. An attractive man, he still managed to look like the stereotypical country cleric: studious, unpretentious, composed. There was a sadness about him, too, around his eyes, like he'd seen too much.

"He was a good man. Now, how about some pie?"

Chapter Three

THERE WAS ANOTHER PICTURE OF ARTHUR CUBECK DISPLAYED ATOP HIS coffin Wednesday morning—the same pose but larger.

His obituary had stated he was well known and admired in the community; but that seemed like a gross understatement when, even leaving the house early with Jesse, there was standing-room only inside the small Unitarian church. The eulogy and affirmations were ardent and heartfelt. Sophie heard later there were friends and neighbors gathered on the lawn and sidewalk outside the church holding their own memorials in small groups, in low voices. A true tribute to a man's life.

She had debated whether to go to the graveside service, but it didn't appear to be a private family affair—she suspected the better half of the town's entire population was there. She stood at the back of the crowd trying to look as unobtrusive as possible, next to Jesse, who seemed determined to greet and commiserate with the whole of said populace.

Arthur Cubeck's son, Hollis, was pointed out to her, along

with his wife, Jane, and two teenaged sons—Terry and John, Jesse believed. Another man, Craig Chamberlin, was Arthur's son-in-law. His wife, Arthur's daughter, Julie, had left Craig—out of the blue—then was accidentally shot in front of a liquor store in Richmond during a holdup a few months later. It was all very strange. Everyone who knew her was devastated. For three years, Craig raised their three pre-to-early teen children all alone, until he married a local girl, Lucy Bevens—and they'd recently revealed that she is four months pregnant. Everyone who knows them is thrilled. The other two gentlemen were, as Jesse recalled them vaguely, Arthur's cousins from Florida. Both had wives, one of which looked like a heart attack in progress—poor woman—and appeared intensely uncomfortable teetering on a padded folding chair.

Jesse was the equivalent of a small-town iPod. But Sophie didn't need the Wikipedia descriptions and connections of those present to commiserate. She found that one could feel the loss of a deceased stranger if one could draw from the sorrow of losing . . . oh, say, one's own mother, if that sorrow was still fresh and raw enough. And hers was.

In the end, it was the very late arrival of Dr. Drew McCarren that distracted her. Approaching from the opposite side of the gathering, he looked as natural in his dark suit as he did in his lab coat. In his business she suspected he attended many a funeral.

Passing through the crowd quietly, he touched a shoulder here, nodded there, and eventually placed both hands comfortably, and comfortingly, on the shoulders of an older lady in large dark glasses. She was medium height and elegant, and she had excellent posture. Sophie wondered if she was a yoga disciple or someone simply accustomed to holding her head high and proud. Either way, the outcome was striking and complimented the rest of the meticulousness—no better word for it—in her appearance. A stylish, perfectly cut black sheath with a long shantung jacket, a thick silver-chain necklace, and an expertly streaked salt-and-pepper hairdo that looked deceptively effortless and extremely becoming on her.

Beside her stood a young woman—slightly taller, more trendy than chic—who looked as easy and contented in her skin as the other appeared staid and proper, though they both stood out in the crowd. Or, they did now that Sophie's attention had been drawn to them. And if these were the sort of women the doctor was used to, it was no wonder he'd paid so little attention to her—not that it mattered anyway.

At least, that's what she was telling herself when his gaze roamed slowly over the grieving townspeople and settled on her—startling her, once again, with the directness of his stare. Was he aware of this unsettling habit of his or was it an unconscious byproduct of his honest and sympathetic personality? She could always look away, clearly, but that wasn't a habit of *hers*.

So they watched each other for that last few minutes of the service, and then he leaned forward to whisper something in the young woman's ear—she gave him a short nod and a light smile in return. The other woman got a swift kiss on the cheek. She reached up and without looking, unerringly palmed his cheek with great affection—and didn't budge when he removed his hands from her shoulders and stepped away.

Once he broke eye contact with her to make his way around the mourners, Sophie was free to breathe again and was careful to keep looking straight ahead as if unaware of him—it was, after all, a funeral. However, and intending no disrespect, she tracked him peripherally while Arthur's family and closest friends laid white roses on the coffin.

His stride was fluid and confident. He had a word, and often a touch, for everyone who turned his way while he circled the mourners. She lost sight of him, but it was only a matter of minutes before she heard murmuring behind her, sensed people moving beside her, felt him at her back—and she hadn't fooled him at all.

"Sorry I missed you yesterday," he whispered over her shoulder.

"Do you always eat pie for breakfast?"

"If it's Jesse's." She could tell by the delighted look on Jesse's face that he'd grinned or winked or done something else charming—like he hadn't two days ago with her. "And if you might be there."

"What. At six thirty? A.M.? On my vacation? Not likely." Was he flirting? Now? At Mr. Cubeck's funeral? Also not likely, so— "Oh. You found a letter," she said, turning to look up at him.

"No. Sorry. I looked everywhere, called everyone I could think of—I don't think there is one."

"Oh. Well, I'm sorry about that. I was hoping." She wanted to steer clear of the will reading and an informative letter would have been her ticket. "Thank you, though, for your trouble. I appreciate you looking into it."

"Sure."

She expected him to leave but he simply continued to stare.

"What? Is there something else?"

He looked confused at first, then smiled and drew Jesse into their chat—formally, as she'd assumed inclusion from the start. "Are you both going out to BelleEllen for the wake?"

She looked to Sophie. "Did you want to go?"

"No. Not at all."

"Good. I have a couple coming in for an overnight sometime this afternoon—from Nashville, on their way to a wedding in Maine. And I sent my three-bean salad and a loaf of banana-date bread out with Gracie Bevens—Lucy's mother—so I was going to skip it. With this mob, no one'll notice."

"They might." He turned back to Sophie. "You've stirred up quite a buzz in town. I've been fielding calls about you since yesterday morning. Apparently, Graham Metzer paid you a visit *after* you'd been to the hospital to inquire after Arthur."

Sophie's eyes drifted toward Jesse, who shook her head in innocence and shrugged. "Small town. Graham drives an ugly old black Lincoln, and he's hardly ever got good news to deliver. People notice where he goes." She crooked a smile. "Besides, I never divulge personal information about my guests . . . until after they leave."

Sophie was becoming as fond of Jesse as Drew McCarren apparently was.

"It might be just as well if you both keep a low profile to-day, to avoid a lot of awkward questions. Even my mother called about you."

"Your mother?"

"You didn't notice her and my sister giving you the once-over? Over and over?"

She turned to look at the women she'd seen him with, and, sure enough, they were watching. Or so it seemed. It was hard to be sure with their dark sunglasses, but it certainly felt like it . . . now. She shook her head. "My radar's on the fritz, I guess."

But it wasn't. She hadn't noticed his mother and sister in particular, but her radar had been pinging like a pinball ma-chine all morning—people taking second glances, gawking and jerking away when she looked up. But it happened in small towns, right?

"Then it's your lucky day." When she looked taken aback, he added, "My sister's okay but my mother . . . well, I love her, but she can get scary when she feels like she's the last one to know what's going on in town."

Jesse gave Drew a motherly smack on the arm. "Pooh. You make her sound terrible. We all like to know what's going on around us. . . . Sophie, she's no different."

"I understand. Marion's small, too. My dad says it doesn't matter how big or small a town is, the people are always the same: the best and the worst of it, often both."

Jesse gave a nod. "Well, that's true enough. I like to believe most people mean well. Now, will you be all right here for a minute while I run over and give my condolences?"

"Of course. Take your time." She expected the doctor to wander off with Jesse and to make it easy on both of them; Sophie turned to walk in the opposite direction to get out of the throng while she waited. It took a *Hey Doc, how ya doin'* to alert her that she wasn't alone—apparently her radar *was* jammed up. She stopped and watched him shake hands and pass comments with a man not much older than himself, then he joined her over AUGUSTUS PEPPER 1918–1984.

"Look, I'm fine. Really. You don't need to babysit me."

"That's a relief. I was never very good at babysitting."

"Aren't you going to . . . ?" She motioned with her head toward the family. He didn't look away, didn't seem inclined to do anything but look at her—which was, after their original encounter, as gratifying as it was disconcerting.

"Line's too long. I'll catch them out at BelleEllen."

"Pretty name."

"Pretty little farmhouse about ten miles east of here. Arthur named it after his wife."

"Jesse told me about her. Mr. Cubeck had a lot of pain and sorrow in his life. His wife. Two daughters. How does someone handle that much sadness?"

"One day at a time, I'm told."

"You'd know, I suppose. Your job and death go hand in hand." He looked shocked; she scrambled. "Sort of. Right?

Cancer patients mostly? You deal with people who die . . . might die, I mean . . . usually. You know, eventually."

His lips twitched. "I'll go with 'eventually.' *Eventually* we all die. And I rarely have patients who don't have at least a fifty-fifty chance of survival. Usually the odds are much better, so I like to think I'm more about hope than death. In fact, my dad's a cardiologist—handles a lot of cardiac patients and his stats are far worse than mine."

"I'm sorry. I didn't mean to insult you."

"I know. At least you stopped short of calling me Dr. Death."

"Oh, no, that's not at all what I meant. I—"

This time he laughed out loud. "Sophie, I'm kidding." But as she began to relax, the more thoughtful he became. "So, who that you love had cancer?"

"I'm so obvious?"

"No. But sometimes hope isn't enough—nothing we do is enough—and then I need to be prepared to recognize and deal with the lack of hope, which turns into resentment and anger."

"And that's what you see in me?"

"Hardly at all. Just flashes, like a second ago. I see you struggling with it."

"My mom. She died last year. Stage-four esophageal cancer. Her pain—" She stopped; she could see he knew about the pain. "My poor dad refused to accept it. For almost two years, he dragged her from one oncologist to another, one hospital to the next, until she and I both put our foot down and refused to go with him. You talk about angry and resentful. . . . There didn't seem to be anything anyone could say to him. He's a psychologist—it was like he'd heard all the words before, so when he needed them, they didn't mean much."

"I'm sorry." There it was again: the understanding and compassion. He knew.

"Who was it for you?"

He smiled at her perception. "My grandfather, a long time ago."

"Is he why you chose oncology?"

"Yep, pretty much. I always knew I wanted to be a doctor. You know, grow up and be like my dad, a big-time cardio-thoracic surgeon at the medical center—at the university in Charlottesville? UVA?" She nodded. She knew the one. "We'd save lives together. He'd be proud of me. We'd be a team and we could spend all kinds of time with each other—which we didn't when I was young." His enthusiasm increased. "But my granddad was there. He took me fishing and to UVA football and baseball games—a huge Wahoo fan." She was about to mention that her father was, too, but she liked the way he was smiling, remembering. "We must have gone to a thousand Flying Squirrels games in Richmond."

"Flying Squirrels." She squinted. "That's what, cricket?"

He laughed. "Minor league baseball. He wouldn't watch anything pro; said the games were better if they were playing for fun or hungry for fame." He gave away to a fond chuckle and added, "When he developed lung cancer and passed away, I took a ninety-degree turn. I decided to cure cancer. I even spent a few years in research and—"

"The Florida cousins are flat-out strange," Jesse announced, coming up behind them. "I asked about their trip up and that one in the yellow tie said they all came in the same car and that it had better be worth the trouble. Can you imagine?"

"They must be expecting quite a wake, huh?"

Jesse laughed and slipped her arm around Sophie's. "You're the sweetest thing. They're talking about the will, I'm thinking."

"Mmm. I figured. But I've been learning about hope recently—thought I'd give it a try." She glanced at the doctor; his eyes warmed and his lips curved upward.

"Well, *I* hope Arthur left them both a dozen rotten eggs for their trouble. Shame on them. Now, what did I interrupt?"

"Dr. McCarren was telling me about his grandfather and why he became a doctor."

"Leroy? Lord, what a flirt he was. He had sweet little pet names for all of Elizabeth's friends; flattering, no matter how homely we were. I'm nine years younger than Elizabeth so, of course, I wasn't a part of her crowd but I was around, and he didn't show favorites. I was Jubilant Jesse—it means full of high-spirited delight. Isn't that nice? I loved him for that. He was a big fella with a roaring voice, and so full of energy. Wasn't he, Drew?"

"Yes."

"We all adored him, but he mortified Elizabeth, I think." She started their walk across the cemetery lawn toward her car. "I imagine it would embarrass any young girl to have such a friendly, playful father, but we all thought she was the luckiest girl alive. Mr. Kingston was a real character."

"I got that from what Dr. McCarren was saying."

"Please. My dad is Dr. McCarren or Dr. Joe. I'm 'Doc' at most, but more often it's just Drew, which suits me fine." He glanced over his shoulder. "And I see I'm holding my mother up. She asked me to go out to BelleEllen with her and my sister."

"Well, it's always good to see you, sweetie. Say hi to your mom and Ava for me," Jesse said, flinging a friendly arm around his neck for a hug. "Don't work too hard."

"Okay."

"I'll say goodbye, too." Sophie extended her hand and, again, took pleasure in the way his engulfed hers. "I've enjoyed talking with you. And thank you again, for looking for the letter."

"No problem. I'm sorry I couldn't find one for you. I hope we get a chance to talk again before you leave town."

"I'd like that, too, but I'll be leaving as soon as I've seen Mr. Metzer tomorrow morning."

He nodded. "In that case, have a safe trip home."

She returned to Jesse's side and he walked off in the opposite direction. Hardly half a minute later, they turned their heads to catch each other looking back, smiled at *what if* and went on their way.

The expected members of Reverend Arthur Cubeck's family arrived at Graham Metzer's office. He herded them into a small conference room with barely enough mismatched chairs, apparently gathered from every room in the building, to seat everyone in no specific order—first come, next seated.

Jesse's overnighters had come and gone early—leaving her with chores to do and no good excuse for Sophie to hang around. She took the time-killing ten-block walk from the B&B and still arrived ten minutes early. It was a warm day but still early enough in June to be pleasant and not miserably humid.

She'd awoken dreading this meeting, wishing she hadn't agreed to come. Sifting through a small catalog of good excuses to avoid it had failed, so she ultimately had to haul herself up and into the shower. A queasy stomach warned her that it might be wise to skip breakfast, and later it decided to churn and growl while she sat and waited for the others to arrive.

Truly, her curiosity aside, she had no real interest in knowing who her birth mother was. Not really, not anymore anyway. Once upon a time and in a moment of teenage rage and rebellion, she'd threatened to seek her out; live with *her* until she was eighteen. She'd broken her mother's heart, made her cry and crushed any further thoughts she had about the woman. She was grateful for her life, but she felt no deep need to thank her in person or to know what could only have been the sad and difficult circumstances of her birth. If the woman had wanted her to know any of it, she'd had plenty of opportunity and many methods of doing so. It seemed pointless—and was very uncomfortable—to expose her now, and in this way.

Hollis, his wife, and teenaged children had arrived before her. Their expressions were perplexed and defensive before and after she was introduced to them. Before they could ask, she answered, "I don't know why I'm here. Your father wrote and asked me to come—not to this, but to see him—but he'd already passed away before I got a chance to talk with him." She faltered. "I'm sorry for your loss, by the way. I should have said that first. But . . . so, anyway . . . I don't know why I'm here."

"What's your connection?" asked Hollis, a wiry-built man who looked to be in his early forties, with thinning blond hair and pale blue eyes. He must have been his mother's son, as he didn't look like the pictures she'd seen of his father.

"To your father? I never met him."

"Your parents?"

"Not that I know of . . . at least not my dad or he would have said something when I told him why I was coming down here to—" She stopped abruptly.

"To what?"

"Talk to your dad."

"About . . . ?"

"Well, I don't know exactly. He said he needed to talk about my mother, my birth mother. I'm adopted. When my parents lived in Charlottesville, going to school, at the university? That's when they got me and we moved to Ohio, right after they graduated. That's where my mom's family was . . .

is still, actually." She could feel the blood begin to drain from her face, her skin breaking out in a cold sweat. Dear God, what if what Arthur Cubeck wanted to say about her birth mother was that *he* was her birth *father*? That would certainly be something to get off his chest—a minister, in a small town, with children older than she was? Oh, yeah. *Now* she really didn't want to be there. "My . . . my parents were told that my birth mother was a young girl, a teenager." *Aw, God!* What had the man been thinking to announce his indiscretion with a teenager to his children, to the public? She could jump in her car and speed out of town, but his reputation would be ruined, forever, and his children—"My dad would have said something if he'd ever met yours—he's good with names, never forgets anybody. A letter would have been enough."

The tension at the base of her neck seeped into her temples and began to throb as Craig and Lucy Chamberlin entered, without their children, and sat on the opposite side of the table from Hollis. They greeted the family quietly and, of course, looked at her curiously but asked no questions. So Hollis's wife, Jane, explained, "She's here to find out who her birth mother is."

They smiled, nodded, looked even more bewildered, and were far more polite than the Florida cousins who came twenty minutes late, squabbled over the remaining chairs, and then turned to Mr. Metzer asking, "Who's that?"

With a gentle smile, he said, "That young lady's name is Sophie Shepard from Marion, Ohio. Ms. Shepard, you met Hollis and his family, so let me introduce you to the others."

He went around the table and when he was finished, Richard Hollister, Jesse's yellow-tie-guy from the day before, reiterated, "But *who* is she? What's she doing here?"

"She came at my request. She is one of the beneficiaries named in Arthur's will—which I will proceed to read without further ado." Hollis leaned forward, looked at her with new curiosity but said nothing. The lawyer sat and cleared his throat, looking anxious, Sophie noted. And who wouldn't with Rude Richard glowering at your elbow? "In the packets before you are copies of The Last Will and Testament of Arthur William Cubeck, which you may take with you."

His copy was in a black folder, which he opened in front of him. He got through the date and the parts about a sound mind and a free will before Richard interrupted.

"I am sixty-eight years old, man, and this is time I will never get back. Get on with it."

Graham Metzer looked to Hollis, who shrugged and nodded, simultaneously frowning at his second cousin. He flipped two pages saying, "Very well. As designated executor of the estate and Arthur's friend of thirty years, I will receive a ten-thousand-dollar stipend beyond the fees entailed by my office in dealing with the will. After an appropriate probate period, during which all outstanding liens, debts, taxes, and charitable donations have been executed, the remaining estate will be divided as follows." Again he cleared his voice and glanced around the room uneasily. " 'Article A: Apart from Article B of this document, my son, Hollister David Cubeck, shall receive a full half of my entire estate without entailment; the other half to be held in trust by Craig James Chamberlin for the children of my daughter, Julie Marie Cubeck, deceased: Charles Arthur and Janet Ellen Chamberlin until such time as they reach their majority and their father sees fit.' " He looked up.

"That's it?" Richard looked at his brother, George, who was looking decidedly worried. "Half and half, that's it? That rat bastard got that money from his mama who got it from *our* grandfather. We have a right to some of it, by God."

With a mutinous look to his right, Graham began to read

again. " 'Article B: The property known as BelleEllen, the house and the twenty acres plotted at the time of its purchase, I do bequeath to Ms. Sophia Amelia Shepard as a token of the enormous obligation I owe her. She may do with it as she pleases. Title fees and taxes for a period of five years shall be set aside during the probate period of this document.' "

She coughed back the laugh that she knew was totally inappropriate for this particular out-of-body experience. This news was absurd and unnatural—and so *not* funny. She couldn't make any sense of it.

It felt like hours before she could do more than sit and listen to nitrogen and oxygen molecules bouncing off the walls and crashing into one another—and it was a feat of courage to shift her gaze from face to face around the table as she prepared for attack.

The sound of Richard Hollister's hand hitting the table was like a sonic boom that woke the entire room and everyone spoke at once.

"What the hell does that mean?"

"Are you sure that's right?"

"His mind must have been very weak at the end. Doesn't that say *of sound mind*? We can go to court and prove he wasn't thinking straight."

"That rat bastard. Damn him to hell."

"I don't understand."

"Maybe you could read it again? Maybe you missed a line?"

"BelleEllen should stay in the family." That statement came down on the room like a giant anvil. All heads turned to Sophie.

"Don't look at me. I don't understand it any more than you do." But she was beginning to understand it quite well.

So was Hollis. He studied her from his end of the table,

looking for a family resemblance, she suspected—his brother-in-law, Craig, seemed still to be doing the math. And for the first time, ever in her life, she felt shame in who she was.

While those closest to the minister grew silent in their uncertainty, his cousins became more adamant: Richard took the lead; the others were his backup singers.

"He figured that because I own a hardware store and George runs a Publix supermarket, that we're morons, that we wouldn't know he was pulling a fast one. But I have a lawyer, too, you know. I knew he was going to hatch some sort of rat-bastard plan to cheat us out of our money."

George's lips moved, but under his booming brother you could hardly hear him. "He always thought he was better than us because Grandpa Hollister disowned our daddy—"

"I'll take you all, and this . . . this"—Richard picked up the large white envelope in front of him and tossed it to the center of the table— "this piece of shit to court."

"—when he was a boy. A teenager. Nineteen, I think. But still, you know teenagers make mistakes." George frowned. "We never did know what it was, that mistake, but teenage boys make 'em all the time. Ask anyone."

"You won't see a dime of it. Not one single dime."

"We have needs, too."

"This isn't fair," the wives chimed in.

"I should have killed that son of a bitch a long time ago when I had the chance. If I'd known he was going to cut me out completely, I would have. You can bet on that."

"They used to be good friends, when they were younger," added George.

"They were, that's true." George's wife confirmed it.

"But see, Arthur inherited his grandpa's money from his mama and got all stuck up and selfish."

Graham Metzer sat listening, patient and stoic, waiting for

the exhibition to wind down; confident the will was solid and unbreakable.

The cousins went on, but Sophie wandered off into her thoughts.

So *this* was what Arthur wanted to confess to her. He was her birth father. Why else would he leave her BelleEllen? What else could his *enormous obligation* to her be?

Maybe if she'd come sooner, she could have told him it didn't matter to her, that she had a perfectly wonderful, truly great dad already. Maybe if she'd come earlier, they could have spared his family the pain of knowing he'd— What? Made a mistake? Impregnated a teenager? Cheated on his wife? Dishonored his ministry?

Gross, appalling sins all. She knew she should be outraged, furious, whatever else someone in her position ought to be feeling—but frankly, at that moment, she simply wasn't.

Her emotions were turning sympathetically toward Arthur. She couldn't stop thinking that his life had clearly been far worse than hers. Far, far worse to be weighted down by sins so huge—even by a man marginally as good and kind and reverent as the town believed him to be. It must have been excruciating for him.

And no doubt he deserved it, no doubt at all. But how much sorrow and torment and penance did one soul have to endure before he received a grain of forgiveness? Even now, in death, his memory would continue to suffer. She wasn't saying he was entitled to forgiveness, only that *she* absolved him of those perpetrated against her—which was no more than creating her life.

And maybe, if she'd come earlier, she could have eased him of *that* pain.

So she sat and let the rhetoric wash over and roll off her until Richard Hollister stood and sent his chair clattering against the wall while he shouted, "You haven't heard the last of this. None of you. I still don't know who the hell *you* are, missy, but I'm telling you, like I'm telling all of you, not to get too comfortable with what that old fool read today because it isn't yours. It'll never be yours."

And with that he stomped out the room, bumping and shoving those in his path, which was almost everyone in the room. His wife, brother, and sister-in-law climbed over and around the furniture to catch up with him; and when the trail became too narrow for the larger lady to get by, Craig stood, taking his pregnant wife with him, to let her pass.

"Thank you," she murmured and followed the others from the room.

This time the silence was more awkward than overwrought, still tense but in a distinctive way. No one wanted to voice out loud what he or she was thinking. No one wanted to know for sure and irrevocably what Sophie's bequest meant.

"Mr. Metzer," she spoke softly at first. "is there any way to. . . . Would it be possible for me to sign the property back to Mr. Cubeck's estate so his family can decide what's best to do with it?" She turned to look at the others, Hollis in particular. "I don't know why he left BelleEllen to me. I don't *want* to know. And I don't want the property. If Mr. Metzer will help, I'll sign the deed over to you . . . and Mr. Chamberlin, I guess. We can work this out. We can make things the way they should be."

Chapter Four

"THEN WHAT HAPPENED?" JESSE WAS PERCHED ON THE EDGE OF HER pins-and-needles chair, biting her nails, wide eyed, all ears—and every other cliché of a good gossip. But who else could Sophie talk to? Besides, she believed her to be a *good gossip* who'd strive to get all the facts and details straight.

"Nothing. Hollis stood up, real slow, like he was in slow motion."

"Shock."

"I hope so." When Jesse frowned, she added, "Shock passes; anger can hang on forever." Jesse wagged her head, concurring, keeping the speak-to-listen ratio low to maintain the flow of information. "He held out a hand in case his wife needed help getting up. She didn't, but she took it anyway and patted it as they walked out of the room with the kids following, without a single word or look back at me. I wanted to sink through the floor."

"I bet."

"But the other one, Craig Chamberlin? I thought he was

going to do the same thing because he hadn't said a word and seemed to be taking his cues from Hollis in all this—but at the last minute he stopped. He tried to smile at me and told me not to worry; that Hollis needed time to process and that it would all work out."

"Mm. He's the guidance counselor at the middle school." Apparently, that explained his forbearance. "So apart from the cousins, no one said anything to you? No one asked questions? No one told you why Arthur left you BelleEllen?"

"I don't think they know any more than I do."

It *had* occurred to her on the walk back to the B&B that Graham Metzer wasn't at all surprised by the contents of the will. Simply because he drafted it? Or did he know the reason behind the inheritance? The details? Had the attorney-client privilege allowed Arthur Cubeck to make a confession, to assuage his guilt, if only for the time it took to tell his lawyer the truth? She decided not to turn around and flip that rock over. She planned to pretend it was none of her business for as long as she could.

"But Hollis and Mr. Metzer will have to hammer it out on their own because I'm going back to Marion tomorrow morning . . . if I can stay here another night."

"Of course. But what about BelleEllen? Don't you at least want to see it?"

"What for?" Her frustration made her answer sharp. She cast Jesse a penitent glance. "I don't want anything to do with any of this. I didn't want to come here in the first place. But I came. I did what a dying old man asked and now I want to go home."

"And you're not curious?" Sophie hadn't had to mention her suspicions. Her landlady had put together her own one-plus-one and come up with three all by herself. It was a relief to be truthful, to be able to talk about it without actually saying it out loud.

She shrugged one shoulder. "Some, I guess. Like, I'd be curious about the ending to a sad movie but not near enough to tear a family apart, to hurt Hollis or damage his memories of an otherwise fine father, a good man. I'm happy with my life. Not knowing isn't going to mess me up the way knowing for sure will Hollis. It's not worth it."

Jesse studied her for a moment, looked slightly disappointed, but seemed to agree. "You're pretty wise for someone so young."

A soft chuckle. "Maybe. This time. When it affects other people more than it does me. But, trust me, there have been many instances where I've proven to be extremely unwise." As in who she was and wasn't attracted to, for example.

Jesse sighed and leaned back in her chair. "You're right about BelleEllen, too, though. It should stay in Arthur's family. Well, you know, with Ellen's children—child. The grandchildren," she said, finally getting the connections right. "Except that Hollis lives in Texas now, where Jane's family is. I wonder if they'll move back here? Or once this is all settled, maybe he'll let the Chamberlins live there. Craig was a big help to Arthur out there, since he first got sick. But then, Lucy might not be comfortable there, you know, because of Julie. . . ." She went silent, mentally attempting to solve the problem of what to do with BelleEllen once Sophie walked away.

But that wasn't her problem. Her involvement would end when she withdrew her claim on the property. And she could do that from Marion. *She* was going up to pack.

"Oh, no. Don't, not yet. I'm going to start dinner soon, but I thought I'd have a lemonade first . . . or better yet, a glass of cheap chardonnay. And I hate drinking alone. Unless, of course, you need some time to be alone and I would certainly understand. You can even take your wine up with you. You've had a crazy day, that's for sure."

Honestly: she was quickly falling in love with this woman. "I'd love a glass of wine—or two."

"Wonderful. It's a gorgeous afternoon. We'll sit out on the veranda and watch my flowers grow." When Sophie hesitated, she grinned. "Otherwise known as the front porch? There's a patio out back but nothing ever happens back there. All the action's out front."

And sure enough, as they lounged in the fan-backed wicker chairs like two southern belles sipping white wine instead of mint juleps, Sophie was regaled with the identity and a short—and occasionally quite long—personal history of every waving or honking occupant in every car that drove by. Sophie ranked those ninety minutes of her life right up there with reading *Rabble Magazine's Most and Least Interesting People of the Decade*, and enjoyed it thoroughly.

"Uh-oh, there's Mike. It must be time for dinner. He's better than a clock. And I haven't even started it yet." Jesse grabbed her wineglass and broke for the door. "I was having too much fun. I completely lost track of the time. Stall him, will you? I'll fix nibbles to hold you both over."

Sophie, on her second glass of wine, was feeling mighty getalongable at the moment—she'd handle the kid.

Soon enough Mike came into view, casually riding his bike down the middle of the street with one hand only on the handlebars. He used the other to pop his earphones; and seeing her on the porch, he sat up straight and put both hands in his pockets with a friendly smile. "Hey."

"Hi."

At a precise point in the road he reached out with both hands for the bars and used the neighbor's drive to launch himself onto the sidewalk. Passing the corner post of his mother's wrought-iron fence, he kicked it and like magic the latch slipped and the gate swung open in time for him to sail through, breeze up the path between his mother's flower beds, across the front of the house and around the side to park in the back.

He must have done it a million times before.

A moment later, he reappeared.

"Wow. Bike skillz."

He laughed, leaping the new growth in the beds to close the gate. He jog-bounced back to the porch to stand before her. "Wait till I get a car."

Her turn to laugh. "That would definitely be worth a trip back here to see."

He draped himself in his mother's chair like a loose noodle. "I can hardly wait. Yours is a solid ride."

They both looked to the new red Liberty at the curb. "Well, I need something solid. We can get a lot of snow in Ohio."

"Yeah, I figured. I meant it's nice."

"Oh, right. Solid. Thanks."

"Problem is, my bike's better for my speed and strength training," he went on. "For basketball? And my balance. Probably my reflexes, too, cuz people are always trying to run me down on it." To her frown, he looked sheepish. "I don't always pay attention." And hearing the sound of his mother's steps coming toward the door, he said in a loud, clear voice, "But don't tell my mom."

"Don't tell your mom what?"

Jesse pushed through the screen door with a small plate of cheese and crackers to snack on. "And don't tell me *nothing* or I'll duct tape your feet to the ceiling and tickle it out of you."

"How much I love your cooking, Ma." He grinned and she bought it. "Which reminds me: I'm starving."

"Here. Dinner'll be ready in twenty minutes. Share that with Sophie now," she said, pausing briefly in the doorway. "How'd you do, honey?"

"Sixty-eight."

"Not bad."

He took exactly half the cheese and crackers and handed the rest to Sophie, who asked, "Can I ask? Sixty-eight what?"

"As mom would say: I don't know, *can* you."

"*May* I?" She feigned the humbled teacher expression and he chuckled.

"Free throws. I shoot at least a hundred a day, practicing. Today I made sixty-eight of them. I'd like to get it up to between eighty and ninety—consistently. Fifty's respectable but respectable's just, you know, respectable. I'm gonna be great."

"I believe you." She considered the boy as she took tiny bites of a square piece of cheddar cheese. She really did believe him.

"I can see why she likes you."

"Your mom?"

He gave a nod. "You're easy to talk to." He raised his brows and lowered his voice. "Which she loves to do, in case you hadn't noticed."

"I like her, too. I enjoy people who are"—she searched for the best words—"well versed in current events."

His laugh was more a hoot. He opened his mouth to respond as a cream-colored Escalade pulled up to the curb and Hollis Cubeck got out.

"Want me to go get my mom?"

The question so startled Sophie that she lost the air she'd been holding in her lungs. "What? No. Why?"

"In case he's got a gun or something."

She gave a halfhearted chuckle and shook her head. "You heard? You know already?" He shrugged; he had informational skillz, too. "He's not going to kill me, especially in front of a witness. He may want to beat me with a baseball bat, but he isn't carrying one, so I think we should wait and see what he wants first."

"So I can stay?"

"No. You should probably go. Thanks, though. But this is between him and me."

" 'K," he said, standing, watching Hollis with a wary expression as he slipped inside the house. She suspected he wouldn't go far, that he'd hear everything anyway and shamelessly she didn't mind.

Hollis's steps were heavy and slow as he mounted the steps; she stood to meet him. There were so many emotions etched across his face that she had to guess at his prime motivation for coming to her: dread.

"Mr. Cubeck. I'm glad you're here. I want to tell you how awful I feel about this morning and that I'm willing to do whatever you think best to make it right. I didn't come here to—"

He listened with a placid expression at first, then held up his hand to stop her.

"I believe you," he said at last, his voice calm and reasonable. "I believe you're as confused by all this as I am. I do. So I came to ask . . . I'd like a paternity test. Please. I suspect we're both making the same assumptions. And if you are family, I think," he glanced away briefly, "well, I think we should honor my dad's wishes." He hesitated. "The thing is, Ms. Shepard—"

"Sophie."

"The thing is, Sophie: it doesn't ring true. What we're thinking. I know my dad. I knew him. Very well. I think we're jumping to the wrong conclusion."

"You do? Oh, thank God. Why?"

He actually laughed at her reaction, visibly relaxing.

"A dozen reasons, the least of which is trying to picture him giving away his own child. Also, he would never, *never* seduce a teenager. But mostly because he wouldn't cheat on my mother." *Well, okay*—Sophie was willing to hang it up right there. "But that isn't to say it isn't possible." *Uh-oh.* "How old are you?"

"I'll be twenty-seven in August."

He nodded, satisfied. "I'm thirty-nine. My mother and older sister died when I was ten; Julie was eight. That's at least two years before you were conceived. My dad could certainly be yours. I didn't know him to date much, at all actually, but I also can't swear he was a monk for the last thirty years. However, if it turns out he is your father, I *can* swear that your mother was no teenager."

She could see why Craig and Mr. Metzer had entrusted the situation to Hollis. He was clear thinking and practical, and far more understanding and charitable than she imagined most people would be in the same circumstances. She had to wonder if these were traits of his father's that he'd learned to emulate or something intrinsic to him. Either way she, too, felt she could trust him.

She nodded. "Everyone I've talked to has told me what a good man he was. I can see you loved him very much. So I have to wonder: Is knowing that important to you, Mr. Cubeck? I mean—"

"Hollis. Please."

She smiled at his grace, then asked, "Aside from me inheriting BelleEllen, which I don't want, do you really need to know for sure? Is it going to change what you think of him, how you feel about him? I guess it's natural for you to be curious, but is knowing going to change anything? I'll be completely honest with you: it doesn't matter to me. My curiosity has never been more than mild and fleeting, even when I was a kid. I've always had the only dad I've ever wanted and I'm far more interested in tomorrow than I ever have been the past."

He nodded, considering her words. "I once had two sisters, and I lost them both. My mother and now my dad are gone, too. I . . . I have no expectations of you, Sophie, but I would like to know if I have a half sister out there—if it's all the same to you."

It wasn't all the same to her. She could ask not to be informed of the results, she guessed, but she'd find out anyway by what Hollis decided to do about BelleEllen, so . . .

Then again, he'd been so cool about the whole thing, it felt like the least she could do for him.

"Knowing I have a half brother could be a good thing, I suppose. You never know when you might need a kidney or something." She grinned at him. "Let's do it."

The next morning, at a nine o'clock appointment in the hospital lab, her contribution to the paternity test was an easy rubbing on the inside of her mouth with a sterile swab. It was over in no time—except for the three-day waiting period for the results, which she'd promised Hollis she would hang around for.

Simply comparing blood types with Arthur Cubeck would have been quick but inconclusive; DNA results were indisputable but they took longer. *Of course.*

Maybe she ought to rent an apartment, she pondered wryly, wondering how many more times she'd have to postpone her departure.

Not that she had anything more pressing to do.

She'd agreed to do some tutoring of first and second graders struggling with reading and math, but that was still weeks away. She'd thought about painting her bedroom and possibly the bathroom in the meantime, but it wasn't her favorite leisure-time interest—and she never did decide on colors. Still and all, she hadn't planned on more than an overnight in Clearfield and she hated being bored.

She could explore the town, but she didn't think that would take more than a day. She tried to recall if she'd seen a movie theater on Main Street, but she wasn't sure. She wasn't much of a window shopper, but if she got desperate . . . She might spend time in Charlottesville checking out the university— ask her dad where to go and what to see; call him when she got there to give him a verbal tour and updates on the changes over the last quarter of a century, which she imagined were considerable. Perhaps a drive in the country? She would take on most anything to avoid having to think about the test re-sults.

And just as she was collecting her purse and preparing to go, a possible solution presented himself.

"Hi."

"Drew. Hi. How did you know I'd . . . or you didn't. I mean, you probably come here a lot, to the lab. And I hap-pened to be . . . well . . . Hi." *Aw, jeeze.*

Kindly, he pretended not to notice her prattle. "Actually, I did know you'd be here. Jesse called. I asked to be notified when you arrived, but I was with a patient or I'd have come down sooner for moral support."

"Oh. Thanks. But it was easy. Just a swab. I was prepared for them to draw blood. After being with my mom and see-ing what she went through, I've developed a reasonably good queasy threshold, so needles don't bother me too much any-more." She stood, thanked the tech, and left the cubicle. "Not nearly as much as hospitals, in general, anyway. You'd think with all the advancements in modern medicine, someone would come up with something for this wretched smell. And don't bother telling me it's disinfectant because every hospital I've been in smells exactly the same, and I don't believe for a second that they're all using the same antiseptics. It's death, isn't it? Rotting bodies and the various byproducts masked by the scents of bland, boiled food, floor polish, and *then* cleaning products. Right?" She looked up to find him staring at her, his expression in check. "No offense." He frowned as if in pain, closed his eyes and gave a short shake of his head. "What?"

His face split into a wide grin, and when he opened his eyes they were bright with humor. "I'm guessing this is a no to a cup of coffee in the doctors' lounge."

"Oh." *Fudge!* "I . . . oh, dear . . . I didn't mean . . . well, I did mean it but not, you know, the smell doesn't make me want to vomit or pass out or anything. It's, you know," she flipped her hand around in the air, "memories. Like spaghetti sauce and chocolate chip cookies, only not as nice. And not together. Eggs, too, smell good sometimes, though I think most hospitals use the powdered kind so they don't smell as good as real eggs . . . actually, they don't smell at all if you ask me but some people might—"

Seemingly unable to control himself any longer, he reached out and clamped her cheeks between his hands to shut her up.

Thank you, God! A short prayer of gratitude for saving her from herself.

"How about dinner instead?"

People were always talking about how green Ireland was . . . and while she looked into Drew McCarren's gaze, she got lost in a comparison she couldn't, in fact, make because she'd never been there. But she would—go—if only to have something to weigh against the color of his eyes.

"Sophie?" She blinked. "Dinner?" She nodded. "Seven?" This time she smiled and nodded. He did the same and released her. "Good. I'll see you later."

"Okay." She thought about telling him how much she was

looking forward to it, thanking him for the invitation—noting his kindness to a stranger in his town, and God only knew what else—but she worried that more than two blathers a day would scare the doctor away. And she didn't want to do that, at least not for the next three days.

She'd taken her car to the hospital, but the facility was only two blocks off the main drag so she decided to leave her car and walk. She was missing her morning runs.

She wanted to buy more toothpaste—if she had to stick around a few days more, her little travel tube wasn't going to make it. Plus, if there was some sort of clothing store she could look for something cheap to run in . . . and maybe a new dress for her date. Maybe.

It might have been the early summer sweetness in the air, the birds singing and the bees buzzing, but Clearfield stirred a light, peaceful sensation deep in her spirit. Like watching a magnificent sunrise—except there was nothing *magnificent* about the town. Quaint and charming describe it better. Quaint, charming and . . . serene.

There appeared to be only two stoplights, barely visible, one on each end of the long Main Street—which was tree lined with bumper-to-bumper parking along the sidewalk. At its heart, it featured a round town square with a lovely, pristine gazebo set on a small knoll. Most of the people had a friendly smile or an easy nod to make her feel welcome. Like Marion, it gave every indication of being small-town America at its finest.

And, like Marion, she knew the more domestically commercial and official town buildings would be grouped tightly midtown, while fast-food, automotive, and industrial interests would sprawl out at each end of the road.

And so she turned left, heading for the businesses across

the street from the gazebo, and sure enough . . . Eddy's Eatery (open 7 A.M. to 9 P.M. for breakfast, lunch, and dinner), Granny's Attic (antiques), Clearfield Credit Union and Arts Council (interesting combination), Lemming's Plumbing and Hardware (pipes and stuff), Pullman's Stationery (stationery) and the Kreski's drugstore—toothpaste.

And because she had nine hours to kill before her date, she took her time meandering through cosmetics and cards, taking up a *People* magazine and picking through paperbacks for a novel to read. She studied the boxes of candy bars while she waited for the customer in front of her to finish at the register. When her turn came, she set her harvest on the counter, then snatched up a Hershey with Almonds and set it on top—for the walk back.

She was smiling when she looked up at the clerk—he was frowning at her. With hair like straw in color and texture, the middle-aged man in khaki pants and a blue plaid cotton shirt sent a sharp, alarming chill down her spine. She got the queer impression that he recognized her in spite of the fact that she was *positive* she'd never seen him before.

The first conclusion she jumped to was her hair.

People were always commenting on or making weird assumptions about it or her because it was red . . . and curly. More a deep burnt-orange color—the kind that eliminates your facial features like an egghead mannequin if you wear black, white, or pastels—a distinction that even imposter redheads know is more about skin tone than hair color. Most folks saw her hair before they looked at her face and were often reminded of redheads they'd known in the past—she was guilty of the same thing with men who have red bulbous noses because her alcoholic uncle Leo had one. It didn't automatically make the men alcoholics or even mean that they looked like her uncle Leo, only that the nose reminded her of him.

No doubt this man was having the same sort of reaction, so she continued to smile pleasantly until he recovered. However, he seemed only to become increasingly agitated, and when a young girl in a blue smock caught his eye, he snapped at her: "It's about time. Come handle this. I have things to do."

And with that, he sent Sophie one last glare and hurried off. His previous redhead must have been a real doozy, she surmised, offering her smile to the girl instead. She reciprocated and said, "Hi. Did you find everything you wanted?"

"I did. Thank you."

But the man had given her the creeps—so should she need more toothpaste, she'd be going to the Rite Aid.

Her original impression that Clearfield was a nice town was re-reinforced by the rest of the residents, however, who were amicable and helpful. She went into several stores with summer fashions in the window displays, found cheap stretchy bicycle shorts and a sport bra in one and might have passed over Betty's Boutique based solely on the unfair rationale that Beverly's Boutique in Marion leaned toward drab fashions for older ladies—until she saw the most wonderful fern green sundress draped oh-so carefully over a small tufted chair in the shop window. She chirped a sigh, went in, and emerged twenty minutes later with the dress, a muted tan-brown shrug, and a pair of light, breezy sandals.

She might have skipped back to her car, she was so happy, but for the peculiar notion that someone was watching her. Like at night, when she scooted faster than necessary from the trash cans to the back door with goose bumps on her arms, sensing the boogeyman who lived in the mind of her inner six-year-old. She always felt foolish and chided herself, but she couldn't stop it. And truth be told, she much preferred being hyperaware of her surroundings than to be walking around like an oblivious airhead.

So she gave herself permission to look back, just a couple of times, and saw no one.

It wasn't until she reached her car that she felt it again. Only this time she had no doubt. After stowing her treasures on the backseat, she got behind the wheel, put her purse on the passenger seat, buckled in, and looked up in time to catch a big blue pickup truck stop at the end of the block, kitty-corner to the hospital parking lot. All she could see of the man inside were his aviator glasses and a thick and jowly face under a green baseball cap. He turned off his truck but didn't get out. Instead, he sat, boldly assessing her. It wasn't another red-hair thing—it was too deliberate, too constant, too composed. Menacing even, but that made no sense at all. She hadn't been in town a week and yet . . .

Suddenly, he seemed to realize that she was inspecting him as closely as he was her. He started his engine, made an illegal U-turn in the street that crossed the front of the hospital, and sped off.

Sophie sat motionless, confused. Certainly, compared to the other odd events she'd witnessed lately, this one was pretty tame. Typical, too, for someone to be curious about the new—and now infamous—girl in town. As far as she could see she had two choices: sit in the car wondering until she was old and gray or shrug it off as one of those peculiar things that happen sometimes.

She chose the latter.

Chapter Five

"OH. IT'S PURR-FECT." JESSE WAS, SOPHIE SENSED, AN UNDEMAND-ing critic who would have said the same thing had she descended in the garment bag she'd brought the dress home in. Still, it was a terrific dress and she felt good in it, which all the real authorities said was, in the end, the important thing. "Tell her, Mike."

He looked away from the flat screen, gave her a hard once-over, a nod, and a grin. "Oh, yeah. Purr-fect."

"Smart aleck." He chuckled and went back to his program. "You look lovely, Sophie. You certainly know how to work with that beautiful hair of yours."

She smiled her gratitude but had to admit, "That's all my mom's doing. She had great taste and she considered me her greatest challenge. One of my first memories is of walking behind her through the kids' department at Penney's and her draping clothes over one side of my face to compare both my hair and my skin with a specific color. We did the same thing in fabric stores. She didn't know how to sew but she'd ask for swatches of this color and that color; and by the time I was insisting on shopping *alone,* she'd put eyelets in all those little pieces of material and strung them on a key chain for me to carry around in my purse." She laughed softly. "She sounds like a complete control freak, doesn't she?"

"No, no," Jesse protested facetiously. "Not at all." They laughed.

"I guess she was. But I'll always think of her more as a perfectionist. A perfectionist who wanted everything to be perfect for me."

"Was it hard living up to her expectations?"

"No, not really. You see, I already *was* perfect—to my parents anyway. Even when I screwed up, which I did fairly frequently, they always made the best of it or found something good about it. Even if they couldn't think of anything spectacular, it was at the very least a learning experience for me. . . ." She gave a soft laugh as she went thoughtful. "It isn't often you find people who believe in you so blindly."

"I think, when your time comes, you'll find that most parents believe in their children. Maybe not blindly but faithfully. By blood or not, the bond between a parent and a child is an amazing thing." She glanced lovingly toward Mike in the TV room, who, with a smirk on his face, was pretending not to hear them. "Or I'd have sold him to a circus long ago."

"They *buy* all those clowns? No wonder they all dress badly."

"Yep. Smart-alecky boys, all of them. Little ones, big ones. Jugglers, basketball players, all kinds. I've checked it out. Several times."

Mike's grin got bigger and he shook his head but still refused to look their way—until the doorbell rang. He flew to answer it, muttering, "Ya'll 'er scary crazy," as he passed.

"Hey, Mike. How ya doin'?"

"Let me put it this way: You're saving my life."

Drew stepped inside, his palms up as in *ta-da* . . . "Saving lives is my job, man." He caught sight of Sophie, and after a slow head-to-toe stroke of a look that made her squirm with delight inside, he frowned and looked back at Mike. "What? You need saving from two beautiful women? Maybe you need a different kind of doctor."

"Dude. One of 'em is my mom."

The man gave the boy a commiserating bob of his head. "Right. In that case, I can certainly feel your pain. Unfortunately—"

"Oh, pooh." Jesse broke in with a laugh. "You two have the nicest mothers in town. Give us gratitude, not grief. Now, where are you taking our girl here? Someplace nice?"

"Burger King," he told Jesse without hesitation. "McDonald's has better fries, of course, but *King* implies a more elegant dinning experience, don't you think?"

While she sputtered playfully, he offered Sophie a wink and his hand, which she took, knowing as well as he did that if they didn't keep moving, they might never get out of the house.

"Now, how did I know you'd be such a culinary snob about this, Jesse?" He gave Mike a fond, reassuring squeeze on one shoulder and pushed the screen door open to let Sophie out. "So purely to keep you happy, I also made a reservation at Tony's. He said he'd hold it until nine o'clock when I called to push it back, which means we should probably get going or we'll end up out on the curb eating leftover spaghetti off paper plates. In which case Burger King *would* start looking good."

"Oh, like Tony wouldn't stay open all night if you asked him. Don't let them fool you, Sophie. Two more unlikely friends you'll never see. Tony's a mountain-sized football player who turned his fondness for food—"

"Whoa. Whoa. Whoa. This is *my* date. If you tell her everything, I won't have anything left to say. She'll think I'm dull as dirt and it'll be your fault."

"Oh, please." She tsked, pretending to be indignant. "Fine. Go. Leave me with the ungrateful child." She threw her arms around Mike's neck from behind and he let her. "Be back before dawn." Mike rolled his eyes and started pushing the door closed. "I don't want to have to explain anything to the neighbors, but I do expect a full report when—"

They were both laughing going down the steps to the sidewalk, still holding hands. Drew stopped, turned to her, and heaved a sigh. "Hi."

"Hi."

"Sorry I'm late."

She smiled. "I appreciated the call. Your patients can't exactly call in to schedule a crisis. I hope it went okay."

He gave a nod. "In case I don't mention it every time I think it tonight, you look beautiful."

"Thank you," she said, happy to hide her heady flush in the twilight—it not being in her color wheel and all. "New dress."

"Mm. It's nice, too." His second compliment caught her off guard and the double flush that came in response was almost painful, though apparently the dusk wasn't as concealing as she'd hoped. He grinned perceptively and moved on, ignoring her stunned silence. "I hope you like Italian. Tony cooks a bit of everything, otherwise he'd never make it in a town this size; but he loves eating Italian, so that's what he cooks best." He pulled the iron gate open and let her pass through. "He's likely to come out of the kitchen, brag about his secret recipes, and even tell you what you should eat, but feel free to order what you want or he'll—" He stopped when she did and frowned at her expression. "What?"

"That truck." She nodded sideways to the big blue one

parked up the block. She wasn't sure if she should stare back at the man seated inside to show she wasn't troubled by his presence—which was a lie—or casually look away to withhold any satisfaction he might be getting if he was indeed stalking her. "I saw it . . . him"—*if the cap he's wearing is green*—"this morning. Across from the hospital." The rest of what she was thinking was too strange to say out loud; and yet, with the sickening drain of blood from under her skin that left her feeling clammy and queasy, she couldn't help herself. "I think he's watching me."

Drew's hesitation to believe her was so brief she almost kissed him. "I'm pretty sure that's Cliff Palmeroy. I . . . well, wait here a second. I'll be right back."

"No, don't," she said, totally without heart, instinctively following him into the street. "I mean, it could be coincidence."

"Then we'll only be a few more minutes late for dinner. We'll say hi and be on our way."

"I feel ridiculous." But only marginally. "I'm probably overreacting."

"Do you do that a lot? Overreact?"

"Well no, not usually but—"

"One of the most amazing things I've learned in my profession is that people often don't give their instincts enough credit. So many of the people I see have known or suspected, but refused to believe, that they're desperately ill until it's too late. And when relatively stable patients tell me they are dying—imminently, at that very moment—despite all evidence to the contrary, I always call their minister and loved ones in. And sure enough, they die a few hours later. My advice: always listen to your instincts." He hesitated. "What's he doing? Sleeping?"

With his arm from the elbow down dangling out the open

window of the truck, Cliff Palmeroy's head was tipped at a backward angle to the left, his cap bill low over his eyes. "See? Stupid. Let's not disturb him."

"He might not be asleep. Could be a coronary or a stroke or a diabetic—" Abruptly he stepped in front of her, putting his back to the truck and turning her around, her back to him, calm but urgently saying, "Call 911."

"What? Why?" Her hands shook as she went for her phone. "What is it?"

"Don't turn around, Sophie."

But even as she dialed the ominous number, she turned and asked, "Why? What's happened? Is he ill?" And putting the cell to her ear, she finally looked up and took a step closer to see if she could help. "Oh, Jesus!"

She saw the man's gaping mouth, the dark bib of blood, thick and wide, down the front of his T-shirt; the explosion of splatter that spotted the driver's window casing and dripped down the door panel—she caught the scent of feces and rusty nails, and the wide-open look of horror in his eyes before she could turn away again.

"What's happened to him? Yes, hello. Hello? Yes. There's blood . . ." She took a deep breath—swallowed several times to keep the salt and bile in the back of her throat. "A man's been injured. We're on Poplar Street, a few blocks down from the hospital. I can't see an address, but we're across from Jesse Halleron's bed-and-breakfast. He's in a truck. There's a doctor here but he's going to need help. There's a lot of blood. What? His name? Dr. McCarren? Oh, the man's name. Cliff . . . something."

"Palmeroy."

"Cliff Palmeroy. Well, I don't—" She half turned but didn't look at Drew. Her hands were shaking—she trembled as if she was standing inside her own personal earthquake. "Is he . . . ?"

"Yes. He's dead," he said directly behind her, reaching to take the phone—which she gave up willingly. He put an arm around her shoulders, no doubt an automatic thing for someone like him but she didn't care; she leaned into him before the shivering took her to her knees. "Drew McCarren. We're going to need the police, too, and someone from the coroner's office will want to see this. Thanks. No, I'll stay. I can hear them already."

Her stomach pitched like waves in a storm—up and down and up again. Salty saliva pooled in her throat again and her mind raced in no specific direction.

Sirens had started to whine in the distance. Closer, far off down the street, they could see red lights flashing as an ambulance sped to their aide.

"Why don't you go back to Jesse's? You don't need to be here. The cops'll want to talk to you, too, but it'll be a while and I'll tell them where you are."

"Are you sure? I'm not as wimpy as I must seem right now. I wasn't expecting . . . it's a shock is all. I can stay. You shouldn't have to deal with this alone."

"There's isn't anything for me to deal with. Once the cops get here, they'll handle it. Go ahead. I'll be along in a few minutes."

There was no point arguing—she'd rather be the full-time poop scooper at Kaufman Dog Park *and* the vomit monitor during flu season at her school than contend with the huge strew of blood.

"And you're sure you've never seen the victim before this morning?" This was the third time Sheriff Murphy posed the same question. He was a tall, sandy-haired man in his midforties—very serious and awfully intimidating in his efforts to be thorough.

"Yes. I'm positive." But that was all she was sure of. Her ankles and the tips of her fingers were numb—and vomiting again was not out of the question.

"And you're certain it was the same man because you recognized the truck?"

"Yes. Well, and the green hat."

"So seeing a man in a blue truck, wearing a green hat convinced you that he was watching you?"

"For crying out loud, Freddy!" A disconcerted Jesse sprang from her chair to begin pacing again. "Pay attention!"

"Mom," Mike said, but she ignored him.

"How many times does the girl need to tell you? This morning, at the hospital, was the first time she'd ever seen him in her life. He stared at her from across the street and then drove off. She thought it was weird but didn't put too much stock in it. She was here with me the rest of the day until Drew showed up for their date. They left the house and she saw him, for the second time in her life, parked up the street in front of the Levy's house. She mentioned both encounters to Drew, who decided to go say hello to Cliff and find out why he was watching Sophie. And that's when they found him dead in his truck and . . . my God, who would *do* such a thing? I know lots of us have *wanted* to at one time or another—he was a miserable excuse for a man but . . . who would do it? I saw Carla at the grocery store the day before yesterday. Poor thing's so flighty . . . if there'd been anything amiss at home she'd have been a wreck. But she was as calm as she ever gets, the kids were with her— Who would *do* this?" She stopped to glare at the sheriff. "Don't make me sorry I voted for you, Freddy. If you accuse Sophie again I'll . . . I'll run for sheriff myself next time. And I won't need a badge to see when someone is so obviously innocent."

Sheriff Murphy glared back. "First off, *Ms. Halleron,* I'm

not accusing anyone of anything," he said, walking toward her. And when he was close enough, he muttered under his breath, "You call me Freddy again and I'll arrest *you*." He turned back to Sophie and Drew, sitting on the couch. "And secondly: sometimes, if a witness repeats what happened more than once, they can recall additional facts like: Did he speak to anyone this morning or did he seem agitated; could there have been anyone with him, in the truck bed maybe, or . . ."

He looked into the foyer when the front door opened and a deputy walked in holding a camera sealed in a plastic bag.

"Hey, Mike," Jesse said.

"Jesse." He nodded, approaching the sheriff. He glanced at Sophie. "Ma'am."

"How's it going out there?" Drew asked, having seen the officer earlier.

"It'll be a while yet." He looked to his boss. "I thought you should see this right away. I noticed it was still on when I bagged it. I meant to turn it off—to save the battery—but this first picture showed up on the screen. I looked at the others. Sorry."

When the sheriff was close enough, they stood, heads together, over the view screen—the sheriff's brow lowering a bit more with each new picture. When he looked up, his gaze went straight to Sophie.

"Are you sure you've never met Cliff Palmeroy?"

"Oh, for the love of heaven!" Jesse plopped down in a chair, shaking her head, but she said no more.

"Yes. To my knowledge, I've never met the man."

"Okay. Can you explain these pictures to me, then?"

He motioned with his head for his deputy to hand her the camera—he also demonstrated how to slide through the pictures . . .

Of her.

"Look." She swung the camera in Drew's direction; she needed someone else to see what she was seeing. "It's me. Coming out of the dress shop this morning." Jesse joined them on the couch, straining her upper body to look, too. Mike stood behind the sofa, silent, peering down over their shoulders. Her head began to throb at the temples. "And walking back to my car. This one, too. Oh. Jesse. You and I on the porch this afternoon. And . . . is this . . . that's my car, my license plate." Fear and frustration made her eyes water as she looked back at the sheriff. "I can't. Explain these pictures. I don't understand any of this."

Deputy Martin took back the camera and the air in the room became brittle and still, all eyes focused on the sheriff. In time, he provided a loud, baffled sigh and they all relaxed— sort of.

"Truth be told, there aren't that many murders committed here in Turchin County, Ms. Shepard. An accident now and again, naturally, but murder? Not so much. It's hard to hide little things, like a murder, in a town this size. *Somebody* will have seen something and then we'll get to the bottom of this."

"Stop looking at her as if she's the something. *Fred*." Jesse squished Sophie tighter between her and Drew. "Go out and find the somebody who witnessed this. No one here did anything to Cliff Palmeroy."

"Jesus, Jesse, I'm not saying any of you did!"

"We know, Fred." Drew's voice was clear and calming. "We, all of us, are shook up and," a quick glance at Jesse, "not quite ourselves right now. I know you have a lot to do tonight, so if you're done with us, maybe we can call it a night and let you get back to work. I'm sure if Sophie remembers anything else she'll let you know."

"I will. I promise. I don't . . . Those pictures, I have no idea why he'd be taking pictures of me but I'll call you—if I think of anything else. Or remember. Or if I can do . . . Well, maybe you should call me if there's anything I can do. I—"

Jesse curved an arm over Sophie's chest, saying, "shhh, shhh," as if to comfort her. And pulling her into a hug, she whispered in her ear. "Don't be too helpful, honey. The most cooperative person is almost always the bad guy on TV—especially when it's the special guest star."

Leaning back between Jesse and Drew, she watched them exchange a scowl of supreme disbelief and a wide-eyed, silently emphatic dare to say different. But neither of them said another word.

"Fair enough." Sheriff Murphy flipped his notepad closed and took two steps toward the door before turning back. He gave Jesse a droll eye. "Is this the part where the unbiased and remarkably tolerant sheriff warns everyone not to leave town without checking with him first?" She huffed and rolled her eyes as he grew sober. "Consider it said, people."

He left but he didn't take any of the stress with him.

Oddly, she became keenly aware of the breathing on both sides of her. Her mind filled with the anticipation of every rise and fall of her companions' chests. At first she tried to synchronize her own respiratory rate with Drew's, but his chest was broader and deeper and she got light-headed. And Jesse's breaths were rapid and erratic—like the increasing tremors in her hands. On an impulse that was as selfish as it was caring, Sophie reached out to stop them; she couldn't handle someone else's anxiety until she'd dealt with her own—and at the moment it was all she could do to simply take in air.

Jesse stood and plumped all the sofa pillows she could get to.

"Maybe a stiff drink . . . anyone else? I might have a shot of bourbon but I have wine and beer, too." Her voice faltered when she muttered, "Not nearly stiff enough, if you ask me." She flicked invisible dust off the end table and put her back to them while she straightened a level picture of an old-time watermill on the wall. "Anyone?"

Swallowing presented itself as a more complicated concept than breathing, but she knew Jesse disliked drinking alone. "Sure. Water maybe? I'm not sure what my stomach can handle yet."

"I'll pass, thanks. I should get going."

Yet he made no move to leave, which was fine by Sophie. No doubt, most any doctor would be clear thinking and self-possessed in a crisis. But it hadn't been most any doctor out there beside the big blue truck with her. It was Drew, who knew what to do, who tried to protect her from seeing what no human should, who sent her to safety while he stayed, alone, until the police came. Self-centered, she knew it, but she was thinking he could stay as long as he wanted to. The longer the better.

She could feel him studying her and looked up to see concern in his eyes. She bowed her lips a bit to abate his worries— it made him scowl and say, "What are you smiling about? So far this has been, hands down, my worst first date ever."

It surprised a giggle from her and then they both laughed softly.

"Attagirl." He bumped his shoulder against hers. "Sheriff's right, you know. By breakfast, everyone in town will be looking sideways at everyone else. Someone will slip up, make a mistake and the truth about whatever happened here tonight will come out. And it won't have anything to do with you."

"What about the pictures?"

He shrugged. "So Cliff had an eye for beautiful women, and you happen to be one. I don't think they can arrest you for that."

"Jesse didn't like him. She made him sound like a not-so-nice guy."

"Mm. I think they went to school about the same time. Seems he was one of those popular jock-slash-bully types who left his game in high school and lost his popularity shortly after that. Stayed a bully, though. And guys like that all seem to have a special talent of picking the weakest person out of a crowd to torment.

"Carla, his wife, is tiny and frail—a sweet, anxious woman who seems always to be sitting on the verge of a mental collapse. He also has two quiet, sullen teenage sons who seem well on their way to becoming just like him." He paused. "Sometimes there are worse things a man can do to his family than beat them, you know?"

She nodded, but she didn't know. Not in truth. At the moment she was almost ashamed to admit that the cruelest her parents ever got was to refuse her a Canadian ski trip with a friend—*and his family!*—in seventh grade. Well, and saying no to extending her curfew all through high school . . . *and,* to letting her get her ears pierced, not until she was sixteen. Still, it was hard to be sorry your childhood was simple and happy and as close to perfect as it ever got—especially in the face of someone else's misery.

Another option occurred to her: "You don't think . . . I mean, he probably wasn't taking pictures of me to . . . you know, later on . . ." She knew what she was trying to say, just not *how* to say it. However, Drew knew both what and how and chose to simply watch with amusement as she struggled. "Stop that. You know what I mean."

He chuckled. "I do. And while different guys get off on different things—shoes, elbows, middle-aged gap-toothed wives— I'd be willing to bet that Cliff Palmeroy's bent was toward something a lot more salacious than those pictures of you."

"Gross, man! There's a child in the room." They both turned to watch Mike unfold himself from the chair near Jesse's office door, and then go wide-striding out of the room, saying, "If Mom knew that I knew what you two are talking about, she'd wash my brain out with soap."

It was true—that old adage about laughter being the best medicine. Every half-laugh and giggle eased the tightness in her chest, dissolved the fuzz in her thoughts. Her smile faded as they returned to Cliff Palmeroy.

"Why did he take them? The pictures."

"We don't know that he did. Not for sure."

"Who then? And how'd they end up in his truck?"

After a few seconds even his expression wilted. It disheartened her—made her chest ache heavily. She sought to lighten the mood again.

"What do you get off on?" The words slipped from her lips like drool from a Mastiff. She wasn't even sure she'd uttered them out loud until his lips quirked and he cast a twinkling gaze her way. Once again she felt the heat rising up both sides of her neck, pooling her cheeks.

"Since you asked . . ." He turned to face her more directly. "Freckles. Not the average, run-of-the-mill round tan freckles that anyone can get. Or sunburn freckles that are bigger, darker, and jagged around the edges, which you, remarkably, have very few of—"

"We used to tease my mom about her silent partnership in Coppertone."

"Smart woman." He kept lowering his gaze away, briefly, but often enough to make her nose twitch and her lips tingle.

"Aha. I appreciate it more now than I used to."

In slow motion he reached up and slid his index finger down the left side of her nose, featherlight and heart crumpling. "These are the ones I like. So tiny and faded, they probably aren't even visible in the winter. But come summer they reappear, a reminder of summers gone by, of a wild little redhead running barefoot and happy in Ohio . . . slick as a fish lip, from her mother's sunscreen."

This time she snorted, an astonished hoot that came all the way from her troubled soul.

"I'm also a sucker for a bright smile and a good laugh; the sound of it. Not those high cackling noises or the lifeless, fake-sounding kind. Like *huhuhuhu*." Truly fake and lifeless and funny when he did it. "But a happy, healthy laugh. Like yours."

She tipped her head, very conscious of her smile *and* that she hadn't thought of the bloody dead man in the truck for the past three or four minutes *and* that he was deliberately making her forget.

Getting her first real taste of Drew McCarren was like stuffing her mouth full of Pop Rocks—unsettling at first, but instantly identified as something uncommon . . . and not to be missed.

"Are you like this with all your patients?"

"Depends," he said easily, not bothering to pretend he didn't know what she meant—that she was getting his best bedside manner.

"On what?"

"What they need from me." He glanced down at her hand, softly fisted on her thigh. He slipped his fingers under hers, caressed them with his thumb, smoothing them out flat. "Most often they only need me to be honest with them. And specific. Sometimes I'm a medical dictionary, defining words they don't understand. Once in a while they need me to be the asshole who forces them into reality—not my favorite role. From time to time I'm the relative stranger who'll hold them while they cry because they feel the need to show their family a brave front. But generally, all they want is a few moments of normality, to *not* see sadness and sympathy in the eyes of the person standing beside their sickbed, to get out from under the seriousness of their condition, to forget for a few minutes and laugh . . . so then I'm a clown."

She shook her head and flipped her hand palm up to meet his, curling her fingers over his. "No. That's when you're a good doctor. A fine friend." When he looked up she added, "Thank you."

He looked reluctant to accept her praise, as if it were just part of the job, but changed his mind. He didn't seem to mind being either of those things in her eyes. Good doctor + fine friend = great start. Leaning forward he kissed the space between her brows as if to ward off troubled thoughts, saying, "Go knock a couple shots of water back with Jesse—or ginger ale. Stay hydrated. Try to get some sleep, okay?"

"No aspirin, doctor?"

"Take ibuprofen, it's easier on your stomach. And I'll call *you* in the morning."

Smiling, she stood with him and they walked the short distance to the foyer together. She held up a hand in farewell when he turned at the door to look back at her.

"Rain check on the date?"

"Yes. Please."

On a hunch, she tracked him as far as the etched glass that covered the top half of the door and found a place to peer out at him. He didn't hesitate at his car but went straight to the crime scene to catch up on whatever news or clues had been gathered.

Releasing a big, noisy puff of air she turned away. Part of her wanted to take the stairs two at a time to pack her stuff and sneak out of town. Head home to her dad. He'd know what to do. He'd handled everything—or at least tell her how.

People in Marion knew her; they could vouch for her character and tell Sheriff Murphy she couldn't possibly have had anything to do with this.

She could also hide under a bed. Wear a disguise. Join a cloistered convent or hitch a ride to the International Space Station, she supposed. But running and hiding wasn't going to answer the questions cycling through her mind.

Who was Cliff Palmeroy? Why was he following her? Why was he photographing her? And if not him, who? What was he going to do with the pictures? Why was he killed? Who murdered him? What did it have to do with her?

At the moment, her involvement was simply a question mark. She had a solid alibi, witnesses to back her up, and a couple of fierce friends to defend her. There was nothing to worry about, yet—and that was *all* her dad could and would say if she told him. And he'd worried enough for one lifetime.

No, she decided, pushing away from the door, heading for the back of the house to join Jesse and her bottle of bourbon. Her parents raised her to be a strong, independent woman with common sense and convictions. Time to test them.

Chapter Six

SATURDAY MORNING CAME AT LAST. NOT THE DAWN—SHE'D WATCHED the sun come up a few hours earlier. But now it was bright enough to make the day official, and she rolled to a sitting position on the side of the bed. Tossing and turning most of the night, her body was stiff, achy, and still tired. Plus, Jesse's bourbon had given her heartburn—an ailment so rare in her life she wasn't prepared with antacids, or even a piece of gum, so it triggered a midnight run to the kitchen for warm water and baking soda. *Yum.*

The run she'd planned for that morning was postponed indefinitely. Oddly, it seemed *too* healthy in light of the murder just a few hours before. Yet, it should have been just the opposite: a run to *celebrate* good health and life. But closer to the truth of it . . . she was still spooked by the sneaky and illicit pictures taken of her by the victim or, at the very least, in his possession. She felt violated, as if she'd been robbed and the thief had rifled through her personal possessions looking for something worth stealing. It was disturbing and scary.

An unusually quiet Jesse served baked eggs with red peppers, Swiss chard, and goat cheese on wonderful heavy dark bread with fruit and coffee while Mike ate two small mixing bowls of Froot Loops. Despite having the same thing on their minds, they didn't have enough information to actually talk about it, so they ate in relative silence until Mike received his paper list of chores for the day.

He looked up after reading it, his face contorted in disgusted disbelief. "Take Kristy Barnes out for a coke? A *coke*? I wouldn't take her out for a glass of water if you paid me ... and paid for the water ... and for the dark room we'd have to sit in because looking at her makes me want to puke! Forget it."

"But I thought you liked Kristy."

"In first grade maybe. Before she got all stuck up and started hanging out with the so-called cool kids, who only like her because her step dad's the sheriff and ... oh. The sheriff. You want me to pump her for information."

"I called this morning and they wouldn't tell me anything—and it happened right up the street, practically in front of my house. I run a business here. I need to be able to tell my guests that they're in no danger, if they have someone in custody or if there's a crazed killer still running around town." Mike's gaze slid sideways to meet Sophie's. She bobbled her head, ambivalent—she could go either way on this Kristy thing. "Not to mention my own peace of mind."

"Yeah, well the sheriff isn't going to tell her anything important. She couldn't keep it to herself if she was the last person on earth."

Jesse crossed her arms over her chest and leaned back in her chair. "All right. But if you hear anything while you're out with your friends, I want you to text me."

"*That* I can do," he said, pushing away from the table with his bowl.

She listened to him leave, then glanced up at Sophie, winced and narrowed her eyes, looked away and came right back with a frown. Sophie sighed inwardly. This couldn't be good.

"What?"

Jesse shook her head, bewildered. "I don't know. There's something about you—I don't know what. I feel like I've seen you before somewhere. Are you sure you aren't someone famous?"

"Ha. Positive. Another life maybe?"

She chuckled. "Possibly. I read somewhere that you meet the same people over and over but in different relationships— like Mike could have been my mother in another incarnation. He is a bossy know-it-all." She thought about it. "But then, who could my actual bossy know-it-all mother have been last time?"

Sophie laughed. "If this is the sort of thing you think about before you've finished the breakfast dishes, does your day get more or less complicated as it goes on?"

"Depends on the day." She stood and started gathering their dishes. "Someone gets murdered on my front porch, it can get pretty complicated."

And if the victim was following you and had pictures of you on his camera?— Well, that would put a crimp in your day, as well, but she didn't say so out loud. Any death was a trauma; murder was a bone-deep shock. But the bloody slaughter of someone you actually knew had to be overwhelming.

Complicated was relative, she supposed.

She offered but Jesse wouldn't let her help with anything around the B&B. Instead, she handed her a brochure of local sights and events issued by the Chamber of Commerce.

Monticello, Ash Lawn-Highland, and Montpelier, the homes of Presidents Jefferson, Monroe, and Madison respectively, were all within an easy drive and well worth a visit—

but, of course, she couldn't leave town. There was an entry point to the Skyline Drive through the Shenandoah National Park not too far off and Charlottesville had the university and a plethora of programs and festivals available to the public, not to mention Miller's—the infamous bar that gave birth to the Dave Matthews Band—but, again, she couldn't leave town.

Even so, all was not lost. Clearfield boasted a Confederate museum just off Main Street on Market, antiques stores, and *"many galleries that displayed local art and pottery"* according to the pamphlet. Plus, if she chose to turn a blind eye to the city limit signs and extend her confinement to those marking the county boundaries, there were two small area vineyards that offered tastings every other weekend from Memorial Day to Thanksgiving with special events during the Christmas season. It was an "other" Saturday, and she could certainly use a tasting—or eight.

While a nice long walk into town would unkink her sore muscles, she took her car to feel less exposed. Safer, too. Jeeps were, after all, originally military vehicles; and if worse came to worst, she wouldn't hesitate to use hers as a weapon, she decided, her attitude unusually fearsome for a kindergarten teacher as she settled into the driver's seat and fastened her seat belt.

Oh, yeah. Her roots may have sprouted from the clay and limestone of Virginia, but her heart was pure Ohio flint, she told herself. *Flint.*

"Hi," she said, pushing into the outer office of Lonny's Service and Tire after filling up her war machine. The scent of old coffee, auto grease, rubber, and car exhaust suggested tires and repair were the establishment's prime objective. The small selection of candy, soft drinks, and cigarettes suggested gas was solely a sideline. And the man behind the counter in the charcoal overalls, wiping his grimy-looking hands on a blue rag, was Lonny—his name tag said so. "Pretty day, huh?"

"Sure is," he said, watching her with a wary eye. He was an older gentleman, well into his sixties, maybe more, but only his poorly cut white hair, bushy gray beard, and the deeply rutted lines in his face gave him away because he stood large, straight, and tall—his hands looked strong and hard working.

"I'm there at that second pump, $42.16." She held her charge card out to him with a smile.

Granted, she could have gone to either the BP station or the Chevron down the street—but not only was Lonny's the closest, it also filled the criteria for her favorite civic crusade: shopping local whenever possible. After all, if she had to spend her hard-earned money, who's going to appreciate it more: the sixteenth-largest public company in the world or Lonny?

He took a few extra seconds reading the name on her card, and when he looked up with a new interest, she mirrored him and smiled again. Small towns were all the same—they made Twitter seem obsolete. Preemptively, she said, "I don't know anything, so don't ask."

That surprised a good-natured chuckle out of him and his natural caution slipped away. "Well, you sure got some blood pumpin' in this old town, that's for sure and for certain. Folks ain't had this much to talk about since the Benson girl come back to life and burnt her people's house to the ground."

"What. She was a zombie?"

"Nah." He shook his head in a sympathetic manner, waiting for authorization on her card. "Went missing years ago, come back to care for her sister's young girl. And the fire were an accident lookin' to happen. Then it did and folks had even more to talk about. Tough little cookie, that one. Took the girl, our sheriff and his kids, and moved 'em all up to Baltimore for some peace and quiet."

Sophie couldn't claim to be innocent of gossiping. Truth: she was as big a nosy parker as anyone in Marion. Being on the other end of the stick, however, was stirring great regret and fostering no less empathy for those she'd sinned against.

"So it turned out well for them."

"Sure did." He hesitated briefly, passing her the charge slip and a pen. "This will, too. You'll see."

She smiled gratefully and bent to sign her name. Looking up, she caught a soft sorrow in his expression—which he quickly covered with a friendly grimace. "You remind me a bit of my baby girl 'cept she had my wife's blue eyes and she weren't near as tall as you. But she was a happy gal growin' up, and that smile-a-yours is a real sweet reminder."

Had, were, reminder . . . "I'm sorry," she said, sensing his sorrow.

"No need. I got plenty of good memories and just the few that are sad. I pick and choose the ones I conjure up."

She liked his thinking. A lot. She sent him her appreciation through her expression and swallowed hard on the envy that filled her chest to aching. Would she have to have snowy white hair and deep furrows in her face before the pain of her own loss disconnected from her other memories, dwindled and let only the good ones shine through? She wanted to ask how long the process took, but judging from the grief she'd seen on his face, she suspected it was an ongoing thing that required a conscious effort.

She glanced over her shoulder and flashed him a quick wave as she began to recognize the repeating pattern in her life: the choice was hers.

The museum was . . . small. The main floor of an old cottage house, it was owned and maintained by the United Daughters of the Confederacy and filled with the usual displays of rifles and uniforms and war gear, but more interestingly the intimate letters, pictures, memoirs, and souvenirs of the soldiers

and their families who once lived in the area. The curator—
nearly a relic herself—was chatty and a fountain of fascinating facts and folktales. Sophie couldn't recall a nicer stroll
through time.

Not that her walk ended at the museum. The antiques shops
she eventually got to were accustomed to tourists, so the pro-
prietors were likewise as lively and informational—and the
artifacts equally as fascinating in a very dissimilar way, like
What the heck IS *that thing*? Or, *Who took such loving care
of this* or *who'd give* THIS *away*? Sometimes simply *wow* or
aww. She'd always enjoyed a good store of fine junk. Today
its diversion value was through the roof.

It was nearly two in the afternoon when—after slowly
ambling the entire length of one side of a well-loaded store,
crossing along the back wall and starting up the other side—
she caught a flash of yellow peripherally and turned in time to
see Drew McCarren's sister barreling down on her.

"I can't decide if it's a good thing or a bad thing that it never
takes longer than fifteen minutes to track someone down in
this town."

"Me?"

"Today, yes." She'd slipped her large sunglasses to the top
of her head like a hair band for her shoulder-length pageboy—
one of those really thick, really shiny dark bobs that curly-
headed gingers tend to wish for as teenagers—revealing the
upper half of her face to be as attractive as the lower half. Her
bright smile sported a single dimple in her right cheek and her
eyes were that curious shade of gray green that Sophie suspected might swing to blue during a shopping montage . . . but
not in a bright yellow sundress. "I'm Ava McCarren. Drew
sent me to entertain you."

"Me?"

"Yes. And don't reject me," she said, skillfully bending her elbow around Sophie's and falling effortlessly into the slow meander she'd interrupted—knowing full well she was an irresistible force and therefore unrejectable. "I have a sensitive ego and am easily wounded, you see, and since my brother so rarely finds the need to ask anything of me, I'm feeling particularly vulnerable because I adore my big brother and would do anything to please him. Not to mention my own profound curiosity about you . . . or the detailed report I'll be delivering to my mother before supper.

"Now, the delivery of information to mother is a daily ordeal at our house, to which an invitation has been extended to you for tomorrow evening, by the way—*to which* Drew stipulates (a) only if you're feeling up to it and (b) only if it doesn't count as his rain check." She took a breath and held it, pretending to make sure she'd forgotten nothing and grinned at her. "So, you teach kindergarten. I loved kindergarten . . ."

Oh, yes. Ava was a tsunami that swept in and took over. And while Sophie seldom complained about making new friends, this one was particularly enjoyable in that she was breezy and light, funny and smart; a talker who listened, and best of all, she felt no desire to discuss the murder.

Instead she diverted Sophie with tales of her great escape from Clearfield to study art history at NYU and the never-ending challenge of convincing her parents that a true artist was not just *of* the world but also needed to be *in* the world. Or vice versa. Ava could never keep it straight. And so, *yada-yada,* she needed to travel to far-off lands, to see new things and people and places in order to feed her artistic spirit and round out her life experiences to fulfill her destiny . . . or teach at some high school, whichever came first.

She lit up talking about a foreign study in college when she spent the better part of a year visiting England, France, and Italy. She received a trip to Japan as a graduation gift three years ago; harped her way to Portugal, Spain, and Greece two years ago; and spent the last eighteen months working her way through the western states studying Native American art. At present, she was home again *staging* a trip to Egypt—a must-see in any artist's reality—which apparently meant tapping a trust fund she wouldn't come into for another six years.

Twinkling good-naturedly, she reluctantly admitted that eventually she was going to have to think about settling down somewhere. "Dad's a soft touch, but he isn't the one who runs things around here," she said, and Sophie understood perfectly. While her own parents had spoiled her rotten, it had been her mother who put her foot down on occasion to keep her from smelling bad. Still, there was something refreshing and sinfully enjoyable in Ava's unapologetic acceptance of her own overindulged lifestyle: she was, she knew it, she liked it, and she didn't want it to change. It was that simple.

"In fact, they make the most wonderful crabapple crisp over at the Crabapple Café and Creamery—up the street there," Ava said, several quick hours later as they stepped into a small bookstore. "Crabapple everything: pies, fruitcakes, jelly, butter, pickles, sauce . . . like for glazing hams? Lord. And ice cream you'd slit your wrists for."

"Crabapple ice cream?" Sophie's face puckered.

"No, of course not—but in every other flavor imaginable, so I don't know why not. They have ice cream cakes, cookie sandwiches, and chocolate-covered ice cream logs. Ah! You can get it in a cone or by the bowl or, in my case, by the bucket." She laughed merrily, as if she wasn't exaggerating. "They have a short menu, sandwiches and salads, in case you want to pretend you're there for lunch but you wouldn't be fooling anyone."

They thanked the waitress for their frosty-cold coffee

drinks and settled back in comfy chairs at a tiny table near the window at The Book Nook—a charming book-and-coffee enterprise they'd stepped into to scout out a copy of an older book title by an author they both loved that Sophie hadn't yet read. They discovered this commonality while browsing The Mystic Maiden, an eclectic establishment with everything from gemstone jewelry—humming over many of the same pieces but buying none—to caftans to incense and amusing bumper stickers that brought them to near tears with giggles. They had much in common.

"Mother wanted me to take you to lunch at her club out at the golf course, but I could see right away you weren't the type."

It wasn't meant to be an insult, but the question had to be asked, "How could you tell?"

"Easy. Drew likes you, so that would make it highly unlikely that you're the country club type. But I liked you, too, right off, so that's a definite *no way*. Now, if you were a friend of Pam or Billy's, that would be an unlikely story right from the start."

"Who are they?"

"You and Drew really haven't had much time to talk at all, have you? Not even the basic sibling stuff?"

"I knew about you, from the funeral. And your mother. Your father's a doctor, too, and your grandfather was a huge Wahoo."

"That's it? Surface dust," she scoffed. "Oh, where to start. . . ." She laughed. "And where to stop before I blow Drew's chances with you."

Despite the way her heart rate kicked up, Sophie shook her head. "I'm going home soon. Chances are you won't be blowing anything."

"Then why are they called chances?" She smirked knowingly. "So now . . . you should know that we McCarrens are pretty much *it* as far as Clearfield royalty goes. There are others in our league, of course, or my mother would be sitting in her club all alone, but as far as our pedigree goes: none's more pure. My mother's family, the Kingstons, were here before the Blue Ridge Mountains. Prosperous, civic-minded farmers for several generations. Abolitionism brought us back to earth, so to speak, but we managed quite well until the modern marvels of farming required fewer and fewer family members to run a large farm. That's when brave, adventurous Kingstons— like myself—ventured forth into the rest of the world and for the most part fell off the family tree altogether. Except for my mother's branch, of course. They stayed and eventually contributed a senator to the great Commonwealth of Virginia. A Governor, too, way back when. A Republican, so we don't talk about him much, but still. . . ." She shrugged. "My grandpa and his younger brother, Charles . . . better known in town as Chucky . . . or to us kids as Uncle Chuckle," she giggled. "Anyway, they took turns being mayor of Clearfield for many years." It was plainly a favorite family joke. "They were a pair." She shook her head, remembering. "Where was I? Oh. My dad. He's old Massachusetts money. He says the only reason Mother went to college was to catch herself a rich husband and he walked straight into her trap. And for some reason that completely escapes me, he adores her. Even now."

"You know, you and your brother don't sound like you like your mother very much."

"Don't be silly, we love her dearly—even if she is the world's biggest pain in the ass." Sophie gasped and laughed at the same time, while Ava simply sighed, disgruntled. "Oh, she's okay. She's just into everything and everybody's business all the time. Anywhere else she'd be labeled a nosy busybody, but here, in the upper echelons of this rinky-dink town, she's a solid citizen, a pillar of public service, an involved parent, a concerned neighbor, a community activist. She's the spoon in the soup pot that moves everything around, stirs things up, and keeps them swirling so nothing burns on the bottom. In any other pond, she'd definitely be an impressive trophy fish. Here, she's *the* fish and that's the way she likes it. It's also why my Dad set his practice up in Charlottesville when he could have gone anywhere. And, yes, I know I had too many metaphors going on there, but one is never enough to describe her."

"So," Sophie said slowly into the breathy silence that followed. "Do I want to accept her invitation to dinner tomorrow night?"

She grinned. "Oh, yeah. For you, she will be the perfect hostess, gracious and charming—that all comes with the meal—the payoff for her being . . . your life story, your connection to Arthur Cubeck, your reason for being here, your plans for the immediate future, and, consequently, my brother."

"Um. Sounds lovely."

"Oh, it will be. The extractions will be painless; simply tell her what she wants to hear. We never know until the last minute if Dad will make it for dinner, but *I'll* be getting the night off from being reminded of what a disappointment my lack of direction, purpose, and ambition are to her. And Drew, who has the most remarkable and annoying talent for letting most everything she says and does roll off his back, will be abnormally jumpy and on guard the whole time to keep you buffered from her . . . which will amuse me immensely."

Sophie shook her head in wonder. "Well, in that case . . ." Then she wondered, "Will I get to meet your other brother and your sister?"

"Definitely not Pam. She's like a clone of my mother but, again," she held up her index finger, "this is a one-fish pond.

Mother was on the verge of eating that little fry when Pam married her college sweetheart and moved to South Carolina. Naturally, she's only a trophy fish down there, but she doesn't seem to mind much." She fell into a moment of thought on that note.

"And your brother?"

Had she not spent the afternoon watching and enjoying Ava McCarren, Sophie might have missed the subtle shades of . . . confusion, wonder, and concession that rippled briefly across her features. "Billy. You never know about Billy. He's . . . well, he's Billy." She hesitated briefly. "You know how people say, *There's one in every family*? Sometimes they compare kids with apples: *There isn't a bad apple in the bunch* or *the apple doesn't fall far from the tree*?" Sophie nodded; she was the apple of their eye in her family.

"Billy's an orange."

"An orange."

"Yeah. He's a fine fruit, no doubt about that, but he doesn't fit in with the McCarren apples. If we had a banana and a pear or a peach to make us a proper fruit bowl, that would be something else. But he's an orange sitting in a bowl of big shiny apples—the unique one, the quiet, thoughtful one; the complicated one, the one's that's harder to eat because you have to peel him."

"What does he do?"

"He's an artist, too." She looked a bit sheepish. "A real one. The best and most beautiful parts of his world are in his soul." She hesitated. "But that also makes him introverted, solitary, and moody sometimes—an historical definition of a great artist, I guess, but it can be hard to live with." She shrugged. "Still, he isn't twenty-seven yet and he's already had two major shows. In Richmond and then Washington D.C. His talent's heading north, you see. Next: Baltimore, Philadelphia, New York. And then the world," she said proudly. She smirked. "He's well on his way to being a phenomenal orange."

Sophie laughed. "I'd love to see some of his work."

"Mother has a couple pieces she's confiscated under the perpetual IYM ruling of 130,000 BCE."

Sophie was not the dullest knife in the drawer. "I'm Your Mother."

"So you know it."

"Quite well, as a matter of fact." They grinned in unison. "I thought it was common knowledge. Right up there next to *'Thou shalt not kill'*."

Not long after that, they parted on the corner of Main and Market Streets. Ava waved and started up Main to her sporty sedan; Sophie slipped around the corner to Market and her car parked in a small lot beside the museum.

She was enjoying the peace of a late-summer afternoon—drowsy and muted; birds chirping, a gentle breeze blowing away the day's heat—and reflecting on all the ways Ava defined the word *character*. Her lips slipped into a soft smile as she recalled Ava's relish in recounting an incident of pure sabotage in seventh grade, when she and a friend "borrowed" three goats from a farmer, labeled them 1, 2, and 4 and turned them loose in the middle school—which was dismissed early that afternoon while the faculty scoured the building for number 3. Their three-day suspension had been well worth it.

She caught the red of her Jeep and sighed contentedly. Wine on the porch with Jesse, another of her wonderful dinners, and she could chalk this Saturday up as one of the nicest she'd spent in—well, since her mother got sick, at least.

Fishing in her purse for her keys, her buoyed spirits sank like an anchor again when she realized her car was listing toward the back of the small lot. She could feel her blood draining from her face and she broke out in a full-body sweat as she hurried around to the rider's side and found both her front and back tires flattened, their rims set deep in the rubber.

One tire would have been a serious bummer. Two flat tires were deliberate and seriously terrifying.

Instinctively, she spun around to check behind her, to scan the rest of the lot, the old thin hedging that circled it, the worn alley that passed between the museum parking lot and the larger stores on Main Street. Nothing. She searched again, this time including every window and door she could see. Nothing. Still, someone was nearby, watching her; she felt it while the tiny hairs on the back of her neck rose up. With great caution she sidled around to the driver's side, unlocked the door, climbed in, relocked the doors and called 911. Again.

Chapter Seven

"Sheriff Murphy fingerprinted my car. It looks like I haven't washed it since I bought it. Dust everywhere. But there were so many prints; whole palm prints in some places. If I hadn't been so"—she shrugged while she searched for the right word. Confused? Angry? Terrified? Nauseous and resisting the urge to cry?—"upset, it might have been more interesting. But all I kept thinking was, Is that dusty stuff going to scratch up the paint on my car?" Her laugh was small but it was all she could muster at the moment. "After that, he called Lonny and had him tow it back to his shop."

"Lonny." Elizabeth McCarren didn't seem to know the name.

She had, however, set Sophie at ease the moment she and Drew arrived at the sprawling two-story colonial home. The place screamed lavish comfort and livability in an understated style—*plenty-o-money but not bragging* described it best, Sophie decided.

Cordial, courteous, and engaging—and not nearly as asser-

tive or intimidating as she'd been made out to be—Mrs. Mc-
Carren was as graceful and put together as she'd appeared the
morning of Arthur Cubeck's funeral.

Plus, she was an artful conversationalist ... or interrogator—
both applied. The cross-examine went exactly as Ava had pre-
dicted and was just as painless; and she'd diverted the dinner
dialogue from any disturbing topics until after dessert and
coffee were served in the airy living room with its high ceiling, huge stone fireplace, and the expanse of windows showing dusk settling on the low, rolling countryside.

"Lonny's Service and Tire?" Sophie said, as if feeding her
clues. "In town? On the corner of Poplar and Main?"

"Yes, of course, I know Lonny's. I simply assumed the
sheriff would send a guest to our town to a more, well, more
modern, up-to-date facility for this sort of thing."

"He probably would have," Sophie said, recalling Mrs.
McCarren's influence in town. "He's been very kind and
helpful—the sheriff. But I asked him to call Lonny. His place
is close to Jesse's and I'd actually stopped to get gas there yesterday morning."

"But he's such an ornery old curmudgeon. He simply refuses to deal with that pile of used tires behind his shop."

Sophie smiled; she didn't care about his tires. "I liked him.
He's . . . wise. And I trust him," she added—a monumental
matter at the moment.

Sophie was a blooming paranoid in a garden of unfamiliar
foliage. She was taking another look at everyone she'd come
in contact with since she arrived in Clearfield—remembering
and reassessing everyone in her head. At one point, she'd
even considered canceling her dinner plans with Drew and
his family, fearing she'd be one of those idiotic women in the
horror films who walk straight into a basement full of ghouls
and maniacs.

Frankly, it seemed to Sophie that simply *knowing* that such idiocy existed was her protection against it . . . *plus,* she'd wanted very much to meet Drew's parents.

"Yes, of course. And clearly his tires are as good as anyone's," Mrs. McCarren said, a jovial jab at the unsightly pile behind Lonny's station. She scored three half-smiles. "It does concern me, however, that the incident is getting so little attention, as if it was no more than some random event."

"Oh, Mother." Ava shook her head, clearly weary of her mother's meddling.

"I'm serious. Taken with the Palmeroy murder, it seems to me to be extremely calculated and purposeful . . . a direct attack against Sophie. I don't know why the sheriff hasn't put her in protective custody or something."

"Don't start jumping to conclusions, Mother. Please. Especially ones so frightening," Ava said with a quick glance at Sophie. "There's a big difference between killing someone and an act of vandalism. Not to mention what a huge step down it is. Murder then tire slashing." She used her hands to show the weight of the crimes. "Murder. Tire slashing. It doesn't make sense. Besides, who'd want to hurt Sophie? What motive would they have to target her? It's a coincidence, not something to scare the wits out of Sophie with. For once, I think Freddy's attention is right where it ought to be—on Cliff Palmeroy's murder."

"I don't believe in coincidence. I believe things happen for a reason." Elizabeth paused, then added, "And please don't call the sheriff Freddy. He doesn't like it."

"Then he shouldn't act like a Freddy. Do you know it's been twenty-four hours since Drew and Sophie found the body and he hasn't got even one good suspect yet?"

"Without a witness it takes some time. Isn't that true,

dear?" Elizabeth looked to Drew for confirmation—and it had the same effect as shaking him awake.

"Of course." He tipped his head to one side, still deep in thought. "But I'm with you this time. This is more than a cosmic accident—Sophie's tires, her pictures in Cliff's truck. I don't like it." Sophie was glad to hear him say it. She didn't like it, either. "And I don't like that the sheriff hasn't whittled down a short list of suspects yet. Cliff was a dick. He made an enemy every time he left his house. The sheriff should be doing a top-ten countdown by now, but he says he's still looking at the evidence and keeping an open mind."

"Open like a wind tunnel. Who elected that guy?" Ava looked pointedly at her parent. "Mother?"

"He's a good, fair, honest man." Elizabeth would always support her candidate. "He'll get to the bottom of this."

"Well, my bet's on the enemies Cliff made at home." Ava set aside her barely touched dessert and picked up her coffee. "Carla could have easily slit his throat . . . if she took him by surprise. He never would have imagined it—never would have seen it coming. But I don't think she'd cut Sophie's tires. What would be the point? And I don't think she'd have the strength anyway."

"Nonsense. A woman is quite capable of deflating a tire— simply unscrew the cap on the valve and press on the widgie- doodle in the middle and the air leaks right out. Easy."

"Sophie's tires were cut, Mother," Drew said.

"Oh. Yes, of course. Well, I still think a woman could manage it, even one as small as Carla. *Not* Carla, naturally, she doesn't have the disposition for it," she said carefully. "But a woman of her stature. The tire walls, near the hubcaps, aren't nearly as thick as the tread. With a good sharp knife and some elbow grease, I feel certain a woman could do it."

A full five seconds passed as everyone in the room sat staring at her curiously.

"Am I wrong?" She seemed willing to debate it, but Sophie didn't know her well enough to play the devil's advocate, and the others apparently knew her too well to try it.

"Fine. Whatever." Ava dismissed her mother's vote for feminism. "But my money is still on the family—one alone or all together."

"Are you going to borrow money for that wager? Because I hear you're broke again, baby girl." A tall, very thin and blond young man entered the room; loose-limbed and laid-back as he bent to kiss Elizabeth on the cheek and take a gentle swipe at Ava's hair, flipping it up and across her face before it settled back in place. *Great hair,* Sophie noted once again. Like everyone else, she watched him pose at the opposite end of the couch from Drew.

His siblings could not look more unrelated, and not in just their physical features and builds. He was wearing dusty, bagged-out jeans and old flip-flops with an open navy blue short-sleeved shirt over a gray T-shirt. If this was Billy Mc-Carren, he was indeed an orange among apples—not as crisp or smooth or as polished as the others. But he did have the family poise and self-confidence in a fashion all his own. The apples didn't overwhelm him; he was unquestionably comfortable in his bowl.

"Not to mention," he continued. "If you don't want to be sued for slander and defamation, you shouldn't make those kinds of bets with anyone but family." His pale blue gaze drifted toward Sophie. "No offense." She shook her head; he was right. "You're her, the girl?"

"I guess so." Being called a girl by a man so very near her own age didn't bother her nearly as much as the way he said it—as if she wasn't what he'd pictured the girl involved in a peculiar bequest, a murder, and a tire slashing to look like; as if she didn't live up to her hype.

"Sophie Shepard," said Drew. "My brother, Billy."

"Hi."

"Pleasure," he said, managing the effort to make it seem so. "I have offended you. Sorry. But 'that girl with the red hair' is the hottest topic in town these days . . . I was just checking." He smiled to smooth out any feathers he may have ruffled. "No one mentioned that you were hotter than the gossip or I wouldn't have had to ask."

She was more uncomfortable than pleased by the statement. The way he was able to turn his charm off and on like hot and cold water from one observation to the next irked her. Sophie's smile was small as she took furtive glances at the others, who looked to be holding a collective breath.

Drew grimaced a smile that begged forbearance. And Ava laughed. "See, Mother? A compliment. Those etiquette classes are paying off after all."

Mrs. McCarren smiled at her guest. "Sophie, the real compliment here lies in the fact that he showed up to meet you at all. I didn't even have to threaten his inheritance."

"Ah, yes. Here we go," Billy drawled. "And as you might have guessed, Sophie, this Blast Billy game is one of the many reasons why I come around so seldom. Amusing as it is to us all." *And yet there would be no need for games if you had better manners,* she thought. Then, as if to put his family in an equally awkward and uneasy position with their visitor, he boldly said, "But speaking of inheritances: What do you think yours is all about? Any idea what the old man was up to with that?"

"Billy." Drew's voice cautioned him.

"I have no idea," she said simply, refusing to allow her pleasant evening to turn tense—or to give him any satisfaction. "But Hollis and I should have the results of the paternity test back sometime tomorrow. I . . . as surprised as I am about it, I find myself hoping he is my brother. I like him very much. But deep down, I don't think he is. I wish, but I don't think so." A small unhappy bob of her head. "I guess we'll know for sure tomorrow."

"I'm sorry, dear," said Mrs. McCarren with great sympathy. "I'm prying, I know, but it seems very peculiar to me that Arthur left you no explanation for his actions, no letter. . . . It's very cryptic and illogical, and very unlike him. Might he have sent a letter to someone else? Left one somewhere? A safe-deposit box, perhaps?"

Sophie shook her head to mean "maybe" and "I don't know" at once, and then spoke the obvious. "Hollis and Mr. Metzer know more about him than I do, and they're just as confused."

"And it doesn't bother you to know that you might be someone's unwanted love child?"

"Billy." Drew scowled at him.

She shrugged. She'd had an answer to this question most of her life. "No. I actually prefer to think I *was* created from love—all children, planned or not, should at least have their roots in love. And my parents always made sure I knew I was *their* child and they never let me feel unwanted. So, no. That part doesn't bother me."

"What part does?"

"Knock it off." There was a feral growl in Drew's warning.

It was good to know he had her back, but she could handle Billy. She was *flint*, Sophie reminded herself. *Flint*. And besides, if she couldn't confront whoever was planting evidence and doing these hateful things against her—well, Billy Mc-Carren was good practice.

"The destruction of old Mr. Cubeck's good reputation

bothers me. Your community thought highly of him. I'd hate for that to change. Hollis says he wouldn't mind having a half sister, but I'm sure finding out that his father knowingly gave his own child away would disturb him. And that would only be speculation anyway, because without knowing who my birth mother was, we'll never know if he knew about me early enough to stop *her* from giving me up. So I'm worried about him—Hollis. BelleEllen bothers me—I don't want it. And, of course, if it turns out that Mr. Cubeck isn't my father, that opens a whole different box of bees.

"Like why he left BelleEllen to you if he wasn't your father."

She nodded. "Yeah, like that."

He squinted at her. "I'm betting he's not."

"Why?—"

"There's betting?" his mother broke in, clearly disapproving.

"Absolutely," said Billy. "And don't bother looking surprised, Mother. You know the best odds are out at your club. All those old guys chewing on their cigars, riding around in their golf carts, betting on everything from their game that day to who'll win *Survivor*." Billy grinned. "I suspect all you ladies are equally as enterprising, but *you'd* never admit it and your friends are too afraid of you to even whisper about it—"

"Knock it off, Billy." Drew turned his attention to his mother, exasperated. "One night without his mouth was asking too much? Sophie could have come to town and left again without ever knowing he existed."

"Hey. You're not afraid she's going to like me better, are you?" Billy laughed and winked at Sophie. "Cuz I don't think that's gonna be a problem, man. She can't stand me."

"Do you blame her? Isn't that what you wanted?" Drew turned to him, more baffled than angry. "Why do you do this? You're better than this, Billy. You're a great guy. You're smart. You're talented. Why do you choose to be like this?"

"Whoa!" Billy stretched out his arms in exaggerated dizziness. "Déjà vu. I'm out there, man. Seriously. I feel like I've had this same conversation with one family doctor or another for the last ten years." He sobered abruptly. Anger smoldered in his eyes. "Doctors who think they know *all* about me— how I think, what I feel, who I am. *You're unhappy. You're depressed. You're weird. Here, take this fist full of drugs. Do it for yourself, not because we think you're nuts and the neighbors are complaining.* Why do I choose to be like this?" He pointed to himself with both hands. "Because this is who I am. This is it, man. This is me." All of a sudden he remembered Sophie. "Wanna know what bothers me, sweetheart?" He didn't wait for an answer. "Normals and nuts. Who's to say which is which, you know? Maybe I'm the normal one and they're the nuts." Pretending to be shocked and appalled, he got to his feet. "Did I say that out loud? Did they hear me? Are they reaching for their nets and straightjackets? I'd better jet. I feel a new label coming on. Not just bipolar, but Bipolar with Paranoid Delusions and Chronic Bad Manners. What's that in Latin, brother?"

"Billy, don't go," Ava said, disappointed and pleading. "Stay. Stay and . . . be nice."

Looking at his sister seemed to trigger an inner valve that caused his anger and aggression to physically drain from his posture. His connection to her was clear—and strong. He gave her a half-smile and glanced at his mother before turning back to Sophie looking almost ashamed.

"I beg your pardon, Ms. Shepard. I've upset and offended you and I apologize. My family and I have diverse opinions— many of them—none of which have anything to do with you. I have behaved badly. I'd like . . . I hope if we meet again I can redeem myself. Good luck with," he flipped his hand vaguely, "you know, everything." He stalled a moment then blurted. "Good night."

"Billy." Ava reached out a hand to stop him and he gave it an affectionate squeeze as he walked past her.

"William?" His mother's voice cracked when he left the room without a blink to mollify her. She rose to follow him, but Drew stopped her with a simple and clearly well established, "I'll go."

With both men out of the room, but not far away as the low peace-making voices in the foyer indicated, Elizabeth, Ava, and Sophie looked from one to the other in silence. They all spoke at once.

"Billy isn't always . . ."

"My son suffers from a . . ."

"I'm sorry I didn't get to meet . . ."

When they all stopped short, the McCarrens were happy to step back and let Sophie finish.

"I'm sorry I didn't get to meet the other Dr. McCarren tonight. I've heard so many good things about him."

"Yes. Thank you, dear. He was sorry to have to miss meeting you, as well, but doctors don't always get to pick and choose their work hours."

"Good thing, too, or they'd never be around when the rest of us need them," she said, too cheery and upbeat . . . too kindergarten-teacher. "Though I'm sure it's very hard on them and their families—a lot of sacrificing on both sides."

"Oh, yes. It can be quite a challenge sometimes. Especially when there are young children at home. In fact, that was my only concern when Andrew indicated he wanted to become a doctor like his father—that he'd never have a normal home life. It was such a relief when he chose to go into cancer research. I thought it would be more of a nine-to-five job like a dermatologist or a proctologist; but, no, he was at it for twelve and sixteen hours a day for months at a time between the hospital and the lab. His social life was pathetic." She gave a sad, but dignified shake of her head. "Nonexistent really. But I recall one woman in particular, considerably older, who had a thing for Andrew . . ."

With Mrs. McCarren chewing on a tasty bone for the moment, Sophie took the opportunity to check on her friend, Ava, who also took that instant to assess her—and after a second or two they grinned, knowing Billy's behavior had changed nothing between them. So the uneasiness she might have felt when Drew returned to the room was minimal—and as his gaze caught and held hers, a swift easy flow of understanding and relief passed between them effortlessly.

"Oh, you're back," his mother said. "I assume all is well with your brother?" He nodded, keeping his eyes on Sophie. "I was telling Sophie about that strange woman you worked with . . . Jade or . . . Jane? Julie?"

Frowning now, he turned to her. "Jasmine?"

"Yes! And when baking him cookies and knitting him scarves didn't produce the reaction she'd hoped for, she started following him around New York."

"No. I told you. It was coincidence. And she wasn't strange. I was always glad of her company when she showed up. She was a nice, lonely woman. A friend."

"Who appears out of nowhere while you're having dinner with your mother? Asks any number of personal questions about you? Fawns like a schoolgirl. She had the most grating giggle."

"Mother."

She sent Sophie the mother-knows look. "She was stalking him. Can you imagine it?"

"No. But lonely people can do odd things sometimes. It's

a sad state to be in. Happens to all of us now and again." She could see that the subject was annoying Drew. "I didn't know you did research. You didn't say."

"Because I don't anymore. Haven't for a while." And because her "oh" was soft and left hanging in the air, he added, "It wasn't for me. I did my residency at Langone—NYU Medical Center—in Internal Medicine and it seemed, in light of my interest in cancer, that my next logical step was to accept a hematology/oncology fellowship to the cancer institute there, with an eye toward being a research physician." He shook his head slightly and his tone warmed to the subject. "The work was phenomenal, brilliant—the true scientists, the biochemists, the molecular biologists—their thoughts and ideas were so outside the box. It was like they had an entire universe of possibilities inside their heads. Even the failures, one after another, were considered minor successes because they eliminated each new hope-filled path as an option, steering the research in an alternate direction, down another hope-filled path. But. . . ." He shrugged.

"It wasn't for you?"

He smiled. "No. It wasn't. For a couple of reasons." His pause was more comic than dramatic. "Is it wimpy for a man to admit he was homesick?"

"I don't think so."

"I was. Horribly. I'd been up there almost seven years by then. I missed the quiet. Central Park had trees and grass and birds, but there were people everywhere and you could still hear the traffic and the sirens. Too many people; too much noise. The noise inside the utility closets at the hospital was subtle and muffled, but it was still noise. And not good noises like crickets at night and the wind in the trees and babbling brooks and—"

"I feel a yawn coming on," Ava announced.

He made a face at her and then raised one shoulder. "Turns out I'm lousy at failure, too. I don't like to lose."

"What. You mean lose to cancer?" Sophie asked.

"Well no, not cancer itself. I know it can be a killer and it'll take some of my patients no matter what I do. But I feel like I have a little more control of it by taking one patient at a time, doing everything possible to help him or her to survive—even if it's recommending them for a clinical trial at Langone when all else fails. But if nothing works, if I've exhausted every avenue, then I want to help them die. In peace and without pain." He sighed. "But during the cancer studies . . . we wouldn't even start clinical trials until our hopes were so strong for each new therapy, we were sky high with confidence and dusting off places to put our Nobel prizes. And to lose, to fail . . . *again*?" He paused, humbled. "It takes a toll. On the patients, on the team. On me."

And it wasn't hard for Sophie to understand his reluctance to pay the fee, having been on that roller coaster ride herself not so long ago. It was tortuous.

"Of course it does, darling." His mother soothed him. "The medical profession is costly to everyone connected with it. It can be detrimental—devastating—particularly on the dynamics of even the strongest family ties and personal relationships.

"Why, I remember one time, very early in our marriage, before I entirely realized what I'd gotten myself into by marrying a doctor—oh my, I was young, barely twenty-one." She gave a soft wistful sigh, smiled and shook her head. "And I was foolish. His life was erratic the whole time we dated, but for some reason that I must attribute solely to my youth . . . and love-blindness, too, I suppose . . . I truly thought it would be different, more stable, and more normal once we were married." She laughed and gradually sobered. "This one time, early on, Joseph took me out to dinner. I'd been moping and complaining that he'd been neglecting me for weeks, so he planned this delightful evening out for us. He got someone else to take his calls. A lovely, lovely surprise for me. And a complete disaster. Halfway through dessert this other doctor calls, very apologetic, but they were getting ready to do an emergency surgery on a patient of his with some sort of problem that included the heart valves— someone perfect for a special repair technique Joseph and a group of surgeons were working on at the time involving the restoration of the patient's own heart valves as opposed to replacing them with pig or mechanical valves. Fascinating . . . but not to me at the time, naturally. Joseph didn't even wait for the check. He simply gave the waitress too much money when we passed her on our way out and drove straight to the hospital. He gave me money for a cab and left me sitting in the doctors' lounge in my lovely new cocktail dress."

She closed her eyes, took a breath, and opened them again. "It's been, what," she looked at Drew to make a quick calculation, "over thirty years and it still sets me off. *And* that wasn't the worst of it. While I sat there fuming, I developed the most ungodly headache. It felt like someone was trying to unscrew the top of my head. Understandable, right?"

Sophie nodded—as did Drew and Ava, who'd obviously heard the story before, as they looked bored.

"I became nauseous, wave after wave, and my stomach was cramping horribly. That's when I decided I needed to calm myself down before I had a stroke. But the harder I tried, the sicker I got. I felt dizzy so I lay down on the floor—much better than falling to the floor, in my opinion, but quite a bit more noticeable than sitting in a chair and suffering in silence. Anyway, when I finally vomited, Grace Levol was with me— she later became my pediatrician; a fabulous woman. She and a nurse got me a wastebasket to be sick in, stayed with me, called Joseph. It wasn't long before I wasn't worried about dying anymore . . . I *wanted* to. I was so sick and so embarrassed and so angry—and do you know what Joseph's response was from the operating room? He told his nurse to tell the other nurse to tell Grace to admit me to the medical floor, keep me hydrated with IV fluids, and he'd come as soon as he was finished. I cried. And *that's* when I knew where I was on his list of priorities."

She nodded her head emphatically and laughed. "It was some time, let me tell you, before I could reconcile myself to the fact that his career and his family were equally important to him . . . like he and my children are to me. I don't love one more than another, but sometimes one will need more of my attention than the others. My husband's work is crucial to so many people and we all make sacrifices—me, the children, *and* him—so that he can continue to save lives. I often felt like a single mother—"

"Okay." Ava interrupted, animated and astute. "Short story long, I think Sophie gets it, Mother. It's tough being a doctor's wife. But Drew hasn't even asked her to be one yet, so let's try another subject . . . like Egypt."

Her mother's smile was closed lipped and crafty. "Let's talk about jobs first."

Drew chuckled and bent toward Sophie to whisper, "I think that's our cue to move on. Are you ready?"

She gave a nod and sent Ava her sympathies. There were worse things than having to discuss the long-overdue necessity of finding a job with an overtaxed parent—but not too many.

"He's a crapshoot," Drew said of his brother, taking the winding country roads at a moderate speed back toward town. His tone was not wholly apologetic; more simply stating the facts.

"We hardly ever agree on anything, but he's the first person I'd call if I got in a pinch. The last one I'd try to borrow money from, though, piker." He chuckled softly, fondly. "My mother and sisters like to say he has an artistic temperament because he's been high-strung and moody for as long as we can remember. But my dad and I are fairly certain it's a mood condition; we think he's bipolar. We've strong-armed him into taking medication from time to time for the depression, but he flat out refuses mood stabilizers. He says they interfere with his creative process. And they might; who'd know better than him?" He glanced at her briefly. "I've never known him to be violent—to himself or to others—but he can be cruel with that mouth of his. I hope—"

"No. It was okay." He didn't need to make excuses for his brother. "I was angry at first but it wasn't anything I couldn't handle, and by the time I realized it wasn't . . . well, it was over and he'd left the room." And thinking it once again, she said it out loud. "He's so unlike the rest of you—you, Ava, and your mother. Does he look more like your father?"

"Pam, Ava, and I look more like him than we do Mother. It's been generally decided that Billy looks like my grandfather's younger brother, Charles. Mother says they could have been twins when he was younger."

"Uncle Chuckle."

He laughed. "That's the one. Ava called him that when she first started to talk and it suited him so well, it stuck. Some of the people in town called him Uncle Chuckle—to his face even. He loved it. He died in his sleep, at least a dozen years ago—he was ninety-eight."

"Gramma York, my mom's mother was ninety-six. Unfortunately, she didn't know who anyone was for the last seven of them. That's a horrible way to grow old—Alzheimer's. Can you imagine how confusing and lonely it must be for them?

Mom was so worried about getting it herself." A pause for thought. "That would be one good thing to know about my birth parents—their medical histories. Oh, and my nationality, maybe. We always said it was Irish. You know, because of the hair? But it could just as easily have come from Scotland . . . any of the northern or western European countries actually. Do you know there are Polynesian redheads? They've even found Chinese mummies with red hair."

He squinted to see her in the low light from the dash. "I think I'd throw out Chinese and Polynesian right off the bat." She sent him a look that said *smartass.* "And what if you're not Irish? That could really throw a wrench in your St. Patrick's Day plans."

"That's true. . . ." She tried to sound worried.

"But if you're German, you'd have Oktoberfest to look forward to every year. And there's that maypole thing in Sweden—Midsummer's Eve . . . or maybe Day, I forget." He glanced at her. "At least you won't be without an ethnic holiday of some sort."

She laughed. "And I can always fall back on being just a plain old American and I'd have the Fourth of July."

"And Mother's, Father's, and Grandparents' Days."

"Columbus Day."

"Labor Day."

"Presidents' Day."

"April fifteen."

"April fifteen?"

"Tax Day."

"Oh, right. How could I miss that one?" She laughed. "How about Black Friday? That one's *huge.*"

"Don't forget March Madness!"

And so the conversation went, light and amusing, until

they pulled up in front of Jesse's B&B and Drew turned off the engine.

"I'm impressed," he said after a brief silence in which Sophie tried to decide how to make her exit—or if she wanted to.

"By what?"

"The last woman to comply with a command performance for my mother came away in tears. I had to give her a Xanax and call a friend to stay with her before I could leave. You took it like a trooper."

She shook her head in disbelief. "You and your sister are awful. Your mother's very nice. Billy's something else, but your mother was nothing but kind and generous." She chuckled. "Ava warned me that she'd give me the third degree but that's understandable. A stranger in town; hanging out with her children—she'd be a negligent mother if she didn't check me out."

"Even if we're adults who can make our own decisions about the people we spend time with?"

Barely two seconds went by before she answered. "Sure. Why not? Don't we all do it, to one degree or another, to everyone we meet. Where are you from? What do you do?"

"Sure, but not: *Do you attend church regularly? Why have you never been married*—and in the same breath, *Do you have any children?* My personal favorite? *Teachers don't make much money, do they?*"

"Was that a real question? I thought she was making a statement. I agreed with her." She laughed but didn't hesitate. "Teacher wages suck. Big time. Do you know that in Ohio, I'll have to work ten to fifteen years before I make as much as a building inspector? Or a dental hygienist? A web designer or even a funeral director? I'll never make as much as a nurse and yet teachers mold the minds of tomorrow. We teach children to use their minds to question and create, and isn't that just as important as keeping their bodies alive?" She took a breath. "I do make more than a fireman, though, and I don't have to run into burning buildings. And despite the fact that it sometimes feels like the exact same job, I do make more than a zookeeper. So there's that. . . ." She tipped her head to one side and smiled. "And I love what I do, so there's that, too— What?"

"Nothing." He looked away but was still grinning. When he could look at her again, her scowl wasn't hard to read. "I was enjoying you all righteous and worked up. I like discovering new things about you. You're quite a bag of mixed tricks, Sophie Shepard."

"Oh, yeah? Like what?" She knew it shouldn't matter what he thought of her. But didn't everyone wonder about the world's general perception of them?

Not that he was becoming her world or anything . . . or even a part of it, really. All it took was: *Oncologist, hospital, more than 400 miles from home* to put him back into a proper perspective.

He adjusted his weight to face her more directly. "Like you appear to be most people's dictionary definition of a kindergarten teacher: cheerful, upbeat, enthusiastic—"

"Don't say perky."

"Wouldn't—perky implies a certain ditziness you don't have. I'd say energetic, full of life. And very compassionate. A stranger, who doesn't get the chance to unburden his heart before he dies, brings you to tears. You're sympathetic to a son's need to know and understand the extraordinary actions of a father he loved and look up to. I did notice that you were a little shaky when we found Cliff Palmeroy's body, but if I hadn't been trying so hard to impress you with my cool, calm, and collected doctorliness, I might have fallen apart altogether."

"Oh, please. That's a lie and a half and you know it."

Smiling, he shook his head. "I was still mighty impressed. No hysterics or screaming and only that short cry afterward, in the face of that kind of trauma? Pretty amazing."

"Ha. Trauma," she said, scoffing, choosing not to remember. "Obviously you've never had to deal with a five-year-old who's accidentally wet himself during his brain vacation."

"Brain vacation?"

"Mm. Young kindergarten people are *far* too grown up for baby things like quiet time or the dreaded nap. But I think it's important to give them a little downtime to unwind and relax a bit after lunchtime. I read online about calling it *a brain vacation*—we all just let our brains relax before we begin our lessons again. They can look at picture books or do puzzles or just lie there and think nice thoughts. At the beginning of the school year they often fall asleep—twenty-minute power naps. By the end of the year most read or color . . . or whisper to their friends until I catch them." Her laugh was tender and affectionate. "You change, grow up a lot in kindergarten."

"And you show them how."

Her shrug was unpretentious. "It takes a village. . . ."

He drew in a deep breath and let it out slow. "Don't move."

She went statue, then barely wiggled her lips to ask, "Why?"

"I need to kiss you." He moved his face up to hers. She felt his breath on her lips when he murmured, "You have two seconds to protest."

Two seconds? That's hardly enough time to even—his lips brushed hers—*think.*

Then there was nothing to think *with* as her mind teetered and started to reel; her stomach lurched in anticipation. He cupped her right ear to secure and support her head; she touched his cheek to make sure he was human, real, and not a dream.

It wasn't a long kiss. It wasn't a sloppy wet or an open-mouthed-and-down-the-throat kiss. It was the gentle press of lips; a slow, careful exploration of their shape and size and softness; a quick test of elasticity and give. It was a shock and a stir and then it stopped.

Her eyes came open to his, deep and dark with only the dim and distant glow from Jesse's porch light.

"I wasn't going to do that." He swept her lips with his again. "I wanted to the second I saw you, but . . . you were supposed to be gone in twenty hours and I—"

"Twenty hours?" A distracting number to pull out of his pocket.

"Mm. At most. We talked at about four o'clock in the afternoon. Jesse's checkout is eleven A.M. so I figured, at the latest, you'd be gone by noon the next day. Twenty hours."

A lot of spur-of-the-moment math for someone with a kiss in mind, she calculated.

"But I didn't leave."

A slow wag of his head. "No. You didn't."

"And we kissed."

"We sure did."

"And it was nice."

"It sure was." Another pass. "Very."

"And probably a big mistake."

"Probably."

"But that's not going to stop us."

She was aware of his chest rising and falling on a sigh. "I hope not."

Sophie grinned at hearing her own wishes out loud and he kissed her again—hot and sure and with every indication of it becoming a new leisure pursuit.

Chapter Eight

IF NOTHING ELSE, SOPHIE'S *FLINT* WAS GETTING A POWERFUL WORK-out.

And it was holding up rather nicely, she decided with no little satisfaction as she sat next to Hollis Cubeck in Mr. Metzer's law office a few minutes after nine o'clock Monday morning. They'd agreed it was the most private and impartial place to meet—and all three of them were anxious.

"I'm sorry to be late." Mr. Metzer fumbled with the latch on his briefcase. "There was some confusion as to who was to pick the results up in Charlottesville this morning, but, as you can see, it was quickly settled." He held up an official-looking envelope, smiling. He sat down behind his desk. "Now, before we open this I want to make sure you both understand that with only Arthur's blood and without a donation from either of the mothers or a third sibling that these results are based on a probability index—meaning there can be no absolute match, only a high or low probability of siblingship. Is this clear to you both?"

"Yes."

"They said basically the same thing when they swabbed my mouth." Sophie twisted her fingers in her lap. Hollis seemed like a nice enough person, but she'd never been a sister before; wasn't sure she'd be any good at it. And Daddy? Bringing home a puppy was one thing, but a brother? "And I read about it online. It's complicated, isn't it? Amazing, too—what they can do; the information they can gather." She caught herself jabbering. "Yes. I understand."

"Hollis, would you like the honor?"

Permission was asked and granted with a single glance between them. He took the envelope and turned it over twice in his hands before looking at Sophie again.

"Ready?"

She nodded. "Are you sure you want to know, Hollis? You have the most to lose." She reached out and touched the sleeve of his shirt. "And I'm not talking about BelleEllen."

His small nervous smile warmed his eyes. "I also have a lot to gain."

Still and all, a blood relative would be awesome. Particularly this one.

He made short work of getting to the lab results and began to read impatiently. He continued to read even as his shoulders sagged and his spine curved back into the chair in disappointment. Because they weren't related or because they were? Sophie held her tongue—literally—between her teeth.

When he looked up and his eyes met hers, she knew. Truth told, she'd guessed as much from the first. Yet, from nowhere, she felt a tear roll from the corner of her eye. She swiped at it with one hand as she reached for Hollis with the other. "Oh, Hollis. Thank you. Thank you for being as disappointed as I am."

He shook his head. "I don't understand. It says it's less than a ten percent match. I was so sure. I even thought I saw a family resemblance." He looked to Graham Metzer. "Could they have made a mistake? Can we get retested?"

The attorney was grave. "You can always retest, of course, but it's doubtful you'll get different results. They're painstaking with this sort of thing to get accurate results. They're very aware of the personal and legal consequences for the people involved if they make a mistake."

They knew what he said was the truth and as acceptance settled in the room, Sophie could almost feel the shift of their thoughts toward Arthur Cubeck. She decided to voice what she suspected they were all wondering.

"If he wasn't my father, then why did he leave me BelleEllen?"

In the silence that followed, she could hear a fly batting against the office window, again and again, desperate to be free.

"Do you know why?" Hollis asked Graham, but it was more like a statement. Sophie's heart smiled—related or not, she and Hollis thought alike.

The lawyer nodded. "I thought I knew. He never said so in so many words. We were friends—we didn't judge each other; we didn't need to make excuses or give explanations if we didn't want to; we knew the other's character and I trusted his decisions. I knew he had his reasons. But to tell you the truth, I assumed as you did. It seemed inconsistent to his nature, extremely, but human beings make mistakes, and they do inconsistent things. It wasn't for me—as his attorney or as his friend—to question him. So as you might guess, at the moment, I'm as surprised . . . and as confused as you are."

They looked at one another—up a stump with no place to go. In her mind, Sophie quickly slammed the door against the questions she saw coming. She didn't want to think them. She'd already allowed her hopes to rise once. It hurt, more than she thought it would, to have them shot down.

"Hollis." She stood swiftly, arms out for a hug. "It was a great idea while it lasted. I would have loved to have had you for a brother." He took her in his arms without hesitation. She let him hold her for a moment, then murmured. "I'm sorry. I'm sorry I'm not your sister."

"Me, too." He gave her a gentle squeeze, held her another second or two, and set her away from him to see her face. "So what's next for you?"

"Well, Sheriff Murphy says I can't leave town yet. Not until he figures out who killed the man Drew and I discovered Friday night."

"Cliff Palmeroy."

"Mm. But he says it shouldn't take long—hard to hide things in a small town, you know."

He nodded. "But I meant what's next for you with regard to your birth parents?"

"Oh." She was afraid of that. She took a step back and his hands dropped to his sides. "Nothing."

"Nothing? You don't want to know?"

"No. Well, maybe. Sort of, I guess, but even if I knew where to start looking, which I don't, I'm not sure what I'd do with the information." She stepped behind the chair, closer to the door, distancing herself. "It was fine with you—great in fact. But you actually wanted me to be your sister. But what if you hadn't?" The ache pulled at her heart again. "What if the numbers had crunched another way and your dad *did* cheat on your mom? How would you have felt then? I'm almost twenty-eight years old. Whoever my birth parents are, they've had nine years since I turned eighteen to try and find me if they wanted to—so clearly they don't."

"You don't know that."

"I don't think I want to. I mean, what if they still don't. I don't want to know that. Is it so awful to prefer my *they-simply-couldn't-raise-me* bubble to the reality that they didn't *want* to raise me?" She took a deep breath. "And for that matter, what if they really couldn't? What if for some reason or another they *might* have wanted me if circumstances had been different? How would I know that the situation had changed? The last thing I want to do is come down on their lives like a dead elephant and ruin what they have, what they were trying to protect or avoid twenty-eight years ago." She shook her head. "Once in a while I have a natural curiosity about them and why they gave me up, but I have no burning need to know anything about them. I had the best mom anyone could ask for; and as soon as the sheriff gives me the go-ahead, I'm going to go home to the greatest dad ever." *That* she had no doubt about. "I'm very sorry about your father, Hollis. I am, but . . . I'm so happy I met you. It was amazing to think you wanted me, a complete stranger, to be your sister; that you were hoping I was a missing piece to your family." She felt her chin quiver. "Thank you for that." She stepped closer to the door. "And, um, Mr. Metzer, good to meet you, too." One last look at the brother she almost had. "Take care."

"Sophie." She heard the sympathy in Hollis's voice—but that was the last thing she needed. What she wanted was to go back in time two weeks and toss Arthur Cubeck's second letter in the trash as she had the first, stay home and paint her bedroom and the bathroom, accept one or all three of the invitations she'd declined to stay with family or friends at Indian Lake for as long as she cared to stay. "Sophie."

She was careful not to let the outer office door slam closed. Overwrought, she was closing the door on her past, shutting away the useless curiosity, sealing the portholes to the pain she wasn't duty bound to feel. Literally, figuratively, and with every fiber of her being, she turned her back once and for all on that long-ago part of her life.

She took two steps, then three, and stopped short. Grimacing head to toe she groaned a whiny, "Aw, Jeeze." She stomped her heel. "Oh, man."

She turned, tramped back inside, and stood in the doorway of Mr. Metzer's office.

"BelleEllen." She looked from one man to the other. "What are we going to do about BelleEllen?"

The lawyer looked to Hollis to answer—as if they'd already discussed the matter in the ninety seconds she'd been gone.

"That depends on why my father felt obligated to give it to you."

"No, it doesn't. No way. . . ."

The most exciting part of Sophie's job was showing up on Meet Your Teacher Night to connect twenty little faces to the names that she'd written on a clown's bow tie and attached to one of the cubbies on the wall the week before. She knew each child would arrive with several special skills, a few weaknesses, and plenty of pressure points. They'd come with one foot in reality and the other in make-believe, with as much pride as fear and with an innate sense that life—and theirs in particular—had infinite potential.

And the *best* part of her job was the part she was best at: figuring each one out.

Not immediately. Never right away. In her experience, no good puzzle unraveled quickly—or easily. Each class of children was as unique as each child in the class. So a plan that worked on most, rarely worked on all. And with change came the fears that some would cope with it, while others struggled.

Attending to their stumbling blocks shared a priority with honing their abilities, and yet limitations and strengths came in a vast array of stages and degrees.

Never easy.

But that was the fun of it, the challenge. Discovering all the pieces and putting them together, finding solutions, adapting. She was good at it . . .

I am, she insisted, staring blindly at the front door of Graham Metzer's law office from the pretty white gazebo in the center of the round town square across the way.

After leaving Hollis and the attorney a second time, still with no clear plan—or explanation—for BelleEllen, she'd paused on the sidewalk, bewildered and discouraged. And really, really cranky. She'd looked up the street at her path back to the B&B and Jesse and more questions she simply couldn't face—then looked down the street toward nothing familiar or comforting. Her gaze shifted forward and elevated slightly and suddenly she was sitting on a built-in bench inside the gazebo, crabby and cross.

She was not an impotent person. She wasn't a weak powerless weenie careening from pillar to post through life. She was goal oriented and methodical. She had ingenuity, logic, and imagination. She was a puzzle solver to her very core. She hated feeling lost and stupid and vulnerable and—

"I think you need more information."

She cried. She coiled. She cursed. "Dammit, Billy!"

"Sorry. There was no good way to do that."

"You scared the hell out of me!"

He nodded. "I thought you would hear me coming. I'm sorry." He turned on his charm and flashed her a cajoling smile. "I am. Are you going to be okay? Want me to call Drew? Tell him what I've done? Let him beat the crap out of

me? I will. I owe you that." Even as he said it, he knew that
she knew he was joking—if she wanted revenge she'd have to
instigate it herself. He wasn't an idiot.

"Tsk." She turned her back on him. "Why are you here
anyway?" She twisted to face him again. "You snuck up behind me on purpose!"

"No. Well, yes. But, no." He decided to sit. "I stopped by
Jesse's to talk to you. She said you were meeting Hollis at
Metzer's office for the big announcement." He shrugged but
she sensed he wasn't entirely indifferent. "On my way back,
I saw you sitting here so I pulled up over there, out of the
way, to give you a ride home when you were done bein' all
mopey—"

"Mopey?"

"Because the brother thing didn't work out for ya." He
flipped his palm upward in the direction of her face to display
his copious evidence. "Clearly. But I have a life of my own,
you know, so I couldn't wait for—"

"Why?"

"Why what?"

"Why did you stop by Jesse's to talk to me? *Clearly* you
don't need to practice being rude so you must have had some
other reason."

His laugh had a mission-accomplished ring to it that
snagged her attention. She watched as the humor in his grin
gradually turned sheepish. "No, I don't need to practice. It's
a natural talent. However, I didn't need to use it on you last
night. I was out of line. I stopped by Jesse's to apologize."

Sophie took a mental step back, recognizing something familiar in Billy's modus operandi—part of it anyway. Where
it was Drew's practice to use humor to engage or deflect or
*re*direct the emotions of other people . . . and possibly his own
as well, it looked as if Billy's mechanism, though not nearly

as charming as Drew's, worked just as well. He pissed people off—intentionally as often as not—and not always without kind intent.

"You did apologize."

"Not really. That was sort of a . . . perfunctory thing to get me out of the room in one piece. This is me begging for your forgiveness—*voluntary*—a rare and notable event by the way."

He didn't deserve it, but she grinned. "You're kind of a jerk, you know."

He bobbed his head, sensing her merciful nature. "You're not buying that it's part of my artistic temperament, I take it."

She shrugged. "Artistic or not, I banish five-year-olds to a chair in the back of the room until they're ready to be polite to the rest of the class. Being an ass doesn't make you a better anything. It just makes you an ass."

"What about a mood disorder? I'm a sensitive guy. I'm probably bipolar, you know." There didn't seem to be any denial or disrespect of the condition in the humor rippling in his voice—only friendly banter.

But she suspected he was also telling the truth, that he was a sensitive guy—an acutely sensitive guy with a not-so-tough shell for protection.

"All right, I'll forgive you on one condition." She had his attention. "Tell me why you were willing to bet that Arthur Cubeck wasn't my father?"

"Oh." He relaxed against the gazebo wall and stretched his long legs out in front of him. Her discouragement met acceptance in his eyes. "Too obvious. If that was why he left you BelleEllen, why didn't he just say so?" Billy attempted to say it in legalese: "I leave the farm to Sophie Shepard because she's my illegitimate daughter and I have felt like a hypocritical douchebag for her entire life because I agreed to give her up and now I'm hoping that by leaving her the family home

I will somehow be making up for it." He shook his head. "Doesn't make sense. Plus, it was too easy to check out. He'd have known you guys would get a paternity test." He shook his head again. "Then, too, if he knew all about you—which I'm guessing he did because he knew your name and how to contact you—then he knew you were okay and happy and all, so he didn't really have anything to make up to you; he would have made this huge big mess just to ease his own guilty conscience." He squinted. "I'm not seeing it that way . . . well, at least not for that reason.

"No. If you're going to do something shocking, it's usually for some distinct reason and you say so up front. Or . . ." he said, a little dramatically. "You do it in secret to keep it a secret, because you're doing it *because* of a secret, because you think the secret is a secret that will never . . . or should never come to light."

He nodded while they both mentally reviewed his hypothesis.

Sophie frowned. "So you're saying that if he'd wanted us to know why, he'd have told us. And since he didn't, we never will."

"No. I'm saying Arthur had a secret. A *big* one. Profoundly personal, but not obvious."

"That involved me."

"Yeah." He furrowed the skin between his eyebrows. "Except . . . well, I caddied for the guy sometimes when I was a kid. Twice I saw him make an honor call when he accidentally moved his ball, and I'm pretty sure no one else saw it. That's kind of how he always was, you know? So, maybe it wasn't something he did personally, but only knew about. And it ate at him."

"Maybe something he heard about through his ministry, you mean?" She shook her head; she wasn't buying it. "What could anyone have told him that was so awful that he felt simply knowing about it obligated *him* to leave me BelleEllen? That's ridiculous."

"Yes, it is. Which leads us back to my original statement." She frowned at him. "I think you need more information, Red."

"Brilliant." He grinned. "And don't call me, Red."

"Arthur did two things for you: he got your attention—in a really big way—and he left you a clue."

"My birth mother." She sighed, disinclined to look in that direction again. The only mother she cared about was the one she missed so deeply that the nucleus of every cell in her body ached. There was no enthusiasm in her voice when she spoke again. "I did promise Hollis I'd at least think about digging into my adoption."

"Good. Where will you start?"

"My dad. He might remember the name of the lawyer who arranged it."

"Excellent." He stood. "And I'll snoop around town, see what I can turn up."

"Why? Why would you do that?"

"I like a good mystery." When the silence that followed demanded more of an explanation, he added, "My town. I know which rocks to look under, who to ask . . . and I owe you one. Come on. I'll drop you off."

"So I said, 'No way. Please draw up the papers to transfer ownership to Hollis and I'll sign them,'" Sophie said, telling Drew, Jesse, and Mike about her visit to the lawyer's office at the dinner table that night. "But Hollis wouldn't budge. He kept saying that if his father felt so strongly indebted to me, for whatever reason, he wanted to honor his father's wishes."

"That sounds like Hollis." Jesse passed a bowl of potato salad back to Mike. "But I don't know how you can walk away from such a mystery. If Arthur wasn't your father, what did he know about your mother that was important enough to call you to his deathbed? What did he know that caused him to feel like he owed you BelleEllen? Aren't you dying to know?" More like dying to be able to stop thinking and talking about it.

As Sophie shook her head, Mike said, "I get that part. You can ask yourself questions and wonder and stuff, but sometimes you feel safer not knowing the answers. And even if you did know the answers, you can never be sure anyone else wants to hear 'em . . . or if telling someone else means you'd be hurting a bunch of people you don't even know. And if *you're* not hurting—just wondering and stuff—and you're mostly happy as you are, why take the chance of messing things up? You know, rocking the boat."

It didn't take the short, shy, and wholly astute meeting of their eyes for Sophie—for any of them—to understand he was speaking from his experience with his father. She wanted to hug him till his ribs cracked. But he swiftly realized he was perched on a thin emotional limb and shrugged indifferently. "Could someone pass that chicken down here?" A quick visual appraisal of his mom's feelings, and he added, "Please."

"That's exactly it," Sophie said, redirecting the spotlight so his supper wouldn't suffer. "Aside from everyone's curiosity—which, by the way, didn't even exist a week ago—there's no real point to digging it all up. What is it going to change?" She bobbled her head and grimaced. "But I did promise Hollis that I'd look into it. A little."

"That's our girl!" Jesse was thrilled. "I knew you couldn't be so . . . dull."

"Well, he's flying home tonight to take care of his own life and I'll be here a while longer, it looks like." She glanced at Drew—who seemed to have his eyes carefully aimed at his plate. What was she expecting to see? Was he to spring onto the table and dance a jig at hearing she'd be staying a few more days? "I mean, I can't go home until the sheriff releases me anyway." Another peek at Drew as he broke open a country biscuit and started to butter it—and she was hoping he'd, what? Fall off his chair, land on the floor in a fetal position and weep a saltwater river of despair at the thought of her leaving? *Get a grip!* "I'm not going to pry up any big rocks or anything, but I thought I could blow some dust off some of the basic information that I already know and see where it goes." She held a fork full of seasoned green beans over her plate. "Like, I know it was a private adoption, so my dad might remember the lawyer's name or have some paperwork with his name on it. And simply because they were living in Charlottesville when they got me, that doesn't necessarily mean I was born there. I could have been born right here in Clearfield. Maybe that's what Mr. Cubeck wanted to tell me." She hesitated. "He'd have to know who my mother was to know that—"

She was about to mention Billy's offer to help her when Jesse broke in. "Yes! That's it. Arthur was a minister." Jesse seemed surprised she hadn't thought of this before. "Oh my. Maybe he knew two young kids who got in trouble and he helped them put the baby up for adoption. That makes perfect sense." She turned to her sense of the slightly more theatrical. "Well, maybe it was a little more complicated. Maybe someone simply left you in a basket on the steps of Arthur's church one day. And maybe he found out who it was but didn't tell anyone." She looked at Sophie. "Arthur might think you'd want to know that. *Would* you want to know that?"

Sophie squinted and mulled it over. "Yeah. Maybe. If someone cared enough to put me in a basket and take me to someone who'd make sure I was taken care of . . . as opposed to simply dropping me in a Dumpster, then yeah, I guess I might want to know. But why would that weigh on his mind? That would have been a good thing—he wouldn't have done anything to feel guilty about. He certainly wouldn't feel compelled to give me BelleEllen for that."

They all looked to be seriously contemplating the color of their food for the next few minutes before Drew spoke. "That's always the rub, isn't it? No matter which direction you take, you always come back to: What did Arthur know about your birth that would cause him to spend half his lifetime in that type of remorse?"

"Maybe if you find that lawyer, he'll know something," Jesse suggested.

"Maybe. Good news is: Sheriff Murphy called and he's releasing my car as evidence. There were no fingerprints on my car that matched any on the truck," she said, avoiding the word *murder* for Jesse's sake. Hers, too, to be truthful. "Lonny said I could pick it up or he'd have someone drop it off in the morning."

"If you do track the lawyer down and decide to go to Charlottesville to talk with him, let me know," Drew said. "I'll make arrangements to go with you. If that's okay."

She wasn't going to pretend that she hadn't been hoping he'd offer to do just that. "Thank you. I will."

Jesse squirmed happily. "And if he doesn't tell you that your mother was a furry red alien from Mars—or something equally disturbing—the two of you can make a day . . . and night of it."

Drew's gaze met Sophie's and he winked. It wasn't until they were out on the porch, saying their goodbyes, that the gesture didn't seem quite so contradictory to his behavior throughout the rest of the meal.

She could tell he wanted to kiss her, but he hadn't come

even close to making a move yet. Maybe he was taking a step back—and maybe he was right to do so. . . .

She was craving the touch of his lips.

"So, you'll call your dad tonight?" He swung his legs slowly down the three steps off Jesse's front porch to the sidewalk. She held her ground at the bright white pillar that supported the roof—she wouldn't chase him all the way to his car for a kiss.

"Mm. But it's Monday—Lions Club night. He's good with names, but I doubt he'll remember the lawyer's name off the top of his head and I can't ask him to look tonight after a long day. So I won't know anything until tomorrow."

"Will it upset him? You digging into this?"

She shrugged. "We talked about all this before I left. He understands. And he knows he's my real dad no matter what."

He nodded as he turned to look up at her. He glanced away, looked at his feet, and looked back at the street again before deciding to speak.

"Look—"

"I know."

"What?"

"We don't have enough time. You and I."

He lowered his head, dejected, but didn't give up. "No. We don't. But . . ." He was suddenly on the step below her looking straight into her eyes. "I know we talked about this last night: starting something that might get complicated, that'll probably hurt like hell to leave unfinished. . . . I thought . . . I hoped the cold light of day would cool me off, bring me to my senses but. . . ."

He looked pained—and he was so uncharacteristically unsure of himself, she couldn't help herself. She grinned.

"Oh." The word escaped on his breath like a prayer—he wasn't alone. "Earlier you were talking about having to stay, like you couldn't get away fast enough. I thought . . . well, I know you'll be leaving eventually but . . . Damn it! Help me out here. Say something. What are you thinking?" He stopped short like he could hear the echo of his words in the evening quiet, then pinched her chance to speak. "Christ, this is nuts. We both know it. We should stop now. Run in opposite directions. We have completely different lives in completely different places. We haven't got a clue to how long it's going to take Fred to find Cliff's killer—but he'll have to release you eventually. You won't have anything else to keep you here. We won't have time to—"

Her forearms came to rest on his shoulders, to ease his burden. She looked directly into the fine green eyes that were beginning to haunt her dreams and smiled.

"We have now."

"My father said the lawyer's name was Biggs, Henry Biggs," she told Hollis the next afternoon. "But that his penmanship is so bad it looks like Hobart Biddles or Horace Bzzzzzz." She'd laughed when her father did it, but Hollis was quiet on the other end of the phone. "There's a Biggs & Biggs listing in Charlottesville—Henry W. and Daniel H. Biggs. They were booked the rest of today, but I got an appointment for ten o'clock tomorrow. Drew McCarren is going with me, so the sheriff says I can go. We should know something one way or another by tomorrow afternoon, at the latest."

"Thanks, Sophie." He sounded tired and relieved. "I know this isn't easy for you. I know you're doing it for me."

"I've never had an almost-brother before. You do things like this for almost-family, right?" She chuckled, tried to make light of it but—"You know, you could have been such an ass when all this started. You've been nothing but great . . .

and gracious. I feel like I owe you this. And it isn't easy for you, either." She heard him sigh. "How's Austin, Texas?"

He chuckled. "We're still weird," he said proudly. "And both boys are off to a high school football camp at the university next Monday. Jane and I will have the whole week to ourselves—we'll probably go into withdrawal and die of silence."

She took a couple of minutes to ask questions about his teenaged sons that he was delighted to answer. Discovering they were only eighteen months apart in age, she was curious to know if they were competitive with each other.

"Oh, sure. They fight constantly and they're pretty gung ho about bringing home the best report card, thank heavens, but out on the football field they know they're more of a force to be reckoned with if they stick together." She started to wander, mentally, when he mentioned double- and triple-A divisions and championships and MVPs and tailbacks and downs. It was a survival mechanism her mother had perfected and passed on to her for every time her daddy launched himself into *football speak*—a peculiar language she not only didn't understand but also didn't give two hoots about.

Not that Sophie wouldn't have noticed Jesse if she *had* been listening. She came rushing up the stairs, did an indecisive shuffle on the landing, turned and started down the hall toward her—pulling at the hem of her cotton shirt, chewing on her lower lip, shaking her head in confusion and distress.

" . . . unless it's an individual sport like wrestling or golf and then, of course, it's a whole new story—it's all-out war."

"Hollis, I'm sorry. Will you hold on a second? Something's wrong."

"What? What's wrong?" She heard him ask, his voice fading as she lowered her cell phone to her lap.

"Jesse?"

"It's Maury Weims."

"Who?"

"Maury Weims. He's gone missing. No one's seen him since Sunday afternoon."

"Who is he?"

"I went to school with him. A year behind. He works at Kerski's drugstore. Phil's the manager. Phil's his brother-in-law. He goes to my church—Maury, I mean. Phil, too. All of them do; the whole family does." She went still, her eyes huge, her skin pale. "And he's one of Cliff Palmeroy's best friends. Cliff, Maury, and Frank Lanyard were tight as bark on a tree in high school . . . Jeremy Bates, too. The four of them." She rubbed her brow, remembering. "They were a walking nightmare for anyone younger or weaker than them. You know how you hear about gentle family dogs turning vicious when they get together with other neighborhood dogs and start running in a pack? Jeremy Bates was a nice enough guy until he started running with Cliff and them. Lucky for him he was smart enough, and had the means and gumption to go off to college. And he never came back. Last I heard he was in California doing something. Real estate, I think, or maybe insurance—I always bunch those two together in the same category, for some reason. Probably because they're always up in your face—telling you that you need more insurance or asking if you want to sell your bed-and-breakfast. And they never include the sentimental value in the net worth, of course, and if—"

"Jesse." Sophie touched the woman's arm gently to break her frightened prattle. "Maury Weims."

"Oh. Yes. He's missing. He . . . um . . . the creepy thing is: Frank Lanyard was the last person to see him."

That didn't seem too creepy. "They're friends, right?"

"Not so much anymore. Not since Frank moved to Roanoke."

"They fought?"

"I don't think so."

"Then why is it so strange that they were together? Especially after a mutual friend of theirs has been murdered?"

"Well, it's not, except now *he's* gone, too. *And* Frank is demanding that the Roanoke police put him in protective custody. He thinks his life's in danger, too."

"Really? From who?"

"He doesn't know, but he's terrified. Who wouldn't be?"

"How do you know all this? Have you talked to the sheriff?"

She nodded. "Better. Mike."

Sophie paused to breathe. "Hold it." She put her cell—and Hollis—back to her ear. "Hollis?"

"I've been listening. Call me back when you know more, okay?"

"Sure." She disconnected and turned back to her landlady. "Mike told you all this?"

"Yes, and I know what you're thinking. But if you want to know something in this town, he's the one to ask. People tell him everything . . . and if they don't tell him, he gets the lowdown from the most reliable sources he knows—and he knows everyone."

Sophie personally knew of two such people in Marion who had the exact same powers of intelligence gathering that Jesse was describing, so she knew the phenomenon existed—and Mike seemed the right sort.

"Okay. So, Frank is afraid for his life because Maury is missing and Cliff is dead—and the three of them, plus the other one—"

"Jeremy."

"Right. The four of them were a young terror cell in high school." She thought it over. "I think I met Maury. At the drugstore. He was at the register. Chubby, scarecrow hair, grouchy."

Jesse frowned. "Maybe you caught him on a bad day. I mean, well, he's chubby and always in need of a haircut, but he's not usually grouchy. He can't afford to be—Phil's the only person in town who'll hire him—brother-in-law, you know; and the Rite Aid is less than three blocks away from Kreski's. Then, too, poor Maury got into drugs and alcohol for a while. Heavily. It almost killed him before he went into rehab. He's been sober—and trying to make amends with people for a long time now. Plus, he had some heart problems a few years back—that almost always causes people to evaluate their lives and start worrying about getting into heaven. Most of us have forgiven him but it's hard to forget, you know? There are still a few holdouts."

"And no one has a clue where he might be?"

"Mike says he told Leigh, his wife, Saturday night that he was driving down to see Frank first thing the next morning. He left before she got up to go to church and she hasn't heard from him since. She called Frank late Sunday and he said that Maury left his house around two-thirty in the afternoon. So by then he'd had eight hours to make the two-hour drive back. Leigh is not a flighty woman, but Mike says that Frank's being late, mixed with his odd behavior since Cliff died, she was immediately alarmed and called Fred."

"The sheriff."

A single nod. "He said he'd tell his men to keep an eye out for him but that being late wasn't against the law, that maybe he ran out of gas or got a flat tire and had to walk to get help." She sat down on the bed beside Sophie, as if too stressed to remain standing. "According to Mike, Leigh called back at midnight and again in the morning. By noon Monday, the sheriff had the Roanoke cops involved and that's when he found out Frank had been asking for protection. That's when he began connecting the dots and started thinking Maury's disappearance might be linked to Cliff's death and stepped things up, called in the state troopers.

"Early this morning they recommended organizing search parties—which Mike wants to volunteer for—which is why he had to tell me all this—which he hadn't planned to so I wouldn't worry—which is so like him, you know. He's always trying to take care of me—which I feel like I'm constantly scolding him for—which is ridiculous because any mother would give their life for a kid like him."

Tears brimmed. Sophie gathered her in her arms. "I love Mike."

"Everyone does."

"And everyone knows what a great mom he has."

"I know." She chuckled and dabbed at the moist corner of her right eye. "But sometimes even that doesn't explain him."

Sophie released her and bumped her with her shoulder, but she couldn't disagree.

They sat on the bed, side by side, laughing softly, clinging to the humor until it wafted away like a summer cloud and they fell into silence—and their own thoughts.

"Are you going to let Mike go?"

"Yeah." She weighed the risks out loud. "He's old enough. We believe in community. He's going with Luke, his oldest friend, and his father who'll keep an eye on both of them. And it's the right thing to do." Another statement she couldn't dispute.

Long after Jesse left to start supper, Sophie sat on the bed, new emotions churning inside her.

Panic, because it was beginning to feel like she was trying to claw her way out of a locked box.

Powerlessness, in that she yearned to challenge someone, fight back, battle past them—but she was swinging at thin air. Who was pulling all the strings?

Pessimistic, because in her mind the Palmeroy murder and Maury Weims's disappearance could very well be a fluke in the time continuum in relation to her appearance in town. Add Arthur Cubeck's actions and the three events were as incongruous as congressional spending and common sense, as terror and reason and yet . . . As far as she knew, she was the only obvious common denominator to each event.

Predestined, as she felt doomed to an end not of her making, without a choice, because it was getting harder and harder to pretend that none of what was happening in Clearfield had anything to do with her . . . especially in the pit of her stomach. From the moment Arthur Cubeck bequeathed BelleEllen to her twenty-five years ago, she was involved.

No, she decided, more and more she was beginning to feel like the catalyst to a chain reaction. A really ugly one.

Chapter Nine

SOPHIE HAD LONG AGO DISCOVERED THAT SOME OF HER *MOST* IN-spired moments occurred in the nimbus space between her dreams and full awareness. It was here, at age nine, that she realized that while the dishwasher remained broken, it was possible to dry more than one dish at a time by simply pick-ing up two together, drying first the top and then the bottom of the set and then switch the plate positions—dry top to dry bottom again and the chore was done in half the time. Bril-liant . . . well, at age nine it was.

Another time, home from college on Christmas break, she became frantic as she looked high and low, for several days, for the ornate key that opened the cedar hope chest her fa-ther built for her. It was decided the lock would need to be picked and left broken or replaced. New Year's Eve, as she lay dozing in bed, gripped in the futility of resolving to eat more vegetables—the thought of them drenched in chocolate an ob-scene prospect—she saw herself dropping the key to her chest into the hidden compartment of a jewelry box she'd gotten for her sixteenth birthday for safekeeping.

In the gap of this semiconsciousness, everything seemed either too like the hole Alice tumbled into or so clear-cut a doorknob could understand it.

Such was the case when she silenced her alarm clock and rolled away from it, still tired and sleepy from the questions that had plagued her sleep—and reluctant to face a day filled with yet more questions.

But they simply wouldn't stop.

Since Arthur wasn't her biological father, what was he to her? What had he done to her . . . or not done *for* her? Who was she? How and why was she conceived, and by whom? Arthur knew, but why had he kept it a secret? What would the attorney in Charlottesville reveal about her beginnings? Kissing Drew was a bad idea, right?

A question for the back burner.

Did the murder victim know what Arthur knew? How were the two men connected? Arthur sounded like an angel; Cliff Palmeroy seemed a devil—what did they have in common? Where was Maury Weims? Did having no future with Drew prohibit kissing him?

She rolled back and scrunched her pillow impatiently.

Who the heck slashed her tires? Was it mayhem or a message? If Maury wasn't a grumpy person in general, was he testy with her specifically? She hadn't had more than eye contact with Cliff Palmeroy—had she? What was he going to do with those pictures of her? He left a frail wife and two angry sons behind—did Maury have children? His wife must have loved Maury very much—she'd been very concerned about him—said she worried when he didn't show up because he'd been acting so strangely since Palmeroy's death.

That wasn't a question. Sophie opened her eyes. That was a fact.

Leigh Weims, who was not a flighty woman according to Jesse, said her husband had been acting *strangely* since the murder. So, how odd did a man have to behave after the death of a friend before his wife could describe it as *strange*? In what way was he strange? What did he do? . . . and why?

More questions. But a couple she could actually get answers for. Would Mrs. Weims talk to her, a stranger, at a time like this? She decided to call Billy; see how well he knew her and if he'd have time to talk with her. Maybe she'd tell him more.

She flipped back the bedding to get up—her mind sluggish and full.

It cleared right up, however, when she made it to the kitchen and found Drew there eating Wheaties and Jesse's cran-banana-bran muffins.

Ear-to-ear grins for them both.

"Hey."

"Hi."

"No pie?"

"Haven't earned one."

A lighthearted scowl. "Are those my cran-banana-bran muffins?"

"There's more over there."

"She makes them special for me."

He nodded. "I noticed. No nuts."

"Extra crans."

"You're allergic to nuts?"

"No. I choked on one once. I feel safer when they're not hidden in my food."

He nodded, satisfied. "One more thing to add to my book."

She set her cup of coffee, a plate, and a knife on the kitchen table across from him. "What book?"

"Didn't I tell you?" he looked surprised. "I'm writing a book about you. It's called, *20 Million Amazing Somethings About Sophie*."

"Nuts make me nervous. That's amazing, all right."

"Give me a break. I've barely started. I'm still on the first chapter. Writing is one of those things that can't be rushed."

"What's that?" asked Jesse, breezing in through the swinging door on the dining room side of the kitchen. "Who's feeling rushed? There's no rush. Mike makes a bigger mess than the two of you together." She nodded toward Sophie. "Plus, she makes her bed every morning so—"

"Oph." Drew perked up, took an imaginary pen from his shirt pocket, and wrote the information on the palm of his hand. Confused, Jesse looked to Sophie.

"He's writing a book about me." She popped the last bite of her buttered muffin in her mouth. "And he can't be rushed."

"Oh." Jesse picked up her mug of coffee and leaned back against the black tiled counter, deep in thought, while Drew picked up their dishes and stacked them in the sink and Sophie finished her coffee. They said their goodbyes and were in the kitchen doorway when she called out, "She hums in the shower."

"Oph." He stopped short, pen and palm at the ready this time. "Sings or hums?"

"Just hums, same song every morning."

Sophie groaned.

"What song?"

Jesse squinted, and with mischief in her voice, she said, "Well, if there's one thing I know, I know my hums." Laughing, Sophie started pushing him down the hall toward the door. "And even taking into consideration the bathroom acoustics and a pitch that makes the dog up the street howl, I'd recognize it anywhere."

"Jesse!"

"What? What is it?"

"One of my all time favorites . . . next to the Chipmunk Christmas song."

Wide-eyed recognition and delight lit his face. " 'Rubber Duckie.' "

"Don't be silly." Heat climbed both sides of her neck as she opened the door. "It's 'Habanera.' "

"Ha. That isn't Jesse's second-most favorite song." He followed her out the door.

"And 'Rubber Duckie' is?"

"Maybe not anymore, but when we were kids and she was our babysitter, Ernie's rubber ducky was right up there with Alvin's hula hoop. Ask Ava and Billy. We sang 'em all the time. And if she put us to bed at night, she sang 'Hush, Little Baby.' In fact, when Mother finally let Billy have a dog, he named it Rover . . . from Jesse's bedtime song."

"You know, I don't think . . . well, I know, I never had a sitter who made the sort of impression or generated the sort of affection that Jesse did in your family—though, it's not hard to see why."

He picked up his pace to beat her to the car door. "Jesse's always been Jesse. And my mother's always been my mother—the opposite of Jesse, who was more spontaneous, less formal." This was a statement, not a criticism of his mother, and one she could easily see. "Jesse was like a spring breeze blowing through our house. We were crazy about her." He stood holding the car door open for her, smirking. "So if she says you hum 'Rubber Duckie' in the shower, I feel confident that she's a reliable source and I'll be putting it in my book as such. Unless, of course, you'd like to prove her wrong."

If his gaze had the power to turn her head in the most conventional of circumstances, a suggestive glimmer in his eyes had it spinning like a top. She grinned, refusing to giggle. She wouldn't mind a shower in his presence—and not merely to prove Jesse wrong, which she wasn't—but she simply couldn't see any future in it. Sadly.

"Okay. Fine." She slipped into the car. "But I have a legitimate excuse."

"Oh?"

"I'm a kindergarten teacher. I need to be able to relate to my peeps."

"Ho! Good one." He laughed.

In her pseudo-rectitude she glanced up at his unrestrained enchantment and felt herself slipping into a familiar space in her heart; an unmanageable place full of dreams and fairy tales that allowed her . . . encouraged her, basically, to fall in love with the most out-of-the-question people. Like the two-week summer vacation romance in fifth grade; the church-sponsored foreign exchange student from Greece who moved in next door during high school; the severe and unrequited crush on her Romantic Poets professor, which was the longest interlude she'd had in college; and, most recently, the rebound relationship for a newly divorced parent of a prior student.

Her love life was an unnatural disaster. She *knew* this—but she loved the skid, the spin out, the loss of her footing in the realm of logic and reason, and she cherished the joy inside. She couldn't stop her fall for Drew. Wouldn't. And she knew this, too.

"I'm Daniel Biggs, Ms. Shepard. My father is Henry," the forty-something attorney corrected her when she introduced Drew. "Dr. McCarren." He waved his hand across his desk. "Please, sit. Be comfortable." He led by example and a friendly smile. "I thought my associate explained—"

"He did. I'm sorry. He explained that the Biggs & Biggs

twenty-seven years ago was your father and uncle, not you and your wife."

"Right. Good." He got right down to business. "So you understand, it's been a while and that there's no longer any personal recollection of the case beyond what's in this file?" She nodded. She understood that lawyers had their own language and that this one was telling her that his father, for one reason or another, was no longer a viable source of information for her.

"As you probably know, Thomas Shepard, your adopted father—"

"My dad."

He nodded his understanding. "He contacted us yesterday and later faxed a standard waiver, allowing full disclosure of any information we have regarding your adoption—which is fairly bare bones, I'm afraid." He handed her a fresh blue file folder with a much older string-sealed manila envelope inside. As she opened it he went on. "I don't imagine we have any more information than your father does."

His voice became distant and muffled as her thoughts grew louder.

Bare bones. *Bare bones?* There weren't a dozen sheets of paper inside. She held them, thin and flimsy, in her hand; thoughts flashing in her mind like a strobe light; not knowing how or what to feel. She couldn't focus enough to read them, too jammed up by how official and professional and bureaucratic and sterile and cold and . . . detached they looked.

"Now in Virginia," she heard him say through the ringing in her ears, "in parental consent adoptions after July of 1994, when the adoptee reaches the age of eighteen, all records are open to all involved parties. Any before that date, still require a court order to be opened and as you can see—"

"This is it?" she asked abruptly, looking up at Drew first,

and then the attorney in disbelief—unaware of the odd crack of hysteria along the edges of her voice. "This is me? This is all it took? There were more papers than this when I bought my car!"

"Sophie?" Drew's voice was soft and solicitous; he touched her arm.

She ignored him, staring at Daniel Biggs as if he were the embodiment of the entire legal system sitting self-righteous and unshakable in a burgundy leather chair.

"How can this be?" she asked. He had the grace to look uncomfortable while her eyes demanded an explanation for the apparent *simplicity* of transferring the care and well-being of a newborn—a human infant, for God's sake—from one set of hands to another.

And it didn't matter that the hands she, herself, had been delivered into were gentle and kind and giving. It didn't matter where she'd come from or the circumstances in which she came to be. It never really had. But she was certain—a little crazily, but *irrevocably* convinced, that more paper should have been involved!

"I know what you're saying." The lawyer's smile was small but hugely perceptive. "An event that changes your life so completely ought not to fit in an envelope. I agree. But keep in mind that those few documents are, in fact, thousands of court cases and volumes of codes and laws and regulations and hundreds of years of experience all boiled down to their simplest form so that we *can* put them in envelopes. I promise you, Ms. Shepard, adopting a child—of any age, in any situation—is never taken lightly." He gave this a moment to settle in. "I'd like to explain some of what I've read and then we can see where we need to go from there. If you want."

"Sophie. My name's Sophie," she said nodding, hoping that less formality would make whatever followed more personal, like it was about *her* and not some random event. She glanced at Drew; he winked and she smiled. She wasn't random to him.

"The order of events are filed chronologically with our parents' initial professional encounter in the very back," Biggs said from his side of the desk without needing to look at the file again. "It seems that our fathers either met briefly socially or yours was referred to mine by a mutual acquaintance because in his file notes, my father mentions Miller's, which is a small bar downtown."

"DMB?"

"The one and only." A soft chuckle and he leaned back in his chair, more relaxed in the presence of another Dave Matthews Band fan. He looked like he could launch himself into a formal dissertation on the bit-of-everything sounds that made the group so unique—and beloved—but he didn't. He took a breath. "This was before the band, of course. Your parents made an appointment to come in and talk about adopting a child—the basic how-to and where-to-start information.

"Adoptions aren't something we deal with routinely, but in a town this size we handle whatever comes in or we don't pay our mortgage. My father did agree to represent your parents legally, but he also explained that it was against the law for him to actively seek out a child for them. They either had to do that themselves—by advertising, by word of mouth inside their religious affiliation, something like that—or go through an adoption agency. He referred them to three separate agencies, listed there, as well as the local Department of Social Services." He paused to recall what else he'd read earlier. "He also noted that your parents had no preference as to sex, race, or age—though, ideally the younger the better. My father suggested they get started on the home study, which is required in every state for every adoption, and can take several months to complete."

"So . . . they were investigated."

"Absolutely. And counseled and informed, and I'm sure they felt like they were being put through a ringer, but as I said before, adopting a child isn't taken lightly. By anyone. In fact, most of what you have in your hands there is a notarized copy of the social worker's report. Naturally, it was included as part of the adoption petition." His eyes lit briefly as he came forward at his desk. "And that's where this case gets interesting." He held up his hand to stop the alarm growing in her eyes. "Not, *not* illegal or unheard of or in any way shady . . . but mildly out of the ordinary in that it all happened at once. The adoption petition was filed and approved, and temporary custody awarded to your parents, all at the same time with the only stipulation being a six-month adjustment period before the adoption was finalized and your parents were allowed to take you out of the state."

"Why?"

"Well, there's always some sort of waiting period—usually given to the birth parents, in case they change their minds." He tipped his head. "But also for the adoptive parents, in case they change theirs."

"No, I meant: Why was it done all at once? That's the out-of-the-ordinary part, right?"

"It is. But again, it's not unheard of," he said patiently. "Under normal circumstances the birth parents aren't even allowed to consent to an adoption until the child is actually born, and typically then it's still three to four days before they can sign the consent forms. Even after that, there is a period of up to three months in which the birth parents can revoke their consent. Now, all this waiting and uncertainty can be extremely stressful on the adoptive parents who might be caring for and falling in love with a baby that could, at any time in that period, be taken from them and returned to the birth parents. In some states, the infant is automatically placed in foster care to prevent that sort of trauma. In the Commonwealth of Virginia there are choices. If the social worker for any reason feels the birth parents are shaky in their decision, they will recommend foster care and the judge will listen. On occasion the adoptive couple, for one reason or another, opts for foster care—usually they've been disappointed before. But for the most part, the adoptive parents take custody as soon as possible—while the ink's still drying on the consent forms.

"This is apparently what your parents did. And the fact that all the paperwork was filed and approved on the same day would indicate some sort of special circumstances."

"Like what?"

"Oh, say, for instance, you were abandoned. The six months of temporary foster care that your parents agreed to would give your birth parents time to reconsider their decision and step forward. Barring that, it also gives the police and social services time to attempt to identify your birth parent or parents to obtain a medical history . . . and, of course, they could face criminal prosecution in the case of abandonment. We don't have a safe-haven law in this state as yet." He hesitated. "Often in these cases, when the birth parents can't be found, the infants remain unadoptable—in a sort of legal limbo until permanent abandonment or deaths in absentia are lawfully declared."

In a heartbeat, he reconsidered his next statement and nodded, letting it go. Unfortunately, Daniel Biggs was a moral man with a dismal poker face.

"But that wasn't the case with me, was it? I wasn't left in a basket somewhere, was I?"

He didn't hesitate again. "No. This copy of the petition to adopt indicates that consent forms were signed, but we'd need the original, sealed, adoption papers to see by whom."

She nodded, confused. "So . . . that sort of negates the spe-

cial circumstances you were talking about. They didn't abandon me or they did abandon me and were caught or came
forward to sign the papers afterward . . . *or* the special circumstances could be something else entirely. Right? Does it
matter? I mean, there was bound to be *some* sort of special
circumstance, one way or another; but if we petition for these
papers you say we need, my birth parents' names will still
be on the consent . . . and on my original birth certificate.
Right?"

He bobbled his head. "On the birth certificate, probably,
but I suspect not on the consent."

"Why . . . would you suspect not?" Too late, she was almost
certain she didn't want to know and held up her hand. "Wait."
She looked at Drew for assurance that what she was about to
hear wasn't going to ruin what she'd come to think of as a
bright and promising future.

"Would you like me to leave? Give you some privacy?"
Drew asked.

"No. Please stay. I'm . . ."

Afraid. *Very* afraid. And now he could see it in her eyes.

"You don't need to know any more. We can leave now. I'll
buy you lunch at Miller's; drive you through the countryside.
. . . We already know Arthur wasn't your father. And Hollis will
understand. You know he will. The time, expense, and hassle—
and the emotional cost of getting your birth records unsealed
would be—"

"A waste," the lawyer injected. They both turned their
heads to stare at him in confusion. "A request for nondisclosure was signed."

"By whom?" Drew asked—in it, now that he'd been invited.

"By whoever signed the adoption papers."

"Why didn't you tell us this in the first place?" He was annoyed.

"I was getting to it. I want you to understand the process, to have an opportunity to ask questions."

"*Whoever*, you said," Sophie stated. She felt numb, like her skin was three inches thick and dampening any sensations coming her way. "Not my birth parents."

"No. Your birth mother's legal guardian made the arrangements for the adoption and signed all the forms—and, I'm sorry to say, also blocked the easiest path to discovering the identity of your birth mother . . . and consequently the father, of course."

"So there's nothing she can do, right?" Drew's voice was thick with relief.

"No. Well, yes. You can file for a release of non-identifying information. Depending on the details taken at the time of your birth, you can sometimes get a medical history and the status of the mother's health at the time. Ethnic origins, level of education, religion. Once in a while you can get the parents' ages at the time of delivery, the age and sex of other children, general geographic information of the birth, even the reasons for the adoption, if you're lucky. Whatever you get, if there's anything *to* get, can sometimes be very helpful in a search."

Drew turned to look at her, brows raised. Did she want to pursue that angle? Did she want to search? But she was stuck on another question—and that moment of resistance she'd noted in the attorney's demeanor.

"My parents always knew she was a teenager. That's why she needed a guardian, right? Because she was a minor?" Her intonation made it a question, forcing him to divulge what he hadn't planned to volunteer.

"Not as a rule. Teenage parents can and are generally encouraged to voluntarily sign their own consent forms." He inhaled heavily. "Unless your birth mother was under the age of twelve." Sophie winced in horror and he rushed on to reassure her. "But that's not the only reason she might have a legal guardian. One would be required if her parental rights had been terminated by a court order—for . . . for long-term alcohol or drug abuse or abuse of other children in the household, sometimes incarceration or abandonment—like we talked about. Also, a parent who has been declared incompetent, and for some reason it's determined that restoration of competency is improbable, would need a guardian."

"Like in a coma . . . or insane?"

His nod was slow. "I'm sorry, Sophie. Even in the best of circumstances, searching for your birth parents can be complicated . . . *or* a box of chocolates as a wise man once said. But whatever you decide to do, I'm here to help in any way I can."

"Thank you," she said softly, slipping into the commotion of her thoughts—into the questions and the dread that accompanied them.

It was as she'd suspected most of her life: she was part of another woman's tragic misfortune. Life is complex and hard, and she was clearly a heartbreaking event best forgotten by her birth parents. She knew this. She understood it. Poking that dog with a stick could trigger a confrontation that was both fierce and furious—and to what end? What would be the point of her knowing about someone else's difficulties—beyond curiosity? What good could she do them now? What would she ask of her birth parents? . . . or the guardian, if she could get no closer to them? It was over and done and sealed up tighter than a shrink-wrapped can of sardines. What difference did it make now?

"Sophie." She felt Drew's warm touch on her arm and looked up. "You don't have to decide anything today. It can wait. You came here on a long shot—to find out what, if anything, Arthur had to do with your birth mother, and it looks like you may never find out. It's likely the relationship wasn't even documented."

"Unless *he* was her guardian." He stared at her, astonished at the idea but not altogether doubtful.

"He wasn't." Again, they turned their heads to look at Daniel Biggs. "At least it seems unlikely according to my father's final notes on the case."

They stared a moment longer before Sophie thought to check her hearing.

"Arthur's name . . . is in the file?"

"Yes. In my father's notes on the case."

"So Arthur Cubeck's relationship to my birth mother *is* documented."

"Yes. In my father's notes."

Drew made an annoyed and frustrated noise. "Which say . . . ?"

"Which say"—the attorney cast a snarky glance at Drew—"your birth mother's guardian was a member of Mr. Cubeck's congregation who asked for his help. I, personally, know that Arthur was a good friend of my father's—they met years ago at a local charity golf tournament, became friends, and played golf every Wednesday morning for years. He often referred people to my father for help."

"But what about Mr. Metzer? He was Mr. Cubeck's lawyer. Why come all the way over here when he— Oh." She pulled up short. "Clearfield. Small town. The rumors. They came here for more privacy." He nodded. "A pregnant teenager in Clearfield would be talked about. When she delivered, the baby would be talked about. Whether she decided to keep the baby or give it up for adoption would be talked about, so what would be the point of keeping the actual adoption quiet?"

The ticking of the wall clock grew louder and louder as they wondered.

Drew spoke first. "Because if someone in town all of a sudden showed up with a newborn, everyone in town, including the mother, would suspect it was hers. It makes sense for the adoption to take place in another town altogether—even more sense if someone knew your parents wouldn't be staying in the vicinity for much longer."

Of course. Perfectly logical. Nothing deceitful or illegal. Nothing to worry about.

"Or no one knew she was pregnant in the first place," Daniel Biggs said. "An illegitimate child can be stressful for a young woman . . . for her family. With or without the family's knowledge, she could have kept the pregnancy under wraps until she delivered. It doesn't explain why the adoption was expedited the way it was, but it's possible."

Okay. Equally as plausible. Deceptive but not illegal. Still nothing to worry about.

"All right." Drew started the wrap-up. "We know that Arthur knew your birth mother's guardian—maybe your birth mother, as well. No way to know that, but he did help facilitate the adoption. We have no idea why your birth mother needed a guardian, but we do have two plausible scenarios for why Arthur thought it best for Henry Biggs to handle the adoption instead of Graham Metzer . . . and I guess we can assume that *he* brought your parents into the picture because they'd recently been in to ask him about adopting a baby. We know we can't get to your original birth records. But you can file for that . . . what was it?"

"Non-identifying information," the lawyer said.

"Right. And depending on how much information you may or may not get, it may or may not be medically useful to you, but it certainly won't do more than help you guess at who your parents might have been. That about cover it?"

Daniel Biggs nodded and looked at Sophie. Both men did.

After a moment she began to speak as if thinking out loud. "You know, I've always wondered if I was . . . odd or an unfeeling person for not being more concerned about where I came from and who my birth parents were. I didn't think it mattered. I mean, for whatever reasons, she didn't think she could keep me, those reasons didn't have anything to do with me. I always assumed that she knew that my being born wasn't my fault; that she didn't blame me for her problems, you know? She did the best she could for me.

"I know people believe what they want to believe. And I know that sometimes we make up stuff to rationalize what we don't understand—like things that hurt. But I truly don't remember ever feeling or thinking that her putting me up for adoption was anything but a gift from her to me." She offered a soft laugh. "Maybe that's how my mom explained it when I was young or something but that doesn't matter, either. It's how I've always felt.

"And now . . . knowing she needed a guardian, for whatever reason, I feel like maybe it was that person's gift, too. He was careful to bring in a good man like Arthur Cubeck to help him—he cared about me. And that nondisclosure thing he signed? Something tells me it wasn't just to protect my birth mother—it protects me, too." She looked from the lawyer to Drew. "I'm being too simple and naïve, aren't I? Boringly detached and objective, right?"

"Not at all."

"I was thinking more along the lines of kind and empathetic," Drew said, looking more impressed than she thought she deserved. "But if that's not doing it for you, how's the fact that your instincts have been tested recently—profoundly—and have proven to be spot on? You know I believe in going with your gut, and if that's what yours is telling you then I'd bet good money that you're right. How you feel is how you feel. You don't need to explain yourself to anyone. And you don't need to make any decisions right this second."

They suspended any further discussion of Arthur Cubeck and her birth mother when Drew closed the office door.

A few minutes later they were on a slow meander through the long narrow hole-in-the-wall type bar that is Miller's on the downtown mall. She challenged him to a game of pool while they waited for their lunch order. Though Drew dominated the game—despite his gallant offers to tie one hand behind his back or, if she preferred, hand drop her balls in the pockets for her—she saved her ego by fending off defeat with an extensive selection of wily trash talk until their food arrived and they were forced to call a tie before it all got cold.

They sat at a small table on the brick walkway outside, hardly aware of the pedestrian traffic browsing the shops along the tree-lined shopping mall. They talked about music and movies and summer vacations. Later, he was patient while she window shopped, and she let him buy her ice cream so he wouldn't have to eat his alone on the way back to his car.

It was too nice a day for the air-conditioning. They'd lowered the car windows and let the wind blow across their cheeks and kink the curls in Sophie's hair. The air was thick with the scent of moist soil, sun-warmed trees, and honeysuckle. The silence between them as comfortable as it was cozy and intimate—until something caught Drew's attention.

He had slowed down rapidly on the highway and took a sloping gravel road off into cool shade and thick green undergrowth.

"Where are we going?" she had asked, bemused by the grin on his face when he told her it was a surprise. She laughed. "You don't think I've had enough surprises lately?"

"This is a good one. You'll like it."

And who would not? He pulled to the side of the dirt road, took her hand when she got out, and led her carefully between the trees to the creek. There was a short drop down to the edge, which he took first, then turned with his arms out to help her. She hugged him with gratitude for his thoughtfulness and then kissed him because . . . well, because she liked kissing him.

"What a lovely, peaceful place." she said, standing barefoot, up to her calves in a shallow, slow moving stream that snaked loose and lazy through the wooded area. The water was so languid she could see the rocky bottom. "Coming in?"

He shook his head, seemingly content to enjoy her enjoyment. "No." He found a rock to perch on. "This one is called South River. It starts from a spring a few miles south of here and flows north all the way to the Atlantic Ocean."

She chuckled to herself and wagged her head. "Geographically, I understand why some rivers flow north but the one I can never wrap my mind around is Niagara Falls . . . flowing north. I always picture it flowing up, backwards, like it's rewinding. This is someone's property, isn't it? Think we'll run into an angry farmer with a shotgun?"

"I can't even imagine a farmer who'd get angry seeing a beautiful woman cooling her feet in his stream."

That dollop of pure maple syrup sent blood rushing to her cheeks. "And this one runs all the way to the ocean, huh?"

"Mm. Until it reaches the North River—clever names, don't you think? They become the South Fork of the Shenandoah River." He pointed upriver. "The South Fork is about a hundred miles long and joins the North Fork in a town called Front Royal and then *they* become the Shenandoah River." He bent his fingers slightly. "It flows another fifty or so miles and dumps into the Potomac in West Virginia somewhere and then *it* empties into the Chesapeake Bay and flows out to sea."

His hand came to rest on his knee as he finished his mental journey.

"It's cool but not freezing. Perfect." She stood on the rock-strewn bottom and wiggled her toes in the silt and clay, the water barely grazing the hem of her sundress. She looked up at him. "Thank you for this."

He shook his head, suddenly ill at ease—as if it were too small a thing to be thanked for.

She studied the water around her. "Fish? Creepy wet things? I'm okay if I can see them but not if they sneak up on me." She grimaced.

His eyes lit with mischief. "I don't know about fish—the water might be too shallow, but there are plenty of bugs, so it's hard to tell. However, creepy wet things. . . ." He grinned—her smile drooped. "No, of course not."

But once she relaxed again, he added, "Well, probably not. You can never tell about creepy wet things." He plucked his invisible pen from the air and began to write on his hand. "Not okay if creepy wet things sneak up on her." He laughed when she kicked water at him, being careful not to get his clothes wet.

Though he'd said nothing about it, she suspected he was staying dry because he still had to go to work; that he'd re-arranged his entire day to take her to Charlottesville so she wouldn't be alone to hear what Daniel Biggs had to say and that this little river interlude was an impulse and just for her pleasure—a distraction, a kindness to show he cared.

A distraction. Her mind followed the ramshackle path back to the reason for it, and she sighed. When she looked up, she found him watching her in concern and smiled as she started toward him. "I bet I haven't mentioned to you yet how beauti-ful I think your eyes are."

His gaze, warm with an unmistakable heat, made her insides pitch with elation. He casually extended his hand to support her over the slippery bank, and then used his grip to guide her between his legs to sit on his knee, her toes still dipped in the water.

She put her hands on his cheeks and saw that while his gaze was calm and compassionate, the contours of his face showed tiny lines of stress fanning the outer edges of his lovely eyes, like so many little tributaries pouring tension into tranquil pools. She placed her thumbs over them, damming them, because she knew the anxiety was for her. She kissed him.

His arms encircled her—easy, effortlessly—as if it was already a long-practiced habit to him. He shared the touch of his lips, the taste of his mouth, and the breath of his life with her and she wallowed in it.

She smiled at the dazed look in his eyes when he opened them and wondered how she could make time stand still for them. Then abruptly, she recalled, "I also forgot to mention, I ran into Billy the other day after Hollis and I met with Mr. Metzer." She smoothed her thumbs across his high strong cheekbones and lowered her hands to his shoulders for more balance. "He apologized again."

Drew nodded. "I know."

"You know?"

"Mm." He seemed more interested in etching her face into his memory than his brother's activities. "My mother called me. She said Billy stopped by the house and asked her questions about life in Clearfield twenty-seven years ago. Women who died in childbirth, girls being sent off to live with relatives for months at a time, unwed mothers being stoned in the streets . . . anything she could recall. She wanted to know if I knew what was behind his behavior and I said he was probably trying to help you. I figured that if he was being a pain in the ass you'd have told me, but I called him anyway. Is that a scar?" He touched the outer edge of her right eyebrow. "How'd you get it?"

"If I tell you, are you going to put it in your book?"

He grinned. "Yes."

She sighed, happily defeated. "I ran into the back porch on my tricycle and hit my head on the handrail."

"How old were you?"

"Seventeen." His laugh echoed through the trees. "Three, I think. I don't remember it."

"Any others?"

She raised her elbow and had to look around for the evidence of an old injury. "Soccer. When I was eleven. Group collision."

Smiling, he raised it to his lips and kissed it. Then he looked at her. "He hadn't unearthed anything when I talked to him."

"And I haven't talked to him since he offered to help. But now . . . I don't know. I don't think he'd find anything. If my birth mother's guardian went to all the trouble to sign a non-disclosure, I can't imagine them leaving any other evidence around for us to find."

"Maybe not, but this is Billy we're talking about. If there is anything out there, he'll find it."

"He said he liked a good mystery."

"No, he doesn't. He hates them. It makes him crazy if he thinks someone's hiding something from him, and he can be as tenacious as a warped door until he finds out what it is." He chuckled as he recalled. "He cried at his birthday party once because one of his friends gave him a Power Rangers puzzle and Mother made him stay with his guests until they'd all gone home before he could start putting it together. Anytime we wanted to get to him, all we had to do was pretend to have a secret."

She scoffed. "I used to wish I had a brother or a sister, but I've just as often been glad I didn't. Horrible creatures. And in that case, I'm even happier Billy offered to help. I was curious about something Jesse told me about Mrs. Weims—that she'd noticed her husband behaving *oddly* after the murder. *Oddly* seems different than sad and grieving, doesn't it? I thought maybe she'd talk more readily to Billy than to me." She made a face. "He offered to be my inside man and I'm glad I have him."

"Me, too." He buzzed her lips with his and smiled. "Is there any way I can help? Anything you want me to do?"

"You mean, beyond all you've done already? More than going to the lawyer's office with me? Including this—bringing me here?" She sighed in satisfaction, and in yearning. She moved her hands to cradle the back of his head as she leaned forward. "Maybe just one other thing."

A gut-clutching sparkle lit his eyes before he closed them to accept her kiss. Her mouth opened over his, hungry and demanding, teasing and coaxing at once—he retaliated in kind.

The soft gurgle of the stream and the sounds of birds rustling in the bushes joined the gentle rhythm of the leaves brushing against each other in the trees until it began to sound like background music. Hands strayed. Breaths became labored. Drew's phone rang.

He groaned deep in his throat and when she would have pulled away, he persuaded her against it—repeatedly—while he removed his cell from his pocket to identify the caller over her right shoulder.

"Speaking of the devil. It's Jesse." He smiled, sent her to voicemail, and nibbled on Sophie's lower lip to get her full attention again.

But not three minutes later it rang again.

Slowly, reluctantly the kisses tapered off and they sighed.

"We should probably get back anyway," she said, grateful for his assistance as she left his lap and picked her way across the rough, slippery rocks to get her flip-flops.

"Hey, Jess."

Hearing the fondness and patience in his voice, Sophie glanced at him. He smiled and winked at her and then his expression flagged. He looked away and then back to Sophie deeply distressed.

"Hold up, Jesse. Who? Jesus. Is he dead?"

Sophie could feel her heart all of a sudden beating so slow and so hard she thought it was stopping.

"Did he see who it was?"

"Who? Is it Mike? Is he hurt?" Drew shook his head. "Maury Weims?"

Another shake and he said, "Lonny Campbell."

"What?"

"Someone attacked him."

"The nice old man from the gas station?"

He nodded. "We're on our way back," he said to Jesse—using the same words and his brow to ask Sophie. "No, she agrees. We'll be home soon. Is Mike there?" He listened, and frowned anew. "Go up to the Levy's. They might know more." He sighed. "I wish I could tell you, Jesse. I don't understand it, either."

Chapter Ten

DREW TERMINATED THE CALL AND LOOKED OVER AT SOPHIE. EVERY muscle in her body was demanding an explanation.

He gave it as they worked their way up the slope and back to the car. "It happened last night. He was taking the trash out to the Dumpster behind the station and someone shocked him with a hotshot, a cattle prod, from behind. He went down but managed to knock them over as well; staggered to his feet somehow, lunged and got shocked again. Hit his head on the Dumpster, but Jesse said he saw the person run off before he passed out. One of his guys found him early this morning."

"So he saw who did it?"

He shook his head. "Dressed all in black with a ski mask, he said."

"Do they think it's the same person who killed Cliff Palmeroy?"

Again, he shook his head—he didn't know.

They were back in Drew's car and heading south in a matter of minutes—and minutes after that she was backhanding uninvited and wholly humiliating tears from her cheeks.

Women of *flint* don't cry until *after* all the crimes have been solved.

"Why is this happening?" She tried to sound angry but came off woefully confused. "I can't even pretend anymore that all this doesn't have something to do with me. It isn't coincidence. First, it's that icky Palmeroy guy following me around. And Maury Weims—he was hostile when he saw me at the drugstore. Hostile. Jesse said it wasn't personal but it was, I swear. I mean, I know when someone's not happy to see me. He wasn't and he's missing. And now Lonny, although . . ."

"What?"

"Lonny was nice, and he liked me. There's no pattern here. Except for me. Everyone I talk to or have any sort of contact with is either dead, missing, or injured or—Oh, God! Give me your phone. Quick."

He did, even before he thought to ask, "Why? Who are you calling?"

"Everyone," she said, busy fingering through his menu. "Jesse and Mike need police protection. I have Hollis on my phone. I'll call him next. He should be all right in Austin, but you never know so I'll give him a heads up. Ava and your mother, too—maybe they could leave town for a while, visit your sister in South Carolina." She stopped and looked at him. "And Billy. Oh, why did I agree to let him help? And Daniel Biggs—we need one of those no-information things he was talking about. Some's better than none." Her attention shifted back to his contact list. "Who else? I don't know who to call first. I didn't want to worry Daddy, but now I have to in case he's in danger, too, and— Oh, my God!" Her hands trembled as she turned to him. "*You!* You have to go, too. I knew this was too good to be true. I have *the worst* luck with men! I've never actually gotten one killed before—even though a couple of them had it coming—but you don't and I sure don't want you to end up dead. Or missing, because I have this sick feeling in my stomach that Maury Weims is as dead as Cliff Palmeroy and I didn't know either one of them. Not like I know you—we kissed!"

"Whoa. Okay." Calm and sensible, Drew watched his rearview mirror and Sophie at the same time as he crossed traffic to the outside lane and slowed to a stop on the shoulder. He put the car in park but didn't turn it off. When he turned to look at her more closely, his expression wasn't very sympathetic. "Listen to me. I get that this whole thing has been confusing and weird and that it's frightening for you. And I can see where you might assume it has something to do with you. I do. But whether it does or not, none of it is your fault. And who knows? There's still a chance that everything that's gone down could have just as easily happened if you'd never come to town. Maybe Cliff was a pervert and God knows the town has vandals. We don't know. And when we get to the bottom of it, if it does have something to do with you, you *still* don't get to claim responsibility for it. You haven't done anything to deserve it. Frankly, I never would have guessed you were so egotistical."

"*Egotistical?*" She was momentarily stunned. "I am not being egotistical. I'm being logical and . . . and pragmatic. You said yourself that I have good instincts and my good instincts are screaming that I'm involved somehow."

"Now? You can hear them screaming *now*?"

"What? No! What. Like now I'm egotistical *and* insane? Stop it. What the hell is your problem?"

"My problem? I'm not the one hearing screams and taking credit for things that I haven't earned."

"*Neither am I!*"

"Oh good," he said on a gust of relief. "You had me worried. I have *the worst* luck with women. Finding one I'm crazy about isn't easy, you know, and if she turns out to be totally nuts it could really, *really* screw up the rest of my life."

"What?"

"I said: Oh good. You had me worried. I have—"

"No. The other part."

He grinned—and she realized that she'd just witnessed his version of slapping a hysterical woman's face. And, okay, she had been a little nuts there for a few seconds but . . . he was crazy about her?

The swoosh of the cars and trucks passing by only a few feet away seemed distant and dreamlike—his voice was a deep, soft rumble in the quiet of the car. "Which other part?"

"The part about *you* being crazy."

"Me?"

"About a woman?"

"Did you think I was talking about you?"

If she didn't, she knew now by the teasing light in his eyes. She squinted and gave him her best scary-teacher stare. He chuckled in the face of danger, undaunted.

"I confess. I do think you're pretty adorable." He used his left thumb to rub a surplus tear off her cheek; looked entirely inclined to kiss her, then sobered. "I hate that you're caught up in all this—digging up the past, what's happening in town. One or the other would be hard enough, but together it must feel overwhelming."

A vague impression grew clearer. It must have shown on her face.

"What?" he asked. He leaned back, as if being too close to her made it harder to think. "What are you thinking?"

She shook her head. "Nothing really. Just a half-thought. We should get back to Jesse. She'll worry."

"She'll be fine and it won't make any difference if we're there or not. What are you thinking? Talk to me."

She wondered if this might be more therapy for a hysterical woman, but his tone was compelling—and she didn't care if was. Thinking out loud might help.

"What if . . . what if someone's trying to frame me? The sheriff already has his suspicions. It could happen."

"No, it couldn't. You have alibis and there's no proof. No motive."

"But what if they plant evidence or do something else? What if it works?" He opened his mouth to protest again. "Just *what if.* . . . What if it worked? What would anyone have to gain from sending me to jail? I don't have anything—certainly nothing someone else would want. I can't say for certain that I've never hurt anyone, but it was never intentional and it certainly wouldn't justify this sort of revenge. And even if it did . . . why here, why now all of a sudden? The only thing I can think of that's changed for me since I got here is that I have BelleEllen now."

An unfamiliar emotion rippled across his features. "I can't think of Hollis as—"

"No. Don't think of Hollis. Don't think of him doing anything to hurt me. He cares about me. He wanted me to be his sister. He did. As much as I wanted to be. Besides, I'm giving it back to him. As soon as he'll let me or I figure out how. I don't want BelleEllen. He *knows* it. It's not him." She hesitated. "Those Florida cousins. . . . The big one? Richard Hollister. He was furious. And he seemed like the kind of guy who'd bite the heads off live chickens for sport."

"And the farm would go to him if anything happened to you," Drew said, a hopeful ah-ha in his voice. She squinted. "No? So Hollis would get it."

"I don't know. But it wasn't Hollis. I'm sure of it." She

crossed her arms mutinously across her belly and stared out the windshield, thinking. And just as Drew—still caught up in the possibilities—reached out to put the car back in gear to drive on, she stalled him with her hand and another thought.

"Wait a second. You know, I barely had any contact with those men. I spent more time with the tech who took my DNA sample the other day. I talked to the little curator in the museum for over an hour. If someone is setting me up, why didn't they pick people I'd spent more time with? More people like Lonny . . . like Ava or Billy, Jesse or Mike, you or your mother? Why not people I actually know, instead of two men who knew each other, but not me?"

He turned toward her again. He took a moment to review the data, readjusted his breakdown of the information, and encouraged her to continue.

"Does it seem like someone might be afraid of what could happen if they had further contact with me? Like if one or both had actually *talked* to me?"

"Like they knew something and whoever's doing this is shutting them up?"

She nodded. "Cliff Palmeroy was following me for some reason. And Maury Weims was . . . cold and unpleasant. Specifically toward me—and I'm not imagining it. He was. He must have had a reason."

"And Lonny?"

She was thoughtful. "Lonny and I . . . chatted. For several minutes. We talked. And I had my car sent to him. We probably would have talked again. Maybe he knows, too. They might have thought he'd let something slip. And what happened last night might have been a warning." Wagging her head slowly, she met his gaze. "You're right. It isn't my fault. Someone else is pulling all the strings for their own reasons. But it does have something to do with me." She paused. "Or even more likely, it has to do with my birth mother. She's what *Arthur* wanted to talk to me about, and my coming is why everything else is happening."

Gravely, he searched her face, accepted the conviction in it, and kissed her—soft, solid, and sure. He nodded. "Okay. It's as good as any other explanation. We'll run it by the sheriff and see what he thinks." A quick promissory peck. "We'll figure it out."

They arrived back at Jesse's to see her red Jeep looking shiny and new at the curb—and the sheriff's brown SUV and two other county cars, grimy with mud and dust, parked in front of the house.

Jesse stood in the dappled sunlight amid the ferns and sweet rose accents on the porch. She wasn't tearing her hair out or screaming hysterically, so it seemed safe to suppose that Mike was well. But she was pale, looked stressed with the nervous flip of one hand in greeting, and her smile was strained: she had more bad news.

"Oh dear," Sophie muttered, sharing a look of dread with Drew. He set his jaw and went for the door handle. He held the gate open for her and neither of them spoke until they stopped at the bottom of the steps, looking up at their friend.

"I'm sorry, Sophie. They have a warrant. I had to let them in."

"Oh." Her shoulders and neck tingled as those muscles loosened and leveled out. "Thank God. I thought someone else was missing or— Have they found Maury Weims yet?" The shrug and short shake of Jesse's head was troubling—very troubling when she had no words to add to it. "How's Lonny? Have you heard anything else? Why would anyone do that to him? Can he have visitors? Do you think he'd mind if I went to see him?"

This time Jesse tipped her head, baffled. "What is it with

you and Lonny? He's such a cranky old fart—he's alienated almost everybody in town. The only reason he's still in business is because he can fix anything. Cars, toasters, freezers, lamps. He fixed Adam Bowman's grandfather's pocket watch two years ago. Adam was so grateful, he replaced all the lightbulbs in Lonny's service-and-repair sign, then Lonny went around bitching about the cost of the electricity to turn it on every night—which by the way, he still doesn't do. Ornery old poop."

This didn't sound like the Lonny she'd met, but her ten-minute acquaintance with him hardly put her in a position to dispute it, except to say, "I caught him in a good mood, I guess. He was nice. I liked him."

Jesse was clearly perplexed still, but voices from inside the house distracted them all.

"So, they're going through my stuff." She couldn't remember how full her dirty laundry bag was; wondered if they'd touch all her underwear . . . or made comments.

"And your car."

An ironic chuckle. "Well, it won't take long. They've already crawled all over my car once and my stuff doesn't fill a whole drawer up there."

"That's what I said." She was plainly relieved that her guest wasn't overly upset. "Well, not the number of drawers, of course, but that you brought so little—not even running clothes, so you had to buy some. It didn't seem to matter."

"Did they say what they were looking for?" Drew asked.

"Incriminating evidence is what the warrant said. So far they've bagged up most of my knives, both of the flathead screwdrivers from the junk drawer, my sewing scissors, and the safety scraper—that thingy with the razor blade inside to get paint off windows? They even took my razor from my bathroom. Ha! I thought they were going to declare a national holiday when they found the X-Acto knife I use to cut away old caulking."

"They're looking through your things, too?"

"They're looking everywhere. Inside the vents, the basement—even I can't find anything down there. The toilet tank, behind the stove and the frig, and the—"

"They're tearing your house apart?" Sophie glanced at Drew—he tipped his head to say they'd already pitched the frame-up theory and it didn't float.

"Ho." Jesse stood taller. "They tried. But I told Fred Murphy I'd call his mother if he didn't put everything back the way they found it." She huffed, hardly as daunting as she pretended to be, and settled in a wicker chair to wait out the search. Drew glanced down at his watch, debated in silence, and then mounted the steps to lean against a support pillar—to prop up his friend. "That was the only fuss I made, though. I figured I'd get more out of Fred with honey than my usual sweet self, so I cooperated as much as my temper would let me. I came out here when they found Mike's Swiss army knife—it was my father's."

"They'll give it all back," he said, sounding certain. "They think Cliff's throat was slashed at with a thin smooth-edged object, likely a scalpel or razor blade, less than two inches long. And if it was anyone's house but yours, I'd have to say it's better to take too much and return it later than not enough and miss something."

Reluctantly the women agreed—or at least didn't argue. Instead, Sophie asked, "What else do you know?"

"All I got was a quick peek at the preliminary autopsy in the ER—nothing's for certain yet." They stared at him, unaffected by his disclaimer. He heaved a sigh. "Because of the shape and location of the lacerations—and the pattern of the blood splatter—they think the killer was in the truck with him at the time of the attack, that the killer was right-handed, that he may have some knowledge of human anatomy, and was either a weak or an unpracticed killer due to the number and the various lengths and depths of the wounds."

"Why right-handed?" Sophie asked.

"Because of the direction of the cuts and which side of the neck they were made on," Jesse explained, clearly up to date on her episodes of *CSI* but shaken enough to look at Drew for confirmation.

"That's right. We know Cliff was in the truck when he died because that's where all the blood was. And if the splatter was on the left side of the truck, the cut had to be on the left side of his neck."

Jesse stood and, without a word, took Sophie by the hand, turned her and placed her behind the steering wheel of an imaginary pickup truck. She pointed to the left side of Sophie's neck. "You're on the driver's side with the window down and the cuts are here. If someone came up behind you on your left and they were left-handed, the cuts would be on the right side of your neck. If they were right-handed it would be too awkward." She tried a pretend incision from Sophie's larynx to her left ear and was startled to see it wasn't impossible. She looked to Drew.

"You can tell the direction of the cut because they're deeper where they start and end superficially." Perhaps he was thinking this gruesome reenactment would supply more facts than their wild speculations.

"Yes, right. I knew that." Jesse turned back to her victim. "So they can tell that the cuts were made from left to right, so anyone standing here, outside his window, couldn't have done it . . . with either hand." She circled the invisible truck and came up on Sophie's right. "Obviously, I can't reach you from over here, so I have to get in." She wiggled in close to the soon-to-be-deceased. "I could maybe stab the left side of your neck with my left hand if I had rubber joints, but not slice it. I'd have to use my right hand and reach across like this." When she did, Sophie's hands automatically reached up and grabbed Jesse's arm to protect herself—and again, the older woman looked surprised and turned to Drew.

"That's a natural response," he said with a shrug. "And it might explain the number and mix of lengths and depths of the wounds. They struggled."

"Should we tell Fred?" Evidently Jesse was hoping that solving the crime would make it go away, flush it from her mind. Sophie wasn't so certain.

He grinned. "Couldn't hurt, but I'm guessing one of his other forensic specialists might have told him by now."

She simpered at him and made a short production of walking away from the murder scene. Sophie remained, completely creeped out.

"What I can't figure out," Drew went on, "is why he's still so fixated on Sophie? Do you know if he thinks everything is related? Cliff, Maury, the tires, Lonny?" He glanced at Sophie, aware of what she thought.

Keeping her eyes averted, she walked passed Jesse to take the other big white wicker chair. She felt drained, sat—then bounced to her feet just as Sheriff Murphy pushed through the screen door to join them on the porch.

"I do," he said, looking around at each of them—one no longer than the other. "I do think they're related."

"And that Sophie's involved?" Jesse jumped on him. "Because of those stupid pictures? Or because of the bloody knife you found in her room? No? No knife? Maybe you found Maury's truck up there—or the black clothes and ski mask Lonny reported. No? So, where's your evidence, Fred? And let's not forget she has an alibi for nearly every second she's been in town. Truly, I don't understand why you're wasting all this time on Sophie when it's so obvious it isn't her. You should be looking somewhere else."

"Like where?"

"Well, how the hell should I know? You're the cop."

His moan was long suffering. "I swear to God, Jesse, you are chewing on my last nerve."

"Then talk to us," Drew said. "Help us understand where you're coming from. If you think Sophie has something to do with this, explain why and maybe she, or we, can elaborate or explain it for you."

The sheriff debated so long, Sophie was sure he was going to step off the porch and leave them to their guessing—or worse, leave her panicking that her most terrible imaginings were true.

Finally, he took up the pillar opposite Drew's, in front of Jesse, and began to count out the steps he'd taken to his deductions. "First, and most obvious, is the location of Palmeroy's murder and Sophie's pictures in his truck—both of which I could have taken as circumstantial until Carla, his wife," he clarified for Sophie, "told me that their camera hadn't worked in years; that he hadn't let her get a new one; that she'd wanted to take pictures of the boys . . . and so on. The next day she tells me the only thing missing from the truck, that she could tell, was a hotshot that Cliff kept in the bed of his truck." He put up a hand. "And don't ask me why he needed a cattle prod for the half dozen head he keeps out there when a cattle cane would work just as well, because I don't want to think about it." His jaw tightened with disgust, and it was plain the sheriff didn't approve of or like the victim, either—not that that let Sophie off the hook.

"So I have pictures of you on a camera that's not his, in the truck with his dead body, and a missing hotshot." He gazed at each face. "It didn't make any sense to me, either. Then your tires are slashed and we all sort of agree that it's vandals. New bright red car in town. They might even have known whose it was because of all the hoopla with Arthur Cubeck's will. I get it dusted for fingerprints for two reasons—to see if it's one of my habitual delinquents—case solved. And because it sets off an alarm in my head that it's the second time in two days that you've been involved in a crime." Again he held up a hand to stall Jesse. "One way or another. Next, when I was ready to call whoever was next on our towing list, you requested that it be taken to Lonny's. Fine, no problem. But now I have you in a suspicious connection to Lonny."

"Why suspicious?" Drew asked before Sophie could.

"You know Lonny. You know his place. Why would anyone—especially a stranger—request *him* to tow her car?"

"Because she'd met him that morning getting gas and she liked him?"

"How would I know that?"

"Okay. Go on."

Sophie glanced at Drew. She was scared—not so much of being found guilty of something she didn't do because, well, because she didn't do anything. But even the sheriff believed she was connected somehow to the evil occurring in his town. And that connection scared her. A lot. How many more people would it lash out at, and why? And how long before that evil came after her?

"Maury goes missing. I don't respond as aggressively as I should have because it hasn't been twenty-four or twelve or even eight hours yet, and I'm busy with the homicide. By noon, Leigh was beside herself and I begin to take notice. I didn't begin to make the connection until I went over to the house to interview her—and this is *after* I find out Frank Lanyard thinks someone might be trying to kill him, too—and she tells me Maury had been acting strangely all day Friday, even before they heard about Cliff Palmeroy."

"I wondered about that," Sophie said, and when the sheriff turned his curious scowl on her, she added, "I heard from . . . through the grapevine that Mrs. Weims thought he was acting peculiar after he heard about the murder of his friend." Both men slid their gaze in Jesse's direction—identifying the grapevine—and back again. "I wondered what he was doing that would stand out as odd behavior after the death of a friend, but if it was all day Friday as well . . ." She paused. "Well, I'm still curious. More, since I saw him earlier that day, before I saw Mr. Palmeroy watching me across from the hospital."

She watched the sheriff review his mental time line before saying, "Leigh said he rushed into the house unexpectedly Friday morning, about eleven or eleven-thirty. He rummaged through their utility closet for their camera and ran out again. She called out the door, asking what he needed the camera for, and he said, 'to take pictures.' He got back in the car and raced off."

"Oh, no." Jesse hid her face from the truth with her hands. "It's his camera in Cliff's truck."

"With my pictures in it."

The officer pressed his lips together in a tight line and nodded. "She called him later in the afternoon on his cell—he was short with her, said he couldn't talk and would call her back. But he didn't. He was late getting home from work, nothing too unusual, but she thought he was coming down with something because she'd fixed something he liked for dinner and he hardly touched it. She said that even once they'd settled in front of the TV, she could feel his tension. She wanted to ask if something had happened at work, but assumed he'd tell her when he was ready. My wife would have nagged the hell out of me," he said as an aside, marveling at Leigh's self-control. He took a breath. "Apparently he liked to have time to 'think out' whatever he was feeling before he told her about it. I guess if you've been married to a guy like that for that long, you figure out quick what works and what doesn't."

"Fred." Jesse's voice was gentle but disapproving. "He's changed a lot since the old days. Leigh wouldn't have taken him back if he hadn't."

"Hmp. You can take the stripes off a zebra but that doesn't make it a horse."

She looked away, disinclined to argue. Sophie's heart smiled. It was just like Jesse to possess the simple fact that some hearts have more pardoning power than others—and that it wasn't up to her to judge the sheriff if his heart wasn't quite as strong as her own. It was a virtue she'd always admired in her mother as well. Forgiveness. She used to say that as hard as it is to forgive someone, it took more energy to hate them—and the weight of hate on your soul was destructive.

"When did he find out about Cliff?" Drew asked.

"One of his kids came home from a sleepover at a friend's house Saturday morning, around ten o'clock. He told them. Leigh said Maury was as shocked as she was at first, but the more questions he asked about it, the more he seemed terrified, as opposed to horrified by it—fearful, not sorrowful. She called him on it; asked him why and what he knew about. He got angry, told her to shut up and to mind her own business. But she was worried; she said she kept at him until he raised his hand to strike her." Both women sucked in air and held it. "But he knew better, she said. He knew she'd leave him forever if he hit her again, even after all these years, so he shoved her away and slammed out the back door instead.

"He was gone most of the day. Next thing she knew, he was

tearing the garage apart. Throwing things around, ransacking through boxes. He was clearly looking for something, but she was still ticked off and didn't want to ask what it was. Eventually, she sent the kids off to bed, turned out all the lights in the house, and went to bed herself."

"She went to sleep? After all that?" Jesse broke in.

Drew reached into his pocket for his cell phone, checked it and put it back as the sheriff said, "She didn't sleep. She said she stood in the bedroom window for over an hour watching his shadow moving around in the garage. When she saw the light go out, she jumped back in bed and pretended to be asleep. A few minutes later, he stood in the doorway of their bedroom—he wasn't fooled—he said he was sorry and that he was going over to Frank Lanyard's place first thing in the morning and went back downstairs. He was gone when she got up for church on Sunday."

Sophie stared up at Sheriff Murphy not knowing what to think—which left plenty of room for thoughts and images to form on their own. The first to take shape clearly: The officer was in over his head; not inept, but untested and afraid of making a mistake, hyperaware of the consequences if he did. She could see the torment and fatigue in his eyes; the curve of his shoulders from the buckling burden of responsibility, and the nervous flicking of his right thumbnail against the side of his pointing finger. She felt for him, but was still more concerned for herself and the people she'd come to care about—like Lonny.

"And last night Lonny is attacked with a cattle prod," she said. "Presumably the one that belonged to Cliff Palmeroy."

"Presumably."

"And that completes a weird sort of circle of evidence that centers on me." They were all looking at her, agreeing, but unwilling to say it out loud. Even the sheriff held off. There had to be a way out of it. "I . . . Do you think there might be some reason their friendship caused them to be targeted? Maybe because they both knew something that someone else doesn't want anyone to know?"

His cell phone rang. He answered it with a quick *what* and an *I'm on my way* and put it back in his pocket as he addressed her. "Like what?"

"I don't know—something about my birth mother maybe?"

"You still don't know who she was, I take it. The lawyer was no help?" She shook her head while he considered her. "Maybe. I can't see Lonny being in cahoots with the two of them in some way, for any reason, but . . . hell, who knows. We have a lot of territory to cover yet. Finding Maury is at the top of the list." He turned and took the first step down off the porch.

"How is Mr. Campbell?" Sophie asked.

Fred Murphy's chuckle produced warmhearted amusement in his eyes. "Let's put it this way: he's fighting an overnight observation at the hospital while the Dumpster he hit his head on is still unconscious." His shot at levity went wide of the mark. He went back to being sheriff. "He's fine. I got one of my guys babysittin' him. He's safe for now."

"May I visit him? I— It's not me. I promise. I'd never hurt him. Anyone actually."

His nod came easily as he got to his feet to leave them. "If you could wait till dinnertime, it'll save me having to send someone over to relieve my deputy so he can eat."

"Sure."

"I'll let him know."

"Wait a minute," Jesse said. "What was he looking for? Maury. In the garage?"

It took only a second for the sheriff to realize he was already in for a penny. . . .

"So far, it looks like it might have been one of *her* school annuals. It could still be there, under something else, but that's all that stands out at the moment. Fact is, it could be anything," he said, slowly descending the steps as if reluctant to rejoin the rest of the world and his troubles therein. "Putting her garage back together isn't exactly where her heart is just now." Automatically and without hope, he added, "Let me know if you hear anything."

He hadn't pulled away from the curb before Jesse jumped up and pulled open the screen door, saying, "Leigh was my class secretary." She gave them an I-just-discovered-gold-in-my-sugar-bowl look. They stared back and she rolled her eyes. "We have the same annuals! If there's a clue in one of them, I'll find it."

Sophie barely noticed the soft bump of the screen door closing, the silence on the porch was so loud. Even Jesse's bossy scolding of the deputies inside to clean up this and put that back where they found it were muffled as she lost herself in the void between knowing for certain that she was somehow involved and the how and the why of it all.

Logically it had something to do with her, her birth mother, and Arthur Cubeck, but all the obvious connections of that triangle had been cleared up. Add Clearfield High School's scream team of bullies from twenty-seven years ago, and the waters muddied again with the dregs of something dark and disturbing. And yet, throwing Lonny into the mix pressed them back into a thick mysterious sludge worse than where they started.

She caught Drew's movement as he pushed away from the pillar and closed the four-step gap between them with his hands extended for her to take—which she did without hesitating. He pulled her to her feet, drawing her into his comforting arms.

"I need to take off," he muttered, his chin near the back of her neck as she lowered her head to his shoulder. Her sigh was of release, of finally grabbing onto something solid and real. "Don't worry. It'll be okay. We'll figure it out. No one's going to hurt you."

She didn't see it until she said it: "It's not me. If he wanted to hurt me he'd have come at me directly. First. I'd be Cliff Palmeroy." She pulled back enough to watch him add it up in his head and concur. It made sense. Why shoot all the ducks in the sky if what you want is the goose swimming on the pond, alone, in the open—an easier target? Returning to the safety of his embrace her voice went soft. "I'm more afraid for you. And Jesse and Mike."

She felt the short shake of his head. "It's not us, either. I don't know how Lonny Campbell fits into it, but everyone knows Cliff and Maury were friends since they were kids. Add their old pal Frank Lanyard and a pattern begins to appear."

"Bullies."

"Hmm?"

"You said Palmeroy was a bully. Jesse said there were four of them in high school. Cliff Palmeroy. Maury Weims. Frank Lanyard . . . and Jeremy somebody—he moved to California. So the connection between them isn't simply their friendship. They were cruel and intimidating together."

"And that would point the finger of guilt at dozens of people in town who'd want to get back at them."

"Sure, but why now?" Again she leaned away to see his face. "Why didn't they take their revenge ten or fifteen years ago or last year or even last month? Why wait until I come to town to get back at them?"

And there it was. . . . As his brow furrowed his eyes filled with the understanding and compassion she'd found so ap-

pealing when they first met. The silent empathy that told her
he was aware of the ache in her heart, the turmoil in her soul—
and he was there for her.

"I don't know, Sophie." He braced the left side of her neck
with his palm and caressed her cheek with his thumb. "I wish
I did." He kissed, first her forehead and then her lips—tender
and caring. "I'll come back about six-thirty to take you over
to see Lonny."

"Don't be silly. It's seven blocks away."

"I don't want you to be alone."

"I told you—"

"I know what you told me. Humor me."

"No. Thanks, but it isn't necessary. I'm tougher than I
look, you know. And I'm not afraid." *I'm flint.* She took a
step back. "Tell you what: I won't walk. I'll drive. I'll lock all
the doors and take Mike's baseball bat—if the cops didn't take
it." He wasn't falling for her stab at humor. She slipped easily
into frustration. "I don't want to be driven! I want to drive!
Alone, by myself. I want to be free to come and go. I want to
be in control!" Her voice cracked and softened. "I *need* to be
in control of something—even if it's just for seven blocks."

He saw it, and smiled with a relenting nod. "Sorry. There
might be more of my mother in me than I want to admit—
she'll smother anyone who lets her."

"No. You've been great this week." Her hesitation was
short. "Actually, you've been the best part—which might not
sound all that special considering everything that's happened,
but even if I'd come here under happier circumstances and
every day was a picnic or a party—or anything but what it's
really been—you'd still be the best part."

She took a breath and he grinned. "So would you say we're
in mutual crazy-aboutness?"

Laughing softly, she settled her forearms across the back of his shoulders. "I think I would. Yes."

"And would you agree that we should set some time aside to be alone, just the two of us, to explore this condition?" He eased her body flat against his; hands at the small of her back, fingers spread wide.

"Didn't we try something like that before with, um, a shocking outcome?"

She felt his abdomen quaver with a silent laugh. "Yes, I believe we did—an unfortunate setback in my opinion."

"Mm. Unfortunate." She leaned in to touch his lips with hers. Soft, warm, and pliant.

"Whatdaya say we give it another whack?"

"Now?" she asked hopefully, only half kidding.

"Later tonight." His voice came from deeper in his throat, like a growl. She liked it. "You haven't seen my place yet. I'll cook. We can take our time. Do it right this time."

"I suggest we step over and ignore all the dead bodies on our way out the door, okay?"

"God, yes." His delight slipped to desire when he lowered his mouth over hers—firm and hot. Urgent.

Chapter Eleven

IN MARION SHE RARELY LOCKED HER CAR DOORS. IT NEVER SEEMED necessary unless she had something of great value on the seat next to her—which was hardly ever—and it was more a matter of *leading them not into temptation* than believing someone might be actively looking for something to steal. And while she sort of automatically glanced more attentively into the shadows of the backseat before she drove at night, it was more for the presence of a boogeyman than a killer.

Though, she supposed a killer was actually a specific *type* of boogeyman for grown-ups—not unlike the kind that'll bite off the fingers of children who suck their thumbs. Rapists might be the adult version of the fiends who wander in the dark looking for little children to snatch up and carry off . . . and thieves and bullies could be the hobgoblins that crawl under the beds of children who don't go to sleep when they're told to.

But they weren't the imaginary goblins used to frighten children into being obedient. They were real, and they were her reasons for locking herself inside her Jeep as she drove to the hospital, parking close to the entrance, and locking it again as she scurried inside to visit Lonny.

While she didn't believe anyone was trying to harm her directly, there was no point in taking foolish chances. And okay, so her inner child still had a healthy fear of the boogeyman. *So what?* she asked herself, walking, eyes forward, passing the metal door to the vacant stairwell—equally as bad as any dark cellar—to the hospital's elevator bay. She was an adult. She could be as peculiar and as paranoid as she wanted to be and no one—

"Oh!" She startled when the elevator doors parted and a woman stepped into the opening. "Mrs. McCarren!"

"Sophie!"

They laughed, both relieved to know they weren't the only jumpy people in town.

"Hi. It's nice to see you again."

"You too, dear. Ava and I were speaking of you this afternoon." She was without a doubt the most put-together woman Sophie'd ever met. Even in simple slacks and a soft summer blouse, she looked like she'd just stepped out of Cate Blanchett's closet. "We were hoping we could persuade you and Jesse over to the house for a light summer lunch on Saturday."

"I'd love that, thank you. I'll check with Jesse when I get back and let you know . . . tomorrow probably." *Because I'm hoping to be out very, very, very late tonight*, she thought, smiling at her date's mother.

"Excellent." They switched places—Sophie into the elevator, Elizabeth McCarren out. "My, you look lovely and bright this evening." She sobered. "You're here to see Drew, if I'm not mistaken. Isn't it lovely that his work is close enough for drop-in visitors?"

"No, no." She waved a small but obvious fistful of deep

purple irises and white peonies from Jesse's garden. "I'm here to visit Mr. Campbell."

"Lonny?"

The door started to close, Sophie held it open.

"You know he was attacked last night, right?"

"Yes, I heard."

Guessing from the tone of disapproval in her voice, Sophie assumed the mere mention of . . . what had she called him? . . . the ornery old curmudgeon, brought to mind the accursed pile of tires behind Lonny's shop—and probably any number of socially unacceptable faux pas he'd committed throughout his lifetime. And with hardly any guilt at all, she began to see the satisfaction Ava found in irking her mother.

"I, ah, he not only replaced my tires the other day but he cleaned off all the dust they used for the fingerprints, and I wanted to thank him. And to say hi, of course . . . well, actually *mostly* to say hi." Apparently a good, deliberate irk required some practice.

"That's very kind of you, Sophie. I can see you have a very caring spirit."

Well, crud. Her caring spirit exhaled uncomfortably, embarrassed. "He was kind to me first. Visiting him is the least I can do."

She smiled fondly at Sophie. "I believe in the corporal works of mercy, too," she said, suddenly in the vein of a theological conversation. "I was brought up on the importance of feeding the hungry, clothing the naked, visiting the sick. And I don't feel you need to be a particularly spiritual person to do what's simply humane."

Sophie wasn't sure what to say to that, if anything, but the longer she said nothing, the more awkward the silence grew.

"No. I agree. People should care about one another." And for bonus points, she added, "Seems like those things ought to be as basic as breathing, and yet we call them *works* of mercy."

For a long somber moment, Drew's mother studied Sophie like she was someone she'd forgotten. She seemed to be taking in the waves in her hair and the arch of her brows, the shape of her mouth and the angle of her chin. A faraway look came into her eyes for as long as it took her to blink, and then it was gone.

"Yes. Yes, indeed. Doing the right thing should come naturally." She tipped her head to one side sympathetically. "But life isn't ever as simple as that, is it?"

Sophie's smile was small. "No, ma'am. Life isn't simple at all."

"And that's why forgiveness is divine, isn't it? Another virtue."

Sophie assumed she was referring to the quote, 'To err is human; to forgive, divine.' She recalled fondly her mother's views on forgiveness and said, "Yes, ma'am. My mom used to say that forgiveness is the choice we make so that our hearts can heal."

Elizabeth gave a satisfied nod. "A wise woman. You've been taught well, dear." Sophie agreed. "Good night, Sophie."

" 'Night, Mrs. McCarren."

"Call me Elizabeth." She turned to walk away. "Say hello to Lonny for me. And don't forget about Saturday."

The elevator doors came together.

"Oookaaay," she said slowly, wondering if Elizabeth's odd drift into the subject of charitable virtues was some sort of test she gave to all of Drew's girlfriends . . . or just the ones from Ohio. She chuckled. Either way, she felt like she'd done well enough to pass. Next . . . the sex test. She squirmed with anticipation.

The elevator opened on the second floor and she stepped out. Reading directions and following arrows, she was pretending she couldn't smell death underneath decades of boiled food and antiseptics when she spotted a khaki-colored deputy sheriff's uniform on a young man down the hall who was bent over the lower wall of the nurses' station deep in dialogue with the nurse on the other side—they laughed at something amusing and Sophie's blood pressure shot through the roof.

Who was protecting Lonny?

Her steps quickened and her mind reeled with a scathing lecture for their lack of concentration on their respective jobs, but the only thing that made it to her tongue by the time she reached them was, "Lonny Campbell?"

"Yes, ma'am. Ms. Shepard, right?" The deputy had a thick drawl and a big friendly grin that she couldn't appreciate at the moment. He turned to face the patient room directly behind him. "Finally got him talked into spendin' the night. He's inside there watchin' *Ice Road Truckers* and eatin' rubber Jell-O."

Her skin cooled as she conceded to his being only eight feet away and in full view of Lonny's door—plus he'd seen her coming, so he would have seen anyone else in the hallway.

"Thank you."

"Appreciate you puttin' your visit off a bit so I kin supper with my wife." He smiled warmly at the nurse. "We work odd shifts and sometimes we can go a couple days without seein' each other. She's done for the day and close to finishin' up on her notes there, then we'll be off. Downstairs to the cafeteria, is all. The other nurses know you're here. So you holler out if you have any problems and I'll be back in half'er three quarters of 'n hour. That good for you?"

"Yes, that's fine." She glanced back at the nurse, whose expression was both curious and pleasant. A cute couple. "Enjoy your dinner."

Before she could tap on Lonny's door, she heard the soft ding from her cell indicating she had a text.

Nearly caught up. Let me know when you're ready.
For my book—how do you like your steak cooked
and how many babies do you want? D

Her head came up quickly to see if anyone took note of her astounded gasp or the happy flush in her cheeks, then dropped the phone back in her big hobo-style purse. Her smile was double wide as she entered Lonny's room.

"Mr. Campbell? Hi." She inched farther into the room. He looked well enough despite the clear-tape dressing on his right temple. "You might not remember me but—"

"Course, I do." His tone was gruff, his voice raspy, as she'd caught him off guard and he was clearly uncomfortable. "Bumped my head—didn't lose my mind."

She grinned. "So I see. Did you get stitches?"

"A few." She watched as he tried to reposition his big body into a more respectable and courteous position for receiving company. But as anyone who knew anything about hospital beds would tell him, comfort—be it physical or psychological—is not what they were designed for. He cleared his throat and said, "Five, they say, and I'm guessing they charge by the stitch 'cause the gash isn't but an inch long and I coulda laced it up myself with just two. Three at most."

"Yes, but that would have left a scar and no one would think you were pretty anymore."

He looked up, taken aback, and coughed out a laugh he hadn't expected. "Pretty. Ho, that's fresh. Never once worried about anyone calling me that one before."

"Really? I find that very hard to believe." Seeing that he was immensely more relaxed, she settled half a thigh on the end of his bed. "What do they call you instead? Handsome? Good-looking? Cute?"

He snorted a chuckle. "Mean and ornery's what they call

me most days. Rest of the time they don't bother callin'." His gaze lowered to the flowers. "Those for me?"

"Yes. Jesse sent them."

He took the flowers with a grumbled utterance, looked at them in bewilderment, glanced around awkwardly, and then plunged the stems into a carafe. "Tell her thanks." He settled his hands in his lap and looked back at her.

There might be a thick layer of snow covering the peak of this mountainous man, and the lines in his face deep as rivers, but the life and humor in his clear green eyes was as vivid and warm as his astute intelligence was keen . . . and clear.

"Is it hurting much? Should you be resting? They said visitors were okay, but I can come back another time."

"No. You're good. My bookkeeper and Tom Johns, who found me, came by early on when they all thought I was dyin' but it only took 'em ten seconds to figure out I was stayin' on, so they left. And it's boring as hell in here." And so as not to appear too eager for companionship, he added, "Got some shows I like on the TV, though. And the nursin' gals are nice." He curled his upper lip. "But someone in the kitchen's got somethin' 'bout boilin' all the food—it's disgustin'."

"I know! What's that about?" She perked up, preheated on the subject.

"Ain't a kernel of salt in the place, neither."

"And it's all the same color. How do they manage that?"

"Same way they make it all taste the same, I'm guessin'." He hesitated. "Cake's good."

"That's true. I like the little frosted brownie sort of cake . . . and the coconut-layered cake."

He nodded. "Ain't had that one yet, but the bacon was good and crisp this mornin' when they finally fed me."

"Yeah, they're pretty good with bacon. Crunchy. I'm not hot on half-cooked bacon."

"Nor them fake eggs and mashed patotas. But can you see crackin' and peelin' and cookin' all them for everbody?"

"No, I can't imagine it's an easy job. And since it's basically the same in every hospital I've ever been in, they probably have some sort of rules or specific ways they have to follow to make special diets." Her expression was empathetic. "And they do serve better food to the staff and visitors in the cafeterias."

He considered her a moment. "You know a bit about hospitals. Are you sickly?"

"No. Perfectly healthy. I don't even catch colds very often." Remembering was still an awful surprise followed by an aching pain. "My mom passed away last year. Cancer. My dad and I got to be hospital food experts."

"Sad. My condolences."

"Thank you." Sophie learned quickly that there was a unique bond between people who'd experienced the loss of loved ones. "The other day . . . You've lost people, too."

His nod was slow, thoughtful. "A long time ago."

"Your wife and daughter." Another nod, but nothing warning her off the subject. "At the same time? In an accident?"

"No." There was an odd tone in his voice—a need to speak laced with defiance. "My wife slipped away from us when our girl was but seven—bad heart." He leaned his head back against his clumsily placed pillow—his scraggly white beard jutting straight out in the air—and closed his eyes briefly as he toppled into his memories. The deep lifelines in his face softened. "Course, we didn't know about that in the beginning. Ha. In the beginning it was more me with the heart problems than her." He raised his head. If his smile was a bit stiff, it was from disuse, not the lack of enjoyment. "I was her cousin's date to a big family reunion picnic after the harvest that year. I didn't know her too well, the cousin, but she seemed like a

nice enough gal. I was twenty-two, fresh out of the navy—
that was the Korean War, ya see. Course, I didn't have much
of nothin' yet, so the family had a wary eye on me; figured
I was up to no good with the cousin, so they missed my jaw
droppin' down to my belt and me near fallin' off my feet the
first time I saw my Cora. She was a sailor's delight with eyes
the color of a noon sky in midsummer."

And *he* was a bit of a romantic poet. Sophie's heart melted.

He went on. "She was wearin' a real pretty yellow sweater
with tiny white buttons up the front and a slimish sort of brown
skirt—I could tell from across the way that she was gonna have
a time getting' up off the blanket she was settin' on—talking'
and laughin' and lookin' like God sent an angel to that picnic."
He sighed, as smitten now as he was at twenty-two.

"And was it love at first sight for her, too?"

"Lord, no. Took some other fella's hand getting' up off
that blanket. Couldn't stand me. So she said at the time." He
chuckled silently. "Course later, when I thought I'd worn her
down by jumpin' through every hoop she set out like a trained
dog, and she says yes at last to bein' my wife, she tells me
different. Says she fancied me from the start but needed to
be sure of me and my intentions—since I was there with her
cousin and all. I tell her I'd kill a bear with my bare hands if
she asked it of me." He picked an invisible twig off his lap.
"Course, she never asked anything of the like from me. Gave
me more than she ever got, I fear."

"Somehow I doubt that." He caught the gentle smile on her
face and looked abroad self-consciously. It made her heady.
She sensed he hadn't talked this much, and particularly on
this subject, in a long, long time. He was comfortable with
her, trusted her; she was delighted . . . and honored.

"She was special, my Cora. Never had an unkind word for

anyone she saw. Couldn't walk by a body in need of help to save her life. She was a good woman."

"I believe you. She sounds amazing."

He nodded affirmative and considered his next words. "It ain't for me to question God's ways a doin' things, but when you get to be an old coot like me, you come to see the plan He's had for you since you took your first breath. Course there's them that say we all make our own choices and I ain't sayin' we don't. But it don't matter if you choose to take the high road or the low road; the rough, windy one or the easy way—you always end up where you're meant to be, I think." He made a brief review of his words and gave a single nod. "That's the way of it, you know. Things happen in life with no rhyme or reason that you can see at the time. Takes time, sometimes your whole life, before you see what good can come of it."

Instinctively, she knew what he was talking about. *Loss.* The loss of those you love. They had that in common. They shared that pain; those fragile, aching spots in their hearts that will always grieve even though their lives go on.

"I'll have to take your word on that one. I'm not seeing it yet. I miss her." The sting of tears made her blink.

"You should. Means ya loved her; means she was a good mama to you."

"She was. She was the best. My dad's terrific, too. I lucked out in the parents department."

"Good ya know it, too. Too many young people don't know how good they got it till it's gone."

"Is that . . . was . . . What was your daughter like?"

"A good girl. Happy girl." He said with no hesitation, as if defending her. Instantly, Sophie knew she'd stumbled into a tender territory. She took no offense and was instantly contrite—she'd intruded. But before she could apologize, he said, "Sweet, she was. Had a smile for everyone she knew, and she never met a stranger. Everyone was her friend. Best and brightest thing that ever happened to me and Cora—named her Lonora after the both of us."

"That's a pretty name."

"She was a pretty little girl. Like her mama. Like you." She let her smile say thank you. His smile was simply a part of his reflective expression. "You see? All part of that plan I was tellin' you about."

"In what way?"

"Had we known when we married about Cora's weak heart; had we known how much worse havin' a tiny baby would make it, I never would have let it happen. Never. The Lord, He tried to tell us in His mysterious way. Made it good and hard for us to get a child, but we weren't hearing Him. We wanted a family. We prayed and we begged for years until He caved in and gave us what we wanted. . . . But Cora's heart, it failed her. And for so long . . . for so long I didn't understand it. It seemed real cruel of Him to bless us with our sweet baby and then take my Cora away. Real cruel. Hurtful, like I'd asked for too much happiness; so when I got it, I had to pay the consequences." He barely shook his head. "But He don't work like that, ya see. He don't punish people for being too happy. That's plain crazy. But He knew what was comin'. He knew. And He sent for Cora ahead of me to save her the pain of bein' here when her baby passed and to be on the other side to welcome her when she did."

Sophie wasn't sure if that was the saddest or the sweetest rationalization she'd ever heard. But having trusted her enough to explain it to her, she decided to trust *him* enough not to question it.

"And Lonora? Why did she have to die to begin with?"

"Choices," he said simply. "Everybody makes choices—some

good, some bad. Some so easy you don't even know you're making 'em; some so hard they rip your heart to pieces. Good people make bad choices. Evil people make choices that hurt innocent people. Innocent people make choices that put them in harm's way. It's always the choices we make that whittle the life we live."

"And my mother died . . . why?"

He pressed his lips together and tipped his head to the right. "Don't know. And if it ain't plain to you yet, might be it's too soon to tell. But it will be the choices you make because of it that'll decide your life from here on."

He had the eyes of a tired old man, but the light in them gave away his wisdom and the faith he had in his convictions. So much so, she allowed her brain to examine and feel its way through the events and experiences—the choices and out-comes in her life—and slowly, but surely, she began to see a pattern.

A singular love and fascination of young children—possibly due to the fact that she was adopted—made garnering a lucra-tive babysitting career in high school practically a no-brainer . . . which then helped her select Child Development for college. And while she preferred small children, making a sustainable living in daycare and Pre-K school wouldn't gel in her predominantly practical mind, so she soon chose Primary and Early Childhood Education as her major.

She elected not to leave Marion because she didn't want to be too far from her parents and friends even though third grade was the only position available at the time. However, she made it clear and well known to everyone who controlled such things that she wanted the first kindergarten position that opened—and when it did, she did.

It was never something she wanted, nor would she say she had a real choice in the matter, but she did take a nine-month leave of absence to be with her mother last year. She blamed those wretched months for an aversion to doctors, hospitals, and funeral homes that was almost palpable. Was it her newly honed compassion for the dying that tipped the scale in favor of hearing Arthur Cubeck's deathbed confession? And her impulse to go sightseeing that caused her to miss it? And everything that had happened since . . . ?

When she glanced at Lonny again she must have looked convinced because he nodded and bowed his lips a bit.

"So everything that's happened to me since the day I was born has led me here, right this second, to the edge of your hospital bed." His nod was slow. "Why?" He shook his head slower.

"Don't know. Might be nothin', might be somethin'. Time will tell, I suspect."

He had the look of a satisfied man—as if he'd seen a need and done what he could with it. He laced his fingers together and settled them on his abdomen—*Done talkin' serious,* it said.

Okay. She had plenty to mull over anyway.

So once again she startled a bark-hoot from him when she grinned and said, "Pretty or not, Mr. Lonny Campbell, you're an odd old duck."

"Ho! There you go! Now you're gettin' it."

The deputy returned from his dinner alone, and Sophie left a few minutes later with renewed confidence that he'd be less distracted as he watched over Lonny.

Though, truth told, now that she'd seen him she suspected the only reason he got hurt in the first place was because he'd been ambushed. He'd have fought off anyone coming directly at him, and he would have won. Weakness didn't fit in his vocabulary.

Then again, what kind of coward would attack an old man from behind? And why?

Her mind drew a blank.

It was so blank, in fact, that she couldn't at first place the soft ping sound from deep in the bowels of her purse. A distinctly dissimilar ping from the ding of an incoming text—she had voicemail.

"Sophie, Elizabeth McCarren calling. It occurred to me a few minutes ago that it might be nice for us to get together alone, before lunch on Saturday with Jesse and Ava. I'd very much enjoy the opportunity to get to know you better. The Crabapple Café isn't far from the hospital and it doesn't close until nine o'clock. I have a couple of errands this evening, but I should be finished between seven and seven-thirty if you'd like to meet me there. I have a bit of a sweet tooth, so perhaps we can share a dessert. If you haven't arrived by then, I'll simply get something to go and see you on Saturday. Um. Yes. Goodbye."

She groaned in dread, passing through the visitors exit to the parking lot.

Alone with *the* fish in the pond, the spoon in the soup pot— the one who kept things stirred up—with no backup, no protectors. She grimaced.

Would her date with Drew, which she deliberately neglected to mention earlier, be a good enough excuse not to go? She twisted to look up at the second-floor windows of the hospital, wondering if a quick call to him would be infantile—or worse, offensive. She was his mother after all.

At her car she leaned back on the door and raised her phone.

Crabapple Café with your mother. Come soon.

About to push send, she changed her mind, went back to erase the second period, and inserted three exclamation marks.

She put her cell back, fished out her keys, and popped the lock with the remote.

The rapid movement in her peripheral vision sent shock and terror to every cell in her body full blast. She panicked. Her hands shook. The keys fell to the ground. Her first thought was to try and beat the odds, go for the keys and the safety of her car. But she wasn't *that girl*. In the movies, the only times *that girl* made it away safely after picking up her keys was if the bad guy was still searching for her elsewhere . . . or momentarily unconscious . . . or superficially wounded— Sophie screamed, bolted for the front door of the hospital.

She didn't get far.

The strong hand that locked on her left upper arm pulled her back against a solid wall of chest as another hand covered her mouth.

She fought.

"Jesus! Shut up. You're going to get me arrested." She tried to shriek that that was the general idea but could barely breathe, so instead she stuck out her tongue and slathered it over the palm of his hand. "What the—" In disgust he tore his hand away. She screamed. He was forced to stifle her once again. "For crissake, will you stop? It's me, Billy. I'm not going to hurt you." As she began to relax, he slowly started to release her. "Unless you lick me again." He swiped his palm across his jeans. "Gawd."

Once free, she turned on him, smacking his chest with both hands. "Damn it, Billy. You scared the shit out of me!" She smacked him once more.

"Again! What's the matter with you?" This time she hit him with only one hand.

Her heart was still thrashing about in her chest and her joints were going soft with relief. "Why didn't you call out? Identify yourself."

"I did!"

"Sooner! Before you start rushing toward me. People are

dying around here. If I had a gun, I would have killed you first and looked to see who it was afterward." She hesitated. "Even then I wouldn't have been able to tell because I'd have shot you in the face because those Kevlar vests are so easy to get and you never know who's wearing—"

"I found something."

"Oh." She took an involuntary step back, like he might burst into flames. At once it was as if she stood in the center of a cyclone that was sucking time from its very beginning into a pinpoint of darkness. This moment would change the entire world as she knew it, her whole life. There would be answers to her questions that could never be retracted, that she could never put back in the box. "Oh God."

She stooped to pick up her keys and turned back to her car. She wasn't sure if she should or how long she could ignore him, but she needed more time. She felt caught up in the whirlwind, off balance, on the verge of vomiting.

And Elizabeth was waiting for her.

Billy circled behind her to stand before her again. "By accident. It was like I was meant to find it. No one in town could remember anything from around that time—1985 or '86. That's almost thirty years ago. I tried birth records. Do you know how many females were born in Virginia in that time frame? In this county alone? Or in Charlottesville? Which is in Albemarle County? Or for that matter, any one of ninety-three other counties?"

Sophie checked the lock through her car window to make sure the tab was up, unlocked. She needed to be ready. Ready to run. Just . . . ready, because she wasn't ready to hear what he had to say next.

"But then I realized I was approaching it all wrong. See, you weren't just some normal average statistic. There was something different about your birth, something surrounding it was hinky, something Arthur Cubeck felt guilty about. Guilty enough to leave you his family farm, even though you weren't family. Pretty damned guilty, if you ask me. So I start thinking of all sorts of different things like: he hit a pregnant woman with his car and ran off . . . or maybe she had her new-born baby in a stroller . . . or he was a drunk driver who killed everyone in your family but you—"

"Jesus, Billy."

"Well, he wasn't a saint. And shit happens, you know. It could have been anything. But it would be an *event* not a statistic. See what I'm saying? It was a real place to start looking . . . that might lead to something else . . . that might lead to who you are."

"I'm Sophie Shepard."

"Yeah. Well, you're someone else, too."

He pulled a folded piece of white paper from his pocket and held it between them. She stared at it—numb. Somewhere in the back of her mind she was repeating over and over, that she was Sophia Amelia Shepard, the best gift a daddy could ever dream of. . . . No piece of paper could change who she was— and yet just hours ago she'd seen the papers that had done just that: changed who she was. No. She was Sophia Amelia Shepard, the best gift—

"Since you were adopted in Charlottesville, I started there in the main library with the microfilm archives from *The Daily Progress*. Obituaries, headlines, some regional stuff—anything where a kid could be orphaned or left somewhere . . . or put in foster care for one reason or another."

"I wasn't in foster care. The lawyer said." She heard a muffled echo in her voice like she was speaking from the inside of a fish bowl. "Special circumstances. She had a guardian."

"See? Sure. I knew it had to be something out of the ordinary. At first I didn't think I'd find anything because all the newspapers around here are sort of connected and print a lot of the same stories except for small sections for the highlights of local news, you know? I spent the whole day over there. Nothing. So I figured I hit another dead end. But then this morning"—he shuffled his weight, as anxious and impatient as he was hesitant and worried—"this morning I started to wonder if maybe whatever happened wasn't a big enough story for the *Progress*. Or what if one of the smaller papers around here hadn't been bought out back then—and even if it had, the local papers always go into more depth on a story. Probably to take up more space since nothing ever happens but—" He shrugged. "Hell, who knows. But I figured it couldn't hurt to look, so I went over to the Staunton library to check out *The News Leader* first before I headed over to Waynesboro for *The News Virginian*." He looked between her face and the paper in his hand twice. It was a long tense moment before he spoke again. "It was a headline. November 12, 1985."

She looked into his eyes—so unlike Drew's but still aware and empathetic. He wouldn't force her to look at it; wouldn't judge her if she chose not to. His steady gaze said: he found the information and the rest was up to her.

But that wasn't what she was saying to herself. Deep in her core, she knew there was no choice. She could flee now, but the facts on Billy's sheet of paper would chase her forever— plague her sleep and change her life whether she read it or not.

She filled her cheeks with air and blew it out slowly through pursed lips, then held out a hand that was clammy and trembling. The muscles in her chest contracted painfully and it was hard to breathe.

There were actually two pages. The first opened to old black-and-white newsprint and a 3x4-inch picture of a happy girl with a lovely bright smile. Though she hadn't had the privilege of braces to correct a slightly displaced lateral incisor, it was also

Sophie's smile . . . set in a more heart-shaped face than Sophie's oval. The bridge of her nose was thinner, and while her eyes appeared to be paler, the shape of them and her eyebrows were also the same. Most shocking of all, however, was the thick, wild, curly hair that Sophie didn't need Kodachrome to know was a deep burnt-orange color.

Immediately, her eyes lowered to the story.

CLEARFIELD POLICE SEARCH FOR MISSING GIRL, 16
Lonora Elizabeth Campbell went missing from her home.

Clearfield authorities have been combing the city and surrounding area since late Thursday in search of a 16-year-old girl who went missing from her home earlier in the evening. The disappearance of Lonora Elizabeth Campbell is being termed "suspicious" by police, who say they know the girl quite well and that while she has developmental disabilities and is known to have wandered off before, "she never goes far and she stays out in the open because enclosed spaces frighten her." The girl's father, Lonny Campbell, discovered her missing at 6:15 yesterday. He reported her disappearance 30 minutes later after searching the neighborhood in vain. Between 75 and 100 rescuers searched through the night and more volunteers have arrived to continue the search today. Lonora is 5'3" 110 lbs. She has blue eyes and red hair. Anyone with any information about the girl is asked to call the sheriff's office immediately.

"She'll be terrified when we find her," Sheriff Charlie Barton said. "If someone she doesn't know finds her they should call for help before they approach her. That'll only make it worse." No sign of forced entry was observed in the family home.

Sophie heard an odd whirring noise inside her head. Lonny's Lonora was her birth mother? She had to be, they looked too much alike. She turned back toward the hospital and looked up at the windows on the second floor. What was it Lonny said about his daughter? *She was a pretty little girl. Like her mama. Like you.*

Lonny was her grandfather! But only a part of her jerked with the thrill of knowing it.

He knew? Why didn't he tell her? He'd dropped hints. *You remind me a bit of my baby girl 'cept she had my wife's blue eyes and she weren't near as tall as you. But she was a happy gal growin' up and that smile-a-yours is a real sweet reminder.* He did tell her . . . without really telling her. But why? Why didn't he want her to know?

Her heart hammered, but she couldn't tell if it was raging anger or an anxious excitement surging through her veins, making her want to hit something and hug Billy at the same time.

"Sophie?"

She shook her head—she didn't want to talk and she couldn't look at him just yet. She bent her head and brought the second page forward to read—a shorter story in smaller print.

MISSING CLEARFIELD GIRL FOUND

Sheriff Charlie Barton reported Friday evening that 16-year-old Lonora Elizabeth Campbell was found dazed and disoriented in the woods around Calvin B. Harvey Park and Arboretum after a 28-hour search by local citizens and the Clearfield County Police. The girl was rushed to Clearfield Memorial Hospital to be treated for an array of cuts and bruises and the hypothermia sustained during her overnight ordeal. She is reported to be in stable condition.

Lonora. Lost and then found as a girl. Lost and now found by her daughter years later—years too late. And now Sophie felt lost—her gaze rose to the windows above—and there was plenty more information to be found up there, she knew. But she wasn't sure she wanted to hear more—wasn't sure she knew what to do with what she had.

"Sophie?"

"I don't know, Billy." She took a step back, opened her car door, and threw her hobo bag inside. "I don't know what it means or what I should think. I need to think about it. I don't want to say or do anything I'll regret—"

"Sophie!"

She turned her head to address the demand in his voice, unprepared to see the helplessness and horror in his face as a large man, two to three inches taller and a hundred pounds heavier, held a big black gun to Billy's head from behind. She froze. It felt like the slightest movement, a bare breeze, would cause the whole world to explode.

Chapter Twelve

THE MAN WITH THE GUN HAD A CREW CUT–TYPE HAIRCUT THAT SHOWED him to be mostly gray haired; he had a pink pudgy sort of face and he wore thick horn-rimmed glasses. He squinted at Sophie—angry, bitter, and unforgiving. He delivered a scoffing chuckle.

"I thought that damned Maury finally pickled his brain about you coming back here to kill us."

"Me?"

"Course he couldn't go to the cops after ya got to Cliff, but he didn't have to make a beeline over to my place so you could follow him straight to me."

"Got to Cliff?"

He wrapped a wad of Billy's blond hair around his hand and dug his fingers into the back of his head to keep it tight, pulling him sideways and tipping his head at her to pass in front of them. She did, her gaze unwavering. The man pushed his hostage a step closer to her, she backed away and he took another step forward. They were heading for the back of her vehicle.

"All you had to do was wait out the cops." She couldn't tell if Billy had done something or not, but the man gave his hair a sharp jerk that made him grimace. Her clammy hands trembled. "They'd pull out eventually, you knew that, and you'd have an open shot at me. Figured I'd strike first—you weren't expectin' that, now were ya?"

"Me? Look, I think you've made a mistake. I don't even know who you—" She made eye contact with Billy as her voice trailed off.

The man peaked an eyebrow. "Finish."

"I—I was going to say I didn't know who you are but . . . now I'm guessing you're Frank Lanyard." If she was the hub of the wheel, then he was the missing spoke.

He pursed his lips and motioned with his head for her to turn the other corner of her car to the rider's side. "You're smarter than her anyway."

"Who?" Keep him talking, distracted—wasn't that one of the safety tips? "Her who? Did you . . . Is Maury Weims dead?"

"That ain't gonna work on me, sweetheart. Can't blame me for this here, what's going on. This time it's your fault."

"My fault?"

"Stop repeatin' what I say and actin' like it's a question, pretendin' you don't know what I'm talkin' about."

"I'm not pretending. What *are* you saying?"

"Open the door." She followed his line of vision to the rider's side front door. It did occur to her to pull it open in such a way as to position it between her and him, to take another shot at running for help . . . but he had Billy. "Now the other."

Opening the back door put her in a makeshift cage of sorts, trapping her between the front door, the car next to them, and the off chance of freedom if she chose scrambling over the seats to the opposite door without getting shot. She stuffed the photocopies under the seat to free her hands.

Frustrated, she went back to distraction. "Please. Tell me what this is about?"

"You." And with that he took a vicious strike at Billy's head with the heavy dark metal in his hand.

"No!" She cried out as the life in Billy's eyes left and his thin body crumpled. "Oh God! Billy!" A flash flood of blood rivered down over his eye and cheek, angling toward his mouth as his head lolled to the left. "Billy. You killed him?" Instinctively she pushed against the door, tipping him and Billy off balance—but only for a second or two. "He's bleeding. Are you crazy?"

"Shut up! And you better think twice about giving me any more grief, girl. I'm up to my neck in this mess, so it makes no difference to me. I can drop him here and put a bullet in his head—up to you," he said as he began to first tip Billy onto the backseat and then shove him in completely. "See? Still breathin'." His smirk was spine chilling. "This here's a McCarren?"

Sophie nodded.

"You best be careful. His mama'll skin you alive if you get him killed, missy."

Elizabeth was waiting.

"Hop in. You're driving."

"Where to? Where are we going?"

Hope gasped its second breath. If they drove by the Crabapple Café there was a chance, a slim one, that Elizabeth might be watching out the window for her. If not, Drew will show up at the café to rescue her from his mother . . . and call to check on her.

Shoot.

With the gun now pointed in her general direction from outside the back door, she did all she could to make it look more awkward than it was to climb over the center console to the driver's seat. She glanced back at Billy, lying on his side, bleeding on her soft gray pleather interior, breathing. Slipping her hand inside her roomy handbag, she said, "Please. Billy needs help. Can't we leave him on the hood of that car so someone will find him?"

"And wake him up so he can set the cops on us? I don't think so. What's that you're doin'?"

"Nothing. Moving my purse out of the way." She slid into the driver's seat.

"Hell." He slammed the back door closed against the bottoms of Billy's feet, bending his legs at the knee. "Give me that damn thing." Grabbing her bag, he flung it at the back window of the Jeep, spilling the contents in a short, noisy clatter.

Turning to look back at Billy again, while Frank Lanyard climbed in next to her, was the perfect opportunity to stuff her cell phone under her left hip, which would, hopefully, muffle any rings, dings, or pings that might occur if Drew tried to contact her. It might take a while for him to get nervous when there's no response, but once he was, the cops were going to need her phone on and in one piece to track the GPS inside.

"What are you waiting for?"

"Directions," she snapped.

Instantly, fear stomped down hard on the anger creeping in around the edges of her emotions. One clever move with a cell phone did not an escape artist make. She and Billy had a long way to go . . . if they were lucky . . . and keeping a civil tongue in her head would, no doubt, be helpful.

"Which way out of the lot," she asked, trying on submissive and finding it itchy. "Right or left?"

"Right."

"Fine." Glancing back at Billy as she twisted the key in the ignition, she couldn't see his face, only the passive in and out of his torso as he slept. The fist in her stomach tightened and turned. It was in her to cry, but there were no tears as yet. She swallowed, but the back of her throat felt stuffed with cotton as she pulled out of the parking lot.

In the few blocks it took to get to Main Street, she went through every scenario she could come up with: speeding, a deliberate accident, jamming on the brakes and leaping from the car while in motion—maybe a daring combination of moves. But every idea produced a red flag: Billy . . . or telegraphing the move by releasing the seat belt . . . or accidental discharge of the gun and the consequences for failure. It wasn't looking good.

They were parked at the stop sign, next to Lonny's place, when he jerked the gun, now aimed in the neighborhood of her liver, indicating a left turn at Main. Looking both ways to make a safe crossing, she noticed her passenger staring at the Service and Tire—hard—a spastic tic in his cheek going wild. Was he angry he hadn't managed to kill Lonny, too?

Her grandfather. The idea of it felt like a size fourteen dress on a size two body—too big and shapeless and yet— *He tried to kill my grandfather, too?*

With even more determination, she solidified her plan to give Elizabeth her one best split second of seeing them as they drove by the Crabapple Café. Seeing, realizing something was wrong when she doesn't stop, and calling for help. It was all she had.

Odd, the things you think about while you're driving toward death.

For instance, it made sense to Sophie that with a lethal weapon so nearby, one's awareness of something as small as a leg itch would be suspended for more important considerations . . . like the way a gunshot face would ruin her open casket funeral.

Problem was: she needed an itch at the moment.

Another thing? Frank Lanyard and his gun weren't as intimidating in a moving vehicle; he wasn't going to shoot her while she was driving, right?

So Sophie dropped her left hand to rub her knee and then put it back on the wheel as she started counting . . . Eddy's Eatery, Granny's Attic. She scratched below her knee, then put her hands back to ten and two on the wheel. They passed Lemming's Plumbing and poor Maury Weims's drugstore— she tilted a bit to scratch lower on her leg—Betty's Boutique and Clearfield Credit Union . . . and she shivered watching the big window front of the Crabapple Café coming up. She asked her mother for help.

Amazed at her perfect timing, she bent low, close to the steering wheel, reached for her ankle, turned her face toward the café and pretended to lean unintentionally on the horn.

Her smug delight lasted barely two seconds before Lanyard's gun crashed down on her right shoulder—she went blind from the pain, and the screaming cry she produced was unlike anything she'd heard before.

She ground her teeth to the shatter point against the intense throbbing, then glared at her captor.

"It was an accident!"

"Like hell." He kept looking back to see if she'd disturbed the evening quiet of Clearfield.

One glance in her rearview mirror and doom settled inside her. She was going to die.

And was this the reason her real mother had suffered so, clung to life with all her might and oh-so reluctantly let go? To be on the other side to greet her daughter a year later, like

Lonny said? She was torn between intense relief and the utter unfairness of it . . . and guilt. If Lonny was right, her mother— her *real* mother—paid the ultimate price in the most excruciating way for simply taking her into her heart as an infant and loving her. Her heart felt shredded. The pain blotted out the discomfort in her shoulder.

They were far enough outside town that there were fewer and fewer places to pull over or turn around, so when she spotted a deserted exit for a gravel county road, she took it.

"What the hell do you think you're doing?" Frank bellowed in tense disbelief. "Keep to the road. Drive on."

"No." *Flint. Flint!* "I'm— We're going to lay Billy right here, out of the way but close enough to the road to be seen."

"The hell we are."

"He needs help and this isn't a discussion." She may have been out of her mind at the moment, but it wasn't *all* gone. She went silent when the big black gun pressed against her forehead.

"Maybe you are as crazy as she was."

"Who?" she whispered, then realized she didn't care anymore. It was about survival now and she had a better chance of it . . . they both had a better chance if Billy wasn't with them. "Billy hasn't done anything. Your beef is clearly with me. I'll go with you. Quietly. If we leave Billy here."

He shook his head, bent his elbow to tip the gun toward the roof. "Let me explain this to ya. You don't get a say. You and old Cubeck made your choices. You two started all this. Now it's my turn. And I choose for you to disappear so you can't do to me what you did to my old buddies. This is self-defense."

"Disappear or die?" His shrug was indifferent. She sneered. "Self-defense. If this was self-defense, you wouldn't be keeping Billy hostage. And you'd be out in the open, defending yourself for everyone to see. Not scurrying off to . . . wherever we're scurrying off to, like the filthy rodent you are." She'd started out calm but ended up a little insane again. "I never even met Arthur Cubeck. And I didn't do anything to your buddies!"

He puckered his lips up and tipped his head thoughtfully. With no change in his expression he simply lowered the barrel of his gun over the back of her seat at Billy. Hope waned. Stupid. She'd tipped her hand and he saw that she cared about Billy's life.

Not that she cared *more* about Billy's life than her own—she was no martyr—but she cared enough that he was leverage.

"Here's what I'll do for ya, honey." His voice was thick with disdain. He drew a large, crumpled white handkerchief from his back pocket—clean or not, that remained a question mark. "You tie his hands up with this. Take your shirt off and cover his face with it. He don't see me, he lives."

"If he doesn't bleed to death, you mean." Her mind flashed back to the three of them in the hospital parking lot. Billy couldn't have seen him with that grip in his hair . . . but he'd tried and Lanyard jerked at the roots.

She looked through his glasses into callous brown eyes and suspected he was lying about letting Billy live, but she couldn't take the chance. It might be the only chance Billy had.

Plus, it was *time*. Time for Drew to discover her gone. Time to think of another plan for escape. Time for the cops to find them. More time to live. Maybe even time for Lanyard to come to his senses, change his mind—but she wasn't feeling that lucky.

"Fine." She retrieved her phone while snatching the rag from his hand, refusing to think about what it had been used for, and jerked on the door handle to get out. Once again she felt the urge to run as she tucked the cell into the back pocket of her denim skirt—but she still couldn't picture herself being faster than a speeding bullet.

Opening the back door, it was Billy's pallor that jumped out at her first, sending a cold chill to the tips of her fingers and toes. She shivered, muttered something incoherent as she reached out to touch his cheek. Warm. There was a strong pulse in his neck and an easy rhythm to his breathing. A slight thaw came as she noted the dry blood cracking on his face and the dark clot congealing in his matted hair.

She heard a car coming up the road and froze. Was Lanyard crazy enough to kill her with a witness? Her gaze shifted toward him. He peaked his brows as if to ask her the same question and made a point of stabbing Billy's ribs with the barrel of his gun. Something evil and dark seeped like black extra-heavy crude oil into the crevices between her fear and her anger; and though she'd had no experience with it until this moment, she recognized it immediately: pure hatred.

Her shoulders drooped in defeat as she listened to her freedom pass behind her. She glanced over her left shoulder—because she had to—but the driver gave no indication of having noticed them. She refused to peek at her captor; simply couldn't give him the satisfaction and rejected the idea of giving up.

Her one best chance was still to come. She'd wait and watch for it.

Both of Billy's arms were in front; hands near his knees and too far from where she stood. A glance at Lanyard caught his gaze on her chest—she wished him dead a thousand times over—unbuttoned the front of her soft cotton top and shucked it off . . . so, so, *so* grateful she'd gone with a pretty, feminine aqua-colored cami instead of an overtly sexy bra for Drew's seduction.

Was he missing her yet?

She took great care in lifting Billy's head off the backseat—trying to ignore the way the blood pulled at his skin before giving it up. She inserted half her shirt below his head and just as carefully put it to rest again before drawing the other half of the shirt down over his eyes, leaving his nose and mouth uncovered so he could get all the air he needed.

Job half done, she looked up for a sign to move on to his hands. Once her gaze caught Lanyard's, he deliberately raked his gawking eyes slowly down her satin-covered breasts, took his time, let them creep back up to hers. It was a sexless stare designed to humiliate her. And it did.

"Tie it up. Tight."

"What?"

"The shirt. Unless you want him to wiggle out of it and die."

She didn't. Pulling the excess material to the top side of his head, opposite his wound, she calculated that it might not be such a bad thing to do. It would keep him as safe as possible *and* put pressure on his wound. She put herself into the task and tied a sturdy knot over his parietal bone—on the order of the rosette wraps she'd fashioned for her mom after she lost her hair to chemotherapy. From another world she watched as she gave it a satisfied pat before backing off to close the door.

Another car, a pickup truck, came around the long curve in the road. She sensed Lanyard watching her but was overwhelmed by the urge to stand and observe the driver as he passed. His eyes never left the road as he passed.

Were they invisible?

Walking around the back of the car to get to the other door and gain access to Billy's hands, it was important to let Frank Lanyard know she wasn't afraid of him, that she was keeping her end of the deal and there would be a penalty to pay if he didn't keep his—she had no idea what yet, but it was worth a good bluff.

In fact, everything she did was becoming very *worth it.*

With her most insolent expression in place, she looked fiercely through the back window, prepared to face the nose of his gun without a flinch. He wasn't even looking at her. Instead, he had his arm between the seats reaching for Billy. She rushed to wrench open the door.

"Do not touch him!" Impulse made her swipe at his hand as he pulled it back after checking the fit of Billy's blindfold. "Keep your hands off him. You said if he couldn't see you, he'd be safe. You've hurt him enough already. Don't touch him."

"Who has the gun here, honey?" He simpered at her and tried once more to debase her with his eyes.

This time it didn't work. The top drawer of her bureau at home was bulging with skimpy lingerie that made this particular cami seem more like a parka. Her glare was defiant. He gave it a mild test, but surprised her by turning away in what looked inexplicably like regret. He rolled back in the seat to face front. "She didn't know when to give up, either."

She took her time tying Billy's hands together—and assuming Frank Lanyard would test for slack, and hoping Billy would be in less danger if he couldn't get loose, she trussed them good and tight. Touching his warm hands, the steady pulse in his wrist, and watching his easy breathing encouraged her to be optimistic. Resentful, too, of the fifty-fifty chance he had of seeing tomorrow.

"You son of a bitch!" The belated realization was like a kick in the gut. "He heard me say your name! You knew. You had no intention of—"

"Keep it up." He sighed, seeming almost resigned to her being a pain in his ass. "It doesn't really matter to me when I kill him, you know."

Looking up at the top half of Lanyard's head above the seat back, she got the impression his attention was mostly elsewhere. A quick scan of the back of the car that she kept vacuumed and clutter-free turned up no weapons—*shocker!*—and backing silently away from the door, she found nothing on the ground that was solid enough to do damage but stones no larger than peach pits.

After another expectant and disappointing examination of the road behind them, there was nothing else she could think of to do but get back in the driver's seat. . . .

She settled in. The leather seat having lost all warmth from the heat of the day was cold against her bare back—a reminder to stay cool and wait for her chance. She reached for her seat belt like it still mattered, like she'd be a cautious, law abiding, well-behaved kindergarten teacher until her last breath was drawn.

And that would be okay, she decided out of the blue with a burst of pride. There were so many worse things to be. She looked at Frank Lanyard.

"So what is it you think Mr. Cubeck told me? Who's this 'her' you keep referring to?" she asked, turning the key to start the car again. Habit had her checking her mirrors—and the lights telegraphing the presence of yet another car coming at them got her thinking of a rescue again. She lit up her own headlights.

"What's that you're doin'?"

"Headlights. Sun's almost set. We'll draw more attention without them than with them on." But if she left the high beams on, she'd annoy everyone who went by—someone could be fostering a good case of road rage and chase them down. You never knew.

"Don't push me, girl. I mean it. I'm in no mood for tricks."

Satisfied with the way her headlights flashed back at them

from the rearview mirror in the car ahead, she pulled back onto the road behind it. She gunned the engine to keep up, but the other driver was already up to the speed limit and was well away from them in no time. She'd get the next one.

In the silence that followed, she took stock of their surroundings—a house here and there, sometimes two or three grouped together between patches of woods and a few open fields; mostly county roads but the occasional rack of mailboxes indicated homes farther along . . . one abandoned shop of some sort.

Where were all the speed traps when you needed a cop?

Frank Lanyard was a loud breather, especially in the silence, as she realized that he hadn't answered her question.

Apparently, the quiet was what she'd needed because that's when it happened. That's when she understood. That's when the puzzle pieces began to fall from out of nowhere and started snapping into place. Click. Click. Click. She frowned into the twilight, winced as an achy chill pushed up each side of her neck, through her jaw, into the temples on both sides of her head. It pulsed. Boom. Boom. Boom.

"Oh, no. It's Lonora, isn't it?" She didn't know why she put the question mark on that—she already knew the answer. "She's what this is about. She is, isn't she?"

Lonny's words gnawed at her mind. . . . *The first time I saw my Cora. She was a sailor's delight with eyes the color of a noon sky in midsummer.*

Right. That was it. Only she wasn't a sailor's delight because he was fresh out of the navy, it was that old adage. How'd it go? "Red sky in the morning, sailor's warning. Red sky at night, sailor's delight." Red. Like her hair. Like Lonora's hair. Like Cora's hair. That's how Maury Weims first recognized her at the drugstore, and he told Cliff Palmeroy. Though Lonora's face had finer, more delicate contours, their similarities were bold enough to set any phasmophobe on their ear—no wonder Maury Weims thought she was a ghost. Her hair, her smile, maybe a dozen other tiny things is why she'd seemed so familiar to Jesse. The people at Arthur Cubeck's funeral hadn't been peeking and whispering because she was a stranger in a strange circumstance in their town—she was a vaguely familiar-looking stranger in a strange circumstance in their town.

"I'm right, aren't I? This is all about her."

"Pay attention there," he growled as the car swerved on the road. "Watch what you're doin' or you'll end up in the back with him." He jerked his head toward Billy and then let it loll the other way. "Ha. That idiot Maury said you and the young doc had something going on, not this one here." He paused. "Course you could be boinkin' 'em both."

Sophie knew five-year-olds who had more talent for the art of distraction in their little fingers than Frank Lanyard had in his whole hulking body.

"I look like her, don't I? I saw a picture." She came up short. Her thoughts became a slideshow: *I'll be twenty-seven in August . . . November 12, 1985 . . . disappearance of Lonora Elizabeth Campbell is being termed "suspicious" by police. . .*

"You had something to do with it. The night she went missing . . . you knew where she was."

She didn't know when to give up, either . . . rushed to be treated. . .

"You hurt her. There were cuts and bruises. It was in the newspaper."

Tell me what this is about? Her throat closed. *You!*

"It is me. Oh God. It is me. You beat that little girl. Lonora. You raped her, didn't you? You did! You pig! Oh God. Oh God! . You're him—the father . . . my father . . . the sperm donor." Even she could hear her voice cracking with hysteria. "Aren't you?"

"How the hell should I know?" he shouted back.

What did that mean? He'd know if he had sex with her, right? There were ten more questions, bitter and sticky on her tongue, but before she could spit them out, he said, "Turn left up there. Beyond that sign."

"No!" Did she say that out loud? Yeah, she did. "No. Not until you tell me. I want to know." He lifted the gun off his lap. "Oh, sure. Shoot me! Go ahead. If you're my father I think I *want* to die."

"Settle down!" His loud voice set her back, in spite of her anger . . . and no minor amount of disgust. "Watch the road. And you damned well *will* turn up ahead there."

She slowed down, squealing her tires on the hard ninety-degree turn she made with equal amounts of fear and anger bubbling in her stomach. Her headlights hit the sign—it was decorative, announcing the entrance to the Calvin B. Harvey Park and Arboretum. She flew onto a dark, unlit tar-and-gravel road that almost immediately slanted uphill.

"Knock it off!" he bellowed in her right ear. She did—but only because she was scaring herself.

"Now," he said, calmer. "We'll talk . . . if you don't drive us off the damn road first. Seems you don't know as much as Maury thought you did. Christ, girl, who taught you how to drive?"

"My *real* dad, that's who. My real dad who loves me and will hunt you down like a dog for this. My real dad who'll—who'll . . . well, I don't think he'll kill you with his bare hands because he's kind and sweet and wonderful and my mom was a pacifist, but he'll make sure you're caught and suffer forever in prison." Her chin quivered and tears of regret gathered in

her eyes for calling him *the worst father in the whole world*
when he nixed that stupid Canadian ski trip with Mike Ful-
lerton in seventh grade. "My real dad held me when I was sick
and gave me a standing ovation for my performance as the entire grain group in the food pyramid on Health Day, and told
me I was too good for Paul Lyton anyway, and let me sleep on
his shoulder while he watched my mom die . . . my *real* mom.
That's what dads do. *Real* dads. They don't—"

"Shut the hell up!" he bellowed, reaching for the dash as the
car veered and came back. "I know what dads do."

Her gasp was loud and ended in an *ack*. "You have children?
Other children?" She blinked hard to clear away her unshed
tears. "And you'd do this to me? I have brothers and sisters?
Which? Brothers or sisters? Both? I bet they don't know what
you're doing right now, do they? I bet they'll be real proud
when they find out. And they will find out. My *real* dad will
make sure of that. And they'll believe him because people like
you can't hide what they truly are, and they'll *hate* you. Hate
you! They won't visit you in prison, they—"

"Christ! Will you shut the fuck up before I stick my boot
in your mouth?" He shifted his weight in the seat, agitated,
and glared at her in disbelief . . . and maybe a little awe. When
the sound of their voices dissipated, he snapped, "You are not
my kid."

"I'm not?" Tears pooled in her eyes once again—a couple
slipped out unnoticed.

"No."

After a whole minute she sniffed and asked, "But this is
still about Lonora, right?" One slow, reluctant nod. "And you
know who hurt her, right? And about me." A long, deep in-
hale of air and a shrug. "That's a maybe. Right?"

"Keep to the right up here at the Y."

Sophie was so confused now, her brain felt like rubber; the

synapses kept firing but they weren't penetrating, weren't being picked up.

There was another ornamental sign at the Y—left for the picnic grounds; they were heading for the arboretum.

"This is where you took her. This is where it happened." Her laugh was pure derision. "The Arboretum? Really? You're taking me back to the scene of the crime? You're a walking cliché, Frank. Plus, I feel I should tell you that a different wooded area, a bit less cultivated, would make it harder to find my remains."

Who *was* she? Truly, she was beginning to think she'd passed to another realm altogether. Sticking up for a defenseless, unconscious Billy was one thing. This was more. More than *flint*, more than rabid teacher. Snapping, prodding, baiting, and screaming at a man intent on killing her was . . . well, crazy. Was that it? Was it more than fear and confusion? Had she lost her mind?

She glanced at Frank Lanyard. It was dusk; the dash lights cast shadows over his face, flashed across the surface of his glasses. He appeared distracted—thinking—or perhaps *rethinking.*

Gradually she began to speculate on the possibility that she wasn't recklessly pushing her luck after all—but that her limits had been extended. He was allowing her to be mouthy and rude because . . . why? He owed her that much? Because it wouldn't last much longer as she was about to die? Or maybe . . . was he beginning to see that he'd made a huge mistake, that she hadn't killed his friends?

No. He already *knew* she didn't kill them because *he* killed them. Obviously. When she showed up looking so like Lonora, he panicked; and thinking his friends would rat him out, he killed them. And now, she was the last bit of evidence to be eliminated.

He seemed pretty certain that he hadn't fathered her—that meant one of the others did. Not that that mattered now. He was there. He knew. He was guilty. And she was going to die.

Her mind raced as she slowed to take the first bend in the zigzaggy road to the top of the hill, and didn't speed up again. *I like my steaks medium rare—pink not bloody. I want four babies—maybe eight. I've never been to an aquarium. I prefer blue ink to black and socks to slippers when my toes are cold.* Those things needed to be in Drew's book. She needed more time . . . a lot of it. A lifetime worth.

Using a soft, tentative tone that she hoped would sound like his inner voice, she said, "I've jumped to the wrong conclusion about people before. We all have, right?" She listened to herself swallow and forged on—feeling her way, not at all sure where she was going. "Usually, because we don't have all the information about them. Or we have wrong information. Somehow that seems worse, doesn't it? Maybe because it infers some sort of lie, I guess, but it doesn't have to be . . . a lie, I mean. Just misunderstanding a word or an action can create wrong information." A quick glance showed him listening but nothing more. "I think we've all rushed into situations without thinking them through, too. Impulsively. Emotionally. Especially if we've been under a lot of stress." She kept stopping and checking him, anticipating an explosion. "Boy, you sure would qualify for that, wouldn't you?" He looked at her. "I get it. I do. I remember high school. The peer pressure and all. Maybe . . . maybe you weren't there; maybe one of your pals did it and bragged. The stress of keeping a secret like that all these years must have been unbearable for you." In her ears, her voice wasn't sympathetic—she adjusted. "I get it. I show up, looking like her, you get anxious. You're afraid the truth will come out; afraid your friends will say something.

You snap under the pressure and start killing them. And I'm still a reminder so—"

"You did that! You killed them."

"I didn't. Why would I—how could I? I didn't even know about Lonora until tonight. But you knew, your friends knew. You killed them and now you're going to kill me."

"I didn't!"

She didn't believe him for a second. He was, after all, intent on killing her. "Then who did?"

"I don't know."

She heard doubt and fear in his tone.

"And they're not friends."

"Oh. I thought—"

"Not since high school."

"Right. You moved away. To Roanoke, which is what? . . . a couple of hours away and that would make it difficult to—"

"I moved to get away from them."

This was interesting. "Why?"

He shook his head. "I couldn't stand to look at 'em anymore."

"You fought?"

Another shake of his head as the road opened to a large gravel parking lot. "Pull up over there. There by those fire bushes."

Did he mean the *green* fire bushes that wouldn't turn flame red until fall? Was he so familiar with the park that he could tell one bush from another . . . in the dark?

Oh. Right. November 12, 1985, she recalled. He was remembering the season. Is that where it happened? There by the fire bushes. So close to the parking lot? Well, that was dumb. Why was the scene so important to him if it was out in the open?

Two seconds later she got her answer. A third, much smaller

sign came into view off to their left, marking a nature trail; and on their right was a loose gravel utility road blocked off with an orange chain and a metal flag instructing them not to enter—both were considerably more conducive to murder.

Her heart jerked and shifted gears; she felt dizzy. This was so wrong. She wasn't ready to die. She had too many things left to do—get married, have babies, ride in a hot air balloon, scuba dive in Aruba, vacation in an ice hotel . . . Aunt Leslie promised to teach her how to knit! Clearfield and a senior trip to Montreal with her French class were the farthest she'd ever been from home and she wanted to see all the castles in Germany, climb Machu Picchu and . . . be there for her dad, because he shouldn't have to lose her, too.

Tears came and spilled down her cheeks but she wasn't crying, not really—she couldn't afford to yet. She needed to stay angry, stay strong, stay *flint*.

"So, um, if Cliff Palmeroy and Maury Weims weren't your friends anymore, why did Maury go to see you after Cliff was murdered?"

"Damn fool lost it, came over to my house half-cocked and hysterical saying you knew and were plannin' to kill us all." He stopped to nod at the steering wheel. "Back 'er up now so the light shines that way."

"At the path?" So he wouldn't have to kill her in the dark?

He nodded and continued on, "Now this whole damned thing is going to blow up in *my* face. The two of them together never did have the sense you could find in a bag of hair. Now cut 'er off and get out." He lifted the gun off his lap once more. "And don't try anything."

Or what? He'd kill her? Didn't seem like much of a threat until she remembered Billy in the backseat . . . and honestly, she didn't consider him for very long. She had her own life to save now and she suffered no regret. She'd done what she could for him.

Still and all, she had no plan aside from *RUN LIKE HELL*. She was about to use Billy to stall Frank for a moment by checking his condition, but changed her mind at the last moment. Lanyard may have forgotten about him for the moment; she couldn't see any real benefit to reminding him. Besides, the sooner she got out of the car, the sooner she could run— and Billy would slip even farther to the back of Frank's mind.

She used her left hand to verify that her cell was tucked deep in the back pocket of her denim skirt, and it wasn't until she reached for the keys in the ignition that she took in the fact that her car—with Billy in the backseat—was Frank Lanyard's only way back to town.

It was just one thing after another!—and all she wanted was to run.

Well, he wasn't taking her new car. Period.

Closing her right hand over the key, she turned the engine off and made it seem a reflex to cut the lights at the same time. When he barked at her to leave them on, she used the sound of his voice to remove the key and pass the remote and the two keys attached to it to her left hand, where she held them firm and noiseless against her palm while she turned the lights back on.

"Sorry," she said, quickly scanning over Frank's shoulder the wooded area on both sides of the path and the half-lit road they came up on. Her best option was to run away from the light, of course, but not down the utility road, she told herself. She'd head into the woods.

Her strategy was to lock the car doors on the run; and if he was close enough that he might catch her, drop the keys— somewhere she could find them again if she could get back . . . *when* she got back.

She moved to get out.

"Hold on."

"What?" she said, short and shocked, so deep into her get-away she'd all but forgotten him. "What. You didn't say to get out?"

"I changed my mind." He opened his door and backed out sideways while she peered through the pale light at the nose of his gun, hoping to see his hand shake with uncertainty—or just nerves for that matter—anything but the unwavering determination she saw in it now.

"Look, I know—"

He slammed the door and advanced around the front of the car to her side, his glasses glinting in the headlights. Was this it—her chance? Lock the doors? Were her windows bulletproof? Who thinks to ask *that* at a car dealership?

That was all she had time for before he yanked open the door, grabbed her arm, and tugged for her to come out. Tears were spontaneous and disregarded by them both. He was as settled on killing her as she was on living—but they shared their terror like a palpable thing. A burden neither of them wanted.

She took her time with the seat belt. Her voice cracked when she spoke. "Look, I know you don't want to do this. I feel it. And you know I don't deserve it. Maury Weims jumped to a wrong conclusion about me and you reacted. That's natural . . . excessive, for sure, but still something we've all done." The belt came loose and rolled back into place. "And . . . and you say you didn't kill anyone, so you haven't done anything too awful yet. Kidnapping and assault. That's all." Her cheap, flat sandals hit the ground. "And I won't press charges. I promise. I swear. It's just assault on Billy and . . . and I bet people beat him up all the time. He can be a real jerk sometimes, you know, and I doubt it's a secret."

She took one last look between the seats at Billy—just his knees and some of his hands in truth—and irrationally wished he'd wake up and hug her before she went any farther with Lanyard. The yearning for compassionate and comforting human contact was overwhelming, like a raging fever that made her bones ache and her body shiver.

Lanyard swung the door closed.

Chapter Thirteen

"PLEASE. DON'T DO THIS."

Sophie gave Frank another chance to back down while she let him lead her, passive at the moment but crouching like a lion inside, toward the nature trail. "I haven't done anything. You know that. You know I don't deserve this. We can both walk away right now. Never speak of it to anyone. Never think about it again. Please."

She squeezed the tears she couldn't stop from her eyes and glanced down at the hand he had wrapped, not so tightly, around her right upper arm—saw the gun in his other hand in the same visual frame, held with familiarity and aimed in the vicinity of her head and neck.

"We—We should be trying to figure out who really killed your ... those men. Maybe whoever it was set us up, you know? You're not the only person who thinks I'm guilty. So does the sheriff." He turned his head to look at her. Her nose was stuffy from crying—she took a deep, raggedy breath through her mouth. "Maybe they knew you'd be scared enough to try and kill me. We could make this backfire on them—figure out some way to expose them. Together." He continued to stare— she felt no acquiescence. "Please. You have children. I'm all my father has left. He—"

"I don't."

"What?"

"I don't have kids."

"But you said—"

"I said I knew about dads, not that I was one."

"Oh." Now where was she . . . ?

"Sister gave me mumps," he muttered, low and private. "In high school. They went down on me."

"Oh." From far, far away she heard her mother's voice reminding her to be grateful for the little things.

The ridges on the keys in her fist dug into the skin of her palm. Run. Lock. Toss. *Now? . . . Now? . . . Now?*

"My old lady's got a kid. A teenager. He hates me."

There didn't seem to be anything she was willing to say about that. She hated him, too.

The nature trail took a slight dip downhill—this was it. He was overweight and older; she could run up the path with no trouble at all.

"Do—Do you love him?"

"Maybe. For a while when he was a kid. Not so much now."

Really? He could turn his love on and off like a gas grill? "My dad has always loved me. My mom, too. She died of cancer last year. My dad needs me." He looked her way but said nothing. This time she didn't even hazard a guess as to his silence and/or what he was thinking. She didn't care. She'd only been biding her time.

Until now.

"Wait." She stopped abruptly. "What is that?"

"What?" He perked his ears and looked around.

"That! Listen." It was the oldest trick in the book—and as he listened intently the full head of steam she'd been building since she first turned around to face Billy and their captor at the hospital exploded.

She used the right side of her body to ram his like a wrecking ball. The terror, the anger, the desperation were enough to shock his grip open and stagger his bulk. He fell. She ran. She ran to save her life.

No more than six yards away, she already felt as if she'd sprinted a mile. She heard him curse; the free gravel on the path rattling as he thrashed around to get back on his feet.

The incline leveled off and the headlights from her car were brighter though not yet directly point on. Could she get to the car, get in, start it and be far enough away to be a blurry target after all? Better yet, was there time to get there, get in, get going and squish him like roadkill? The light would be in his eyes . . . he'd be out of breath . . . was there time? How far behind was he? Could she make it?

The only crunchy-gravel steps she could make out were her own. She strained to listen for the sound of his but still couldn't be sure of the distance between them. A quick glance over her shoulder revealed nothing. Her heart was skipping, fluttering, aching inside her chest. She was nauseous, couldn't gulp enough air—and running had little to do with it.

The bright beam of headlights hovered along the ridge of the next rise. She had to decide. The woods? The car? She thought she could hear his labored huffing, his heavy steps, but where *was* he? How much time did she have?

One more, slightly longer look over her shoulder—she saw the dark figure of the big bad boogeyman of her childhood, at a distance, and that gave her hope.

Until she took a misstep, veered off the path into the woods and the decision was taken out of her hands.

Tripping and stumbling through the underbrush, she wanted to kick herself for taking her attention off her goal for even that one moment, but simply didn't have the time— every instinct she had was screaming, *Forward!* There could be no turning back if he was behind her. The nature trail was no longer an option.

Her eyes adjusted quickly to solid black objects inside the shadows cast by the now dim headlights as she bobbed and weaved around trees. Holding her arm straight in the air she pressed lock on the remote, over and over, until the short honk echoed in the not too far away—locking the doors and giving her a general bearing of where she was. She ducked behind a tree, took a good hard look in the direction from where she'd come, tried to memorize it in a heartbeat, then pressed the keys to the base of the trunk of the tree. She *would* be back for them. She bolted away—farther from the path and downhill— but when she recalled his age and shape, she swerved to go up hill again. Blindly. Toward the park road? Or back to the parking lot and her car? She had no idea. But moving was her only defense; moving meant safety and it meant she was still alive.

It wasn't long before the frenzied chaos in her head broke momentarily to let in Frank Lanyard's thrashing and cursing behind her. She doubled her efforts—and the effort doubled her adrenaline; her lungs were screaming but all she could hear was the rush of her heart. Her muscles trembled. Slipping, falling, she felt her skin rip and tear, puncture and bruise, but there was no pain. Only *forward, forward, forward.*

She came across a rock, barely waist high but not one she could jump over. That's when she realized there was more light in the woods than her car would provide; looked up and saw a giant full moon that was both enemy and benefactor at the moment. With the briefest of inspections, she couldn't tell if she could go around the rock so she started to climb; topped it without incident—despite the slippage of her sandals—to find it was a short drop off to a steep tilt on the hillside. So steep, she was afraid to continue her ascent upright. She bent at the waist and scrambled like an animal with four legs, head down, feeling her way through brush and over rocks and roots and branches.

She was sure it wasn't a good thing to be so loud—the tornado sounds of air coming and going through her lungs; her heartbeats echoing throughout the park, and the noise of her clumsy climbing had to be making her easy to track. Could she risk a breather to catch her breath and quiet her heart enough to check on him? Salty saliva pooled in her mouth and her stomach roiled. She groaned and spit, refused to vomit, and used her arm to wipe spittle off her chin and the unstoppable tears from both cheeks.

Her vision cleared and promptly went black as she plowed, head down, into something solid.

Her scream petered to an injured cry that resonated from one end of the woods to the other as she slowly realized her skull was split wide open . . . but she was still alive. She could move, too, though flailing wasn't meeting the urgency triggering her muscles.

Her eyes were open, but not seeing. She focused, tipped her head to make out dark beyond darker as her head began to throb. Putting forth a shaky hand she touched the darker—rough, solid . . . a tree! She remembered and understood immediately.

Forward! Forward! Panic broke back into her mind even as she touched the point of impact on her head—sticky and stinging and rolling into her eyebrows—even as she started to scramble again.

"Whoa!" A heavy boot landed in the middle of her back. Her belly hit the ground and her legs sprawled.

"No. Please."

He said nothing—couldn't if his rapid wheezing was any indicator. They were both spent and breathless—though Sophie believed she could go farther given the chance. Not that she saw another one coming any time soon. The surprise hit-and-run wasn't likely to be unexpected a second time.

"Please. Don't do this. Don't kill me, please. I don't want to die." She cried full on, without pride or caution—there simply didn't seem to be a need for it anymore. She was caught.

Tears and blood and dirt mingled in her eyes and on her face while his breathing grew slow and quiet again and he was ready to move on.

"Come on," he said, his tone more resigned than harsh. He reached down and found her arm—the pressure under his boot pressing the remains of her air from her lungs. She knew a moment of suffocating alarm before he grabbed her upper arm and stepped back, pulling lightly, helping her to her feet. She kept slipping—the pitch of the hillside, the disorientation from the grunge in her eyes making it difficult to see. He was patient with her, steadied her, waited for her to right herself. "Don't do this again. Come on."

She could only assume he knew where he was going. She was aware only that it was downhill, away from her car; away from the parking lot and the road, away from safety.

She staggered. Often. He'd stop and stabilize her, not unkindly, but didn't loosen his grip.

Her breathing was more like raggedy sobs, and in a surreal moment it passed through her mind that she was admirably well hydrated to still have tears wetting her cheeks. And then, and again oddly, she was reminded that both major and minor facial wounds were notorious for bleeding profusely—and she had an instant 3D-HD flashback of the moment she learned that fact in the first first aid class she'd taken in Girl Scouts . . . at the fire station . . . before they ate the brownies that were made by one of the firemen . . . that weren't even burnt on the bottom like Mommy's. . . . Daddy.

"Please," she repeated, her voice a raspy whisper. "Don't. Don't do this." A despondent thought: "I . . . please . . . Do you have a cell? A cell phone? I only want to call my dad? That's all, only my dad. To say goodbye? Please? I need to tell him that I love him." She swiped at a fresh deluge of tears. Her own phone, snug in her back pocket, was a temptation, but also still her last best chance of being rescued. "I'm begging you. Please."

Without warning he shoved her to the ground and snapped at her. "Stop that!"

They were in a ditch or a gully; she sensed enclosure—but perhaps it was simply the anticipation of a grave. She sat up. The moonlight wasn't enough to make certain.

"I'm sorry." But she wasn't. At all. She smacked the palm of her hand over the blood spout on the top of her head to stem the flow of blood. "If you have to do this, if you're going to kill me, let me talk to him first."

"Shut up and let me think."

About the phone call? Lord God, he was human after all. "I won't mention your name or—or what's happening. I promise. I just need him to know I love him. It'll only take a second. I promise."

"Forget that. And stop talking! I need to think!"

About what? The mistake he was making? About letting her go? About how best to do it, to kill her? She held her breath. Disturbing any molecule in the humid night air might sway a lenient thought.

He paced in short distances. It was an eon before he stopped to look at her and another before she sensed he was staring straight through her. What *a weird man,* she thought, distracted by his behavior. What was he thinking? What was he seeing in his mind? Why was he so far away? And then . . . *how* far away was he? Was this a miracle, another chance at escape? Which direction gave her the best odds? Oh! And maybe the old-dirt-in-the-face trick would hold him an extra second or two to—

"It wasn't my idea, you know," he said, out of the blue, his tone petulant and rather juvenile—as if he'd gone back in time. "I told them not to do it. Jeremy and I both did. But once Cliff got something in his head, there was no stopping him. And that fool Maury did everything Cliff told him to do." He paused, focused more intently on wherever he was in his recollections. "I guess we all did." He shook his head in what looked like regret, the moonlight bouncing off his glasses. "I knew. The second he took his foot off the gas and I looked up and saw her walking up ahead, I knew what he was going to do. He talked about it all the time. Not right out, not in words exactly. But you could tell by the way he looked at her all the time. He'd say he thought she was pretty but you knew . . . in my gut I knew he meant something else. But I never thought he'd do it. I never thought . . ." He took a deep breath in and exhaled slowly. "That's it, isn't it? I never thought. Kids don't, though, do they? They don't think."

He didn't seem to want an answer—which was good because she was toying with the idea of making another break for it.

She lowered her hand from the stinging wound on her scalp, waited, let it drop to her lap when she realized the river was dammed up.

"Or they think too much," he went on. "Like in daydreams, so that sometimes the lines between what they think about and what they know they can't really do get blurred. You know what I mean?"

"No." Short responses to keep him talking—the more he blathered the less air he'd have to chase her with.

"Oh." Stymied, he paced some more. "I'm just saying that maybe I knew what Cliff was thinking because I thought about it, too. Once in a while. Not like Cliff. I always knew it was wrong; that I'd never do it. I knew even thinking about it was wrong . . . but, hell, I was just a kid." She caught the expectancy in the air but said nothing. Her reticence was making him anxious and jumpy. He heaved a sigh. "That's not a good enough excuse, is it? It's not. I know that. I've always known that. That's why Jeremy left, and why I left. I couldn't look into their eyes anymore. I kept seeing the way we were that night."

There was a long pause. He was asking and answering his own questions—a good sign. And yet while it was perfectly fine with her if he slipped over the edge of sanity, she did need to speculate on how it would affect his reflexes. Faster? Slower?

She hesitated, her mind jerked backward. *We . . . that night . . .*

"You know I don't think we thought she was even human. I don't. Not that night. It was like she was too stupid to understand what was happening or maybe we thought she was so simple-minded she wouldn't remember the next day so it didn't matter."

She tipped her head to one side. What the hell *was* he talking about? Her skin began to crawl in a whole new way.

He went on. "And you don't know about people like her, do you? Not really. You can't tell what they're thinking. They say and do whatever passes through what little brain they have and—"

He stopped short and it looked like he swayed a bit, like he was feeling dizzy. After a moment he looked her way again. "That's not the point, though. Is it? Her being simple-minded made it easy but nothing could ever make it right."

"Simple-minded," she murmured softly, remembering . . . *that while she has developmental disabilities and is known to have wandered off before. . .*

"Yeah. You know. Retarded," he said, frustrated, filled with shame and hopelessly without honor. He backed away immediately. "Not completely, though. I mean, she could read some, and write, and she could figure most things out if she had enough time. Slow, they'd say."

He nodded—seeming to think it a much better word.

"Yeah. But for the most part no one cared. She was what she was. We all knew about her. She was harmless. Sweet even . . . real friendly, happy all the time. Most of the time she just . . . *was*, you know? She'd roam around smiling, saying hi to everyone by their full name. Hi, Frank Lanyard. Hello, Maury Weims. Good morning, Leigh Kerski. Sometimes she'd sit herself down in the middle of a group of us and pretend she was part of the conversation. No one minded. Now and again she'd say something—either completely off the wall or so true and smart it made your jaw drop—then she'd get up and wander off." He gave an unconscious half-laugh. "There was no reason for her to be afraid of any of us. She was like a class pet or a school mascot; she was one of us. We all knew that loud noises scared her and she didn't like being touched. And for the fuss that followed either one of them two things, it just wasn't worth messing with her." But, he recalled, "Unless you were in need of a quick distraction.

A pat on her back or taking hold of her arm was better than throwing a live grenade into an angry mob."

Sophie sat in silence, feeling dead inside.

He was lost in recollection. "She liked to walk around. Her old mama kept a real close watch on her, but once in a while she'd give her the slip and off she'd go. You'd see her strolling down Main Street and soon enough here'd come her mother, huffing and puffing to get her. She wasn't well, though, the mother. She passed early on. After that you'd see her dad or the housekeeper or a babysitter trailing after her.

"If you came across her alone somewhere and asked her what she was doing, she'd say she was *traveling*. And as far as I know, her destinations were always some wacky place she'd get into her head like DisneyWorld USA or she was going to Paris for springtime or to Boston to see what happened to the tea or the moon or . . . or some street where a character from a book lived." He raised his hands in amused wonderment—the gun a loose appendage. "See, she knew stuff but the pieces didn't always fit tight, you know? She was a couple years younger than us, but I heard that one of her teachers used to have her draw some of these places she traveled to . . . I heard she drew pretty good."

It felt like he was awaiting her approval for divulging so much information to her. She wished him in hell.

He cleared his throat. "Looking back, it's almost like it was meant to happen." He flustered quickly. "Not meant to happen—we never meant for it to happen, but like a setup, a trap we fell into." He paused again. "Well, no. That makes it sound like we had no choice. We had lots of choices. . . ."

Choices. *Everybody makes choices—some good, some bad. Some so easy you don't even know you're making 'em; some so hard they rip your heart to pieces. Good people make bad choices. Evil people make choices that hurt innocent people.*

Innocent people make choices that put them in harm's way. It's always the choices we make that whittle the life we live, Lonny had said.

"I remember hearing the gravel crunching under the tires as he pulled off the road behind her," Frank was saying. "The tension was already so strong it felt like a fifth person inside the car. We all knew something bad was going to happen—I did, at any rate. I didn't know what, I swear. But I knew it was going to be wrong because of . . . because of how she was, you know?

"When he told her it was getting too dark to be walking along on the highway alone, I thought maybe I was wrong, maybe I was all wrong. He wasn't going to play any tricks on her or tease her or make her cry. She told him she had eyes like a cat and could see in the dark just fine and there was something so . . . I don't know . . . evil, I guess . . . in his voice when he said, '*Is that so?*'

"It wasn't until he asked her where she was traveling to, and she said she was walking to the very top of the mountains to see the snow, that me and Jeremy looked at each other. He knew, too. And when Cliff said he'd seen the snow and offered to give her a ride up the mountain, Jeremy told him to stop, told him to leave her alone. Cliff laughed and called him a candy-ass. Then he got out and opened the back door for her to get in. She did resist, at first, but only because she didn't want any of us to sit too close to her. Cliff told us to move, to give her plenty of room. We should have gotten out, let her have the whole backseat." He stopped.

"No. We should have thrown her over our shoulders and run like hell in the other direction. That's what we should have done, that's what I wish we'd done." He pictured the alternate scenario in his mind. "But we didn't. We knew how it would be if we didn't go along. We knew we couldn't leave him and we knew we couldn't leave her with him. Trapped. We were trapped.

"We moved way over and she smiled and got in. 'Hi, Jeremy Bates. Hi, Frank Lanyard,' she said." He used his left hand to wipe her words off his lips. "Cliff got back in and pulled back onto the road and she sat in the backseat yakking about mountains and how the higher they got in the sky, the less air and the more snow they had and how some mountain climbers had to use air tanks like the one someone at her church used, and she went on and—"

He stopped abruptly, grew thoughtful and paced a few steps back and forth before speaking again.

"You know, I don't think I ever heard her talk like that before. Do you think . . . ? Do you think she knew what was coming? Maybe she could sense it, like feel trouble coming. Think she was talking like crazy to keep herself calm or something?"

She felt no compulsion to answer him. Even *she* knew what was coming and her upper lip was already curled with repulsion and disgust.

Had she the wherewithal to examine the furor powering through her body at the moment, she probably wouldn't have been surprised to note the shocking lack of fear in her system. He was looking smaller and weaker with every word he spoke. Clearly, the girl was autistic to some degree. Clearly, she was a trusting innocent. Clearly, he'd known she was in danger and he'd done nothing to help her.

She was all fury and anger and rage as she leaned slowly to her left and bent her legs up under her right hip. She wasn't going to die tonight, not without a good fight and not without tearing part of his face off first.

"I thought, when Cliff turned into the park here, that he was planning to set her down somewhere and let her stumble through the park all night. You know, because of the cat-vision thing? That wouldn't have been the worst thing we ever did to someone and I could always come back and get her later . . . or Jeremy could. Hell, it might even be good for her—teach her to stay home at night, not to get into cars, to run screaming from people like Cliff . . . like us." He shook his head. "She had to have known what we were like back then. She wasn't that dumb. She saw. She heard. She could have figured it out."

"You pig."

He looked her way through the faint moonlight but said nothing—acknowledging that there was nothing *to* say. And while she obviously agreed, she was sorry she'd spoken. He was confessing his sins, distracted from the here and now— the time zone in which her left hand clutched as much thick, rich forest dirt as she could gather while she used her right to search for something big enough and hard enough to split his skull wide open and turn the contents therein to a slimy mush before she spit on them. Conversing in *Supergrossout* with five- and six-year-old boys was paying off in a most satisfying manner.

"No. You're right. What she was thinking didn't matter. Not to us. We were like animals—all of us. Always looking for someone pathetic to hassle. And as long as I'm telling it all, for you I'll admit I enjoyed it as much as anyone. I did. I loved that look on their faces when they first noticed us noticing them." A loud bark of a long lost laugh. "Pure, raw fear."

"When they first noticed *us,* huh? I bet that when you were alone, when you weren't with all your pals, people looked straight through you."

He looked away, wiping at something on his face.

"And Lonora? How did she look at you?"

She couldn't seem to stop engaging him. And she needed to move to expand her search area. She bit the tip of her tongue to remind herself of the danger and remained still, waiting for him to speak again.

It took a while.

"She was confused, I guess." He spoke so softly she almost missed it, straining to hear the rest. "Yeah. Confused. At first. No." He shook his head. "The whole time. She didn't understand. The whole time. She just didn't get it." He looked at Sophie, but he wasn't with her anymore. "We stopped in the lot up there. I remember thinking that she was getting off easy. Setting her loose to wander in the dark for a while wasn't so bad. If she were some kid, one of our regulars, we'd have taken all his clothes, too. So, I laughed with everyone else when Cliff opened her door and waved her out like she was royal or something.

"She stood there frowning for a second, then explained to him—like *he* was the idiot—that he'd taken the wrong road, that this wasn't where the mountains were. Sure it is, he said. He pointed into the darkness. Over there, he said. She looked but you could tell she still thought he was in the wrong about it. That's . . . that's when it all turned to shit. So fast. Like a nightmare you couldn't control, that you couldn't wake up from. Cliff touched her neck to try and turn her head in the right direction. She screamed and her whole body wiggled like an eel trying to get away from him. I don't think he'd meant to hurt her. I don't think he did—he barely touched her and she went nuts. And that scream of hers—seemed like it echoed for miles. Scared the shit out of all of us. Cliff just automatically slapped a hand over her mouth to shut her up . . . but he was touching her again and she went wild trying to get away from him. He tried holding her for a couple minutes but finally let her go. Pushed her away from him. Put his hands in the air like a promise not to touch her again. Told her he was sorry. She'd be okay.

"She—She stopped screaming but she was shook up; her hands were shaking and she had this crazy look in her eyes. We'd all seen it before. You know, from setting her off by accident."

Sophie stopped midbreath and went still except for the tips of her fingers as they pried loose a rock from the dry earthen floor that fit perfectly into the palm of her hand. A good manageable size; she tested the weight of it—it would have to do. She finished exhaling and took another breath.

"When Cliff didn't get back in the car, Maury got out. The two of them . . . they weren't like Jeremy and me. They weren't. They fed off each other, like they needed one another to even breathe. I'd say they were worse than us, but even as young as I was, I knew watching was as bad as doing. Watching was my part in the game, see? Like sports: half the fun of playing is having people watch you, root for you."

Lanyard stopped to review the analogy. He gave it a nod, walked a few paces and stopped in a beam of moonlight.

"And maybe you're right. Maybe I did need them so people wouldn't look straight through me like I wasn't there. But they made me feel like I could be somebody. They made me feel alive, like I mattered. Even fear and hate were better than people feeling nothing for me. It wasn't fair, you know. I was as good as anyone else, but they couldn't see me. No matter how I tried, they couldn't see me until Cliff and Maury and Jeremy came along. *They* saw me. I was their friend."

She got the impression that he expected her to commiserate or show him some compassion, but instead he swiftly realized he was drowning in the contempt that was rolling off her in ever growing waves.

"Even *she* got more attention than me!" he shouted.

She had nothing to lose. She met him head on. "She probably deserved more!"

"She wasn't normal!"

"And you are?"

He started toward her in a charge. She clutched her rock, grabbed more dirt. She was only vaguely aware of the instinctive, feral changes occurring in her muscles as they coiled and drew strength from no place she'd been before. He stopped unexpectedly. Her war cry died in her throat. He huffed and puffed and stood staring at her. She stared back.

"Stop screwing with me." He shook the gun at her like an index finger. "I don't have to do this. I could be done with this and halfway home by now. I don't have to tell you anything."

She laughed without amusement. "Yes, you do. You've been dying to tell someone for years. All this time it's been your ugly, foul little secret that's chewed holes in everything in your life. You think telling me that you raped Lonora that night will make it all better and—"

"I didn't. I didn't rape her, I swear."

"Somebody did!" She held her arms out as proof.

She wheezed, sucking in air. In a queer, sort of fractured moment she realized she wasn't standing on the outside looking in or hearing a story of horror from long ago. It was not two different, separate and completely unrelated events that linked her with Lonora, though her mind had clearly buffered it for her that way. Until that moment, until she said it out loud.

It was a blow that shattered her heart to possess at last the fact that she wasn't the product of an innocent puppy love gone askew or a passionate but illicit love affair—love of any kind as she'd always imagined. She was the byproduct of Lonora's torture and anguish, of senseless cruelty and violence.

The putrefaction of her childlike hopes and dreams oozed around inside her like noxious venom.

She was going to kill him.

"I . . . Cliff motioned Maury to go get her. He went slow, talking soft and telling her it was okay. She was okay. He'd get close and she'd shy away from him but he was patient, took his time. We, Jeremy and me, we got out of the car. I figured the game was over, that we were trying to get her back in the car to take her home. I remember thinking they'd want to give her the whole backseat to keep her quiet, which meant me or Jeremy—probably me, because girls liked Jeremy so he was a bigger deal than me . . . and I'd end up having to stay behind because there was only room for three with the bucket seats up front, and, of course, they'd think it was hilarious not to come back for me so I'd have to hike home or hitch a ride once I got down to the highway, so . . . so I was already pissed off but—but Maury jumped her; got around back and grabbed her from behind and . . . God Almighty," he said as the hand holding the gun lowered to his side and he tipped his face to the moon. It wasn't a curse and it wasn't a prayer. It was an admission of his own weakness.

Sophie gathered several large pebbles into a pile beside her.

"They laughed. Maury was having trouble holding her while she cried and screamed and fought, but he was happy to be making Cliff laugh, so he held on but even he looked surprised when Cliff walked over and backhanded her so hard they both staggered. I heard Jeremy make a noise—I might have, too, because we looked at each other. She stopped screaming but now she was sort of whimpering and cowering . . . and there was blood on her lip."

Sophie ignored an intense urge to cover her ears—something stronger knew that she owed it to Lonora to listen, to be *her* witness.

"She was so pale that her face was bright red where he'd hit her. We didn't know what was happening but we knew it'd gone far enough. We were walking over to say so, to stop them, when she broke loose and started running. Cliff yelled to get her but I couldn't move. It was like I wasn't there, it wasn't really happening. I could have been watching TV.

"But I knew I wasn't when Maury tackled her. And Cliff rushed up, straddled her, hit her again to shut her up . . . and again." He produced a loud sigh. "She kept fighting him, hitting him with her fists and screaming, telling him he was hurting her—like he didn't know it. She was so loud. I kept looking around. I kept thinking someone from town would hear and come to help her. Cliff yelled at Maury to come hold her hands but once he let go of her feet, she started kicking and rolling, still hitting and screaming. He hollered out for me and Jeremy to come help—to hold her arms and shut her up."

Sophie hissed air between her teeth as pain pierced palm. She relaxed her hand on the rock she'd been holding so tightly it gouged her hand. The stinging felt good, oddly comforting. She wrapped her fingers around the rock again.

"I swear I was still thinking we were trying to calm her down so we could get her in the car and take her back to town. And maybe if she hadn't . . . well, she bit him and—"

"God, you're pathetic," Sophie said, her voice calm and cold as she bent forward, shifted her weight, and sat back on her legs in the dark. "Now you're going to blame her? It was *her* fault? How about you just kill me now? I'm sick of your whiny excuses for not helping her."

"It's not excuses. It's how it was. I wanted—"

"Yeah, I know how it was. Same as now I suspect. People don't change." Staying low she brought her right knee up, placed her foot on the ground directly beneath it, and pressed her chest against her thigh using a fist filled with dirt on one side and a hand full of rock on the other for balance. "You were a spineless coward then and you're a spineless coward now."

"Shut up!"

Leaning heavily on her fist, she put aside her weapon briefly to pluck up a stone from her small arsenal and pitched it into the brush on her left. It rustled wonderfully. He, along with the barrel of his gun, jumped and swung to his right to frantically search the darkness. She took up another and tossed it as hard as she could beyond his shadowy bulk, and when he turned his back on her, she grabbed her rock and made her move.

A bitter wrath and desperation mingled in a sizzling explosion of strength and single-minded intent. Her maniacal shrieking burst into the treetops and resounded down into the valley. *Flint* met bone with such a pleasing and sustaining *thunk!* that encouraged her to strike again. His yelp of pain was delightful. Her senses were so honed on the moment, she actually heard his fist plowing through the air toward her—she ducked and it passed overhead. Next she remembered thinking *Crap!* as she flew through the air with her fist still full of dirt . . . and a subdued *Uh-oh* when she heard the renting of the seams of her cami as he grabbed the front and yanked, fist in the air—

Chapter Fourteen

THE FIRE IN HER FACE WASN'T NEARLY AS DISTRESSING AS THE ENOR-mous truck parked on her chest. Her breaths were shallow and rapid; she was dizzy, and again there was the fire burning through the bones on the left side of her face.

She groaned and pushed at the vehicle—it groaned and rolled over onto her legs, bent at an awkward position. She cried out and began pummeling the side of it. It turned over again and she was free.

In the seconds it took to scramble to her feet, she recalled every second of the night—except for bringing Lanyard down atop her. The blistering pain in her cheek was distracting but not so much that she missed the sound of his body shifting slowly on the ground or the jolt of her instinct to flee kicking in.

She'd kill him later.

She turned into a sudden beam of light that smarted in her eyes and blinded her at once. She teetered, sidestepping it, us-ing her arm to shield her vision.

"Sophie, you're all right now, dear. Come over here next to me." The voice was female and familiar. "You're safe. He won't touch you again."

"Mrs. McCarren?"

"Yes, dear. Step away from him now, please."

Not a problem, except she still couldn't see where she was going. She did know where Frank Lanyard was, however, so she sidled in the opposite direction. She tipped a bit when the light abruptly lowered to quickly inspect the condition of her body before it veered away toward Frank.

"Look what you've done to this sweet girl, Frank Lanyard." There was no mistaking the elegance of her walk as she advanced on the downed man.

"Mrs. McCarren? Elizabeth?" Clearly, he'd knocked Sophie senseless. "Is that you?" A swift perusal of the woods held no answers. "Where's Drew? Are you alone? Where is everyone?"

The lady seemed not to be hearing as the beam of her shoebox-sized flashlight swept the floor of the gully until it settled on Frank's gun, which she bent down to pick up. She kicked Lanyard's butt and said, "Sit up, you oaf. I barely touched you."

Elizabeth McCarren knocked out Frank Lanyard? Sophie wondered if she was still unconscious, dreaming. Or maybe she simply found a bigger, better rock and did Sophie's job brilliantly. She could live with that—literally.

When she stuffed the gun in her belt like a desperado, Sophie was utterly dazzled.

"I am so glad to see you. I wasn't sure you'd understand what was happening when we drove by the café." Together they watched Lanyard push himself up to a sitting position. "My S.O.S. left a lot to be desired, I know, but I didn't have a lot of options. I hoped you'd see that something was wrong and call the sheriff . . . or maybe Drew. I sure didn't expect you to come alone. I—"

"Take your shirt off." Elizabeth ordered Frank, swinging a stick at him. "If you've done more harm to this child than what I can see from here, you're going to be sorry. Don't people like you ever learn?"

Sophie was liking Drew's mother more and more. *She* was a good parent. She—

"He raped Lonora!" The volatile mix of emotions scorched her once again. "Him and his friends . . . Cliff Palmeroy and Maury Weims and the other one. They raped her. They found her walking along the road. They brought her up here—"

"Yes, dear. Calm yourself." She flashed the light in Lanyard's eyes. "Give Sophie your shirt. She's freezing."

She was cold, Sophie realized, looking down at her not-so-pretty-anymore camisole. She was also entirely exposed. She covered her breasts with her arm and waited for Frank's shirt.

Bowing her head as she buttoned up the front of the shirt, she marveled at the sensations she'd missed and the pain that had slipped away unnoticed while she fought for her life— that now returned full force. The raw fingertips under broken nails; dirty bloody scratches everywhere; deep aching muscles that were already swelling and pushing tender bruises up under her skin. She used a featherlight touch on the puffed-up laceration above her right brow and worked her jaw—which she assumed would be even more painful and considerably more difficult to move if it was broken.

Out of the blue, Frank yowled and fell over again. Several seconds later he cried out, "She didn't know! Maury said she did. But she didn't know."

"So you had to brag about it before you killed her?" Elizabeth's voice was civil and unruffled as she watched Lanyard, bit by bit, return to a sitting position in a white T-shirt that had seen many better days. "You are unbelievable."

"She deserved to know," he said, belligerent. He rolled his shoulder to remove a kink that made him wince. "It's why she came."

"She came to hear Arthur's confession, not yours, you idiot."

He shook his head, confused. "Why not tell the cops? How did he know it was us in the first place?"

"Who said he did?"

"How else would she know who to kill?"

"I told you. I didn't—" Sophie started to tell him, *again,* that she hadn't killed anyone but Elizabeth cut her off.

"Now never you mind, Frank Lanyard. You're in enough trouble." She pointed her stick at him as a threat. "And now I have to figure out what to do with you."

Sophie knew.

"Look," she said grinning, patting her bottom and beyond pleased with herself as she jerked the cell phone from her back pocket. "We can call for more help." With Drew's mother at her side, the two of them could handle anything. "Oh, Elizabeth, you have no idea . . . I know so much more than what Mr. Cubeck wanted to tell me. He knew Lonora Campbell was my birth mother. That's what he wanted to tell me. Billy found it; he figured it out. Oh! Billy! I forgot!"

"Yes, I know about William. I was quite beside myself when I realized he was embroiled in this. I should have anticipated it—so like him to be meddlesome. And you mustn't feel responsible. What's done is done. Hopefully, no real harm has been done and we can turn it to our advantage. Go on, dear. Tell me what else you've uncovered."

Sophie was heartened. If Elizabeth knew about Billy, he must have been conscious when she arrived—and well enough for her to leave him, to come rescue her. Maybe she called for help first or left him calling for help. Maybe it was already on the way. Maybe it would work out after all.

"Well, Billy showed me a picture of her, from the newspaper. I guess she could have been any relative with a strong family resemblance but . . . well, not *that* strong. I knew immediately who she was." Instantly riled up again, she glanced at Frank and pointed her cell phone at him. "He must have guessed that Lonny would recognize me, too, and that's why he attacked him. But now I know, too. I know everything. I know what you did. We're calling Sheriff Murphy. He'll arrest your ass and you'll die in jail after we testify to what you've done. To Lonora. To me. I hope you're getting used to the dark because if it's up to me—"

"No, dear." With a long, resigned sigh and weariness in her voice, Elizabeth said, "Give it to me for now. We need to get our story straight first."

"Our story? It's not straight?"

"Gracious, no. Not anymore. Now it's a big old mess, thanks to Arthur." She groaned. "And William. He'll be like a shark in bloody water now."

Elizabeth McCarren walked toward her, the flashlight and her stick held loose in one hand. Not a particularly big stick if it's what she hit Frank with, but Sophie was living proof of what a woman replete with adrenaline could manage.

Actually . . . not a stick-stick, Sophie noticed, as Elizabeth came closer through the darkness with her hand out to receive the phone. More like a rod, a thin metal stick with a handle . . . like the wide end of a broken fishing pole . . . or maybe a cattle prod.

Cold sweat popped from every pore in Sophie's body. She heard the sheriff's voice in her head. . . . *The only thing missing from the truck was a hotshot that Cliff kept in the bed of his truck.*

That didn't mean it was Cliff's prod. Lots of country people used them on their cattle—not the nicest or kindest way to get cows to move but certainly common enough.

Still, it was a strain to imagine someone like Elizabeth Mc-Carren having one conveniently locked away in the trunk of her luxury Lexis on the off chance that she would need one some day to subdue a killer . . . or herd cattle for that matter.

Hope was becoming harder and harder to hold as Sophie realized that Elizabeth didn't know Billy was in the parking lot. She hadn't called for help. It wasn't coming.

Sophie's hand shook as she relinquished the cell. Her gaze passed from her savior to her captor and back again. Was it too late to ask for a do-over? As repulsive as he was, Frank was beginning to look like a lesser threat.

"Nice hotshot."

"I know. Isn't it wonderful?" Elizabeth smiled happily—insanely so—and gave it a whirl. "If I'd known how handy they were, I'd have gotten one long ago. And let me tell you this: the social hour at the Clearfield Service Committee meetings would no longer exceed the length of the business discussions." Her eyes widened. "And Maxine Pollock would think twice about spreading lies about Botox injections around town." She gave it a neat little snap like a whip master and sobered abruptly. "It's not a toy, though. That's important to remember."

"Yes, ma'am." They heard Frank move, disturbing his cushion of brittle dry leaves. The ladies looked at him. Sophie narrowed her eyes. "I bet it hurts like the dickens."

"Yes, indeed, it seems quite painful—and it can be quite deadly under certain circumstances." Sophie's heart shuddered before it sank deeper into her abdomen. Part of her wished Elizabeth would just stop talking. The more she said, the more insane she sounded. "It's the electricity, of course, and I feel positively foolish for not making that connection."

"What connection?"

Elizabeth made a cheeky grimace. "I had a bit of an accident with it recently. I should have Googled it for more information *before* I used it but, of course, everything is clearer in hindsight, isn't it?" Sophie had to agree. "You see, theoretically, the high voltage/low current combination isn't supposed to be strong enough to kill a human or a large animal such as a cow or a goat with short-term exposure—no more than cause incapacitating pain. But it isn't until you get to the small print that you find it isn't recommended for people with heart conditions or pacemakers." Her shrug was graceful. "Forgetting that Maury Weims had both is a mixed blessing, I suppose."

"Had?"

"Oh, yes. For years. I believe my husband treated him when he had his first coronary . . . in his thirties. Quite young."

"Oh. So . . . And why is that a mixed blessing?" She needed to hear the words out loud to accept it.

"Well, I see now that it was for the best, of course, but I didn't intend to kill Maury. I only meant to scare him. I thought that by putting Cliff down—cutting the head off the snake, so to speak—that the others would fall into line and leave you be. The secret would be safe. I needed Maury to keep his mouth shut. The man had no spine, Sophie. Cliff Palmeroy, a foul man start to finish, led him around like a trained monkey. He did everything Cliff told him to do, even back then. This one, too." She set the flashlight on the ground, aimed the blinding beam straight into Frank's face. He scooted to one side. She didn't bother to bend over again, but simply tapped the battery box with the toe of her expensive summer flats to pin him again. Lanyard covered his eyes. "Maury Weims was pitiful and inept, but nowhere near as dangerous as Cliff. And I'll tell you this: as much as I like Phil Kerski, and admire his dedication to his family—hiring his sister's husband when no one else in town would—I was compelled to switch to the Rite Aid pharmacy for my prescriptions because simply seeing Maury Weims nauseated me. Truth. If I wasn't ill when I went in there, I was when I left. Running into either of them could trigger one of my migraines . . . I keep my Celebrex in my purse for that exact reason."

Sophie glanced around for something to sit down on—she was feeling a bit sick herself.

For even beyond the gradual awareness of the two murdering maniacs in her presence, there was a numbing exhaustion creeping deep into her bones, anesthetizing her wounds and clearly blunting her normal reactions because she detected an irrational sense of safety with Drew's mother. For the moment anyway—for as long as Elizabeth felt safe, felt no threat coming from her. And once again, paramount, was her need for time—to recoup her strength, reassemble her mind, and to request that God arrange for an official police rescue this time.

She must have looked ready to drop, too, because Elizabeth picked up the flashlight, took her arm, and led her gingerly over to a fallen tree a few yards away, saying, "You poor thing. What you've been through . . . let me help you. There, that's better isn't it?"

Sophie nodded, huddling inside Frank's shirt. She wasn't that cold but she was shivering.

Elizabeth sat next to her and reset the beam of her flashlight on their prisoner. She set the hotshot on the log and brought the gun out. Sophie nodded again. Their mutual loathing of Frank Lanyard made the gun the more plausible weapon if he was foolish enough to attempt an escape. And there wasn't a doubt in the air, anywhere, that she'd miss her mark.

Elizabeth settled primly and sighed softly. "Filthy business this. I'm sorry Arthur dragged you into it, Sophie. I told him, more than once, that it was a bad idea to send for you. As an old and dear friend, I felt that the least I could do for him was to ease his conscience and let him die in peace. I promised him that I would protect and care for you when you arrived." There was a soft laugh. "I never dreamed it would become this complicated. Lord, that man and his ridiculous will. Who knew what would be in it?" She rubbed her forehead with the back of her gun hand, clearly vexed. "I was sick with worry. It wouldn't have been nearly so nerve-racking had I been able to count on Arthur, just this once, not to be rash. It was one thing to break the promise we made to Lonny Campbell when you were born, but we both knew that pulling on one little thread would unravel everything so we agreed to leave none exposed. It was best for everyone. But he was so remorseful at the end . . . and *so* unpredictable."

"What promise?"

"Well, you see, by the time it was discovered that little Lonora was pregnant, Lonny simply couldn't bear the idea of everyone knowing the whole truth of what happened to his baby. He said he wouldn't give whoever did it the satisfaction. And who could blame him?"

"I didn't get her pregnant," Frank shouted to them. "My sister gave me the mumps."

Elizabeth angled her gun at him, limp wristed. "Don't make me come back over there. I will bring the cattle prod and I will make you wiggle like a fish out of water if you open that mouth of yours again. Nod if you understand what I'm saying."

Nodding, he muttered something about a *crazy bitch*.

"Now, where was I . . . Oh, yes. As Lonny's minister and as president of Clearfield General Hospital's Charitable Foundation that year, Arthur and I decided we could safely step in and help Lonny by finding a better home for her and arranging private medical care for her during that last trimester of her pregnancy."

Safely? An odd adverb to use, but not the question uppermost in Sophie's mind. "A better home than Lonny's? I'm surprised he let her go anywhere else."

"Oh. Yes. How could you know . . . ?" She paused and was thoughtful. "I suppose, in light of what you and William already know, there's no point in keeping the truth from you. I may as well tell the whole of it—since he's bound to figure out the rest anyway."

Bound to figure out the rest? There was more? More than Lonora being her birth mother? More than her rape? More than Elizabeth killing those responsible? Sophie felt something shriveling inside her—it felt like the last of her hope.

"That sweet child was extremely traumatized," Elizabeth said—soft, gentle, and full of compassion. "Anyone would be, but she was so mentally fragile to begin with—she suffered an acute stress reaction to the incident. She was dazed and disoriented and combative initially, when they first found her. But she rapidly deteriorated to a dissociative stupor as she became more and more depressed and detached—she wouldn't . . . or couldn't respond to any sort of stimulus. Lonny was lost. They tried drugs and electroshock therapy." Her voice cracked with emotion. "No one could say how long her stupor would last, so Lonny was forced to admit her to a long-term convalescent center."

A parent who has been declared incompetent and for some reason it's determined that restoration of competency is improbable would need a guardian, Daniel Biggs had said. Lonora had always needed one.

Sophie's groan was involuntary.

"Oh my goodness, you're not thinking of those gruesome old asylums, are you?"

No. She was thinking of the horror Lonora endured—physically but more permanently in her mind. She was thinking of the misery Lonny suffered from that day to this one. She was thinking she must be stuck in a nightmare that would end when the alarm went off and she woke up back in Marion, the summer sun shining bright and warm through her bedroom window.

"They aren't like that anymore." Elizabeth made a face. "Even the state facilities aren't so bad anymore. But they are state hospitals, so when Arthur and I stepped in we pushed for a nicer, private long-term care facility. At least until after the baby was born." A soft giggle. "That would be *you*, of course. She was going to need the extra care for a while."

"But she was ill. Why didn't they . . . you know . . ."

"Terminate the pregnancy?"

Sophie nodded.

"Well, to be honest, there was talk of it. I, personally, encouraged the idea, thinking it would be the best solution for everyone involved. No offense, dear, but the girl was on this drug and that drug; she wasn't eating or drinking; they were using a feeding tube and IVs and catheters and whatnot. Bearing a child is difficult enough under normal circumstances, and these were not." She casually crossed her legs, like she was having a Sunday-afternoon chat. "But once Lonny saw that first sonogram—more than halfway through the pregnancy, mind you—well, he wasn't sure what to do. Tests were done and he was persuaded to take it a day at a time and let her carry it as long as possible, if there was no threat to her health."

Lonny. Most of her life, she'd assumed that her existence was a gift . . . the ultimate gift from a woman who had other options. That the gift had come from her grandfather in the worst possible situation made her heart ache as it stretched to make a special place for him.

"Arthur made the arrangements for the adoption—not everyone is willing to take a high-risk baby, you know. Lonny wanted the baby to go as far away as possible. He didn't want Lonora to know, ever. He didn't trust anyone in town anymore and couldn't assume that no one would mention it to her. So, we three and the doctor and nurse who did the delivery and the judge who pushed through the paperwork—who was a friend of the lawyer who handled the adoption—well, we were the only people who knew about you."

"And Lonora?" Her voice was low with dread. "Lonny said she died but . . . but not when. Did she ever recover . . . or was it because of me?"

The older woman bowed her head and didn't speak for so long that Sophie wondered if she would. Her voice was soft and deeply aggrieved when she said, "No. A few months after you were born, she started to look better. She didn't speak or smile the way we all knew her to, but her eyes lit up for Lonny and she'd watch people walk by or birds fly overhead if she was out in the garden. She was taking notice. They were trying to get her to use a walker and talking about different meds and psychotherapy—and then she was gone."

"Gone?"

"To heaven, I believe." She stood, belted the gun, picked up the hotshot and took a few paces into the periphery of the beam of light to stare across at Frank Lanyard a few feet away. Conversationally, she added, "I don't buy into that business about suicide ruining your chance at heaven, do you? One moment shouldn't define your entire life. It's ludicrous."

Sophie swallowed hard on the rock of emotion stuck in her throat and shook her head—no, she didn't buy into it either, not anymore certainly. Sophie stood to follow Elizabeth but the ground rolled and she felt herself weaving like a drunk. Readjusting her stance helped but not by much. She knew the next, most logical question should be: *How?* But why introduce logic at this point?

Also, she didn't want to know.

"And Mr. Cubeck . . ." she said. "When he found out he was dying, he decided I should know all this; that Lonora was my mother and what happened to her?"

"The secret weighed heavily on him. Yes."

"Why?" Her mind felt thick and stiff; still, she sensed something was wrong, missing. "I mean, why would he think I'd want to know any of this? What good would it do me? And Lonny is still alive. Why would he betray him like that?" *And* come to think of it, "Why would he leave me BelleEllen? He knew the kind of dust that would stir up. He said he owed it to me, but it sounds more like we owed him for helping us— Lonny and Lonora and me. It doesn't make sense."

Elizabeth tipped her head to the right as if trying to fathom an odd puzzle. "No, it doesn't."

"It sure as shit doesn't." Sophie stared at Frank Lanyard— pictured a wiggling fish and cringed as he said, "Who the hell figured out it was us? That's what I want to know. If she was crazy and not talkin' to anyone, not even her old man, how'd *you* know it was us? How'd you know who did it? How'd you know to kill Cliff and Maury? How'd you know about me? *Why didn't you just call the cops?*"

Elizabeth took two steps and gave a jab at Frank's leg that had him roaring out a curse and falling on his side. He jerked twice, and when he could pull his leg up, he rubbed out the cramp. Stubbornly, or stupidly, he asked again, "How'd you know?"

The leaves in the trees stopped rustling in the wind to hear her answer. Crickets and toads took notice and went silent, listening for a response. Sophie wasn't as quick to catch on, but the rhythmic roaring of her heartbeat inside her ears had her breathing deep and slow, calming herself for whatever came next. . . .

Which was Elizabeth lunging her lance into Frank's belly and holding it there while Sophie screamed, "Elizabeth! Stop. You'll kill him. Stop it!" And no one was more surprised than she to find her hands clasped over the older woman's, lowering the hotshot away and pleading, "Stop. Please, stop."

The flashlight cast eerie shadows in the night, but Sophie was still able to see the vagueness in Elizabeth's face, like she'd only this moment arrived from another planet.

"Actually, Mother, I'd like to hear your answer."

The women turned their heads and responded in unison. "Billy!" "William!"—one in relief, the other in stunned dismay.

Somehow Sophie crossed the uneven terrain in seconds. "Oh my God, you're alive!" She threw her arms around his neck, *never* so glad to see someone in all her life. She pulled back, squinted to see the wound deep inside his hairline that was clotted closed and discolored, then pulled him close again. There was an entire crying jag caught in her throat as she croaked in his ear. "I was so afraid you'd die. You were so pale. I didn't know what to do."

His chest jerked with a silent half-laugh as he held her tight. "So you locked me in the car while you figured it out?" Sophie nodded. "Thank you."

"Your mother is . . ." What? Unwell? Acting oddly? Crazy as bat shit? A killer?

"I know. I heard."

Exhaling heavily and setting her aside, he spoke in a less private voice. "You look like hell." Startling a short laugh from

her, he used her chin to tip her face to the light and check out
her head and face. Exchanging small reassuring smiles—they
both might live, it seemed—they gradually gravitated back to
his mother and Frank Lanyard, who were staring at them.

"Mother."

"William, what are you doing here?"

"He brought me." Frank hadn't moved since Billy arrived,
but his wide, panicky eyes and an occasional groan were proof
of life. "I was with Sophie when he hijacked her. Looks like I
slept through all the excitement after he knocked me out. See
here?" he said, trying to distract her.

However, once Elizabeth saw the laceration her instinctive
reaction was to turn to Lanyard and inflict more pain for his
newest crime, but when Billy's voice grew louder, she stopped.

"Sophie locked her car and the honk woke me up. It took
me a while to get untied." He took a cautious step in her direction. "You could have helped me, you know."

"But I didn't see you, sweetheart, or I would have."

Sophie admired how unruffled and rational she sounded,
even as her insanity sparkled in her eyes.

"You know that."

"I saw you drive up. No headlights. Very stealth, Mother.
I was impressed. You probably didn't see me because you had
your I'm-on-a-mission face on."

"She rescued me, Billy," Sophie said, stepping up behind
him, not willing to let him get too far away from her.

"I did. Just in time, too. This . . . animal had her on the
ground with a rock in his hand. He was going to kill her. I
took his gun." She patted the weapon in her belt and then
put her hands on her hips, hotshot jutting out behind. "I was
thinking we could use it to make it look like he killed himself out here. Everyone would think he killed Palmeroy and
Weims before he kidnapped Sophie . . . and you, too. You'd be

a witness to that. And no one would think to question a Mc-Carren's word. After he knocked Sophie out, he took her for dead. But then he realized that he'd never get away with any of it, so he killed himself. That's when you and I arrive on the scene." She grinned over her shoulder at him. "*After* I discover you in Sophie's car and untied you, of course."

"Of course." Without looking back, his open palm connected with Sophie's chest to hold her in place as he continued to slowly approach his mother. "Clever. It's a good plan except for the why. The sheriff is going to need a motive, Mother? Why would he kill his friends and a young woman he doesn't even know?"

After a moment's calculation: "But he does know her. Who she is, anyway, because she looks like her mother. That lovely red hair." A benevolent smile for Sophie. "And he thought she knew about them. He thought *she* was killing them off. But he could just as easily be afraid the others would break down and confess when people started asking questions about her. Maybe blame him for instigating the attack on Lonora. . . . Which he didn't because he's a weak, spineless hanger-on who only does what he's told."

Like lightning, she pierced the air with her rod and struck him again, and again.

"Mother!" Billy shouted too late.

"She was unconscious when he took his turn." She made a snarling sound. "Unconscious."

Sophie's dry eyes burned and scratched as she lowered her lids over them to close out the picture forming in her head—there was no more room.

Billy's weak laugh was meant to pacify his troubled parent. "You know those things leave marks, don't you? Really distinct marks. Nobody's going to believe he sat out here electrocuting himself before he committed suicide."

He had a point.

"Yes. I see it." She put the hotshot on the ground at her feet, saying, "We must remember to wipe it clean and put his fingerprints all over it so they'll know he used it." She went for her gun.

"No, leave it, Mother. You don't need it right now. He's not going anywhere. And the fewer prints you put on it, the fewer we'll have to wipe off."

Another good point. She nodded, clearly still willing to accept rational input.

"Okay. So." Billy picked up the thread. "He's killing everyone who knows what happened. And he tries to kill Sophie because he *thinks* she knows, too, and that that's why she came to town. For revenge."

"Yes."

Looking confused, he took another step her way. "And how would Sophie find out?"

"Arthur. Arthur knew! That's why he wrote to her to come."

"But how did Arthur know?"

"He. . . ." She shook her head. His common sense was beginning to frustrate her. "Listen to me. You have no idea how difficult Arthur could be. It's been twenty-eight years and I had to talk him out of confessing almost every single one of them. He kept track of her . . . and didn't tell me for years. He went to her high school graduation—against my advice and my explicit wishes. This last time, after he got sick, he sent for her and *then* told me what he'd done. I wanted to kill him. Have you ever heard of anything more selfish? He was going to die and leave *me* holding the bag."

"Holding what bag?"

"The bag of truth!"

Billy's hesitation was brief. "What truth, Mother?"

Sophie wasn't sure if Billy saw the lights moving through

the trees in the distance behind Elizabeth, but it might explain some of the new tension and urgency in his voice. "The truth about how you and Arthur knew who was there that night? And what they did to Lonny's daughter? The truth about how you know when this guy took his turn at her?"

"What?" His mother looked as if he was speaking Mandarin with his soft southern drawl.

"Did one of them confess to Arthur or to you? Is that how you knew?" He was less than two steps from her. "Or were you both there?"

"No. No." She shook her head. "I believe someone may have—"

"You and Arthur were there. You saw the whole thing."

"No!"

"You saw and did nothing." Billy was shattered, his disillusionment shining in his eyes, ringing in his voice.

"We couldn't!"

"You couldn't? Really? Why not?"

Elizabeth said nothing, so Billy continued to press her. "What exactly were you and Arthur doing up here? That is, what were you doing *before* you saw what was happening and did nothing?"

Her eyes shifted to Sophie and then back to Billy. She was caught. Her neck stiffened and she became noticeably taller as she straightened her spine, holding her head high. A proud and beautiful creature caught in her own trap. She was angry.

"Your father was never home! He's still never home! I was young and lonely. I was alone and isolated with only Andrew and Pamela to look after. Soon they were in school all day. I was so lonely. I took up gardening—alone—everything died. I took on more community responsibilities, more charities, more and more activities. And invariably Arthur would be on one committee or another with me.

"My . . . our favorite was always the clean-up committee. Ellen had been gone for years by then. We'd talk after. Have coffee sometimes. He and I, we both took all the jobs no one else wanted because we had no one to . . . we had no one. We loved our children, naturally. But they don't provide adult companionship. We were young—your age. We spent time together. We were lonely. We had needs."

"You had an affair." It wasn't a question. Elizabeth said nothing, stoically ambiguous. "You were up here somewhere going at it. You heard her screams. You went to investigate. You found them. But if they saw *you*, you'd have to explain what you were doing here—with Arthur. Dad would divorce you and Arthur would end up preaching to the pews. You'd both lose everything. So you hid. You watched. You did nothing."

She had the grace to look away . . . far, far away. "Arthur would have. He wanted to. He begged me. He promised to leave me out of it, to say he was here alone. But you open a door to evil and it'll walk right in. I couldn't risk it. I loved my family. It would have devastated my husband, my children. Destroy my home. Yes, everything. I had to protect all that. I had too much to lose. We both did. I said no. It broke my heart; killed me. Arthur cried. He covered his ears and curled up on the ground beside me. It tormented him. Always." She looked back at Billy. "We were so young."

Far afield, the first twinkling of searchlights flickered like stars in the night. Faint, indistinguishable shouts floated on a mild breeze.

Then and there, Sophie made a solemn vow: She was going to eat all the maple bars she wanted, whenever she wanted. Life was fragile and uncertain and she needed to do everything she wanted to do when she wanted to do it and not wait because the only thing certain in life is uncertainty and she loved maple bars and she was sick of not eating them because they have no nutritional value whatsoever, unlike cauliflower—*the* most incredible bland-tasting white stuff since notebook paper.

Pleased with the new declaration, with the rescuers almost upon them *and* with the budding belief that she would likely live through the night, she turned to Billy to share her elation . . . only to find him staring at her strangely.

Hadn't he seen the lights? Was he hearing impaired?

She glanced over his shoulder at Elizabeth, who looked spent and deep in thought. It occurred to her that being rescued, while wonderful, would drill his mother's life deep into the ground. And the reality of her being a murderess?

She tried to form an understanding, encouraging and now-she-can-get-the-help-she-needs expression on her face because she truly did empathize with those who were Elizabeth's collateral damage—her family and the families of the men she'd killed—attempting to protect *her*, Sophie realized and accepted sadly.

Billy continued to stare.

"What?"

"Your birthday. It's only a few weeks before mine."

"So?" she said, wondering if he'd taken the ride around the bend with his mother.

He merely nodded, and while they stood locked in pensive eye contact, she watched his thoughts and emotions come and go; add, subtract, and divide. In slow-witted stages, she picked up his trail: noted the similarity in their ages and recalled his orangeness in the apple bowl. After a few minutes, his lids fell like the final curtain on a stage and when they opened he was a changed character.

"You were young, you said." He turned back to his mother. "Young like me, you said." She frowned. He made no sense. She had no playbill. "Young like Sophie, too. Right?"

She darted her eyes in Sophie's direction. "I suppose."

"Sophie and I are the same age, Mother." She smiled—that was nice, but it wasn't going to solve the problem of disposing of Frank Lanyard, now was it? Billy lost it. "For God's sake! Was he my father?"

"Who?"

"Arthur Cubeck!"

"What?"

"Sophie and I were conceived on the same night, right?"

Chapter Fifteen

ELIZABETH WAS CLEARLY SHOCKED.

Then she stunned them when she burst out laughing—hysterically.

Sophie forced her sore, shaky legs to walk to Billy's side. She slipped her hand into his.

Still seeming vastly too amused, Elizabeth asked, "Did this just now come to you? This revelation?"

"No." He spoke stiffly. "It didn't. Pam used to tell me I was adopted. All the time. I thought she was just being mean, but after a while I—"

"Pamela is a royal bitch and you know it," she said, not with her usual sophistication. She chuckled at the absurdity of his assertion and shook her head.

Sophie heard her name in the wind. Clearer. Closer.

"I'm glad you find my question entertaining, Mother, but I'd still like an answer. Who is my father?"

"Oh, darling," she said, smiling broadly, straining for control. She took a step toward him and he stepped back.

"Stop it!" His hands convulsed with anger and Sophie yelped with pain. He let go immediately. "In case you haven't noticed, I'm not laughing."

"So I see. But you will be. It's the best part of the story. Honestly." With her arms out in hopeless irony, she shouted to the treetops. "Nothing happened! It's classic. It's comical. We flirted back and forth for *for-ever*. Harmless. Fun. It didn't mean anything. We were lonely, is all. But then we kissed. We were so appalled we couldn't look each other in the eye for weeks . . . until it happened again. It was exciting. Thrilling. It was like playing at being teenagers again. We'd go out for coffee after the most tedious meetings imaginable and hold hands under the table. We'd whisper and blush, steal kisses in dark corners. We'd get so frustrated . . . needy, you know?" Billy was stone still. "One night we just went . . . too far. We never meant to hurt anyone—it just happened. I remember feeling so free and happy and filled with anticipation . . . he drove straight through the chain blocking the access road." Her lovely animated face melted like heated wax. "It was barely dusk. I could see the longing in his eyes, his desire for me. I felt beautiful again. I wanted it to last forever, that feeling." She was as empty as her sigh. The vacancy in her eyes as she turned toward the thrashing noises of their rescuers said it all. She didn't turn back before she continued.

"Nothing happened—her first scream shattered everything between us. Afterward, I was so guilty I seduced your father every chance I got trying to make it up to him. And when I found out about you, I never wanted a child more than I wanted you, Billy. You were my gift to my family for failing them so miserably. You saved us. You made my family normal and safe again.

"But Arthur and I . . . well, we were already in hell before we heard her cry out a second time." She turned back to them with a small smile on her face and the gun in her right hand. "We never made it back, sweetheart."

In a grotesque slow-motion scene, like so many frames from an old silent film, Elizabeth raised her right arm into the air, one jerky movement after the next. Her wrist twisted and her hand pulled the gun around until it gradually lined the nose up with her ear. A large dark form passed by low in Sophie's peripheral vision. Billy. His mother's amazing grace was still evident in the motion of the backlash that followed the sound of an underwater explosion. Sophie actually *saw* the bullet floating in the air. . . .

But that's all she saw.

"Sophie." It was Jesse. "Sophie, honey?"

Her eyes opened, wide with fear. But a split second later she knew she was safe with her friend, and that while most of the noise and commotion was several feet away, she could continue to hide away . . . leave the lights off . . . let the phone ring . . . ignore it all.

"Sophie." Drew this time.

Blinding light. Tender facial poking. The light went away, but the squeezing and gentle bending continued until he said it again. "Sophie?"

Another blink showed her the crowd was breaking up. She got that movie's-over, time-to-go-home feeling and took another quick peek. People were pairing up, forming small groups. Jesse was holding Billy—he was sobbing, clinging to her. Frank Lanyard had three policemen with him. People huddled low to the ground . . . *Elizabeth*. She turned her head and looked up at Drew.

Those eyes. . . . His wonderful, caring eyes. The deep pain inside them; the terrified concern. The questions he couldn't begin to ask. The tears pooling on the rims.

He said her name again and she lifted her hand, smeared dirt on his cheek and said, "I'm so sorry."

"Oh, Sophie." He rolled her up into his arms and lowered his forehead to the curve of her neck. He wept.

When Billy fought going back to town in the ambulance, his brother became insistent.

"The sheriff wants you to go. He said he'd meet you back in the ER and get more details. There's nothing else you can do here."

"She shouldn't be left alone."

"She won't be. I promise."

"I should stay. Sophie needs you. You go with her and I'll stay with Mother."

A darting glance at Sophie on the stretcher in the back of the ambulance reassured him. "Sophie's going to be fine. She needs medical care and so do you. Please. Go with her. Keep an eye on her for me, will you?"

Billy looked back at the second emergency vehicle containing the shrouded body of his mother—devastated, aching for the power to turn back time.

"I pushed her." He confided in a low voice to his big brother. "I was angry. I wanted an answer. I pushed her too hard."

"Stop. It's not your fault. You didn't know. Hell, no one knew." Though Drew had no clear answers of his own for what had happened, he grabbed Billy's forearms to get his attention and did his puzzling out loud, on the fly. "This started before you were born. And she . . . she always had Arthur to share their secret with. When he died, she was alone. Imagine having to carry all that guilt alone." It was clear that neither brother could conceive it. "The first time Cliff Palmeroy looked in Sophie's direction, she started rolling, taking down everyone in her path who was a threat . . . to Sophie or to her and Arthur's secret, I don't know. Both. We may never know. And you just happened to get in her way." He moved both his hands to Billy's neck and gave him an affectionate shake. "You kept her from killing Lanyard. And maybe Sophie, too. And I promise you, I don't think you pushed her into doing anything she hadn't planned on doing anyway. I don't."

It was a long minute before Billy grabbed at Drew's shirt-sleeves and they gave each other weird, rigid little jerks before embracing.

Sophie let her heavy eyelids close. For a fraction of a second, she contemplated drumming up a bit of blame of her own—but there was none. This wasn't one of those unpleasant situations in which there was plenty of blameworthiness to go around. This was an instance of one drop of evil being added to any amount of weakness becoming the perfect recipe for a great deal of pain inflicted on a lot of innocent people.

A hand touched her shoulder and she looked into Billy's core-deep misery. She wormed a hand from her warm cocoon of blankets and rounded her fingers over his. Without words, he was quick to get that he wasn't alone; that for all time, she would be a part of his nightmares, that she would factor into the most traumatic hours of his life—and he hers. They recognized this perpetual bond in each other's eyes—took comfort in it; promised hope and support.

Even without a siren, the ride back to the hospital was remarkably short. The lights were on; people were waiting for them. She'd long ago lost track of the time, but it was still dark when her eyes rolled open once more with the wobbly rocking of the stretcher as they entered.

Fading fast, beyond exhausted, Sophie only half listened to the med-speak.

Her here, *him* over there . . . a third *victim* on the way.

Seriously? She tried, but couldn't raise a kernel of care that they were misidentifying Frank Lanyard as a third victim— the sheriff would sort all that out. . . .

Start an IV. Allergies? Current medications? Does pushing here hurt? Cut that. Get an X-ray. Next of kin? Clean this up. No stitches. Grip tighter. Where's the pain on a scale from 1 to 10?

Kin? Next of kin?

Draw blood for a full panel. Steri-Strips. Chronic medical conditions? Pregnant? Last menstrual cycle?

Next of kin?

Surgeries? Primary physician. Shivering—more blankets.

It all stopped so abruptly it was jarring. She opened one eye to the back of a woman in blue scrubs and whimpered in the blessed peace. Safe, warm, peaceful.

Except for that word that played over and over in her head. *Kin* . . .

She opened both her eyes. Nothing felt real. Actually, nothing felt at all. She was numb, body and soul . . . except for that word. *Kin* . . . She took in the curtained cubicle and the short end of the counter surrounding the nurse's station a few yards away. The IV in the bend of her arm was tender; the oxygen blowing in her nose had turned the mucus membrane inside dry and stiff and crusty. She took note of the wires for the heart monitor, the clip on her finger, and the clean hospital gown lying loose on her shoulders, and, apparently, over her denim skirt beneath the covers.

Kin. She ached for her dad's strong arms and low soothing voice. But short of that . . . she had a grandfather on the second floor.

As if on cue, the flurry that ensued with Lanyard's arrival allowed Sophie to fling off the oxygen before rattling the divided rails on the stretcher—both locked tight.

It was one of those nights. . . .

The space between the rails was too small to squeeze through, so scooting to the bottom—stretching the monitor wires and IV tubing beyond their company recommended distances—allowed her the freedom to move around unsteadily. She first found the off button on the monitor and then removed the IV the way she'd seen the nurses do it a hundred times for her mother, using a tissue to block the blood and hold pressure to the site.

Spying—and straining air through her teeth at the pain in her arm muscles when she raised them to tie up the back of her gown—she located an exit and began a shadowy escape.

"Sophie!" She jumped a foot and scowled at Billy for scaring her. Again. She put her finger to her lips so he whispered loudly. "Where are you going?"

"Shhh."

"What are you doing? You shouldn't be up. You're a mess. You can hardly walk. Shit! Fine. Wait a second. Wait. I'll go with you." He rattled the rail on his stretcher—it sounded like a train passing through.

"Shhh." She waved him off and left him sputtering.

"Sophie!"

On the other side of a metal double-door was a corridor with all the customary signs and directions so often taken for granted in hospitals. She ruminated in a rummy daze: ← X-ray. Physical Therapy. Rest Rooms. Cafeteria. Chapel. Gift Shop. ATM. Phones →

Brilliantly, someone made all the exit signs bigger and bright red. They were → too, so she peered around the corner before walking softly down the next hall to: EXIT. Elevator. Stairs. No mental effort required there.

She pushed ^ for the elevator.

Sophie hated hospitals: the smells, the colors, the chairs,

the peculiar silence under the noise by day . . . and the empty inactivity the darkness inevitably brought that, to her, always meant that nothing was being done to cure her mother. Tonight, however, the stillness was a stroke of luck.

She was leaning heavily on the wall of the elevator when the doors opened. Her feet were swollen, like walking in soaking wet house slippers. Squishy. The queasy hollow in her belly was a reminder that she hadn't eaten in a while—a long while. Had it been only yesterday? Yesterday seemed like years ago.

From the elevator to the wall directly opposite, she stood for several minutes—eyes closed, catching her breath—before leaning forward to check out the terrain between her and the far end of the nurse's desk and the patient room mere steps away.

All clear—even the chair outside the door was empty.

Frankly, the closer her drunken gait took her to her destination, the narrower her tunnel vision became and the more she surrendered herself to autopilot. The closer she got, the less she saw, and the less she cared about being seen. The closer she got, the stronger the connection pulled at her and the more deep-down certain she felt.

The TV was still on—a war in black and white—and a low glow from a panel above the head of the bed shone down on the old man's white hair, casting his gray beard into shadow. The head of his bed was barely elevated, giving him room to stretch out; his eyes were closed.

It was most likely the pounding of her heart that woke him—and he didn't seem surprised to see her . . . only the condition she was in.

"Dear God, girl," he said, rolling sideways to get out of bed. "What's happened now?"

Somehow she was there, at his side, with a powerless hand on his shoulder. Still, even that light touch had the strength to stop him, calm him and lay him back against the bed. He looked up at her, concerned and confused until his gaze caught on hers. Slowly, without a sound, he came to recognize the truths now in her possession.

Her small smile was big work so the light in her eyes did most of the talking. "Can I call you Grandpa?"

"You bet."

With a satisfied nod, she lowered herself onto the bed with her back to him, put a leg up and rolled his way. The steady sound of his heart in her ear and the comfort of his arm across her shoulder felt like home.

"Ah. Wakin' up, are you?" Lonny sat in the chair next to her bed. Not in his usual blue overalls, he wore a soft-looking flannel shirt tucked into baggy khaki pants; his hair, slicked back over the stitched wound on the crown of his head and his beard was combed as if he were trying to make a good impression. "Hey there."

One corner of her mouth lifted and she acknowledged him. "Hey, Grandpa."

He chuckled. "I like it."

"Me, too."

"How you feelin'?"

She didn't know. She looked down at the fresh IV in her bruised and scratched-up—but wonderfully clean—arm. Reaching for the sting on her forehead, she found it loosely dressed. She'd been bathed and her hair freed of dirt and debris. Still, she wasn't feeling much of anything.

"Young Doc McCarren came lookin' for you. Got you patched up and then the nurses got you all presentable before they let me in to see ya again. You look better anyway."

"How is he? And his family?"

"If the rest of them look as blindsided as him, they ain't

doin' so well. Hurt and grievin', he is. Bad time for the lot, I suspect."

"Is Billy all right?"

"Seems so. Doc said they finally had a reason to be grateful for his hardheadedness. He told me yours was likewise as hard, and it concerned him some."

Drowsy as she was, she recognized Drew's bedside manner. Anything he could think of to relieve an old man's concerns and infuse him with hope—even when his own world was falling apart.

"Your Daddy's gonna want to know about this. I'd be happy to give him a call."

She tried to picture her father's reaction to what happened to her and frowned. She had a mental flash of the woods, of the mud on the palms of her hands, and the grave urgency she'd felt to talk to him one last time—begging, her spirit broken. How could she explain that to him? He needed to be notified—he'd be angry and hurt if he wasn't—but how much did she have to tell him? How much did he need to know?

Did she have to decide *now*? Maybe she'd rest a little and sort it out a little later—when her mind was clearer . . . when her emotions weren't rippling a hair's breadth below the surface of her skin.

"Thank you, but I think I should call him. He'll want to hear from me that I'm all right."

She assumed Lonny had been told. The who, what, when, and where. But did he also know the why?

She turned her head to look at him. One glance into her eyes had him shaking his head and humming a negative noise. "No point to goin' back there, my girl. Over and done a long time ago. And if those responsible ain't been livin' in hell all these many years, they'll surely have it in the hereafter." He looked away briefly. "I been bitter and full of hate so long.

. . . When you first come to town, I didn't want nothin' to do with you. You weren't my sweet girl and you weren't her dear mama. You were someone else's child; you had been all your life. Nothin' to do with me. Till you walked into the office that day and I saw for myself that you had their smile . . . that wild red hair."

"A sailor's delight."

His features softened. "Always."

"Why didn't you tell me?"

"I thought about it. Hard. And then I wanted to. I thought maybe you needed to understand that when you were born, I was trying to protect my girl—like I shoulda been doin' all along instead of assumin' she was safe here." He hesitated. "Plus, to be honest, I didn't want any part of the person who did that to her around. When Reverend Cubeck and Elizabeth McCarren came to help me, I thought God sent 'em. We decided to keep the birth a secret. It was best.

"But then that day? Seeing you in the office? Well, I called Elizabeth and told her how I was feelin'. I asked her, did she think it would hurt you any to know me? Would it help you any to know why I did what I did? She said to keep quiet." He hesitated. "Then she came 'round to my place the other night to remind me, case I was getting weak about it. Caught me off guard."

"Were you? Getting weak?" He nodded. She did, too. "Why didn't you tell the police?"

"I'd be puttin' you in harm's way, she said, at risk from whoever killed Palmeroy. She wanted me to see that if I told you, you'd either hate me or want to stay a get to know me. And the longer you stayed, the more danger you were in. I was afraid of both them things." He glanced away briefly. "She told me she was watchin' out for you, protecting ya. If I'd known—"

"She did. She saved me. I don't think she ever wanted to hurt me." She turned her hand palm up on the bed and he filled it with his big paw. "I'm sorry it's all been dredged up again. I know it's stirred painful memories."

He gave a short nod, frowning. "Can't deny it. But those are mine. Not yours. You got some healin' of your own to do. Just don't let this turn your good heart to stone. Don't let it touch you at all if you can manage it. Ain't none of it your fault. Ain't none of it yours to bear. Learn from your ol' grandpa now. Learn to forgive, you hear?"

A nod and a gentle smile assured him that she'd try. "For the record? I wouldn't have hated you. I've always . . . understood. I've wondered why sometimes, but I always knew it was more about the situation than her or me." She closed her eyes, to rest them, for only one second. "I never blamed her. And I wouldn't have blamed you." She got the impression she was floating and hoped she added, "I'm grateful" out loud.

Sheriff Murphy stopped by briefly for what seemed to her more of a personal than professional visit—his questions few, his assurances sincere. And it didn't keep her awake when no apology for suspecting her of murder was offered. He was a good man doing the best he could at a hard job—who would apologize for that?

"Mike said that his friend Junior told him that there were several burn marks on the body and the inside of the car smelled like the hot dogs at the ballpark and burnt rubber, which is sort of interesting, I guess, but I'm still glad it wasn't Mike or Luke who found him."

"Who?" She pulled her eyes open and turned her head in the direction of Jesse's voice.

"Oh. There you are. How are you feeling? I heard once that

unconscious people can still hear, so it's good to talk to them."

"I'm fine. And I was sleeping, not unconscious."

"Trust me, anyone who can sleep through me talking for forty-five minutes is definitely unconscious."

"You've been sitting there talking to yourself for forty-five minutes?"

"No. Drew was here for a while."

"I missed him?" Disappointment gripped inside her chest.

"He said he pops in and out and you're usually sleeping. I told him he should wake you up, that you'd want to talk to him, but he says sleep is what you need now, to recover."

The explanation didn't help. She missed him. "How long have I been sleeping?"

"Most of the last sixteen or seventeen hours—all day. Drew said it wasn't uncommon. He said the sudden drop in the adrenaline you used to survive can really wipe you out. And that it isn't only your body healing; your mind is recouping as well. Shut down for repairs, he said." She grinned. "Mike said rebooting."

"Mike's here?"

"Was. He went down to see if the cafeteria's still open." She shook her head. "He didn't miss dinner—of course—and he ate two bologna sandwiches walking me up here, and he's still hungry. I figure when he graduates from high school, I'll just be swapping my grocery bill for his college tuition."

Sophie puffed out a soft laugh. She adored Jesse and happily placed her name close to the top of the list of her twelve *most* favorite people. Yet, she had to resist the urge to roll over and go back to sleep.

"I was thinking," Jesse said. "Did anyone call your father to let him know you're okay? Would you like me to?"

He'd come, Sophie knew. He'd need to see her. Was she ready to see the fear in his eyes? Was she up to watching him go pale with worry and the frantic concern he'd try to hide as he took in her condition? Was she willing to put him through that right now? He'd want to know.

Maybe after a little nap. . . . "Thanks, but he'll worry less if he can hear it from me. I'll call in a little bit."

Still and all, it would be lovely to sit on his lap and cry, to feel him stroking her hair and to hear his soothing offer of ice cream to make her all better. She could pretend to be very brave and let him put pink Band-Aids on all her boo-boos. She missed his smile and the deep tender love that softens his expression whenever he looked at her. She missed him.

She squeezed her eyes tight to ebb her tears and spoke quickly. "Have you heard anything about Elizabeth's funeral?"

"Monday morning."

"Can I go with you?"

"Absolutely. But are you—"

"Yes. Yes, I'm sure. It was all for me, Jesse. She saved my life." She felt awkward and self-centered when it occurred to her: "Unless they don't want me there."

"I don't think anyone's blaming you, honey." She studied Sophie's face. "And you shouldn't blame yourself. You didn't do anything wrong."

"I know," she said. And she did know it—but even the most innocent catalyst was a part of the explosion. She moaned. "I suppose everyone knows everything about everything by now."

"I'm afraid so." They shared a moment of sad regret.

"Which reminds me . . ." Jesse's warm heart would not stay down for long, at least not in front of Sophie. She dove deep into her bag and pulled out a set of clean clothes that Sophie recognized and a set of pajamas she didn't. "I thought you might need these and feel better in these. And I wasn't sure what you'd need, so I brought what I'd want." She set a large ziplock bag of toiletries on the nightstand. She chuckled. "I figured since Fred and his deputies had already been through your stuff, you wouldn't mind me doin' the same.

"*And* I found this." Jesse faltered. "I tried to call you to tell you about it. I thought it might be important. So when you didn't answer, I called Drew. He and Fred and half the county were already combing the countryside for you."

"Why didn't they use the GPS to locate my phone?"

"I think they tried. But it was either off or dead."

"But I'd just used it. Minutes before— How'd they know where to find us?"

"Billy called. I think if they'd known he was with you, they would have tracked his phone. But they didn't know."

She closed her eyes and turned her face straight up, whispering, "Billy."

It occurred to her: "Drew must have known we were in trouble sooner than I thought, when both his mother and I weren't at the café when he got there. Elizabeth didn't know that I'd told him we were meeting there."

"When Mike and I joined the search, he was sick with worry. In all his life I've never seen him so upset. You . . . and his mother."

Sophie didn't have to travel far to remember the fear of losing a mother . . . or the misery when it happened.

"I wasn't sure if I should bring this," Jesse said tentatively. She reached back into her bag slowly. "I found it . . . but I can take it home if you don't want to look at it, but I thought you might be interested because once I saw it and remembered and realized what I'd been seeing . . . you know, in you, that seemed so familiar to me, like I'd seen you before . . . remember I said that the other day? You said in another life maybe, and then with the murder and Maury and all, I didn't think about it again—and you probably didn't either—until Fred mentioned that the only thing that seemed to be missing from Maury's garage was—"

Sophie smiled at her friend. "Jesse. Is it a picture of Lonora?"

She nodded. "She was a freshman when I was a junior."

"I'd love to see it." She reached for the thin volume Jesse held against her chest.

Jesse opened the old school album to the place she'd marked. "Here. That one. That's her."

She took the book in both hands and strained her gritty eyes to focus on the black-and-white photos lined up across the page. Even if it hadn't been the same photo used in the newspaper, she didn't need Jesse's finger to point Lonora out.

Smiling thoughtfully, Sophie touched the image in wonder. She'd never seen, nor could she ever imitate, the utter euphoria in the girl's expression—the eager delight of a contented child. It made her pretty face exquisite—without reserve or concern or the knowledge of evil.

"Elizabeth said she took her own life," she said softly.

"I didn't know." Jesse matched her tone. "When it happened, people were shocked and angry that anyone would do such a thing to her—most of us assumed that it had to be a stranger. No one who knew her would hurt her. She was . . . I want to say special but I don't mean just *special ed*. She was truly special. Kind. Sweet. Happy. She thought everyone was her friend and no one I knew would want to disappoint her or make her think different."

She paused to recall. "I remember my mother telling me that she'd been attacked in Harvey Park and beaten badly; that it was more important than ever to avoid strangers. Later we heard that she'd died in her sleep. That's all. But thinking back on it now, I think people were still trying to protect her. I bet plenty of people knew plenty of details about what happened to her that night, but they were never discussed that I know of—no gossip or speculation. And dying innocently in her sleep was a kinder ending for her, even if people knew the truth about—" She pulled up short and looked at Sophie, suddenly shamefaced. "Maybe we were just protecting ourselves from the truth. Maybe we just didn't want to think about . . . that sort of evil being so close to us."

Maybe both of those statements were true—*who could blame them?* Sophie wondered. She gave her friend a drowsy smile. "I think you were right the first time."

It was clear that Jesse wasn't as sure, but she didn't push it—Sophie looked exhausted and needed to get her strength back.

"Can I get you anything before I go?" She stood up, and Sophie returned the yearbook. She made a quick decision, reopened the book, and ripped out a page. "I'd give you the whole thing but they're in it, too, and they're best forgotten."

"Thank you, Jesse." She reached up and took her hand. "For everything. Thank you."

"You're welcome. Are you sure you don't want me to call your dad?"

"I'm sure."

"What. The party's over?" Mike stood in the doorway, arms out in astonishment. "I missed it?"

"Hey, Mike."

"Where have you been?"

"Looking for a *get well soon* incentive." He produced a Hershey with Almonds bar while his eyebrows did push-ups. "Your favorite."

"How'd you know?"

"I empty your trash, remember?"

"You're not supposed to *go through* her trash."

"I don't—didn't. The wrapper was on top and dumping the trash is generally an eyes-open operation. But if you want me to wear a blindfold from now on, it might take me longer than usual to get it done." He grinned to disavow any impertinence and walked the candy bar over to the tray table. Placing it within her reach, he gave Sophie a good hard going over. "You've definitely looked better, but this isn't nearly as bad as I thought it would be."

"What kind of compliment is that?" Jesse frowned.

"It's not?"

"No."

"I saw this guy on YouTube who survived a train wreck—*he* was messed up."

"So, I don't look like a train wreck?"

He grinned and wagged his head. "More like the third car in a ten-car pile up, I think. What do you think?" he asked his mother, straight-faced.

"I think I'm going to take you home before they have to put Sophie on antidepressants."

A good chuckle made her ribs hurt, but it was worth it.

She'd hardly noticed the nurses coming and going, doing the vital-sign checks and testing her mental functions—and as soon as she announced her name, the year, and where she was before, she was asleep again before they left the room.

At one point she dreamt one of them stroked her cheek and kissed her on the forehead. The bizarre vision roused her enough to confirm the emptiness of her room with a quick slit-eyed scan before she slipped back into oblivion.

"She's sleeping." A woman spoke in a hushed voice.

It was morning. The last time she looked at the clock on the wall it said ten o'clock. A nurse had been by earlier and *strongly* encouraged her into a recliner and set her breakfast of almost-cooked fake eggs and great crispy bacon in front of her while she put fresh sheets on the bed. As it happened, the chair was a comfortable alternative to the bed, so the nurse gave her a pair of ugly socks, put a blanket over her lap, and she dozed. Heavily.

She didn't budge for the voice at the door. She didn't recognize the soft voice, and she wasn't up to unknown visitors—though her current position would indicate otherwise, she supposed. At least, not until she heard a man say, "I'll hang. I'm not going home until I see her."

"Billy. Come in. Please. Both of you." Ava stood behind her brother in unnatural reserve. Sophie pushed herself up in the chair. "Ava."

Her mind was an empty chamber. Why hadn't she prepared things to say to the McCarrens? Come to think of it, what had she planned to say to Drew when she saw him? Their pain, their confusion—there was nothing she could say that would change it for them, nothing to make it right again. It wasn't an enormous leap to assume they were as emotionally overwhelmed as she and that whatever fell from her mouth would make no difference anyway.

"Ava. I don't know what to say. I'm so sorry about your mother. I'm sorry for your loss." Ava nodded, finding it difficult to meet Sophie's eyes—while Billy, with tiny strips of tape across the wound at his hairline, strolled to the other side of the chair to sit on the bed. Sophie held out her hand and he took it like an old, dear friend. "How's your head? How are you?"

"I'm on my way home. I have a little concussion headache, but other than that I'm fine. You look much better."

"I am. I think. I sleep a lot." He nodded, seeming to identify. "So I'll probably get to go home today, too, then. As soon as I get the okay. From my doctor," she said, looking at him askance, hoping he'd say something about Drew.

"Dr. Kelsey's slow, huh?" He shook his head, mildly annoyed for her sake. "That was the sheriff's dumb idea, not letting Drew be your doctor. Said it wouldn't be ethical or legal or something, so he asked Kelsey from the ER to keep an eye on you. You know, since you weren't going to be here long and he already knew all your stuff—from that night."

"Oh." It made sense but it didn't explain why Drew hadn't come to be with her.

"Course, Drew's been keeping an eye on *him,* so it's basically a twofer." He grinned. "Plus, he gave me reports on you without breaking any confidentiality rules, since they wouldn't let me come down to see you for myself until now. Worked out great . . . except for Kelsey being slow."

"Oh." Still not the answer she was hoping for.

"Drew hasn't been in to see you, has he?" Ava asked, her voice soft and atypically timid.

She shook her head.

"He hasn't?" Billy was open-mouthed.

"He's been by, I heard, but I haven't seen him. He doesn't wake me up."

"He's been kind of busy," Ava said. "With my dad and stuff. It doesn't mean anything. He worries about you. I'll make sure to tell him to wake you up next time."

Sophie looked up into Ava's face. "I was wondering if it would be all right . . . would you mind if I attend your mother's funeral?"

"Really?" She looked surprised.

"Unless you think someone might object. Your dad or your sister. Drew. I'd like to go but I'd understand—"

"Well, sure. Yes, you can come. Of course. You don't hate her?" The question came on an impulse.

"No. I don't hate her." Ava's eyes darted to Billy and back. "Ava, she saved my life."

There was another uncertain glance at her brother and her voice dropped low. "She didn't save your mother."

So much of Sophie wanted to put all she'd learned that night away somewhere, lock it up and forget about it. Not possible, she knew—not even when some parts of it seemed so simple. "It was a mistake. She made a mistake. A huge mistake. And she spent her life paying a huge price for it."

"What she did . . . I mean, I feel lost—and I'm so angry and disappointed and ashamed of her at the same time, but she's my mother—"

"But that's all you need to remember. She's your mother. She loved you. And you love her." She hesitated, wanting to console her friend. "A very wise man recently told me we can pick and choose our memories. Choose the good ones, Ava."

"How can you forgive her for what she did?"

"I don't know." That very same wise man told her: *It's the choices we make that whittle the life we live.* And her mother's words came, too. *Forgiveness is the choice we make so our hearts can heal.* Sophie was making a choice.

"I was taught to forgive. I was brought up believing it was the right thing to do." Sophie smiled. Ava didn't. "I'm not very good at it, though. Someday, maybe, I'll try to forgive Frank Lanyard. But I can hold a grudge as tight as anyone. I can be really spiteful. And I play dirty sometimes. I'm not special. I'm as human as anyone. But the truth of the matter is: What your mother did all those years ago, it just doesn't feel like something that's mine to forgive.

"It's Lonny's to forgive. And Lonora's. Maybe even those four animals who might have had different lives if she'd stepped forward. But me? If she'd gotten involved, I wouldn't be here. How can I hate her for permitting me to be?"

It was a conundrum, all right. One they could all appreciate—and did, in silence, with furrowed brows.

"I think, too"—Sophie said after a moment, reckoning out loud—"she tried to make up for what she did. Helping Lonny care for his daughter, making sure I went to a good home. She even did what she thought would keep me safe when I came back here. She tried. And in the end it took her mind and her life. How could anyone ask her for more?" She looked at her and passed on Lonny's advice. "Forgive her, Ava."

The rest of their visit was an awkward mix of renewed offers of friendship, long pauses, and attempts at not-so-easy optimism.

Standing, with minimal help to hug them goodbye, Sophie was relieved to note that the places of true pain scattered over her body were now simply sore, stiff aches like the rest of her.

She was healing—everywhere.

It was hard to tell if anything she said was a comfort to the McCarrens, but it went a long way in clearing up the muddle in her own mind.

If she believed that everything happened for a reason—and she did tend to lean in that direction—then Cliff Palmeroy spotting sweet Lonora Campbell traveling to the top of the mountains to see the snow that evening was meant to happen. Because of who those boys were at the time, the choices they made that night twisted that harmless encounter into something diabolical. Then, from a completely different direction—through a completely different series of events—Elizabeth and Arthur's lives collided with theirs. And the choices *they* made skewed the episode down yet another path . . . to her.

How was *that* for making sense of the senseless? she mused, returning to bed for another nap before lunch.

Lonny returned in the early afternoon with some good news.

"Sheriff Murphy had your car towed back to my place the other night."

She'd forgotten all about it. Her lovely Liberty. "I dropped the keys."

"Locksmith cut ya a new one." And before she could mention it, he said, "Got me a young detailer who owes me a favor. He'll have the backseat lookin' like new in no time."

"Thank you."

"He returned this, too." From his pocket he produced her cell phone. Dead as Aunt Debbie's dog.

Her mind flashed on Elizabeth reaching for it: *Give it to me for now. We'll need to get our story straight first.* Sophie chose not to remember more.

Best of all, Lonny brought a photo album. Sophie was captivated and studied the photos of her great-grandparents and Lonny's brother Sam and his family—soaked up every detail of the images of Cora and Lonora until they started to blur with eyestrain.

"Rest well, Granddaughter," he said as he was leaving.

"Will I see you again tomorrow, Grandpa?"

They grinned. "You bet."

It was a busy afternoon.

Graham Metzer stopped by to pay his proper, attorney-like condolences—but as an aside, also professed his profound astonishment in Arthur and Elizabeth's behavior. He'd known them both for years, and the story that had been related to him was too much to imagine.

"I took the liberty of calling Hollis. I hope you don't mind. I knew he'd want to know . . . not so much his father's part in this business, but about you. He sends his love, and I hope you won't think it presumptive of me, but I promised I'd call him again, once I'd seen you, to let him know when you might be up for his visit."

"Anytime. And thank you Mr. Metzer. It would have been . . . horrible having to tell him the truth myself. Thank you." He smiled and started to take his leave. "One more thing? Please. BelleEllen."

It was all she had to say for the man to bow his head in understanding and agreement. He'd make the arrangements for the transfer.

Mike appeared in her doorway a few minutes after Mr. Metzer left. They watched an episode each of *American Chopper* and *Mythbusters* on Discovery Channel; he ate the Hershey with Almonds he'd given her, drank her box of apple juice from lunch, and split. She loved Mike.

And she told his mother so when she walked in an hour later.

Jesse came bearing flowers, a chocolate-and-vanilla milkshake—Sophie's pick—two magazines, and twenty minutes of amusing gossip that had nothing to do with anyone the patient knew personally before Dr. Kelsey and a nurse arrived.

The doctor was a friendly thirty-something man who said he was glad to see her more alert than the day before.

"I'm sorry I missed you," Sophie said with an awkward chuckle. "So completely. I don't remember you at all."

"I get that *all* the time," he said in mock dismay. "I am an unsung hero if there ever was one. I'm savin' lives left and right down there and no one remembers me."

He laughed then and told her it was common—that disproportionate sleeping and vague recall are part of the body's defense mechanism. She was going to be just fine . . . and he wasn't too offended.

He examined her cuts and bruises—particularly those on her feet and knees. The scalp wound was a gusher but not grave, he said. He flashed a penlight in her eyes, had her squeeze his hands, and eventually informed her she was well enough to be discharged in the morning.

Finally, he sat beside her on the bed to remove the Telfa dressing covering a laceration on her forearm. He debated leaving it exposed then started to replace it with . . . a pink Band-Aid.

"Hey. That's not. . . . Where'd you get that?" His eyes lit before he could smile. She was already sitting up and staring at the door. "Dad?"

The door began to open slowly, tentatively at first and then he was there. Tall and a smidge too stout; a Caesar's crown of graying hair and warm brown eyes behind round wire glasses—unwavering devotion in his expression.

"Daddy."

"Baby."

She was out of bed and in his arms before the first tear slipped.

Chapter Sixteen

"Jesse gave me the blue room across from yours. It's a lovely old house. You can see she's put a lot of work into it," Tom Shepard said, promenading with his daughter on his arm down the second-floor corridor of Clearfield General Hospital shortly after the dinner hour.

Dr. Kelsey's only stipulation to her discharge the next morning was more walking. This was their third go-around.

"Isn't she great? And Mike? Have you met him yet?"

"His mother warned me about him, but he was out when I arrived."

"Warned you," she scoffed. "Wait until you meet him, Dad. He's a great kid. Really funny. An *ardent* basketball player. And don't let her fool you—he's her pride and joy."

He smiled, having already assumed that.

Sophie couldn't stop looking at him and was fully aware that it was more fear than happiness that kept her from looking away. She couldn't get close enough or hold him tight enough. And he was content to let her lean as heavily on his

calm, gentle strength as she needed to . . . because that's what
a *real* dad does.

"She certainly seems fond of you."

"The feeling is mutual. I don't know what I would have
done without her this whole time." How do you explain
someone like Jesse? How do you describe a friend who knows
you well enough to call your father when you can't quite bring
yourself to do it—even though you want to. Was it even possible? She giggled. "She'd tear into the sheriff if he even *looked*
like he was going to accuse me of murder again."

He chuckled. "Well, let's face it: You are quite sinister-
looking for a kindergarten teacher."

Ha! She was *flint*!

"Right. To a shy five-year-old. For the first week of school.
Maybe."

They turned a corner laughing—and her legs wobbled a bit
when she saw Drew at the nurses' station up ahead. She had
a flash of déjà vu taking in the white lab coat and the small
laptop that held his rapt attention.

Not walk-into-a-wall handsome, he was tall and fit with
the customary number of limbs and short, dark wavy hair. A
truly ordinary man. And truly magnificent to her. Truly. It
was as if a blurry film had been peeled away, leaving her world
brighter, clearer, more defined—in every sense.

"Oops." Her father steadied her misstep. "Getting tired,
honey?"

By the time she realized he'd spoken, he'd already seen
whatever look she had on her face and tracked her gaze to
Drew.

"Yeah. A little." Too sorry to say it, she knew her fatigue
would depend on Drew. If when he turned and saw them, his
eyes sparked in the way that caused her pulses to skitter and
it was clear they were still in mutual crazy-aboutness, then

she'd be up to a marathon. If they didn't, if they weren't, she wasn't sure her heart would ever get up again.

The cuts on the sides of her feet remained tender to walk on. She knew it wasn't necessary to conceal the way she limped, but somehow it seemed critical to appear less weak, less injured . . . less pitiable. Sympathy was not what she wanted from him.

They strolled into his peripheral vision and he looked up— she didn't miss the slight hesitation in him before he turned his head to look at them.

For a moment his uncertainty was not enough to hide the light in his eyes, that glow that was more than the fire and life inside him, beyond his empathy and compassion. They were brilliant with delight and desire. His affection made her heart swell and buoyed her spirits. His ardor thrilled her, made her shiver.

For a moment.

He didn't even glance away, merely blinked and it was gone—and he was Dr. Andrew Kingston McCarren, an extraordinarily kind and understanding physician and an all-around great guy . . . but not more.

"Hey, Sophie." Dr. McCarren was quick and thorough with his appraisal. "You're looking much better. How are you feeling?"

Did she look as devastated as she felt? She caught herself staring, looked away and muttered. "Better."

So she was going to be in a train wreck after all, she thought, seeing the headlights coming down the track in her mind. And there she was: aware, waiting, feeling helpless to stop it.

"Good. That's good news." For a long moment they tried to ignore the uneasiness raining down on them. "And you must be her dad." He held out his hand. "Drew McCarren."

His hand was taken readily. "Tom Shepard. I'm deeply sorry

for your loss, young man. I know your family's in a terrible place right now."

"Yes, sir. Thank you." The strain in his voice brought her gaze to his face. He had more to say, but the words were stuck in his throat.

"I don't know how to begin to express my gratitude to you and your family for all you've done for my daughter."

"Please. There's no need." Stiff. Brittle.

Her father backed down, not wanting to press on anything painful. "At least let me thank you for calling to let me know about it."

Drew gave a short nod and said, "You're welcome. I—"

"You. You called him?" Yes. Yes, of course, he would—without asking, without uncertainty—because he knew her, knew her heart.

He darted a glance in her direction, noted the emotional quiver in her chin, and shot back to Tom Shepard. "I figured she'd want you here and you'd want to know so . . . it was nothing." He jammed his hands into the pockets of his jacket and immediately pulled them out again. "Ah. Well. I'm happy to hear you're on the mend. I guess I should get going." In a swift automatic motion, he snapped two keys on his computer and pulled the cover down, explaining, "Patients to see. Good to meet you, Mr. Shepard."

"Doctor." He shook Drew's hand again. "I'm in your debt."

He was wagging his head when his gaze slipped into Sophie's eyes. He squinted as if deliberately hardening his eyes—but he couldn't hide his deep remorse. He swallowed, then swallowed again. "Take care, Sophie."

"Drew. Don't."

His smile was small and resigned. "I'm sorry. I can't do this."

When he turned, snatched up his computer and started to

walk away, Sophie cringed at the noise in her head, like finger-nails on a chalkboard. Or, come to think of it, maybe on *flint*. She was not some poor, helpless thing caught in the headlights of a train. She was *flint* . . . damn it!

A fleeting look at her father and he graciously started melt-ing into the woodwork.

"Drew." He stopped, shoulders drooping—his escape foiled. She strode forward and spoke in a soft, private voice at his back. "I know you're hurting. I know what it's like to lose your mother. There's no other pain like it. I know. But, please, don't shut me out. We can talk. I can help you, if you let me." She waited. She watched his back expand and con-tract with short, tight breaths. "So. You're just going to walk away? Feeling the way we feel happens so often in your life that you can afford to throw it away without even talking to me?" She heard him sigh; watched him bow his head. "Talk to me. Please. Turn around and tell me why you're doing this."

He set the computer back on the counter as a nurse rounded the corner into the nurse station. One look at the two of them and she suddenly recalled something she'd forgotten to do else-where.

"Come on, Sophie," he said, swinging from formal to frosty. "Too much has happened. Everything is different; it's changed. What did you expect? That life would simply go on as if Thursday night never happened?"

"No. But I didn't expect you to be like this."

"How'd you expect me to be?"

There was a clear line between what a person hoped for and what they were reasonably allowed to expect. She knew that. She'd hoped he'd hold her in his arms every second of the day and night till she was ready to let go. She'd hoped that nothing would change between them. Realistically, though, at the very least, she'd expected they'd work their way through it together and . . . yeah . . . eventually get back to where they left off.

"I expected you to be heartbroken. I expected you to trust me with your feelings. I expected you to know that I love you and I want to be here for you. And I expected that you of all people would know that it wasn't your life that ended." She paused, knowing that last one might sting a little, but he said nothing. "I guess I expected too much."

"Maybe I'm just more of your bad luck with men." And there it was . . . he looked at her sympathetically. Her fingers itched to slap him.

"Maybe you are," she said gently, slow to reconcile. "But it isn't because of what happened the other night. I'm sorry about your mother, Drew. More than I can tell you. But nothing about that night is my fault." He opened his mouth to speak but he'd had his chance; she cut him off. "Nothing about that night is *your* fault. And nothing that happened that night twenty-eight years ago is our fault. We weren't involved, never have been. None of it *ever* had anything to do with us. So mourn your mother, you should. But don't kid yourself. If you are more of my bad luck with men, it's not because of what happened—it's because you want to be."

Her tone dared him to contradict her. When he didn't, she sidestepped him and limped back to her room—head high and heartsick.

Tom Shepard stood when his daughter broke into the room, swinging the door closed behind her as she hurried straight into his open arms.

It didn't seem fair that Elizabeth McCarren's funeral was less populated than Arthur's. True, she was not the leader of a congregation of Unitarians, but she was a member of the local

Presbyterian Church—and she sat on every charitable committee in town. And while there were plenty of people there to stare and whisper when Sophie walked in with her father, Jesse, and Mike, she had braced herself for far more.

On the other hand, which was far more generous, perhaps so many of the good citizens of Clearfield stayed away to spare Elizabeth's husband and children any excess emotions that didn't directly pertain to their loss—like having to deal with curious, prying eyes, awkward comments, and unconscious but judgmental body language.

That's the explanation Sophie chose to believe anyway. That muggy, overcast morning she deliberately chose to think only good thoughts, dwell only on pleasant memories, and hope the McCarrens—and Elizabeth's soul—found the peace they so needed.

And that was all she was going to think about—though Drew was ever-present in her heart.

Sitting in the back of the church to cause as little disruption as possible made it easy for Lonny to find them—and *his* arrival disrupted those gathered . . . a lot. So much so that the family turned their heads to look back. Lonny stood like a noble snow-capped mountain and gave a respectful nod to them and their sorrow—and in return received their silent, humble welcome. He took a seat in the pew beside Mike, but not before he locked eyes with Sophie, who beamed at him with great pride and love.

After a moment, Sophie looked to her left to catch her dad's reaction—he winked and beamed at *her* with great pride and love.

Perhaps it was because a happy, contented life was all she'd ever known that she found it . . . well, not exactly easy but also not grueling or complicated to find closure to the past two weeks. Maybe Mike was right; maybe she was simply rebooting to her original default mode because her qualms at having her past and her present meet for the first time were mild and few. Her romantic relationships were clearly an on-going, head-banging nightmare of epic proportions, but that might be due to the fact that her bar was set extraordinarily high by the men who'd already proven their love and trustworthiness to her.

And so it was that when Lonny came to see her at Jesse's after her release from the hospital, and she introduced him to her father, the initially awkward meeting was as short lived as she'd expected it to be, turning quickly into acceptance and appreciation for the sacrifices they'd both made and the gifts each had given. *These* men knew love was a rare and unconditional miracle, meant to be cherished and foolish to ignore.

Her dad, not as reserved as Lonny, was the first to launch into the "I remember this one time" stories of Sophie's childhood that her grandfather seemed to guzzle down like homemade cider. After a while Jesse and Mike stepped out on the porch to join the gaiety and a cool summer breeze, which had Sophie unwinding in a heightened but unfinished satisfaction.

One more person would have made it a perfect afternoon.

And so it was at the funeral the next day that the two men—father and grandfather—nodded and smiled in friendship as their lives were now forever intertwined.

They hadn't planned on attending the interment—assuming the McCarrens would appreciate the privacy—nor were those congregated invited from the pulpit. But when Billy found them after escorting his mother's casket safely to the hearse and requested they come, they couldn't refuse him.

In sorrow and profound regret, Elizabeth's dearest friends and relatives gathered at her grave. Her immediate family grouped close together, the women comforting one another and weep-ing behind their dark glasses; the men standing stoically in theirs. Sophie's group stood across from them but behind the other mourners.

The minister's final words were not vague or ambiguous. He spoke of Elizabeth's great devotion to her family and to her community; her empathy toward those less fortunate and to those who found the obstacles on the paths they'd chosen too great to overcome. He briefly addressed her humanness and invited only those without sin to throw stones at the memory of the woman whose sole purpose in life was to love her family and to give friendship and comfort to her neighbors.

Knowing that her reluctance to approach the family before leaving was mostly selfish, Sophie sought out Billy first.

No words were necessary. They simply embraced. And where he had once appeared from the darkness, held her and imparted his courage and strength to her, she now passed an equal portion of hers to him.

He felt it and squeezed her tight before releasing her. "I hear you're leaving today."

"Yeah. This afternoon. Daddy wants to drive over to the university and look around a bit. Show me the ol' alma mater. We'll leave for home sometime tomorrow."

"You're leaving?" This came from Ava, who was accepting Tom Shepard's condolences a few feet away. "So soon? Now? But we've hardly talked and I want to. Not, you know, about . . . all this but . . . like before."

Sophie grinned and grabbed her up. "Like friends. Yes." She held her a few more seconds, then pulled away to look at her—dark glasses notwithstanding. "I have a grandfather here, you know. I plan to see a lot of him, so I'll be back. Soon. I'll call."

They were hugging again, in empathy and farewell, when

the last three McCarrens approached, having already spoken to everyone else. Drew, hanging back, made the introductions to his father, Joseph, and his sister, Pam.

Pam was stiff and formal due to the stress of the moment, her natural manner, or a prejudice toward Sophie—it was a mystery. She thanked her for coming and wished her a quick recovery and a safe trip home before excusing herself to follow her younger siblings back to the car.

Dr. Joseph McCarren had removed his sunglasses and slipped them into his jacket pocket before holding his hand out to Sophie. When she took it, he covered it with his other one and with an expression so forlorn that it pulled at her heart, he said, "I cannot tell you how I regret what has happened."

She was acutely aware of his many losses—his friend, partner, and wife, the sanctity of his marriage, his faith in what he believed to be true and real in his life.

Her nod was more agreement than acceptance. "I regret it as well. Please accept my deepest condolences."

He seemed to sense her understanding. His expression softened and he said simply, "Thank you."

After a polite inquiry about her health he, too, wished her a safe trip back to Ohio.

And there she was, alone with Drew.

The air was humid, cloying, sticking to her. It was clogging her nose and throat—she was suffocating and she couldn't tell if Drew could see she was dying because she couldn't make herself look at him.

"Sophie—"

"My condolences," she blurted. "I deeply regret my part in your mother's death, but you have to know it was unintentional and that I never wanted to cause her, you, or the rest of your family any pain." Her brief glance at his face was his only chance to see the truth in her eyes. It was time to walk away. "Take care of yourself."

"Sophie."

She stopped and turned back slowly, tamping down her scattered emotions. She hadn't practiced saying anything else and wasn't sure she could trust herself.

"What?" He waited so long to speak, she looked at him and spoke again, sharply. "What?"

"I just wanted to say, again, how sorry I am."

It was in her to scream. She wanted to shake him so hard his head would rattle, kick him in the shins and then hold him so gently, so tenderly and for so long that he'd eventually come to realize that she was a part of him and that they shared a love that was special and true and not to be ignored. But she hadn't practiced that either.

"Me too, Drew." She stretched up on her toes and kissed his cheek. "Bye."

Seeing that Mike and her father were in Jesse's car, she chose to climb into Lonny's truck and closed the door. She felt low as a worm in a gopher's basement.

Lonny studied her. "I'm old. Chock-full-o-wisdom and sage advice, you know."

Her lips bowed but couldn't hold a smile. "I know."

"Never had anyone to use it on till now," he said casually. "They say all the very best of them guru types don't go round spoutin' off their clever, deep-thought answers to just anyone — they play it close to the vest and wait to be asked."

The silence inside the truck grew so loud, it started to pop and crack before it came to her that he was waiting to be asked. She slipped him a sidelong glance, chuckled involuntarily, and then let her frustration fly, growling, deep and angry, in her throat. "Oh! He makes me *so* mad."

Lonny's nod was somber and scholarly as he started up the truck. "I can see that."

"All he can say is 'I'm sorry, I'm sorry'," she said, lowering her voice to illustrate how dull Drew sounded. "He won't talk to me. He won't tell me what he's feeling. And it's right there on his face. I can see how he's feeling but he won't . . . talk to me. Not that I want him to actually talk about it—like *speak*—I know lots of people can't. But he could at least let me be there with him, for him. He's in so much pain, Grandpa. I want to help but . . . well, he's sorry!" She crossed her arms over her chest in a huff. "He won't tell me if he thinks what happened to his mother is my fault or if he feels like he has to take responsibility for his mother's actions. No explanations. Nothing. He just says there's too much between us—and that he's sorry.

"Well, I'll make him sorry. I'll make him rue the day he met me because if he thinks I'm walking away to make this easy on him, he is quite mistaken. I may be just a kindergarten teacher, but I know stuff. And one thing I know for sure is that you don't give up on love."

His gaze left the road briefly to meet hers. He nodded his veteran insightfulness on the subject like one of the magi and she continued.

"I'll go home. For now. I'll give him a little space and a little time to think . . . and to grieve . . . but I'm not just going to disappear. I'm not going to let him forget. I'll come back—to visit you and Jesse and Billy and Ava." She spread her arms at the obvious. "I'm going to be here. A lot. And if he thinks he's sorry now—ha!—he doesn't know sorry yet. *I'll* make him sorry. I'm flint. And I'll make sure—"

"You're what now?"

"Never mind." Her cheeks heated and she lost most of the

wind in her sails. "I'm just . . . really frustrated. And really sad."

"Course you are. I'm disappointed myself. I always figured that one to be a real smart fella, being a doctor and all."

"Well, he is smart. Just not about this." She sighed, feeling better, calmer for having let off some steam. "He'll figure it out. On his own, the hard way, but he'll figure it out." She paused and then cringed. "Ah, jeez. I said rue, didn't I? Can you believe he made me say rue?"

Lonny looked at her, pressed his lips together, and shook his head gravely. "No, indeed, I cannot."

Day 18. That was her thought between the outer fringe of her REM sleep and the vague awareness of the shuffling in the hall outside her bedroom door. She identified it as *Dad* with her eyes still closed and groggily reminded herself that while she'd given up her own apartment when her mother became ill, and stayed for a handful of reasons after she died, it was time to move out again. He was a *noisyearlyriser*—and she dreamt next of dinosaurs.

The clanking and the clipping and the inconsistent bird noises swelling into her room through the open window beside her bed had her scowling before her eyelids parted on the too-bright sunlight lasering in on the rug, dragging with it the too-sweet reek of fresh-cut grass, diesel oil, and corn chips that had, not so long ago, been the very essence of a long, lazy, lovely summertime to her. Lately, not so much. Lately, not much pleased her at all—and being a poopyhead was not her natural state of being. It felt heavy and hollow at once. She'd been trying to be her usual happy self, but privately, she was feeling pretty poopy.

After a brief muddle through her mind during which she concluded that it was still *Day 18* since she'd left Clearfield, she turned her back to the window, beat her pillow with her fist, and went back to sleep.

Tried.

He's talking to someone, she groaned mentally. It was like having a fly in the room. Buzzing and stopping, then buzzing again. She flopped onto her back and stared at the ancient four-sided patch-crack in the ceiling—a parallelogram that looked like a square from one side of the room and a rhombus from the other. If her dad was talking to someone down in the kitchen, he hadn't gone to work—which meant it was the third weekend she'd had to endure since she last saw Drew. Every week seemed like a year.

Her uncle Fred often dropped in early Saturday morning for coffee—before his errands in town, to get his motor started, he'd say. Her dad made really strong coffee so Fred always said either that it grew hair on his chest or it got his motor—

Except yesterday was Thursday. Day 17. Is it a holiday weekend? No. Something's wrong.

She was out of bed—her frizzy topknot in serious bed-headed disarray—and her wonderfully worn Buckeye T-shirt and shorty sport shorts were still bed-warm by the time she reached the top step and stopped short.

She knew the voice. It made everything inside her go liquid, like melting ice, as she listened.

" . . . I thought if we ever found her, we'd find her dead." Drew went silent for several seconds. "That's the first time I've said it out loud. Sounds even worse than it does in my head—and thinking it was . . ." She lowered her head and took two or three steps down to hear better. "We'd barely spotted the light in the woods when we heard the shot. I thought it then. By the time we got there, Billy was crying over a body and I thought it then, too." His voice lowered with emotion. "When I realized it was my mother and that she was dead, I was—well, shocked doesn't exactly cover it. I was horrified . . . and confused and . . . and for just a second I was . . . no, it was more than a second . . ."

When he was not forthcoming with a word, her dad offered, "Grateful? Relieved?"

"Grateful." He tried it on like a new shirt. "I was grateful. Not grateful that my mother was dead, of course, but grateful that it wasn't Sophie. And there's a hair's difference between that and being grateful Sophie wasn't dead, too. You see? And it seemed wrong—in my head—like I'd chosen between them. But that's how I felt, and then I felt guilty."

Part of Sophie wished she could watch his face during the long pauses in his account, though she knew the emotion in his frank expression would be crushing to see. She went two steps lower, wondering if she could catch a glimpse of him without interrupting—suspecting it wouldn't be any easier on him to tell her these things than it was to tell a relative stranger—who happened to be her father . . . who happened to make his living being easy to talk to and listening with care.

"When I heard Jesse calling her name and seeming to expect her to answer . . . well, I don't know. Somewhere in there— between seeing my mother and what Lanyard did to Sophie and hearing what Mother did and almost losing Sophie and not being there for either of them—I wasn't sure I wanted to, or even could, keep feeling the way I did about her. It was . . . too much. It felt out of control. *I* felt out of control."

Out of control. His feelings for her made him feel out of control. Believing he had no feelings for her made *her* feel out of control. *Oh, surely there was a happy medium here somewhere,* she thought, her chest tight with optimism.

The next step moaned slightly, briefly, but not enough to disturb them.

"It took me too long to understand that I felt differently about them because I love them differently, in different ways . . . for different reasons. And to remember that emotions don't parade by, one at a time, so you can pick and choose. They come all at once in massive proportions. And you can't always tell them apart or decide to feel one more than another. You just feel them all, all at once. I've seen it. A million times. I just couldn't see it in me." He paused. Sophie could all but see him collecting himself, though the stress in his voice remained. "Of course, by the time I did, it was too late. I'd pushed her away.

"So I came to tell her . . . I want Sophie to know that as enormous and scary and almost unbearable as it can be to love her sometimes, living without her is worse." His voice lowered as he said, "I hurt her. I know that. I came to say I'm sorry."

As the silence in the kitchen grew, Sophie waited, anticipating the soft throat-clearing that always signaled what her father seemed to deem his turn to talk.

It came and he spoke calmly. "I agree with you. And it doesn't seem to me that anything you've told me is unnatural. Extraordinary circumstances produce extraordinary emotions, which in turn produce extraordinary reactions. I think, in fact, it would have been extraordinary and quite unnatural if you hadn't felt overwhelmed and out of control. I also believe that it'll be considerably easier to acquire Sophie's forgiveness than it's been to forgive yourself—but one is not more important than the other."

There was an abrupt change in her father's manner.

"Now, first, I feel I should tell you that while it is unexpectedly gratifying—and sentimentally satisfying—it isn't necessary for you to explain yourself or to inform me of your intentions toward Sophie . . . even if she is living in my home. However, that said, if you can relieve this blue funk she's been in lately and get her to stop scribbling your name on the grocery lists, you have my blessing and I will be forever in your debt. Tuesday evening I spent thirty minutes after work looking for 'Drew laundry detergent' before I realized what she'd done."

She heard Drew's chuckle and was again startled to think that every time she believed she could not love her father more, she did.

"Also, while Sophie has been blessed with an easy ability to forgive, I would advise you not to use the word *sorry* when you apologize. She's had several very peculiar reactions to it lately. Although, if I'm not mistaken, it might not be necessary to use any words at all because I'm certain I heard the step, sixth from the bottom, creak in the hall a few minutes ago and"—Sophie heard a kitchen chair move across the floor— "I'm fairly certain she's been listening."

Drew was at the bottom of the steps before Tom Shepard finished speaking.

Being embarrassed at having been caught eavesdropping was nothing compared to watching the joy in his eyes turn a little amused and hungry as he drank her in head to toe and back again.

In the six feet between them, regret and forgiveness bounced freely back and forth between leaps of faith and bounding love, soaring hopes and the mounting fervor of promises that were just as binding unsaid as said.

And then they smiled, as friends . . . and more.

"I'm redeeming my rain check." He held up the invisible chit for her to see. "You owe me a date."

Insights,
Interviews
& More...

About the author

2 Meet Mary Kay McComas

About the book

3 Author note

7 Discussion Topics for Book Clubs

Read on

8 More from Mary Kay McComas

Meet
Mary Kay McComas

Kathleen Branigan

MARY KAY MCCOMAS started her writing career twenty-five years ago. To date she's written twenty-one short contemporary romances and five novellas; *Something About Sophie* is her third novel. She was born in Spokane, Washington, and now lives in a small town in the beautiful Shenandoah Valley of Virginia with her husband, three dogs, a cat, and her four children nearby. ❧

Author Note

ASK ANY AUTHOR and they'll tell you that the question they are most frequently asked is: Where do you get your ideas?

In fact, it is asked so frequently that Google has more than twenty-six pages (at which point I stopped counting) dedicated to explanations as wide and varied as the authors who attempt them.

Luckily for you, I agree with most of these explanations. Ideas come from everywhere and nowhere, from personal encounters to dreams to—as Stephen King suggests in his wonderful book *On Writing*—simply asking "what if."

On rare occasions, ideas arrive in a short summary with a beginning, middle, and an end that the writer must flesh out, warp, and manipulate into a story—a story with substance, with conflict and resolution, and vivid images that will, hopefully, resonate with the people who read it. But more often ideas come as a kernel or two that must be ground into flour between a rock and the top of your head. Long story short, so to speak: they don't come easy.

The idea for *Something About Sophie* was of the former breed. A fully developed concept that I kneaded like clay, then pressed and squeezed into a story of my own. And this is how it came about . . .

I live in the country. It takes seven hours straight to mow my entire lawn, front and back. I don't have a gardener or even a lawn service, and before my ▶

3

kids were old enough to take their turns, I did it.

It is a wonderfully mindless job. Going around and around and around I pondered many a seed of a story that gradually grew and produced fruit in the form of one of the many short contemporary romances I wrote for the Loveswept line at Bantam Books. (Note from my agent: many of Mary Kay's romances are available as e-books from Amazon and Barnes & Noble.)

For seven hours a week it was just me, my lawn tractor, and my choice for album-of-the-day played full blast (so I could hear it over the mower, of course) over and over so I could belt out the songs with unabashed off-key enthusiasm.*

I did a lot of mowing with Motown—The Supremes of the sixties before Diana went solo, a little Marvin Gaye and *Greatest Hits* by Mary Wells (who didn't record enough, if you ask me). And of course, The Four Seasons—who better to scream out those high notes with than Frankie Valli? I was soulful with the amazing Aretha Franklin. I was killer with *Thriller*. And who doesn't love Bonnie Raitt, Cher, Bette Midler, George Strait, and Fleetwood Mac? And Dan Fogelberg? Billy Joel is my favorite piano man and little Dolly Parton's big

* Portable MP3 players appeared in 1999 so, yes, the tapes and CDs mentioned played repeatedly, unshuffled, at least seven times before I put the mower away. I *really* love the music I love.

voice was on repeat. Plus, here it is in black and white: I love ABBA and the Bee Gees—my children accept this about me.

In the summer of 1994, a year after the release of Garth Brooks's fifth studio album, *In Pieces*, I was all about "Standing Outside the Fire," "Callin' Baton Rouge," and "American Honky-Tonk Bar Association." I mangled them all. "The Night I Called the Old Man Out," "One Night a Day," "Kickin' and Screamin'." The whole album is lawn mower legend.

Except for "The Night Will Only Know."

"The Night Will Only Know" is not the sort of song you sing along with—not happy or upbeat or even broken-hearted sad. It's disturbing. And haunting. I listened.

It tells the story of two people who are having an affair and accidentally witness the attack and murder of a woman. The next day the woman's death is reported as a suicide, which always confuses me since it's hard to hide an attack, but it adds to the evil in the story. The thing is, the couple didn't step in to help her and didn't step up to tell the truth later because to do so would bring to light the sin *they* committed that night. They chose to save their secret. But wait, it gets worse. Not only is the night privy to their deception and a daily reminder of their cowardice and failure, but it also keeps the secrets of the murder that took place, why it happened . . . and ▶

Author Note *(continued)*

who got away with it. Is that twisted or what? It's so wrong and so morally depraved—and so *human* in that heroes are heroes because the rest of us are not—because looking away is not uncommon and because we all might be tempted do the same thing, only hoping we'd be different.

Of course, this isn't the sort of fare a writer of short contemporary romances would cook up for inspiration. But it is certainly a scenario to be dumped into the cauldron of ideas on the back burner, stewed for eighteen years, and eventually ladled out as my version of southern small-town gumbo . . . *Something About Sophie.*

I hope you enjoy Sophie's story. I hope it does justice to the thought-provoking song written by Stephanie Davis, Jenny Yates, and Garth Brooks that so stirred me.

With *Sophie* following *What Happened to Hannah* and set in the same rural Virginia town, I see a trilogy in my future with *Don't Ask Alice*. Please watch for it.

—Mary Kay McComas

Discussion Topics for Book Clubs

1. Was there a specific theme (or themes) that the author emphasized throughout the novel? What do you think she was trying to get across to the reader?

2. Did you feel sympathy for Elizabeth? Truthfully, what would you have done in her place that fateful night?

3. How many times did Sophie's view of and feelings for her birth mother change? How do you think she felt about her when the story ended?

4. *Something About Sophie* is a dark tale. Talk about the lighter parts. Was there a good balance?

5. The real cause of Arthur's death was never brought to light. Might there have been other crimes left in the dark? Knowing what you know of Elizabeth, could Lonora have been her first victim?

6. Does Elizabeth deserve absolution from her children? Did it seem unnatural that Sophie was so quick to forgive?

7. Do you have a favorite scene? What about it appeals to you? If you could rewrite any part of the story what would it be and how would you write it? ᔐ

More from
Mary Kay McComas

What Happened
to Hannah
a novel
Mary Kay McComas

"McComas weaves stories that brighten the heart."
—NORA ROBERTS

Don't miss the next book by your favorite author. Sign up now for AuthorTracker by visiting www.AuthorTracker.com.

WHAT HAPPENED TO HANNAH

To save her own life, Hannah Benson fled her hometown as a teenager. She's never looked back, not even to find out what happened to the mother and sister she left behind. Twenty years later, the past comes calling when the town sheriff, Grady Steadman—Hannah's high school sweetheart, phones her with life-changing news: her mother and sister have both died, and she's the sole relative of her fifteen-year-old niece.

Hannah had become used to the idea of going it alone, but she can't shake her responsibility for her young niece. Returning home to bitter memories and devastating secrets, Hannah has to find a way to take on this new challenge without ruining lives—or risking her own sanity. And when her painful memories of this small town become mingled with the new, happier memories she's creating with her niece—and the rekindled feelings she has for Grady— Hannah finds out once and for all if she's strong enough to save her own life one more time.